Fall
Through
the
Sky

Jennifer DiMarco

Books in print by Jennifer DiMarco:
* Escape to the Wind
At the Edge
Fall Through the Sky

*not published by Pride

Fall Through the Sky
copyright 1991 by Jennifer DiMarco
published by Pride Publications

ISBN 1-886383-16-2

First edition February 1997.

Cover art by Chris Storm.
Interior and cover design by Pride Publications.

Printed in the United States of America.

There is only one
possible dedication for this book.

For Cris
For Mama
For Tyger

Without you,
there would be no story to tell.

Author's Acknowledgments

Until about a year ago, I thought this novel would never be published. In truth, it never would have had it not been for the passionate artists and visionaries here at Pride Publications. I owe this accomplishment to them — something I will never forget.

My editor Cris Newport has worked tirelessly on numerous Pride projects but never has a novel presented her with such a challenge as the original 150,000 word *Fall Through the Sky*. Through long nights and countless arguments with the hot-headed author, Cris' patience, insight and expertise did not waver. Thank you for not throwing in the towel, Cris — on this book, or on me.

My Mama, Carol DiMarco, first gave me the desire to write, and the space to complete the *Wind Trilogy* — *Escape to the Wind, Fall Through the Sky* and *Drinking Silver Wine* — back in 1991. Her encouragement and her love are the solid foundation of my writing and my life. I also thank my Mumu, Connie Wurm, for tempering my craziness and focusing my dreams. Through her examples I have learned to find some peace in all things. Mama, Mumu, I have become who I am today because of both of you.

Angela Marie DiMarco, my (taller) baby sister makes appearances in all of my books and this one is no exception. She has made a huge impact on my life and my heart, and I am very proud of her. Angel, you are destined for great things.

Artist and friend Chris Storm, who has designed many stunning Pride covers, created the art for *Fall Through the Sky* no less than five different times — all without complaint. Chris' wit had me laughing on days I wanted only to scream. Together we'd like to dedicate this cover in memory of Catherine Hopkins who created the cover art for *Escape to the Wind*.

Speaking of *Escape to the Wind*, I cannot over-look the almost one hundred reviewers and interviewers who took the time to speak to me or review the book, especially Gayle Detweiler and Grant Michael Menzies whose passion for *Escape to the Wind* is still with me today. Thank you to the periodicals, radio and television programs that gave space to an eighteen-year-old's story.

Thanks also to Deborah Holland, my proof-reader with an iron will and a heart of gold; Jeane Candido, for continuous understanding, lively debates and for being my best friend; Michelle Clark for her invaluable suggestions, great macros and her friendship, and all of the readers who keep Pride Publications alive.

I will never be able to fully express how honored and over-joyed I am to be part of this publishing house and this industry, but let me say to all of you, thank you for this gift.

Sincerely,
Jennifer DiMarco
Pride Publications President and Author

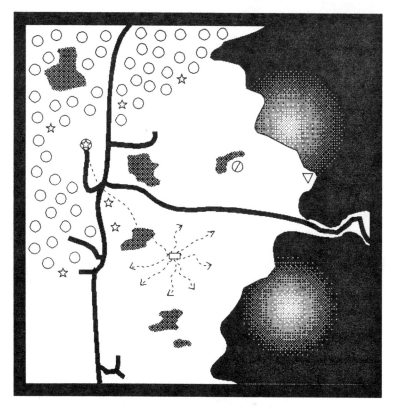

The layout of the land as this book begins....

✪	New Seattle, Dome #342
⊘	Dome construction site where first P3M were freed
▭	The Valley
☆	Dome construction sites where P3M remain
○	The Patriarchy's fifty other domed cities
🪨	Great Stone groves and Great Stone Forest
▬	The Skyway, standing remains of old freeway system
-------	Underground tunnels orginating from the Land of Sky
▽	Where the Village of Wind once stood

This map does not show the lone Great Stones that pepper the landscape or the fact that there are actually dozens of tunnels from Sky and also several non-Patriarchy domes in this general vicinity ruled by other nations or independent citizenry.

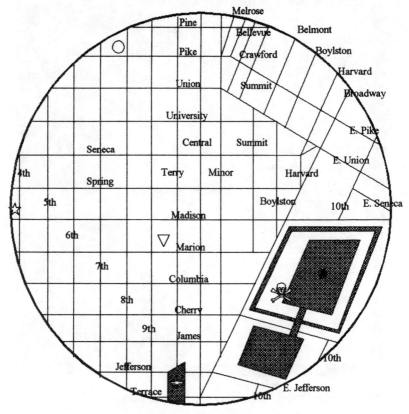

Dome 342
New Seattle

Major Landmarks

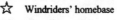

☆   Windriders' homebase

▽   Spiders' homebase

○   Wheels' homebase

✳   The Ramp

☠   Patriarchy's walled compound,
     Jarth's tower and prison

Character List

The Windriders
The gang lead by Tyger in "Escape to the Wind."
Tyger: Windborn leader of the Windriders. Past employee of the Patriarchy.
Ardyn: One-time rival of Tyger for the love of Sarya.
Tryl: The cowgirl. Jyln's lover.
Jyln: The medic. Tryl's lover.
Tylon: The inventor.
Petre: One-time Patriarchy soldier now changed by the Wind.
Ravyn: The first Windrider inventor. Returned to New Seattle.
Byn: The youngest Windrider. Returned to New Seattle to escape the Wind.
Sarya: Tyger's one-time lover, died from exposure to the Wind.

The P3M
One-time members of Tyger's gang who were betrayed by Tyger to the Patriarchy and were enslaved to build the Patriarchy's domes.
Spider: The oldest among the P3M, she was one of the first Windriders.
Fox: The medic.
Tamarin: Wolf's playful brother.
Wolf: Tamarin's serious brother.

The Sky Folk
Inhabitants of the Sky base.
Iahala: The Pagan Wisewoman.
Aliqui: Iahala's grand-daughter. Teacher of the Phoenix fighting art.
Kestrel: Sarah and Abraham's biological daughter. Lead Flyer.
Mlinz: Sarah and Abraham's biological son.
Mouse: Windborn rescued from the destruction of the Village of Wind.
Sarah: Co-leader of the One believers.
Abraham: Co-leader of the One believers.
Falcon: Rescued Windborn. She has been missing from Sky for several days.

The Spiders
A gang allied with the Windriders, led by Terri, a one-time Windrider.
Terri: Leader of the Spiders. One-time lover of Tyger.
Joanna: Second in command of the Spiders. Ravyn's lover.
Belle, Curn, Darja and Jamie: One-time members of the Eyes, a spy ring.

The Patriarchy
The nation of domes ruled by Christopher Jarth.
Christopher Jarth: Leader of the Patriarchy living in New Seattle.
Wenright: The lead Patriarchy scientist.
Sart: The deceased second in command of the Patriarchy's special squads.

Fall Through the Sky

Jennifer DiMarco

What Has Gone Before

Everyone knows that humans were cowards. They hated the
unknown because they feared it. They hated difference because it wasn't
what they knew, and they destroyed it. A little at a time, and then a lot all at
once.

When difference was gone, so was the world. All the flowers, all
the birds, all the grass and trees. All the waterfalls and rainbows, all the fish
and butterflies... and all the humans. After tolerance broke, all that was left
was dust and sand, a scorching sun and a disfigured moon, earthquakes,
radiation and the Wind.

The landscape was golden white sand filled with shining chips of
mica. There was no green – no grass or trees. Even the occasional cactus,
twisted and strange, was blue or silver. Where trees once stood, the Great
Stones had risen. When the End came, entire groves, entire forests were
uprooted and thrown together – melded into shapes harder than any petrified
wood – becoming marvelous stone-like creations. Massive sculptures
standing stories high, molded and shaped into impossible configurations,
laced with deep tunnels and turns in every direction.

It was from these Great Stones that the Song came. Under the New
World's bronze sky streaked with hints of color, the Song rose and fell
across all the land. The Wind soared through the tunnels of the Great
Stones, and together Wind and Stone made music.

Those who lived before the End died when it arrived. None were
left to walk the earth, but they all rode the Wind. Without beginning or end,
the never-ceasing gales were said to be the souls of the departed, born again
as the singing, crying, screaming Wind. Immortalized.

But this was no ordinary Wind. It had three Phases – the Dreams,
the Fever and the Change. Each more deadly than the last. And each Phase
had its own spirits – the Innocents, the Furious and the Resigned – each with
its own place and time.

The New World was a dangerous beauty, filled with hidden
wonders and strange creatures with manes, talons and scales all in one. Of
the two-legged beings who replaced humans – the Windborn, the Originals
and the Clones – two of them – the Originals and the Clones – could not live
long in the Wind.

Clones, with their identical offspring and fragile bodies, were not
suited for the Wind. Clones had once been humans, but the End had
changed one to the other long ago. And now the world seemed set to destroy
these offspring of humanity. Clones could not thrive, could not truly survive
in the Wind. Eventually, or suddenly, they died. The Wind, in all its Phases,
was too powerful for them. And so they wandered aimlessly, taking refuge in
the deepest tunnels and crevices of the Great Stones where the Wind did not

torment as much. They were a lost people without a purpose.

Without a world.

But not all of the Clone offspring were Clones themselves. Nearly once in each litter, a Clone mother gave birth to a baby who did not match with the rest of the replicant brood. The baby was an individual. A freak. This breed, these mutations were called the Originals. A word spoken with distaste by Clones. For even though people said that prejudice had died with the Old World, it had not.

Original babies were often left behind by the nomadic Clones or killed. But on the occasion when a mother kept one of the strange ones, she found that even as the Wind bore hard and Clones began to die, the Original would thrive. As the Original grew, he or she resembled the beasts of the New World rather than other Clones. And like the New World animals, Originals could survive in the Wind. Eventually, all Originals were abandoned by the Clones.

So for sometime after the End of the Old World, Clones roamed in the Wind, sought shelter in the Great Stones and lived only to die. But that time is over now. Christopher Jarth ended it.

Jarth was a Clone boy, born of a Clone mother into a litter of replicant brothers and sisters. It was Jarth who first went to the ruins of Seattle and found the cubes – metal and stone boxes covered with hidden computers and filled with dormant cells. Four cubes, one for each direction, set in a circle one mile in diameter.

He discovered that the cells inside the cubes were alive and very, very hungry. They needed power, so he fed them blood. He gave the cubes living animals, Beasts, to feed upon and it worked. When fed, the cells grew, rising forth from their four boxes, reaching upwards towards the sky, arching over and meeting each other far, far above the center of the circle. So he fed them more, and the thin bands of cells grew wider and wider until they came together on all sides, sealing tight one mile of land beneath their pulsing dome of guardianship. A living dome sealed away from the Wind. A dome that could be retrofitted with filters and fans. A place away from the Wind where the Clones could live. And with the life of that first dome, Jarth gave birth to his government. The Patriarchy.

Before the End, thousands of domes had stood. These domes were alive – they were conscious of other cells in other domes all across the world. With the aid of computer monitors and machines, nations could discover – through the cells' instinctive knowledge – how many other domes there were, where the domes were located... and the population of citizens within each one. This information was used for a myriad of military and political schemes during the incredible distrust before the end. And now Jarth had reawakened one of these ancient domes, linking him instantly to a global network of 391 other domes, thrusting him into power.

Soon Jarth had fifty-one domes standing in what was once the state of Washington in the United States of America. Fifty-one domes that made up his nation called the Patriarchy, ruled by Christopher Jarth alone. And dome 342, the city of New Seattle, housed his mighty headquarters.

When Jarth and his followers awoke the first dome, the monitors linking him with the other domes globally became operational. Through them came a strange link, a twisted knowledge. Through this link Jarth learned that all across the world there was a war raging. Not a war to end life, but a war to preserve it. With no weapons and no bombs, the winners were proclaimed by who could survive, by who had the most lives within their domes, whose population was the highest. If population was low, a siren would sound. When population was high, a brilliant light would shine. Domes were rated in order of greatness – the more citizens, the higher the rating. Jarth, like any normal Clone man, felt compelled to enter the competition. But there was more to this contest than simply the knowledge that he could become the best. That "more" was the understanding that should another real war begin, the nations which survived would be those with the highest populations, the ones who could afford the most losses. Jarth understood this aspect of the competition all too well.

Across the globe, other rulers controlled other clusters of domes – other nations – but Jarth, with his Patriarchy, was a newcomer. The Patriarchy had entered the race late and Jarth was behind. So he stopped killing Original babies, because every life counted, and he developed the Allegiance Divided.

He split New Seattle, dome 342, in half with a cultural border. One half, called the Central District, contained brightly colored streets where Clone women and their Clone children lived in simplistic frivolity. The steel compound of the mighty Patriarchy where all Clone males were raised also towered here. The Central District was alive during the day, filled with light and laughter and the promise of a bright future.

But when darkness fell, the Central District became quiet, deserted, and the other half of the domed city, the Industrial District, awoke. This half of the city was compiled from the ruins of Old Seattle and ruled by the Originals who were tossed into the streets when they were still children. Some believed this was better than killing them, some did not, but no one argued. All that mattered was the population count. And the Originals took care of their own. In the Industrial District, gangs took the place of families and turf wars occupied the lives of these nocturnal Originals.

The Patriarchy supported both communities. In the Central District, the men and women were strictly segregated. Jarth gave the Clone women enough drugs, pleasantries and playthings to keep them from questioning the normalcy of a life filled with litter after litter of artificially inseminated children. Reproduction was their sole purpose and they were socialized from birth to accept their fate. The men, taken from their mothers at age five and sent to live in the Patriarchy's compound, were trained as soldiers. They were kept busy with their studies and duties, including supplying the Industrial District's Ration Bins with rations and mock weapons. Of course, not even the Patriarchy had weapons that could kill. Violence was acceptable. Death was not. Births were wanted, not deaths. Never deaths. Even the Original gangs, racing their homemade motorcycles, riding the dome's air currents on silver disc Windboards or swinging by Threads from one building to the next, never wanted to kill anyone... except maybe Cristopher Jarth.

Jarth was a symbol of protection for the Clones and slavery for the Originals because he controlled travel to and from the city. And while the Clones found solace in the dome's protection, the Originals found imprisonment. Only Jarth and his soldiers traveled in the lands outside and between the domes. The lands ruled by the Wind. And even though everyone knew it was impossible to survive for long on the outside, it seemed to the Originals that anything would be better then oppression and hatred.

During one visit into the Wind-swept world outside New Seattle, Jarth and his men, carefully encased in protective hovercraft, happened upon an entire village of Originals living strong and fine in the midst of the Wind. The village inhabitants were defiantly more than Clone, more than Original even, with taller, stronger statures and heightened awareness. It was as if all the Original children abandoned over the years by the once nomadic Clones had come together, changed by the Wind. They had grown older and had their own children... children born changed. Their hair was fur-like and multi-toned; their ears were pointed like an animal's and their hands hid retractable claws. Most amazing of all, and most disturbing, were their eyes, which bore no visiable pupil or sclera, but were one solid color with the rich intensity of a jewel.

Jarth and his men felt fear and jealousy, and so they felt hate as well. Jarth decided to massacre the entire village before he and his soldiers could be spotted by the villagers. But it was too late. They had already been seen by a child.

Her name was Tyger, and when she came forward and offered her life in exchange for the lives of her people, she thought Jarth would keep his promise and spare her people's lives as long as she obeyed him. Jarth took the young Windborn woman back to New Seattle, and after tests and training and threats, she did what he wanted. Believing all along in his promise. Believing that her people were safe outside, in the Wind.

Obeying Jarth meant murder. But to Tyger the death of a few was surely worth saving the lives of the many. Jarth needed Tyger. And Tyger believed she needed him. Jarth sent Tyger into the Industrial District with orders to start a gang. And when that gang was completed, she waited until the Wind entered its third Phase – the Phase of Change. Then Tyger and her followers escaped to the Wind. Or at least that's what the gang-members believed. In truth, Jarth let them go, staging an accident that would open a small part of the dome, allowing Tyger's band of Originals to flee New Seattle.

Once in the Wind, only some of the Originals survived Phase Three and metamorphosed, able to live in the Wind. Jarth and his Retrieval Squad would come after the gang then, and those Originals who were struggling with the change were left to die. The newly changed, called P3Ms – Phase Three Metamorphosed – were taken by Jarth to work sites where they were forced to build new domes so that Jarth could expand his empire. Tyger would be returned to New Seattle to start the cycle again.

Finally Tyger could stand no more. After six years, she rebelled because she could no longer bring those she loved into the Wind to die or be forced into slavery. Without Jarth's help, Tyger escaped from the dome with a band of followers called the Windriders. She planned to return to her village home, the Village of Wind, where they would be safe. But through a cruel accident of fate, Tyger misread the Wind's Phases and the Windriders entered the Wind when it was still incredibly deadly to everyone but Tyger. Some of the Windriders retreated to the dome to escape death and others died in the Wind. With sickness in their midst and the Patriarchy on their trail, the Windriders fled to Tyger's village only to discover the deepest horror of all: Jarth had lied. He had not spared Tyger's village, but slaughtered them all years ago, despite his promise. Despite Tyger's loyalty.

In her anger and despair, Tyger contemplated her own death and was tormented by memories of those who died because of her. Eventually, she came back to herself, knowing that the Windriders were depending on her. Inspired by a dream, Tyger lead the Windriders southwest. Along their way they were able to rescue four P3M from a Patriarchy work site – four changed Originals that were once Tyger's friends and gang members: Spider, Fox, Wolf and Tamarin. Together, their travels bring them to a miracle. A deep valley of green grass and a majestic waterfall. The Patriarchy had legends about this valley. They had long ago proclaimed it evil, sworn they would never set foot inside. So Tyger knew, finally, that she had brought the Windriders to safety. They hoped this would be their haven, but no one knew what awaited them beneath the surface of all the beauty....

And what of the Wind? The never-ceasing power of the New World. In the Valley, it didn't seem to blow. A world without the Wind

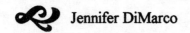

seemed almost impossible. What did it mean that the Valley was still?

Scientists of the New World had tried to comprehend the Wind and failed but every child knows, from its mama's bedtime stories, that with its razor claws and needle teeth, blazing eyes and mighty roar, the Wind is a tiger.

* * *

 Part One

Tyger of the Village of Wind raised her head and brushed locks of orange and black hair out of her solid emerald eyes. She smiled. She loved heights, and she especially loved danger. The rugged cliff face below the ledge where she stood dropped over two hundred feet to the Valley floor and rose the same distance above her. Bronze and streaked with silver, the towering walls that circled the Valley were peppered with nooks, ledges and layers, their bases meeting the soft green of the meadows below. It was as though before the End there had been no Valley at all. But when the End came, this grassy sward of earth had dropped straight down four hundred feet to escape the wrath of mankind. Now these stone walls were loyal guardians of this last piece of the Old World.

Tyger looked all the way down into the bowl of the Valley, enjoying the feeling of vertigo. She guessed the Valley was a mile long, perhaps half that wide. From where she stood, the flowers below looked like star-shaped jewels scattered across the green wash of grass. She could identify them by their rich colors – blue spire and tiger petal, daisies and roses. Both New World and Old World flowers.

They had come to the edge of the bowl the day before and begun their descent just after dawn. It was now afternoon. Slightly above Tyger, scattered in pairs across the rock face, were the other Windriders: Tryl and Spider were the closest. Behind them came Jyln and Fox, then Wolf and Tamarin. Bringing up the rear were Tylon and Petre. Ardyn stood beside Tyger on the ledge. Tyger could see Ardyn just inside her peripheral vision, the woman's raven hair stirring in the breeze. It seemed the farther they climbed down into the Valley, the lighter the Wind became.

Tyger pressed her palms to the sheer wall at her back. It seemed that the wall pulsed beneath her hands, just like the Great Stones, and she wondered if they were one and the same. A sculpture of angular spires, smooth surfaces and rough plains, the walls were striped with the history of what had once been.

Her eyes wandered to the small sandy shore of the pool beneath the waterfall, down and to the left of where she stood. No picture or film reel had shown her how beautiful water would be. This cascading curtain was glorious. Tyger found herself wondering, as she had when she first set eyes on it, where all the water disappeared to. The falls were a constant stream but the pool beneath was small and strangely still. She could see the sandy bottom from here: a golden white sand just like the rest of the New World. How could it be that the falls met the pool with such force but caused so little reaction across the surface?

It was then that the swarm returned. This time they came out of the sun's light and soared straight toward the face of the wall where Tyger stood. With their wings like colored rice-paper catching the rays of the late day sun and their slender bodies tucked in flight, the Butterflies were the most spectacular thing Tyger had ever seen.

As they moved closer to her and the rock wall, she was stunned by their size. Their leader was at least six feet in length, eight including wings. Their leader.... Tyger saw again the bright gold of that Butterfly's wings and the rich blue markings like eyes on the wing tips. As this beauty flew almost close enough for her to touch, she was transfixed for a moment with a vision of Sarya and the smell of sunshine.

How wonderful it would be if Sarya had truly been granted her wish.

The golden leader dove straight at the cliff face then caught an updraft, rode it gracefully, paralleling the wall, then led the swarm back up into the skies. As the leader flew directly over Tyger, she saw something strange. There was something about the black lepidopterain body that was not quite as it should be, it appeared almost....

Tyger jolted as Ardyn screamed. Entranced by the Butterflies, Ardyn took a step backward on the ledge, her neck craned as the rock edge collapsed.

Tyger cried out as Ardyn's body toppled over the side. She dove, catching Ardyn's right arm as Ardyn's left hand scrabbled for a purchase in the stone.

Ardyn looked up at Tyger and her rich brown eyes spoke the words that neither could say. Ardyn could not hold on. Her wrist, newly healed, wouldn't stand the pull much longer.

Tyger's striped hair fell over her straining shoulders and she pressed more tightly against the stone. "I'm not letting go," she said through clenched teeth.

A strange grin flashed across Ardyn's face. "I tripped over my own feet. Not quite a warrior's death." Ardyn cast a side glance down into the Valley. So close to freedom.

Tyger set her jaw. "I'm not losing you, too," she growled. Tears of frustration spilled over Ardyn's chestnut skin and Tyger reached for her other hand. "If you go over, I'm going with you." But Tyger's strength was no match for the force of gravity and she shouted to the others as she slid closer to the brink. Tryl was already moving fast towards the ledge, lunging dangerously across the stone face, the rest of the Windriders close behind her.

Tyger dug in with her booted feet but there was no hold. Despite it all she wanted to wipe the tears from Ardyn's cheeks. Tyger had only seen her cry once before, when Sarya had died in their arms. She refused to let this be another funeral.

Ardyn stopped struggling because the more she moved the more Tyger was endangered. "Tyger." Her voice was barely a whisper, and then the tip of the ledge gave way and Tyger felt her body slide over.

There was a large *thump*; someone landed on Tyger's legs. Tryl's strong hands began to pull at Tyger's waist. Tyger tightened her grip on Ardyn and managed to grasp her other hand. Tyger's long hair fell over her eyes, but she could feel Ardyn holding onto her and that was all she needed.

Tryl grunted and pulled at Tyger, sweat streaming down her body. Her cowboy-style hat tumbled from her head, falling past both Tyger and Ardyn and tumbling into the air. Tryl's muscles bulged under her tee-shirt and pressed tightly against her vest. Tryl was a warrior, but also an Original, not yet completely changed. She had stopped Tyger from slipping but could do no more.

Spider landed on the ledge with the grace of a P3M. Her metamorphosis was complete and her body had been hardened through slave labor. She sank down beside Tryl and the two women began to pull together. "We can do this," Spider hissed.

With their help, Ardyn was finally able to pull her body beside Tyger's. Spider and Tryl moved back. Ardyn had just gotten her knees under her when the sound of stone on stone, grinding and crumbling, filled the air. A hard *crack* and the entire front of the ledge gave way completely.

Among the Windriders someone screamed as the two women plunged downward. They fell within inches of the wall, Tyger's body twisted about Ardyn's. A thought flashed through Tyger's mind, *One of us must live*. Tyger had always known she would make penance someday, somehow for all the wrong she had done. It seemed now she would pay with her life.

Tyger's head grazed the wall at the same moment her body struck solid stone. They had dropped thirty feet onto a twisted outcropping of rock protruding from the wall. Pain shot down her neck as her skull exploded with lights. Darkness took her.

Ardyn lifted her head from Tyger's chest. There was blood on her face. Tyger's blood. She shifted and knelt. Her arm stung, the skin ripped away where she had covered Tyger's head. She pushed her jacket sleeve back down over her wound.

Tyger was still, blood dyeing the fiery colors in her hair brown. Ardyn looked up. Large handfuls of Tyger's hair had been ripped out and hung from a jutting rock a few feet above them. But if it hadn't been for Ardyn's arm, Tyger's skull would have been split.

"Tyger?" Ardyn whispered. Tyger did not stir. Ardyn was not used to being afraid; she was a brave and stubborn woman, but she felt a sudden need to know Tyger still lived. She wrapped her arms around her and began to lift.

Jyln's voice reached her from above. "Ardyn, don't move her!" The medic was perched in a nook in the wall, just barely able to see the two women around the curves in the stone. "If she hit her head, you mustn't move her."

From directly above Tyger and Ardyn, Tryl called. "We're going to try to get to you. Are you all right? We can't really see you from up here!"

"Okay," Ardyn answered. "Jyln, what can I do til you get here?"

There was silence for a moment. No one was used to Ardyn and their leader getting along. Finally, the blonde-haired medic answered, "Stop any bleeding. Try to see where she's wounded. If anything's broken."

Above Ardyn, voices floated across the air – Tryl and Spider were arguing about how to get down to them, the other Windriders being drawn into the argument. At this rate, Ardyn knew it could take the Windriders hours to reach a decision.

Ardyn looked down at Tyger and set her jaw. She tugged her tee-shirt from her jeans and began to tear the bottom into strips. Patches of Tyger's body were scraped raw, tears in the rich chocolate-colored skin. Ardyn touched Tyger's hair. The long mane was now torn short and it fell back from her slightly pointed ears and strong features. Even lying unconscious, Tyger looked like a warrior.

"Are we going to spend the rest of our lives saving each other?" Ardyn whispered as she wrapped Tyger's head carefully. She and Tyger had once been bitter rivals for Sarya's love, but Ardyn had never wished Tyger dead. And now, after all they had seen and been through together, she wasn't going to let her go this easily.

Without thinking, Ardyn leaned forward and touched her lips to Tyger's. She heard herself say Tyger's name even as she drew away, shocked by her own actions. Tyger's eyes fluttered opened. Intelligence and strength flooded the emerald depths and Tyger looked up at her. Did she know what Ardyn had done to revive her?

Tyger reached back and touched her head. A low growl rose in her throat and then she saw Ardyn's torn jacket sleeve, putting the pieces together. "You saved my life."

Ardyn gave her a smirk. "I landed on you."

Tyger laughed and then groaned, holding her head in her hands. "Every time I try to kill myself, you always wind up saving me." She tried to sit up.

Ardyn pushed her back down. "It's just like you to figure you're paying off some spiritual debt or something. When are you going to realize you've already been forgiven?"

Tyger said nothing. She knew that penance and forgiveness were two totally different things.

* * *

Standing on the ledge, Tryl and Spider continued to disagree.

"Untie the bundles and drop them some rope? Give me a break, Spider! This isn't dome construction! We can't just do everything with ropes and pulleys. It would take Windborn strength to heave them both back up here!"

Spider knocked Tryl on the side on the head with a flip of her hand as if to knock some sense into her. "We wouldn't pull them. Just anchor the rope. They'd climb up, cowgirl!"

Tryl smacked Spider up-side the head. "What if Ardyn's re-broken her wrist, hm? And who knows what's wrong with Tyger!"

Under her silver bangs, Spider narrowed her solid metallic eyes. Tryl's irises were a richer gray-blue than a normal Original's but her eyes had changed no further yet. She met Spider's gaze steadily. Spider looked over the edge again. The wall seemed completely featureless, angling out in a dangerously smooth slope. There was no way Tyger and Ardyn could just continue the climb down from where they were. Spider looked back at Tryl, her doubt clear. "You got a better idea?"

Tryl grinned. "As a matter of fact, I think one of us should jump down to them. Find some way to climb back up here – an easy way, where she could hold Ardyn across her back, then drop down again and carry Tyger up."

Spider started to laugh, a raspy sound from high in her throat. "You know, I think you lost your brains with your hat! Look up, cowgirl. We've climbed at least two hundred feet, has even one step been easy? I don't think so. And what makes you think you can jump down without being hurt if Tyger couldn't?"

"Tyger could! She fell unexpectedly. And I didn't say it had to be me–"

"Who else but you would follow one of your hair-brained schemes?"

Tryl gave Spider a snarl and began an angry retort. Jyln interrupted her. "Need I remind you two that Ardyn and our leader are wounded down there? Can you forget your blasted differences for a second and come to a consensus, please? I don't know how much time we have til it gets dark."

Tryl and Spider fell silent. It was true. Spider, Fox, Wolf and Tamarin had escaped from a dome construction slave site; Tryl, Jyln, Tylon, Ardyn and Tyger had escaped from New Seattle, and Petre had gone AWOL from the Patriarchy, but among them all, none knew this land or how soon the Valley below and the rocks they perched upon would grow dark with night. Calmer now, Tryl and Spider began to plan again.

Leaning back into the nook, Jyln continued rifling through her med-pack. Fox sat beside her in the small space. She peered around Jyln, squinting. "I think Tyger is moving," she announced.

Jyln looked out. Tyger was trying to sit up. "Keep her down, Ardyn! We'll be there soon." Then under her breath, "I hope."

"I'll keep her down, Jyln," Ardyn called back, laughter in her voice.

Jyln wondered what was so funny.

* * *

Ardyn grinned. "I never thought a Windrider was going to tell me to hold you down."

Tyger chuckled. "That's because they were too busy holding us apart!" Tyger peered up the wall, trying to get a glimpse of the others. All she could hear was Spider and Tryl arguing. "We could be here for days...."

Ardyn reached out and impulsively brushed an uneven strand of hair out of Tyger's eyes. The leader smiled at her but Ardyn's eyes looked distant. Tyger asked softly, "What are you thinking?"

Ardyn shook her head in surprise, clearing away the visions. Tyger had never asked anyone what they were thinking. Most of the time, she told them what to think. But Ardyn had never let Tyger choose her path. Her faraway looks had first infuriated Tyger but now they intrigued her. "How we always used to be at each other's throats."

Tyger knew Ardyn was lying by the flush of her cheeks. She held her curiosity in check. "I was a beast," Tyger admitted, liking the shock that flashed across Ardyn's face.

"You're confessing you were less than a woman?" Ardyn was amazed. Tyger rarely admitted she was wrong, even if everyone else said she was – which they never dared, of course.

Tyger grinned up at Ardyn. "You used to say I was."

Ardyn caught on, grinning back. "So now I'm supposed to say I was mistaken?" Tyger looked away with a shrug. She let her gaze wander across the bronze sky with its wisps of pale lavender clouds.

"Tyger," Ardyn's voice held a smile, gentle in a way Tyger had never heard before. They looked at each other and the Windborn thought that the Original's eyes were an even deeper, richer brown than they had been a moment before.

"I was wrong," Ardyn said, and in her words there was truth and apology, and something more. Tyger was stunned. She had always secretly believed that Ardyn had been right. Tyger had been a beast all those years when her loyalty was torn between her loved ones in her village and her loved ones in the city. And Ardyn had been her sole accuser.

Tyger sat up slowly, grimacing. She lay her hand on Ardyn's.

"Your rebellion was the only thing that kept me humble. What am I supposed to do now?"

Ardyn smiled. "I'll insult you once in a while." They laughed together.

"Stop all that! Tyger lie down!" Jyln's voice startled them both and they jerked away from each other like secret lovers. Jyln was glaring down at them, peering at them from around a rise in the wall. "Ardyn, you have to keep her still. We've very close to a decision now.... She can wait. Even if she does have the impatience of a puppy!"

Ardyn and Tyger laughed harder. "She's not a beast!" Ardyn exclaimed, but Tyger barked before she lay back down.

* * *

Jyln leaned back into the tiny cave. "They're hysterical," she mumbled. She peeked out at Spider and Tryl who were still picking apart each other's plans, their words punctuated with occasional shoves. "We all needed a rest anyhow," she said, frowning good-humoredly at Fox. Ardyn would care for Tyger, no matter how strange that notion seemed.

Fox shook her head and smiled. Tyger's stubbornness was part of her charm. Fox leaned out and called over to Wolf and Tamarin, "Have you found a way down from over there?"

Tall and slender, Tamarin shook his head, his thigh-length braid of dark orange, gold-streaked hair shaking behind him. "We're still searching, but it doesn't look good."

Wolf leaned over the edge. "The wall slopes out from where they are. Doesn't become climbable rock again for forty feet."

Tamarin slumped down beside his brother. They had looked nothing alike when they were children, and metamorphosis had changed them even more. Wolf was Tamarin's opposite. He was short and stocky with a burly rather than lithe strength and short wild black hair touched with accents of white. He was steady and quiet where Tamarin was bolder and exuberant. Tamarin sighed, "I'd say we should nap awhile, but Tyger and Ardyn would probably kill each other."

Wolf was silent. Of all the Windriders perched above Tyger and Ardyn, he knew he was the only one that could see them clearly. The only one that had seen Ardyn wake Tyger. He leaned back from the edge, the hint of a grin on his face. "I think they're doing fine together."

* * *

Not far from Tamarin and Wolf, Tylon and Petre sat on a small ledge, their backs against the wall. They were quite a pair, Tylon barely changed at all and Petre almost completely metamorphosed.

Petre had once been a Clone but a flawed invention of the Patriarchy had accidentally allowed his body to change. His senses, however, had not changed. He did not have the heightened awareness that other P3M have, only his own instincts and emotions.

He looked out at the other Windriders, then back at his climbing partner. Tylon was just a bit more than an Original, as if the Wind had filled him on the inside and decided not to show on the outside. Tylon was the engineer of the Windriders, though since Ravyn had returned to New Seattle, his heart had not been in his work. Normally he would have been trying to solve the problem at hand, but today he just sat.

Everyone looked up as the swarm of Butterflies returned and swooped down over Tryl and Spider. Tryl threw a rock at one and shouted. They had started all this. The swarm wound down towards Ardyn and Tyger, hovering there. Tyger sat up slowly, placing a protective arm around Ardyn shoulder's. The two women looked dwarfed by the Butterflies.

After a moment, the golden leader of the swarm led others away. Diving straight into the curtain of the waterfall, they all disappeared.

"There must be a cave behind the water."

Petre jumped a little at Tylon's voice. He looked at his friend. Tylon's pale blue eyes were fixed on the falls and Petre noticed that they were nearly the same color. So blue. Once, Tyger had said that the Patriarchy in the Wind was obscene. Petre agreed with her. "I would die before I saw Hovercraft in this Valley," he murmured with soft passion. Tylon turned to him and his eyes were very wide. Petre sank back in alarm. "Tylon, what—"

Tylon's hands were suddenly on Petre's shoulders, a huge smile on his face. "That's it, Petre! A Hovercraft. Of course!" Tylon called to the others, every face turning towards him. Could he do this? Could he solve this? "The Wind is faint here in the Valley, so cross-currents are not strong. But what about other currents? The swarm glides on something. They rode a stream of air right up along the wall. A thermal." Tylon explained, "We removed the engines of the Windboards a long time ago, and the gentler Wind that reaches down here won't be enough to keep a board airborne. But a thermal is a column of heated air that rises off stone or hot earth. The wall slopes out from Tyger and Ardyn. The jutting layers of rock could be giving off enough heat to create a strong current."

"We've got a thermal column, so what?" Spider said. "We want to go down, not up."

Tylon continued. "When we were traveling here I noticed how the Wind would change and react differently in different places and over different terrain. I'm not sure, but I think that if just the edge of a Windboard is inside the thermal column, then the Windboard will... hover. The more of the current the board catches, the more it will rise. Too much in and it will shoot up and out of control. But just the edge should keep it steady enough for–"

"For Tyger and Ardyn to step on," Tryl interrupted. "Give it a little push and it'll rise up here! All right, Tylon, my pal! You did it!" Tryl gave Spider one last celebratory shove.

Tylon looked over at Petre who was looking at him with only half-hidden awe. "I would never have thought of it myself. Petre said something that reminded me." Petre looked away from the other young man, his face flushed.

Until now the group had been hauling their Windboards across their backs. They were light-weight so everyone had strapped their belongings across them. Wolf and Tamarin bent and began to untie the bundles from one of the boards. They stood together and held it up. "Ready!" Wolf announced.

"Go!" Tamarin cried, flinging the board out over the sloped wall.

It sliced through the air, the sun catching the thin edges of the silver disc as it hovered for a moment, and then plunged to the rock, skidding down the slope and launching itself over the edge to plummet to the Valley floor.

Ardyn cleared her throat. "Were we supposed to grab that?"

Someone groaned.

"Oh, for Wind's sake, people!" Tyger shouted. Everyone looked down at her. She was on her feet, and looking rather steady. Ardyn stood beside her, her hands in the pockets of her leather jacket. Tyger put her hands on her hips. Around Tyger's head, Ardyn had tied a long strip of her tee-shirt. The white cloth was stained in the back where Tyger's hair had been torn from her scalp. "If I had been bleeding to death down here, I'd be stiff and cold by now! We don't need you to come rescue us. We'll just climb down from here."

"How?!" hollered Tryl. Aggravated, Jyln didn't give Tyger time to answer. "Tyger, you shouldn't be climbing around."

"Oh?" Tyger laughed. "I'm just going to live here on the wall?"

"You don't know how bad your injuries are!" Fox tried.

"Hey! I know my own body, thank you. I got an unwanted hair cut, a few bumps and scrapes. Nothing I have to lie still over."

Jyln rolled her eyes. "You wouldn't lie still if you had two broken legs and your head was lying next to you!"

"How are you going to climb down from there?!" Tryl and Spider blurted together.

Tyger grinned, only able to see their faces peering over the ledge above. "We'll slide down the slope, catch the lip at the end, and then go hand-over-hand down the wall."

Tryl raised her eyebrows. Tamarin muttered, "Wild!"

"You'll be sliding too fast! You'll fly right over the lip just like the Windboard did!" Jyln was red-faced now. "Ardyn, you've always been the sensible one, won't you two just stay there and wait til we come down? We'll have a new plan..."

"In a few days!" Ardyn had to laugh. "I'll go with Tyger."

Jyln threw up her hands in dismay. "I give up. Someone else try."

Tryl and Spider exchanged glances. "We'll race you down!" Tryl called.

"You're on!"

Laughter echoed through the Valley, bouncing off the walls. High above them the Wind sang. The Wind that the Windriders had escaped to, the Wind that had filled their veins and changed their bodies. The Wind they left behind.

* * *

Tyger stood and looked out over the Valley. It was much more real now that she stood within it. Climbing down, the goal so far below, her mind almost told her she would never reach it – it was just a dream.

"Am I dreaming?" Ardyn whispered behind her. Tyger shook her head slowly, and Ardyn moved to stand beside her.

Petre had named this place the Valley of Freedom when they had first arrived. The Patriarchy called it the Roaring Valley. But Tyger gave it no name at all. She was sure it already had one. This Valley had a life and a purpose. A purpose the Windriders would come to as naturally as breathing the Wind. "I think the whole Valley is breathing. Like a living thing."

"Yes. It is alive," Ardyn agreed. "Beautiful."

And powerful, Tyger thought. The towering walls rising to the sky and keeping everything at bay. Silent guardians. Tyger and Ardyn stood together and watched as the Windriders walked out over the rolling expanse of this new land, determined to touch and feel everything. To prove it was real.

Tryl kicked off her boots and walked out into the soft green grass. "This is so strange," she mumbled. Tryl turned to Jyln and beckoned to her. "Come on, you'll like it. It's, uhm, soft but firm."

Jyln laughed and tossed off her low boots. She ran at Tryl, tackling her into the grass. "Sounds like you," she said through laughter as they began to wrestle like cubs or kits. After all, they were only nineteen.

"I love you, Jyln of the Windriders," Tryl bowed her head but just before their lips met, Jyln threw her off. Tryl was tall and strong, but Jyln was quick in both body and wit. Soon she had her pinned. She touched her nose to Tryl's. "I love you, cowgirl."

Tryl pouted. "When I dove for Tyger, my hat fell over the edge. I fought for that hat at the Ration Bins."

Jyln kissed her. "You're still my cowgirl." Jyln rolled off her lover and stretched out, her head on Tryl's stomach. Tryl ran her fingers through Jyln's hair and together they watched the clouds.

"That one looks like the side of a Windboard," Tryl said.

"Flat and thin? They all look like Windboards today."

Tryl pointed. "No, that one looks like a Thread."

"Yeah, flat and thin!" Jyln laughed.

The ground seemed to vibrate just the slightest bit, and Jyln and Tryl sat up as Spider sauntered over to them. "Here, you can have your brain back." Spider flipped the dirty cowboy hat at Tryl. They were always going to be like this. Playfully clashing.

Tryl was, for once, speechless.

Jyln grinned up at Spider. "Thanks." Her eyes were bright on the other woman. "The Patriarchy didn't give us much. Things are special."

Spider didn't look away from her gaze. "Yes. I remember."

"Hey," Tryl placed her hat on her head with a settled pat. "Why don't you join us, Spi?"

"I think I will... Tr."

Tryl looked up at her frown. "Gotcha."

Spider sat down in the warm grass and tilted her head back. The sky was a wonderful treat for all three of them. Until Tryl and Jyln had escaped from New Seattle, they had never seen the sky, and until Spider had escaped from the slave site, the sky had always been obstructed by beams and metal work.

Jyln stood and began to walk silently through the grass, staring at the new stuff. She tossed her hair over her shoulder, looking from the sky to the grass, letting the last of the sun touch her skin. Spider watched, her heart pounding. Jyln looked over at her. She knew.

"How'd you find my hat?" Tryl's voice was almost innocent. Young. Besides Tyger, Spider was the oldest among them at twenty-one. Spider sighed and looked away from Jyln. "I went searching for it."

Tryl seemed surprised. "Why?"

Spider frowned. She took a deep breath and looked directly at Tryl. "Because, Tryl, I respect you." Spider went to stand, to walk away, but Jyln dropped down between them. Her hands came to rest on their thighs. She looked at Tryl and then Spider, slowly. "I want you to like each other," she said. "I really do."

Tylon leaned over and picked up another piece of rock, placing it with the others. He stood at the base of the wall they had come down, his clothes covered in dry, red dirt from the climb.

Petre walked with him, watching and talking. "I've never even seen pictures of rocks like that."

Tylon shook his head. "Neither have I." They looked down at the collection of almost clear rocks. They were small and chipped but appeared to have smooth, angular sides.

"What do they look like in sunlight?" Petre asked.

Tylon shrugged and picked up the largest of the group. They walked away from the lengthening shadow of the wall and Tylon held up the strange stone.

At first it seemed as though nothing happened, but then the finger-sized rock filled with light. Tylon was so enthralled with the discovery that it was Petre who first saw the colors on the wall behind them. "Tylon, look..."

Tylon turned. There upon the wall was a spectrum of colors, moving ever so slightly in one direction and then another. As Tylon stared, he dropped the rock into the grass. The colors disappeared.

"Where did they go?" Petre looked from side to side.

Tylon looked down at the clear stone lying in the grass. "But that's impossible. It's a rock!" He bent and lifted it up into the light again. The colors returned.

Tylon began muttering to himself as he lifted one after another of the clear stones into the light, moving them this way and that, watching their projection of colors on the wall.

Petre spotted a rather large clear stone hidden in thick shadow and went to it. He bent to retrieve it when someone called his name. He found his gaze wandering up the wall. A cold breeze brushed by him, lifting his short curls. He squinted into the darkness. He heard his name again. "Who's there?" Petre looked higher and suddenly there were faces. Faces in the wall. Staring at him. Calling.

Petre grabbed his chest, a sharp pain tearing through him. "What–?" But the vision was gone as quickly as it had come. He'd had only enough time to see that they were P3M and they were crying.

Petre shivered, staring at the wall. He thought he saw Jarth's face, Jarth's sharp eyes. He trembled. *I'm changed now*, he told himself. *I am P3M, not a Clone. I have nothing to fear from him. Nothing*. But he could not stop shaking. A hand came to his shoulder and Petre jumped.

Tylon turned Petre towards him. He searched his gaze. "Petre, you're a Windrider. Even if Jarth finds us, we'll stand together. We'll fight."

The name Windrider had always meant strength to Petre, and it was good to be reminded he was part of that strength now. He belonged. He pushed all the faces from his mind and his shaking stopped. Petre had no way of knowing that his calling had just begun. "Thank you," he said.

Tylon squeezed his shoulder. "That's what brothers are for." He paused, "You know what you need? Something to keep your mind busy. Today..." Tylon laughed a bit sarcastically. "Well, my idea was wrong, but *you* inspired me. You've had training – the only good thing the Patriarchy ever gave you. We could make good team. Ravyn and I always worked together, why don't you and I?"

Petre smiled, but pride made him ask, "Do you really think I can help, or is this just a courtesy?"

Tylon's face became solemn. "Both. You're my friend. And you're the only one here who isn't a warrior first. You think like I do and that's hard to find." Tylon looked away. There was a certain sense of loss behind his words. "Ravyn and I were the best team there ever was. When she went back to New Seattle to save Byn, I thought I'd never find my place again. But I can see that I'm still who I always was. Except now, I have to be me alone." He turned back to Petre. "That's why I want us to be a team. Because I know that we can work together, and I don't want to be alone."

"I can't be Ravyn," Petre said.

Tylon just looked at him. "I don't want you to be. I want you to be Petre."

Fox bent over and smelled a huge yellow rose. It smelled like the sunshine felt but sweeter. Before she could straighten up, Tamarin leapt over her back.

"Taa-da!" He bowed with a flourish. "The Great Tamarin proves his powers of flight once again!"

Fox straightened. She glared at Tamarin, with only a little mischief in her gaze. "The ever-modest Tamarin still hasn't learned that tamarins didn't fly."

Tamarin leapt to Fox's side. "Come on, Foxy. I was just having some fun."

"You're never trying to have anything else."

The young man frowned. When enslaved by the Patriarchy they had worked so hard during the day that night had been about exhaustion and little else. But he remembered many nights looking across the fire at Fox and wishing he wasn't so tired.... The Patriarchy had randomly shuffled the P3M from work group to work group, to stop alliances from forming, so Tamarin had found himself gazing at many beautiful young women, but he had always remembered Fox. He was drawn to her.

Fox knelt down and looked at the long stem of the rose. She tentatively touched one of the thorns. "You see, this flower has its own swords."

Tamarin sank down beside her. He touched the stem and then took

Fox's hand. Fox gave him a bemused smile. His eyes were very deep, a comforting solid gold with no white or black. "She's such a beautiful flower that she has to have thorns. She doesn't need anyone to protect her. She can take care of herself." He looked at the roses. "But if no one can get near her... I wonder if she's lonely?"

Fox blinked in surprise. Tamarin and soft poetry were about as opposite as one could get. It was a nice change. She reached out a hand and turned Tamarin to face her.

"Kiss?" he wiggled his eyebrows.

Fox laughed and pushed him down. She was one fox that would not be caught so easily.

Wolf sat cross-legged in the middle of the meadow. All around him stretched the rolling carpet of green. The Valley floor was so smooth that standing anywhere he could see it all. He liked that feeling. No one could sneak up on him.

He ran his fingers through the grass. It felt like fur. The Earth's fur. He fingered a single blade. The Earth was a Beast, running through the sky, and they were all riding its back. He grinned and looked over at Tyger who stood across the meadow talking with Ardyn . The Earth was probably a tiger.   Wolf had always felt a certain kinship to the wild animals that roamed the world. All Windborn and P3M did, of course, but his was especially deep. When he fantasized about killing Christopher Jarth, he always imagined that he would let the Natives, the Beasts, share in the deed. His vision of Jarth's bloody end was so clear in his mind – after he tore Jarth limb from limb, Wolf would leave the pieces for the Natives to feast upon. It was only fitting considering that Jarth had slaughtered hundreds of them, and still did, to awaken and feed the living cells that lay within the walls of his cursed domes.

Wolf's thoughts went to his other kindred then. The other P3M who were scattered across the land, enslaved and forced to build domes for the Patriarchy. Tyger had found Wolf, Tamarin, Fox and Spider's work site, but there were others. Six more sites, each with four or five workers. *Not workers,* Wolf snorted. *Slaves.*

In that moment, as he lay upon the soft, green earth, basking in the evening sun, his brothers and sisters slaved over metal beams and cables, building shelter for Jarth and his weak breed. Wolf decided he would save them. He would save the P3M. He would talk to Tyger and she would find a way to free them all. Somehow.

Then something landed on his cheek. Wolf let out a startled grunt and jerked upright. He pawed his face and brushed something silky and alive. It fluttered down onto his pant leg and Wolf smiled, his dark thoughts whirling away from him like smoke.

There, its hand-sized wings quivering in the air as it walked up Wolf's breeches on six tiny legs, was a Butterfly. Red and green with streaks of pale blue, it looked up at him with black eyes intelligent as his own.

"You must be a baby." He pointed toward the waterfall. "You're late; the others already went into the falls."

The Butterfly lifted into the air, and as if understanding Wolf's words, it circled his head twice and darted off to the water. Wolf watched it fly. Unsteady but still graceful, it seemed more beautiful than anything he had ever seen.

"These are my Windriders." Tyger was as content as a proud mother. She looked out over the Valley and watched each of them for a moment. They found a place for themselves no matter where they were: the city, the slave sites, the Wind and even here, in this new land.

"Your Windriders," Ardyn smiled.

Ardyn looked out over the expanse of flat meadows, and Tyger admired her strong profile, the dark sheen of her midnight hair. Tyger had realized a long time ago that Ardyn was beautiful, but that knowledge had been lost when hatred came between them. Ardyn blinked and turned slowly to face her. She was flushed and Tyger realized it was her gaze that brought the unfamiliar warmth to Ardyn's cheeks.

Tyger was about to speak when a small Butterfly flew over their heads. The two women watched as it was swallowed up by the falls.

"How...?" Ardyn began.

Tyger took a deep breath. "Only one way to find out." She walked over to the pool. Ardyn followed her.

They stood on the white-gold edge of the falls. The falls, smooth like a ribbon of rippling silk, streamed down from a hundred feet above them, cascading from a mouth in the stone wall. Maybe five feet across, the falls didn't appear to be too dense, but enough water fell that the stream was not translucent. The clear, blue-tinted water pooled calmly beneath the rushing falls with minimal movement marking their union. The pool never grew larger than twenty feet across even though water poured into it non-stop and there seemed no other outlet. Here and there, there were streaks of white foam that moved like clouds across the surface of the pool and the sand around the pool was soft under their shoes and felt like the New World.

"I don't see a cave," Ardyn said, trying to peer through the blue curtain to the stone behind.

Tyger walked around the edge of the pool, moving toward the wall. "Neither do I. Can't get the right angle to look behind it." Tyger grinned and raised her eyebrows. "You know what this means, don't you?"

Ardyn opened her mouth to protest.

Tyger grabbed Ardyn's hands. "Come on, Ardyn! We want to know the secret, right? Well, the only way to do it is to wade in and get behind the falls." Ardyn looked unconvinced. Tyger teased her. "Fish used to do it all the time. So did people! I think it was called swimming, but it doesn't really matter, we can name it all over again."

Ardyn gave a playful snort. "Yeah, how about *crazy?*"

Tyger laughed and let go of Ardyn's hands. Smiling, she began to undress. "Be reckless for once, huh? I'll tell everyone I made you do it. An order from your leader."

Ardyn said nothing. She stared wordlessly at Tyger, the woman's dark-skinned body breathtaking in its power and grace. Tyger always wore just breeches and boots, but Ardyn had never seen her fully bare like this. Tyger was all supple muscle, like warm clay, with broad shoulders and hips, firm thighs and taut arms. Like the meadows, Tyger's stomach was smooth and flat, muscles moving beneath the skin. As the Windborn moved back and forth, trying to gauge the depth of the water, Ardyn's eyes moved to her breasts. They were small and gently sculpted, rising and falling with each breath, the dark nipples hard in the chilly air.

Tyger looked back at Ardyn. She pretended to ignore the obvious flush in Ardyn's chestnut-colored skin. The trace of a smile flickered across her lips and Tyger beckoned with one finger. "What's wrong, Ardyn?" Her voice held the memory of their old rivalry. A dare. A tease. "Scared?"

Ardyn raised her eyebrows. "You wish." She began to strip off her clothes.

Tyger bounded into the pool. Without undressing further, Ardyn ran after her. Tyger waded in towards the falls, the water reaching up over her waist. "A woman sure can get you out of your clothes easy. Just question your warrior's will and you'll toss it all off!" Tyger laughed.

Ardyn growled back. She waded after the Windborn, her jeans clinging to her and her sneakers heavy under the water. "If you're so sure of yourself, Tyger, then why are you running away from me?"

There was a double meaning in the words and Tyger stopped suddenly. "I'm not the one running," she said. The water now covered her breasts, and her hair, severed to shoulder length, was wet with the mist of the falls. She got ready to dart away as Ardyn drew near, but then relaxed as the woman looked down at the water, distracted.

"This is wonderful! Like walking in thick air."

Tyger nodded, her eyes on the water. "It is. I never imagined–"

Ardyn shouted and rushed her. The Windborn moved aside at the last moment and Ardyn lost her balance. Before she could fall, Tyger snaked her arms around her. Ardyn shook her hair from her face, her feet back under her. Tyger let her hands fall to Ardyn's hips, but did not move away. "Speaking of wonderful things, I never imagined..."

This close to Tyger, Ardyn didn't seem to know where to put her hands. Finally she reached up and touched a wet lock of fiery hair. "I'm going to miss your mane."

Tyger ran her hand over the wet strands and the new bandage that Jyln had made for her. "I don't know, I was ready for a change." Tyger wondered if Ardyn understood her double meaning. It was time to push the past away.

"Hey! Look there!" one of the Windrider shouted from nearby.

Tyger and Ardyn moved away from each other as Tryl and the others came running towards the falls. The cowgirl was pointing up into the darkening sky, one hand on her hat as she ran. All eyes turned skyward. There, across the pastels of the evening sky, came a thick swarm of hand-sized Butterflies. Their wings fluttered awkwardly and their tiny bodies dipped and swirled in the strong Wind, but they were coming into the Valley with the certainty of those coming home. And there was something else as well. Tyger heard it first, her keen Windborn ears finding the sound. "They're singing," she said.

"Singing?" someone asked, but then the flock came closer and they heard it too. The song was soft and as the Windriders stood spellbound, they recognized the flow of notes, the twisting, overlapping melodies. The Butterflies were imitating the sounds the Wind made when passing through groves of Great Stones. In the groves, the Wind played each monument like a magical instrument. Each song different because each Stone is different. And when they all played at once, the air was full of a sweet and wild music.

The flock of young Butterflies seemed to be singing many of the Wind's songs in succession. They would sing one set of highs and lows, twists and turns, and then pause, as if listening, and sing another. Tyger's eyes searched the sky beyond the flying young Butterflies. "They're repeating the song of one of their elders, but where is it?"

The Windriders turned and looked at Tyger in confusion. Petre was first to ask, "Repeating? I only hear the songs once."

Tyger looked at him with surprise. "Can't you hear it? The song is given to them first in a voice more precise, more mature. Then they repeat it."

Petre looked at her; sadness flashed in his eyes. Tyger remembered that though Petre had the body of a P3M, he did not have the extra senses that most metamorphosed had. She opened her mouth to comfort him when Tylon spoke, "I only hear the flock, too."

Tyger looked over at him and then at the others. Even Spider, Fox,

Wolf and Tamarin, fully changed, nodded in agreement. Only one song. Tyger frowned and looked back to the sky. She knew there were differences between being Windborn and Wind-changed, but she was still learning what those differences were.

The flock was steadily heading their way, gliding down into the Valley and carrying their songs with them. Although Tyger continued to hear two singers, she still could not see the first.

"They're headed for the falls, just like the others," Ardyn said.

The Windriders watched as Tyger turned and gazed at the falls, her mind turning the puzzle over and over. Behind her, the Windriders murmured as the flock of Butterflies drew closer. There was a secret here. A secret the Butterflies knew. One that Tyger wanted to know as well. No longer satisfied to wait for an answer, Tyger took a step towards the curtain of water and suddenly she was gone.

Ardyn watched Tyger step forward. The curtain of mist seemed to enshroud her for a brief moment and then she disappeared.

"Tyger!" Ardyn lurched forward, but something appeared in her peripheral vision. Something huge. Something falling from the sky.

From over the rim of the Valley came a Butterfly with wings that stretched sixteen feet: white wings with a design like eyes on the tips that were black with a golden, round iris. The great creature overtook the flock of young, cutting directly through the Valley and dropping down in the midst of the gathered Windriders.

He was not particularly magnificent. In fact, he was quite plain. Despite the stories and rumors and legends, there was nothing amazing about him at all. Ardyn guessed he was about sixteen years old and close to five-foot-five inches tall. His hair, tight, crisp raven curls, fell to narrow shoulders. His eyes were brown and the skin on his bare young chest was ebony. He wore soft pants the colors of his glider and sandals that laced to his knees. In his hand he held a crystal flute. He was, as simple as it seems, completely ordinary, and that in itself made the Windriders' jaws drop in amazement. The bare fact that he stood, alive, before them made him the most marvelous discovery in the entire Valley. This newcomer was no Butterfly. This was a Human on a glider.

None of the Windriders had ever seen a Human before, nor even pictures of one – hadn't all Humans died with the End? – but instinctively they knew the boy for what he was. The blood in their veins told them. As the Windriders watched, he stepped away from his cloth wings and the thin crystal rods that had supported him beneath. He stood for a moment gazing at the Windriders. *How strange we must seem to him*, Ardyn thought, *with our blazing eyes and heads of thick hair*. The Windriders were all taller, stronger, their skin a variety of tones from cream to deep gold and chestnut. They were older than the newcomer as well, some by as much as eight years.

The young Butterflies, all ten or twelve dozen of them, flew randomly about the gathered group like children freed to play. Ardyn came to her senses first, her anxiety, her fear, about Tyger's disappearance making her bold. "Our leader stepped into these falls and now she's gone. Where is she?"

"She fell through the Sky," the boy said as if that were explanation enough.

A growl rose in Ardyn's throat. She plunged through the water and surged up onto shore. Reaching for the boy, she lifted him from the ground with one hand. "Don't give me riddles, boy! I want answers!"

The boy moved swiftly and a sharp pain shot through Ardyn's arm. She dropped him in surprise. He rose slowly to his feet, tucking what appeared to be a thick rod of crystal back into his belt next to his flute.

Ardyn started toward him again, but Tryl and Spider stopped her. She fought against them. "Damn it, Tryl! Don't you remember Tyger's stories about water? It may seem like liquid air, but you can't breathe it! She'll die if we don't do something!"

Tryl snapped back at her, "Get a grip! If you kill this boy we'll never find her." Ardyn shook off their hands.

Jyln turned to the boy. "We're the Windriders," she said, her voice calm. "We know nothing about this valley. One moment it was beautiful, the next, deadly. You say that Tyger fell through the sky, what do you mean? How can we get her back?"

The boy laughed out loud. "Hardly deadly! The River Sky makes life, it doesn't take it away. I thought you already knew that." His eyes touched each of their faces. He continued, "You don't have to bring her back. You can go to her."

Jyln opened her mouth to speak, but Ardyn pushed past her. "You mean go into the falls?"

The boy looked at her, a bemused smile on his face. "Well, you could–"

Ardyn had had enough of these riddles. Before the boy could say more, she turned and dove into the streaming blue water of the falls.

Tryl threw up her hands in disgust. "She's as bad as Tyger!" The Windriders laughed almost nervously. Now Tyger and Ardyn were missing.

The boy was smiling at them with wide eyes.

"What are you staring at?" Spider asked, grumbling but not unkind.

"I never thought I'd see others who weren't Human." He paused and then asked, "You aren't Humans, are you?"

Jyln shook her head. "No. We're... P3M. Originals, Clones,

changed or almost changed by the Wind. Tyger is a Windborn. She was born changed." There was power behind those words and all of them felt it.

His expression shifted. "Windborn ...? Tyger?" he repeated. Jyln nodded, her brow creased. The Windriders stirred. Something was in the air. Something was about to happen.

The boy turned quickly, rushing to his glider. "Come, we must hurry."

"What–?" Tryl looked to see if anyone else was following this.

The Human grabbed the front tip of his glider and turned a clear stone plate. The wings collapsed inward, and he slid his arms through two strong straps, hefting the glider across his back. When he turned back to them, the folded glider swinging, he brought his flute to his lips and the dancing Butterflies dove into the falls, their wings hugging their bodies, looking not unlike the boy's collapsed glider.

For a moment, the flock was a stream of dark colors in the falls and then the Windrider understood. "A passage into the earth," Tylon murmured. "The water falls through... into the ground."

The boy tucked his flute away and turned to the Windriders. "I will bring you to the Windborn Tyger. Someone has been waiting for her. Waiting for a long time. We will bring him to her as well." The Windriders exchanged stunned glances. The boy went to the stone wall beside the pool. He took a crystal pendant from his neck, sliding the crystal into a tiny opening in the wall.

After a moment, a deep rumble sounded from somewhere behind the wall itself. The boy removed his crystal and turned to the Windriders. "I shouldn't be doing any of this. I have no right to bring strangers in, or even show myself to you. But no one has ever come into the Valley before, and," he hesitated, looking partially away as something dark danced across his face. Then he straightened resolutely. "I think you are needed." He smiled at them then, a sad smile. The wall behind him began to move and as the Windriders watched, a slab of stone slid aside revealing a long downward sloping tunnel. The tunnel was lined with crystals, all alight with bright swirls of color that danced and moved to their own silent music. Or was it silent? If Tyger had been there she would have heard the slow, flowing melody.

The boy looked at the group and then at the entrance. "The Elders are supposed to be the ones to welcome newcomers, but no one has ever found us on their own before." He laughed, "I've gotten myself in over my head so I might as well enjoy the swim!" They did not understand his joke, so he cleared his throat and, with a toss of his dark curls, he said, "My name is Mlinz, Sixth Generation Survivor and second in command of the Flyers." He urged the group forward into the tunnel of colors. "Windriders, welcome to Sky."

* * *

Once the water closed over Ardyn's head, she squeezed her eyes shut. Her heart pounded in her ears. She felt herself falling, shoved forward, downward by the sheer power of the water.

Bright walls of the earth sped past her, worked smooth by the water. Ardyn tried to relax into the current that threw her, but her lungs were screaming for air. She fought the impulse to draw breath, focusing instead on Tyger. On being Tyger's equal. On finding her.

But her body's instinct was stronger than she had imagined. Struggling against need, she was only twenty feet from the end of the passage when her lungs filled with water.

* * *

Tyger hit the surface of a deep pool, her body pushed down by the force of the water behind her. She struggled and pushed off the stone bottom, away from the falls. Her head broke the surface and she gasped for breath, her lungs burning. The falls crashed down just behind her and she let the power of it push her into shallow water where she could finally stand. She was in an underground cavern, the falls coming through the ceiling into the pool that branched off into a dozen different streams, racing off in every direction. A thick mist rolled off the water, filling the cavern with a rich, eerie presence.

Where was she? Tyger waded out of the water. The air was moist and tasted slightly of salt or stone. She drew her hand through her shortened hair and wiped water from her eyes. She took a deep breath, enjoying the new, clean scent that surrounded her.

Her solid green eyes peered into the thick mist. Beyond the rolling clouds of vapor, Tyger could see streaks of color on the cavern walls. Were the colors illuminated? Glowing? The whole area was a contrast in different shades of shadow with streaks of color. Beneath the streams, the rivers of water running off from the pool, there was also color. Was it painted marks? Natural?

A new scent met her nostrils. Alien. Unique. It cut through the smell of the water and stone, or perhaps Tyger's nose simply picked the scent from the others. Testing her footing, she made her way cautiously forward, letting her heightened senses guide her. She followed the new smell. This way it barely lingered. This way it was strong.

The scent washed over her suddenly and Tyger could feel the vibration of footsteps. She heard boots splashing in water. Tyger spun and locked eyes with two Human women. She crouched to spring just as their net dropped over her.

"This is no Butterfly, Ali!" one of the Humans called to the other as she threw her body across the net, trying to hold down the thrashing Tyger. Water soaked them as they rolled across the cavern floor.

Aliqui grabbed her crystal Element Rod from her belt and it came alive with power. "I'll try to stun it, Kes! Hang on!" She jumped, landing on the net just as Kestrel was thrown from it. The younger woman hit the wall and swore. Grabbing hold of the beast beneath the net, Aliqui brought her El Rod back to strike. Tyger brought her legs up and thrust Aliqui into the air with all her might. The woman flew back and landed in the pool with a huge splash.

The net was made of a silky cloth that clung when wet. Tyger, batting at the mesh, had climbed half way to her feet when she was struck by Kestrel's running tackle. Off balance, Tyger grunted and toppled. Kestrel tried to keep Tyger under the net but Tyger's patience ran out. A snarl rose from deep in her throat. Her claws emerged. With two swipes the net lay shredded. Still growling, Tyger lifted Kestrel off the ground and stood, holding the Human woman above her head. A beam of light cut through the mist, illuminating the area. Tyger blinked, forcing away thoughts of the Patriarchy's searchlights. She squinted into the glare, trying to see the figure behind it.

"Put her down," Aliqui commanded in a steady voice. Tyger grinned at her. She could see past the glare now and she stared with open curiosity. She'd never seen a Human before. Aliqui, a head shorter than Tyger, was built like a warrior. She wore soft breeches and a vest over cords of muscle. Her straight black hair was cropped short but she had a long tail in back, braided with beads and small feathers, that had flipped over her shoulder. Her skin was chestnut colored. Like Ardyn's.

Aliqui frowned. In one hand she held her glowing light crystal and in the other a larger crystal with a blazing red beam rising from it.

Tyger studied the weapon. It looked almost like an Energy Cylinder, the weapon she and her Windriders used in battle. But where the E.C. had a steel shaft that held its hidden power, Aliqui's weapon did not look like a man-made object. And it wasn't just one crystal shaft but rather four slender shafts bound together, each a different color. Tyger took a step forward to get a better look.

Aliqui held her ground, but the El Rod's beam wavered. She looked into Tyger's eyes and then let her gaze wander over all six feet two inches of her naked form. "Put Kestrel down," she said again.

"Catch." Tyger laughed as she tossed Kestrel into the air. But instead of throwing her at Aliqui, Tyger threw her into the pool. With a cry, Aliqui dropped the light crystal and lunged. She swung her sword-shaped beam.

Tyger danced into balance across the slippery stones and Aliqui charged her again. The beam whizzed by Tyger's shoulder, slicing the air where she'd been a moment before. The Human woman looked surprised and Tyger laughed. The woman struck again and the beam hit the wall with sparks of color. Tyger slipped to the side, grabbed Aliqui's arm and flipped her into a stream. The woman sputtered and glared at Tyger who stood, knees bent and ready to continue, like a child waiting to play.

Aliqui jumped up. The beam changed. No longer a red sword blade, it was a living whip, bright blue, writhing and fast. She snapped it at Tyger, who dropped and rolled to escape. As Aliqui approached again, Tyger lashed out with one foot. But Aliqui was too quick. She leapt, bouncing on Tyger like a wild animal.

Tyger avoided Aliqui's attempts to pin her arms. "You attack an unarmed woman just because she falls into your domain? That's not very hospitable of you, Ali!"

The Human continued to struggle. "You struck first!"

"I don't take to nets!" Tyger rolled, throwing Aliqui away from her. They faced each other again, Tyger's grin widening with enjoyment of the game. Aliqui, on the other hand, looked grim, determined. Rising from a crouch, Aliqui charged. Intent on Aliqui's attack, Tyger was surprised when she felt first Aliqui's weight and then Kestrel's as the other Human attacked from behind. With a howl of delight, Tyger dropped to the ground. She wrestled them both across the water-streaked stone, using them against each other. Aliqui managed to draw her El Rod once more and this time Kestrel took the cue and reached for hers as well. But before either Human could use her weapon, the flock of young Butterflies came darting through the falls and burst over them like wind-blown bubbles, fluttering about Tyger as though she were a long-lost friend.

Aliqui and Kestrel fell still, afraid they would accidentally crush one of the precious youngsters but Tyger laughed out loud as the soft, wet wings and the songs of the Great Stones surrounded her. And just at that moment, Ardyn fell through the ceiling of the cavern and splashed into the pool.

Everyone turned toward the newest arrival. Aliqui's light, still lying on the ground, illuminated Ardyn, rising bold and strong out of the pool, ready to fight. The water she had breathed was not deadly as Tyger had cautioned but somehow, through some miracle, as sweet as any air. It had invigorated her and she moved swiftly toward Tyger with a shout of recognition.

The Butterflies scattered and disappeared into the mist.

Aliqui turned toward her new opponent as Tyger snatched at Kestrel and held her in check. Aliqui sliced forward with her El Rod and Ardyn ran directly into the beam, her body thrown to the ground.

Shaking her head, Ardyn's eyes blazed with confusion and anger. What had hit her?! Aliqui grinned wolfishly and Ardyn rose to her feet.

Aliqui struck again, but Ardyn was moving swiftly and the beam narrowly missed as Ardyn's well-placed kick caught Aliqui in the solar plexus. The Human doubled over, but not before she struck out once more, throwing Ardyn down again.

"Invisible!" Tyger shoved away her astonishment as she realized that Ardyn couldn't see the El Rod's beam. Tyger thrust Kestrel aside hard and threw herself into the fray. "Not very fair to fight with invisible weapons, is it, Ali?"

The woman spun to face Tyger, her beam becoming a whip once more. She ran at Tyger. Tyger waited until Aliqui was close enough to touch. As Aliqui struck right, Tyger moved left and kicked. Aliqui lashed high with the whip, but Tyger ducked and struck upward with her fist.

"Now this is fair," Tyger growled.

Ardyn, rising slowly to her feet, could not see the beam Tyger dodged, but trusted Tyger could best Aliqui. Ardyn looked for the woman Kestrel. The roiling mist hid the Human from sight as Kestrel leapt at her.

"The fight's not over, stranger!" Aliqui brought the whip down and it grazed Tyger's arm with a sizzle. Tyger stepped inside the next blow and grabbed Aliqui by the collar. She dropped her in a deep stream and Ardyn tossed Kestrel in after her. Tyger turned as Ardyn's shoulder touched hers.

"Glad you could make it," Tyger said.

Ardyn grinned at her. The two Humans were already rising from the stream, their clothes dripping, their faces twisted by expressions of effort. "Determined, aren't they?" Ardyn smirked. "I couldn't let you have all the fun."

Ardyn dropped into a ready crouch. The Humans approached, their crystal weapons producing whip-like energy. Tyger warned Ardyn.

Tension crackled in the air between the two pairs of warriors and when Aliqui spoke, her voice cut through it like a knife. "You can see El Rod beams," she said to Tyger and then motioned to Ardyn. "That one's almost a Changeling, but you're not. You're too fast and too strong."

Tyger said nothing, her body poised and ready to spring, her expression playful but dangerous.

Aliqui continued. "You're not a Butterfly, you're not an animal and you certainly aren't Human...."

Tyger grinned. "No, none of those. I'm Windborn."

Aliqui drew back. Kestrel took a sharp breath. The energy of their weapons flickered. Kestrel spoke first. "All his stories begin the same: *She had emerald eyes and hair like the fur of a tiger. She was the bravest of the village. She was a warrior-child. And something more, something they didn't want us to know....*" Kestrel looked to Aliqui. "Ali, it must be–"

Shock and distrust rose instantly in Tyger. With a growl she grabbed both women and pushed them back against the wall. "What do you know about my village? Who tells you these stories?!"

Kestrel opened her mouth to speak but Aliqui cut her off. "Tell this beast nothing! That Tyger is dead. Mouse and Falcon have said so themselves. This can't be their–"

"Tyger! Tyger!"

Tyger spun away, dropping the two Humans as the cavern was flooded with the light from twelve glowing crystals. A young Windborn boy, his silver hair streaked with the colors of fire, his solid silver eyes brighter than the lights, ran to Tyger with outstretched arms. Tyger felt a shout break from her throat, from even deeper than that, as she took the boy into her arms, as she hoped this wasn't a dream.

"We thought you were dead!" he cried.

"Mouse..." Tyger buried her face against him, unable to speak. Unable to think or move.

Led by Mlinz, the Windriders poured into the cavern through a connected passageway, coming immediately to Tyger like metal to magnet. Behind them came two Elders of Sky whom Mlinz had also brought.

Tyger finally spoke, her voice husky with emotion, her smile as fierce as her fighting had been moments before. "Windriders." The boy lifted his face from her hair. "This is my brother, Mouse."

There was clamoring confusion as friends and strangers talked at once. How could this be? All the Windborn of Tyger's village has been killed by the Patriarchy. Hadn't they? Why had Mouse assumed Tyger was dead? And where had Tyger been all these years? Tyger raised her arms, quieting everyone.

She set Mouse on his feet and calmly made introductions all around. "This is Tryl, Jyln, Tylon and Petre. Spider, Wolf, Fox, Tamarin." She turned to Ardyn last, motioning her closer. "And this is Ardyn."

Mouse blinked his wide beautiful eyes shyly at the Windriders, obviously embarrassed to be the center of so much attention. "I'm pleased to meet all of you," he said, his thirteen-year-old's voice both melodious and intelligent. His slender Windborn body stood five-foot-six already. "I was young when my village was attacked and I don't remember everyone. Did all of you escape, too?"

Tyger smiled. "My friends were adopted by the Wind, Mouse. They weren't born of it like you and I." Then Tyger laughed hard and loud, her voice playing throughout the cavern. "By the Wind, how is it that you're alive?!"

"I don't know where to start..." Mouse looked up into his sister's eyes. "How could I believe you were dead? I should have known better."

"Mine is a long story," Tyger said.

Mouse nodded. "Mine may be just as long. But we have all the time we want now." Mouse turned to the three Humans who had arrived here with the Windriders. "Tyger, this is Mlinz. He brought the Windriders into Sky and then brought us all to you. He is my dearest friend." Tyger bobbed her head in thanks and the Human boy smiled at her.

Tyger watched Mouse's face changed almost imperceptibly as he introduced the other two. "And this is Abraham and Sarah Tarahson." He looked up at Tyger and she could tell that his next words were not what he believed. "They are the leaders of Sky."

Tyger looked at the man and woman. They smiled at her, clearly nervous. Dressed in the bright swirling colors of Sky, the woman's ginger hair was just beyond shoulder length, her skin very pale. Dressed in similar colors, the man's dark curls were tight, clipped short like a soldier's, his skin as dark as Mlinz's. There was something unreal, something awkward about the two and Tyger immediately disliked them.

"If you must know the short of it, Tyger," Abraham's voice was not too deep. "We saved your brother, and a number of other children from your village."

Despite the joyful news, Tyger frowned. "Actually, I would rather my brother tell me his tale. Thank you, Abraham." She spoke with measured inflections, conveying her authority. If these two were leaders of this land, then Tyger wanted it clear from the start that she and hers were not part of their charge. Tyger wondered why Aliqui and Kestrel had not joined the gathering.

Sarah extended her hand as was the Human custom. "Welcome to Sky, Tyger. I'm certain you'll love it here during all your... visit."

Tyger did not take her hand. Already they were trying to get rid of her!

Aliqui pushed forward then through the crowd. She glared at Abraham and Sarah, the anger and resentment on her face clearly visible. When she turned to Tyger, she showed apology and welcome. "Tyger, and Windriders, you will have all the time you want to share stories. I'm sure I'm not the only one curious to hear how you came to us. We will hold a celebration of welcome in the Gathering Place. Kestrel and Mouse can bring you there. I ask only that you wait until *all* our Elders have arrived before you begin." She paused and shot a glance of pure hatred at Mlinz, addressing him even though her words were meant for Tyger as well. "For you see, one of our esteemed Elders has not yet been informed of your arrival. Our Wisewoman, Iahala, will be overjoyed to know that Mouse's sister has come to Sky."

Aliqui smiled at Mouse and he smiled back at her. Tyger saw a shared understanding pass between them, a shared history. To Tyger Aliqui said, "It was through Iahala's guidance and wisdom that the Windborn children were rescued from the Village of Wind. Her insight and the Flyers' bravery."

"The Flyers, of which Mlinz is one!" Abraham said suddenly, defensively, as if Mlinz's participation gave him the right to claim the rescue.

Aliqui looked at Mlinz again, her words barely contained her disgust. "Yes. Of which Mlinz is one." She turned back to Tyger. "If you will, please wait until I have returned with our Wisewoman. I would not want you to know only one side of Sky."

Tyger tipped her head in agreement. "No," she said. "Neither would I."

* * *

In every place, there is history. In every place there are secrets. Magics. Stories. In the Wind, in the Great Stones, in the domes and even in this land called Sky, far, far beneath the ground.

To every Original and every Clone on the planet, Humans no longer exist. They believe the Humans have all perished with the End. When the Old World became the New World, when the blue heavens turned bronze, there seemed to be no place for Humans. Their time was done.

Yet several thousand have survived the End. They have survived in their underground world called Sky. A world of passageways and caverns, small communities, stretching, weaving like a web beneath the surface of the earth, encircling the globe. These few Humans don't talk much about why they lived when millions died. But there is a reason. They try to forget and to be simply glad that they are here. They think of themselves as the Earth's heart. They have an existence that is almost perfect and yet deeply divided from within. And Humans know, perhaps better than any breed, that a people divided can be a people conquered.

At the core of Human life there is a wellspring of belief. To be Human means to believe in the unknown. It is this fact which keeps the people of Sky from an idyllic existence. Their difference of belief. In Sky there are two sects: the One Believers and the Pagans. They co-exist in a tenuous peace, in a questionable harmony.

The One Believers are lead by Sarah and Abraham Tarahson, a married couple. They are the fifth One Believer couple to bear the names Sarah and Abraham since the End. They were raised as heirs to their names and their position as leaders of Sky. And with their names they bear a certain lineage, a certain burden upon their shoulders and a certain destiny. Secrets and shame. The One Believers despise the New World. They fear, and so they hate, the bronze sky, the white-gold sand, the Great Stones... and all the new children. The Natives, the Clones, the Originals. The Windborn.

The Pagans accept the New World. They wish that Humans could be strong enough to live in the Wind, under the new marvelous sky. They are allied, nearly kindred, with the Great Butterflies who were born with the End. Their leader is an ancient Wisewoman named Iahala. Born long, long ago to the Snoqualmie tribe, there are few others on the planet who can match her knowledge or her age.

Iahala remembers the Old World and she remembers the End even though she was born over a hundred years after it. Like Sarah and Abraham, whose heads are filled with the deeds and memories of four other Sarahs and Abrahams, Iahala also remembers the lives of her ancestors, their thoughts, their feelings, their dreams. Technology can offer so much for so little. Iahala remembers the myths and the legends, and through them she remembers both the past... and the future.

It is Iahala who waits for the proper person, the proper time, to reveal all the world's secrets.

Upon the smooth stone floor stood a circle of tall stones, each embedded with crystalline eyes, engraved with figures, words and symbols that shimmered and sometimes moved. The stones were solid tones of deepest red or blue, purple or white, each emanating its own aura of heat or cold.

In the center of this circle, upon a woven blanket of green, gold and brown, sat Iahala, the Wisewoman of Sky. Her eyes were closed, her strong, weathered hands held open over a single shaft of crystal. The crystal stood upright in an ancient wooden bowl, filled with water and a bit of clay. The bowl was very likely the last piece of wood on the planet and it was sacred to her.

Native American, born of the Snoqualmie tribe, Iahala stopped counting the years when she passed one-hundred-twenty-years-old. What is age, really, when everyone of Sky knows that she remembers even before she was born? But that was no magic, that was knowledge. A knowledge that came from books, holo-recorders, interactive virtual reality programs and, of course, the IkioiHashi link. Her education was perhaps the only thing about Iahala that wasn't magical. The rest of her sang with mysticism.

She was dressed in a long robe, woven in the same tones as the blanket, and her long black hair, shot with white and silver, hung in a single thick braid down her straight back. From her thick woven belt hung a short talking stick, one of the ancient symbols of a story teller and of power. Most talking sticks told many stories with their carvings but this one told only one: one story with four parts. One story that would end and begin all others.

She had given years to the study of this talking stick, passed down to her from her father and his mother before, but today she had other concerns on her mind. Iahala was chanting. She was intoning the Soul's Song. She was Spirit-Calling.

As Iahala chanted, ten adult Butterflies swooped and swirled about the robust old woman sitting on the ground. The room was filled with the matured creatures, and as they soared up the high stone walls to the open ceiling, the only fully open ceiling in Sky, their wings were silhouetted by the colors of the setting sun. They fluttered down again to weave in and out of the standing circle of stones. At long last, exhausted from play, they settled atop the stones and their wings stilled. In the many nooks lining the stone walls, the small, young Butterflies lay sleeping. This place was safe. From the circular hole in the ceiling high above, the last of the light seemed to slide from the sky.

The golden Butterfly, the same Butterfly that had entranced Tyger and Ardyn earlier that day, twitched its antennae and looked around. Its wide eyes were actually black, but blue eye-spots glittered on its wings. It looked down at the Wisewoman and cocked its head. Her concentration was complete; even the ten unexpected visitors did not disturb her.

A spirit had called to Iahala and now she was answering. This was a magical and important time because the only time a spirit could call the Wisewoman was when the spirit was that of an innocent. And so this ritual took priority over all else. That included the Butterflies, and they, especially their golden leader, did not like being ignored. At just the crucial moment, when Iahala chanted the Word of Welcome and opened her hands for the spirit to come into the crystal, into refuge, the Butterfly with the blue eyes on its wings did what adult Butterflies never do – it sang.

It was only one note, but one note was one too many and Iahala's steady concentration was shattered. With a exasperated sigh and a motherly frown, she looked up at the golden one. She saw herself reflected in its glossy large eyes. "I know you are here, Gold One, but other things call to me. You must let me finish, then my time will be your own."

The Gold One twitched its antennae and shook its head, uttering another single note. In the bowl, the crystal vibrated in sympathy. Iahala's frown deepened. "Stop that. This is the best Spirit Crystal of the harvest. We can not afford to lose it just because you are jealous and want attention."

The Gold One fell silent and looked stubbornly away.

Iahala allowed herself to smile. Oh, for the good old days, when butterflies were the size of quarters. When they didn't have egos of their own!

The Gold One cast a glance in her direction. She chuckled and apologized. Even her thoughts weren't her own around this one! She turned back to the task at hand and had just closed her eyes when the hidden panel slid back and Aliqui burst into the room. "Grandmother! I know it's wrong to disturb you but–"

Iahala had already risen. Clearly the ritual was not destined to be completed this day. "What is it, child?"

Aliqui almost smiled, despite the gravity of her mood. She was twenty-six years old, no longer a child, but she liked that her grandmother still called her that.

"Mouse and Falcon's sister is alive. She is here now with her followers, Changelings called the Windriders. Tyger is here in Sky!"

Iahala's shock and delight were clear on her face. One hand wandered to her talking stick, moving to one of the symbols, then quickly away, as if even wishing was too much. Before she could speak, Aliqui rushed on. "Mlinz went out again today to bring in the Children because Mouse was still not well. He found the Windriders in the Valley. Tyger had fallen through the Sky, so he brought them in. I'm sure he thought the sight of Tyger would bring Mouse from his sorrow, but when he took Mouse and the Windriders to her, he also took Abraham and Sarah. He called them, but not you!" Aliqui's anger was obvious. Unlike her grandmother, she could not always control how she felt. Disgust and betrayal were clear on her face.

Iahala took her hand gently. "Child, Mlinz is their son. Just because his sister, Kestrel, has turned from their beliefs and embraced ours does not mean he will as well. They are the inherited leaders of Sky and many still follow their word."

Aliqui set her jaw and brought her chin up. "But many follow your words, Grandmother. You are Wisewoman. You know the Earth and the animals of the New World. The past in all creatures sees the past in you. Abraham and Sarah live life out of their Book. They cannot see the New World, only the Old."

"I have no words, Aliqui. My words are the words of the River Sky. People follow the River, not me."

Aliqui looked skeptical and Iahala said no more. She knew her proud granddaughter would never hear what she didn't want to believe. "Abraham and Sarah don't even honor the Great Butterflies but still Mlinz rides with the Flyers. How can someone like that be entrusted to protect and care for the Butterfly Children – as well as defend Sky? He's second in command of our own protectors!"

Iahala waved at the sleeping children – the young Butterflies – and the perched adults. "Sarah and Abraham may not honor them, but Mlinz does, regardless of his other beliefs." Iahala touched Aliqui's anger-flushed cheek. "And you know as well as I that Abraham and Sarah do not approve of Mlinz's place with the Flyers. The only reason the boy flies is to please Mouse."

"They approved of his participation today. They tried to claim that the rescue of the Windborn youth was a result of Mlinz's flying!"

Iahala took a deep breath. "Does it matter who claims what? We did what we could. We saved as many as possible."

Aliqui looked at her grandmother, her eyes burning. "It does matter, Grandmother! Sarah and Abraham voted to let the Windborn *die*. It was you who said we should try the rescue. You knew something was going to happen!"

Iahala nodded, remembering the dream in which the Great Butterflies urged her to save the Windborn children. Aliqui was still talking, her voice tight with anger and indignation, "...and if it wasn't for your beliefs and your respect for the Butterflies, all the Windborn would have perished. Your way is the *right* way. Why doesn't everyone see that?"

Iahala held up her hand suddenly and Aliqui fell silent. "That is dangerous thinking, child. The kind of thinking that brought us the End." She let her words linger until Aliqui nodded.

"You're right," Aliqui admitted. "I'm sorry."

"It is fine to have fierce beliefs, Granddaughter, but we would be no different than Abraham and Sarah if we imposed our beliefs on others." Iahala paused and then changed the subject. Her voice became very gentle. "Does Mouse's sister know about Falcon yet?"

Aliqui looked away and then shook her head. "They're waiting for us at the Gathering Place. Once we're all there, I'm sure she'll be told."

Iahala nodded sadly. She managed a grin and took a deep breath. "So, the larger-than-life Tyger is not dead after all."

Aliqui put her hand to her ribs. They were still sore from when Tyger had thrown her into the pool. "Yes, and she is definitely larger-than-life."

Iahala looked at the younger woman and noticed some of her bruises. "Did my bristly-tongued granddaughter already get herself in a fight? I would think, the way Windborn are, that you would get along with her."

Aliqui grinned. "She didn't like Abraham and Sarah the moment they approached her. They were already trying to get rid of her." Aliqui laughed. "You should have seen them when they first set eyes on every six foot, bare-chested warrior inch! They must have thought she was a minion of their Hell."

Iahala shook her head. "Don't be so quick to put that above them. They didn't want to take in the Windborn children. Full-grown Tyger might seem an evil herald for their twisted True End. They always whispered their dark truths about Falcon." Dread fell across Aliqui's face. Iahala touched her cheek. "But we will deal with omens and ills when they are before us. Like water, we must wait until we come to an obstacle before we overcome it. Now, tell me how you and Tyger came to clash."

Aliqui let herself smirk. "Kestrel and I were at the Genesis waiting to make sure no more adult Butterflies got in. When she fell down the falls, we tried to net her. We thought she was a Butterfly."

Iahala laughed. At the mention of Butterflies, the Gold One sang one note again, and Iahala turned. She had almost forgotten. The leader looked at her with its wide lidless eyes. Trouble and miracles always seemed to come in pairs.

"I haven't forgotten you," Iahala assured it. "I'll be back. Just wait for me."

The Gold One's wings quivered and it glanced skyward, out the open ceiling that led to the Valley above.

Iahala nodded. "Or go flying. Either way I'll be back to finish later." She motioned to the Spirit Crystal. Iahala turned to Aliqui as they walked from the room, Iahala's talking stick swaying at her side. "I knew it would be a powerful day when the grown Butterflies fell through the Sky and returned to the nest, but I never guessed that a tiger would fall through as well!"

Aliqui laughed with her and the wall slid shut behind them, sealing off the room called Skynest.

When the Human women were gone, the Gold One twitched its antennae. It looked at the place where the open door had been and then down at the Spirit Crystal and then at the door again. It moved its antennae once more, then floated down and landed on Iahala's blanket. Carefully, it arranged many of its delicate feet upon the blanket. The other Butterflies watched in curiosity.

The Gold One leaned forward and gazed into the crystal.

It was empty. The spirit who had called to the Wisewoman was not waiting safely inside the crystalline depths to be born again because Iahala had never been able to utter the Word of Welcome with firm concentration. The Gold One had always interrupted her.

And it was the very same Gold One who leaned forward now and sang. As before it sang only one note, but this time the note was different. It was the Wisewoman's Word of Welcome. The word that would bring the spirit into the crystal sanctuary which awaited it.

At once there was an answering sound, like a cry of happiness. The Butterflies saw a sudden streak of gold and blue that fell like a shooting star through the open roof. It struck the crystal and its colors filled the clear emptiness.

The Gold One with the blue-eyed wings looked down into the crystal. The colors without and the colors within were identical. It tilted its head and walked around the bowl, watching the living thing, mesmerized.

The Gold One looked up at the wall where the door had been one last time. It looked back down at the swirling gold and blue waiting to be born again. It twitched its antennae once, then it leaned forward and ate the crystal.

* * *

Tyger reached out a hand and touched the rock wall. She had grown up playing in the Great Stones, stone much like that of the Valley walls, but this stone was alien to her. She touched one crystal line of pale blue. She wasn't sure yet if she liked the feeling of being so far underground, surrounded by all this color-streaked rock. They had already been walking for a long time, winding through what seemed to be a never-ending maze of tunnels. She flexed her hands as if making sure her claws were still there.

And what of her sister? Aliqui had mentioned Falcon but why had Falcon not come to greet her with Mouse? Was it more politics and customs? Tyger felt a dark dread crawl over her that she could not force away. But answers would come soon enough. She had waited six years; she could wait a little more.

She looked ahead of her at the quiet Skyfolk. Aliqui was nowhere to be seen and Tyger assumed she had gone ahead to bring this Elder, Iahala, to the Gathering Place. Abraham and Sarah walked at the front of the procession and Tyger sensed a deep discomfort in them that she only understood as bigotry.

Then her eyes lit on Mouse again, walking with Mlinz and Kestrel, and she could not help but be amazed. Even though Mouse was of the Village of Wind as Windborn as she, dressed in pastel breeches and a matching short-sleeved shirt, he looked like one of Sky. But his steps were light and balanced, his body held straight. Tyger credited those qualities to his true heritage.

Every now and again, Mouse turned to smile at Tyger, his expression always a mixture of surprise, delight and uncertainty. For the present, she could only smile back at him in reassurance and wait for a time when they could talk more privately.

"He looks like you," Ardyn whispered close to her ear. Tyger felt the other woman take her hand. She had been testing her claws again but Ardyn's touch calmed her. "No one's going to hurt him, warrior. Relax."

"I look at him and I see the Patriarchy taking me away all over again." Her tone was fiercely protective with a foundation of anger as solid as the stone they walked upon. "He was only seven or eight when it happened. Still so small. Now look at him. He's as tall as Wolf, and walks like a young man. What has his life been like? Jarth took his childhood from me. His childhood and mine. My parents never saw their children grow up." She turned toward Ardyn and her eyes were flat with hatred, her voice a monotone. "I *will* make him pay, Ardyn. More than he already has.

Destroying Sart and his squad isn't enough. I just need time. Time to plan."

In that moment Ardyn felt Tyger's rage rise up like a living thing between them. It was a huge and powerful presence with its own heartbeat, its own destiny. Then Tyger flexed the muscles in her shoulders and arms, sending a ripple of motion and control through her body. Taming the rage. For now. She looked at Ardyn then and grinned as if trying to reassure her that she knew the difference between her fantasies and reality. What chance did Tyger really have of bring Jarth down? Tyger glanced down at their linked hands. "I'm allowed my dreams, at least."

Tryl jogged up to them and they released hands suddenly. "Hey, we're all memorizing these passageways. Just in case we have to get out of here. But we'll need a crystal thing to return to the outside. It opens doors." She motioned to Tyger's dripping hair. "We didn't all get wet entering Sky."

Tyger grinned. "Maybe it was a key. How did it work?"

"It fits into a space in the stone. Talks to the stone or something. Makes a door open. Mlinz has one." Tryl made a face, "What's a key?"

"Something that opens doors and locks them too. That's why the Patriarchy never let us have them. I'd like to get a look at these. Sounds like they do a bit more then most," Tyger mused. "Maybe Mouse will have one."

"So," Tryl breathed, "we can't get caught down here, right?"

Tyger looked back at the cowgirl, recognizing the fear behind her eyes for the first time. Tyger gave her a strong stare. "No one holds the Windriders against their will."

Tryl smiled and fell back to walk with the others. Her voice drifted up to them. "Tyger says it's no prob. They try to keep us here, she'll kick their Human butts. She says not even these key things can trap us..."

Ardyn shook her head. "They think you can do anything."

Tyger shrugged. "I can."

For now Ardyn decided to believe her.

Mouse looked back at his sister talking to the dark-haired woman, Ardyn. Mouse knew the signs of a powerful leader, and he knew that his sister was one. "I thought I was the only one left," he said in almost a whisper. "But Tyger... of all my people to live...."

Walking beside him, Mlinz looked at Mouse. "Are you angry that she lived and not your parents?"

"Mlinz!" Mouse admonished, his tone a harsh whisper. "I would never choose between them. Never!"

"I just meant..." Mlinz frowned. "Just, Tyger wasn't even there when it all happened. She had left you, and your parents died."

Mouse frowned back at him. "You make it sound like she

abandoned me, abandoned the village. It wasn't like that."

"How do you know?" Mlinz asked.

Mouse brought his chin up. "I know."

Kestrel glanced back at the two. Her eyes lingered on her brother, Mlinz, and she felt the old anger at his betrayal rise up in her again. "Only you would suggest that someone would rather have their sister die than their parents," she snarled, her voice icy. "If I had a choice I would be an only child and an orphan."

Mouse reached out for Kestrel's hand and she slowed down to fall into step beside him. "Don't say that, Kes. You don't mean it."

Kestrel's voice was full of bitterness, "I do mean it." She shook her head at Mlinz, meeting his equally angry glare. "You know there are three leaders in Sky, Mlinz, and that Iahala is one of them. Yet today you conveniently forgot that. I'm ashamed to share your blood. You follow the ways of thieves and liars. The god of our parents is your god and an ugly one. May you be damned even as your One damns the Windborn."

"Enough from you!" Mlinz barked, his eyes flashing. He drew breath to say more but Mouse put his body between them.

"Yes, enough." Mouse sighed. He looked at Kestrel. "More than anyone, don't you think I understand how difficult it is? I follow Iahala's ways and honor the Great Butterfly, but I also love Mlinz. Abraham and Sarah do not accept me. They hate it that Mlinz is part of my heart, that he studies the Phoenix fighting art, that he is a Flyer. More than either of the two of you, I am caught between the two beliefs of Sky.

"But no matter how angry Mlinz makes you, never wish to be alone, Kestrel. No matter how much you disagree with your parents' teachings, do not wish your family to be taken from you." Mouse took Mlinz's hand. "If you cannot respect each other, at least try to respect that you have chosen different paths." Both of the siblings looked chastised. They didn't apologize to each other. That would be asking too much. The three walked on.

Mlinz held Mouse's hand tenderly. "Blessed are the peace-makers," he whispered, quoting the Book. Mouse smiled at him and Kestrel only sighed.

At the head of the procession, two of the designated leaders of Sky walked resolutely forward, unaware of the conversations and skirmishes behind them. If the two leaders thought of how their own daughter had chosen another spiritual path, how their son loved another man, it was not visible on their stony faces. Their belief in themselves and the rightness of their way was unswerving, as it is in all fanatics. Abraham knew the Land of Sky hung in a fragile balance. The Pagan's Great Butterflies had returned to the nest and that meant change. Something would happen. Something soon.

His faith demanded he wait for the second coming of the One – and they had been waiting for millennia – but the Pagan's miracles happened in the here and now. It didn't seem fair to him that his faith be tested so sorely. The inhabitants of Sky were influenced by the Pagan's everyday miracles and he feared the way of the One was losing its power, its hold on the people. And behind that lay a greater fear – what would happen should the worship of the One cease to be the spiritual heart of Sky? Moral decay and eventual collapse? A welcoming of the Windborn beasts? A tainting of Human blood? He worried and his face twisted with the thoughts wrestling inside his mind.

Beside her husband, Sarah narrowed her eyes and walked faster. Iahala had been a thorn in her side her entire life. For that matter, the old woman had been a pain to the Sarah before her as well! But Sarah bore Iahala like a true believer. She had borne the accusations, the questions about their authority, the validity of their leadership of Sky. She knew it was hard for Humans, harder with every passing generation, to have faith in something they could not see, something they saw as based in the Old World, a world that had been dead for almost three hundred years. Matters weren't made any easier when Iahala's deities, Mother Earth, the Elements, were here now, visible and changing before everyone's eyes. It was hard to have faith in a One who seemed to have turned His back on the world. Hard to believe. But that was how faith was tested, was it not? Tempered to sharpness. Didn't the Book tell them so? And hadn't the Book predicted the End long before any Pagan visions revealed it? Why did no one remember these facts as well as they remembered the stories of Butterflies and spirits?

Iahala's presence had divided the Land of Sky all across the globe. And everyday it seemed more were swayed to the Wisewoman's evil arts and false worship. Sarah knew that things couldn't continue the way they were now. The Wisewoman's beliefs were spreading, along with her granddaughter's fighting art and basic trust in the Pagan prophesies. Sarah had worked all her life to get the people of Sky back to the strict ways of the Book. Worked to convince them that their same-love relationships were wrong, that their false gods were wrong. What did it matter that society before the End had accepted these practices? The Book condemned them and that was enough for her. They must recognize themselves as sinners. They must repent.

It had taken her years, but she had done it. She had raised the fear that needed to be raised. The fear of the One and Only. The One who had created Humans in His image. Humans, not Butterflies. And certainly not Windborn. That fear must not fall victim to Pagan magic.

Sarah turned to Abraham and as if on command the man looked over at her. "This cannot be allowed to happen, Abraham. This is one step too far."

The man nodded, for there was nothing more to say.

* * *

When Tyger walked into the large cavern with its rings within rings of stone benches, her eyes were drawn at once to the Wisewoman. Iahala sat comfortably on a pillow on the floor. She looked up at Tyger and her deep hazel eyes seemed to see much more than the Windborn woman who stood before her. In Iahala's eyes, Tyger saw knowledge that brought power, a knowledge of the Earth and its children. A quiet understanding that was comforting and imposing but could easily be threatening as well.

How this could be? Tyger wondered. How could a Human know these things, and how could they care? Humans were the ones who had tried to kill the Earth. Humans were the ones who had abused and abandoned Her. At least, that was what the legends told. For the first time in her life, Tyger wondered if the legends were true.

Tyger walked slowly past Sarah and Abraham, Kestrel, Mlinz and Mouse who had come into the Gathering Place before her. Her eyes and Iahala's were held together by a mutual respect and an even deeper connection as Tyger went to the Wisewoman and sat down beside her. Iahala's dark eyes searched Tyger's brown face even as Tyger's solid emerald eyes moved over Iahala's chestnut brow, high cheekbones and proud chin. Questions moved like a thousand clouds across their faces.

Moving into the room, the Windriders stirred behind Tyger, startled and confused by their leader's silence. Murmured conversation swelled like a breeze behind Tyger and yet she did not speak or rise. She knew it was Ardyn who sank down beside her first, and then the others followed suit. Sitting before this ancient Human, Tyger experienced a poignant sense of homecoming that made her heart ache for her village and her people. In this Elder's eyes, Tyger knew she could be a child, a warrior, a hero, a savior. Tyger simply did not know what the Wisewoman's magic would show her.

Iahala reached out and Tyger did not stop her. Iahala touched Tyger's head, stroking the fiery mane of hair. Her eyes seemed to say, *Wait, your questions will be answered.* The spell faded then and after a moment more, Tyger turned and presented each of the Windriders by name. Then Iahala turned to Aliqui who stood just behind her and Kestrel who had come to sit, saying, "And you have met my granddaughter and our Lead Flyer, have you not?"

Tyger nodded. "We have. I have great admiration for anyone who fights to defend her home. They both fought well."

Aliqui and Kestrel nodded in acknowledgment of Tyger's praise.

"Well, now that that's done," Abraham said, clearing his throat loudly. Tyger had almost forgotten he was there and fought back her rising anger. Iahala had a sense of ritual that Tyger recognized and respected, but these other "leaders" seemed as soulless as the Patriarchy. Abraham stood, towering over Iahala, glaring down at both of them with poorly masked disdain. Tyger's expression did not hide her displeasure as she stood, purposefully rising to her full height to look down at him.

Abraham cleared his throat again. "Now that you know everyone, Tyger," he said, spitting out her name as though it were quaint or beneath him, "why don't we all find seats – off the floor – and begin this Gathering."

"We have found our seats," Tyger answered him, motioning to her Windriders. She did not sit back down until Abraham stepped away from her. The two Human leaders took their seats together on a bench across from where Iahala sat. Tyger lowered herself cross-legged onto the floor beside Iahala again, watching Sarah and Abraham with open distrust.

The tension in the room was palpable. The circle had already been split unevenly in half. The only one clearly sitting with Abraham and Sarah was their son, Mlinz. Mouse straddled a kind of center line between the two camps wedged between Mlinz, who sat beside his father, and Kestrel, who was at Aliqui's right. All around them, the outer rings of benches circled them, empty. Either the people of Sky were spread far and wide beneath the Earth, or not many Humans had survived after all. Or perhaps both.

"So, Tyger," Sarah began, her tone at once cautious and patronizing, "where are you from?"

"From?" Tyger seemed momentarily confused by the point of the woman's question.

"Yes. Where are you from? Clearly not from the long gone Village of Wind."

"Clearly," Tyger glared at her.

"Yes, very sad that. So where are you and your... people from?"

Your *people*. Sarah said it like the word *possession*. They might as well have still been the Patriarchy's captives and not a family who had struggled together through hardship, death and loss. Sarah spoke to them all as if they were not real, not alive, not equals. She could not see their hard-won loyalty, the circumstances that Humans had created which made Originals slaves and created the Windborn only to be feared and hated.

"From?" Tyger felt her face twist into a snarl. "Do you expect some story of a paradise? Some place we look forward to rather than escaped from? We came from the world *you* made and it is not a pleasant place–"

"You ignorant savage–" Sarah shot back. "Listen to you talk about what you know nothing about!"

"Ignorant?!" Ardyn's hand came suddenly to Tyger's arm, and Tyger realized she had half-risen towards Sarah. Ardyn was looking at her with a mixture of confusion and alarm. Why was Tyger rising to this woman's bait? Harsh words continued to tumble inside Tyger's mouth even as she eased back down. There was just something about Sarah, something that boiled Tyger's blood. Iahala spoke through the roiling emotions, "Quick anger will not serve you here, Tyger. We in Sky know very little of the world beyond these walls. Be patient with us."

Tyger knew that Iahala's words were not for Sarah's benefit. The Wisewoman's eyes spoke to Tyger again, urging her to tred carefully in this new land for some of it was made of glass. Glass that an angry Windborn could easily shatter.

Tyger nodded her head once, "Of course," feeling Ardyn's hand still steady on her arm. The tension in the room dispersed. Tyger could feel her Windriders letting go of their own rage around her.

"Let us all remember," Iahala said gently into the stillness, "that all actions and words have consequence, whether in this life or the one that follows." She looked directly at Sarah as she spoke but the other woman simply looked away.

Tyger took a breath. "I would like to hear the tale of how my brother came to be rescued." Her words were somewhere between a demand and a request.

Iahala looked at Mlinz before anyone else could speak. "Why don't you tell it, Mlinz?"

Mlinz blinked with some surprise as if uncomfortable at being singled out before so many. A quick look at Mouse seemed to settle him and he began the recount. "A little more than six years ago, Iahala the Wisewoman had a dream in which one of her Great Butterflies told of a horrible event about to occur. Christopher Jarth, the leader of a Clone nation called the Patriarchy, was going to destroy the village of the Windborn, the Village of Wind. Every Windborn would be killed unless we could help them." Mlinz paused here as if trying to decide how to continue. Tyger wondered what he was leaving out. "We put a call out through all of Sky, asking for Flyers to come and aid us. We are not the only Sky base. All over the world there are pockets of Humans who survived the End. But we had very little time and barely a dozen Flyers could get here. That's only a dozen or so Humans who know how to fly a glider – a Wing. From our home, our Sky base, the Flyers were Aliqui, Kestrel and myself. We flew out together on the day that the dream had foretold with the others who arrived in time. We drank flasks of water from the River Sky to keep the Wind from harming our bodies for the River bears certain... attributes that protect us. When we reached the Village of Wind, it had already begun."

The boy paused and a visible tremor ran through his body. "We were too late for so many, but we were able to save some of the smaller children who had worked free of the Patriarchy's electrical net." Tyger's mind raced ahead as the boy paused again. She looked at Ardyn, Tylon, Tryl and Jyln in turn. They had all shared a vision-dream about what had happened at the village that terrible day. The day the Patriarchy's Hovercraft had dropped the huge steel net and electrocuted the gathering of villagers like beasts. But in the dream, there had been flashes of color, bright colors diving down and then away. Colors that were different from the shining silver of the Patriarchy's craft. Now it was clear what those colors were. They were the gliders of the Flyers saving the children.

Tyger tuned back into Mlinz's story as he said, "We brought the young Windborn here. We tried to make them feel at home, tried to help everyone accept them. But their home was in the Wind and ours is underground in Sky."

His voice became sorrowful. "All the Windborn quickly became Flyers even though they were unusually young. Being Flyers brought them into the Wind, but it seemed that wasn't enough. Over time they fell sick and, and they began to die...." Mlinz faltered. His chin sank to his chest. Reaching blindly for Mouse, he found the other boy's hand and gripped it fiercely, ignoring the openly hostile stares of his parents.

There was an awkward pause, then Kestrel's voice spoke into the silence. "No one knew what to do. The children didn't seem to want to live anymore. Nothing we said or did could bring them away from their sadness."

Tyger thought of Lion who had been brought as a slave into New Seattle. The Patriarchy thought she would agree to kill Natives, New World animals, so that the Patriarchy could have protective skins to shield themselves from the Wind. But Lion would not participate in their evil work. So she killed herself. Without knife or weapon, chained in an empty cell, she simply wished her death and freed her spirit to the Wind.

"We saved them from one death, but brought them another," Aliqui added.

"It wasn't the people of Sky who made this happen, Tyger," Mouse said. "It was sorrow. We were the last of our kind and we were just children. We all wanted to die. At least then we'd be with the others."

Tyger nodded. She knew there was more to the story, more that Mouse could not or would not share. At least not yet. Now, though, she understood that Aliqui, Kestrel and Iahala had helped give Mouse the will to survive, and Mlinz had been his savior. Tyger found it serendipitous that the word *Mlinz* meant guardian.

"Sorrow," Tyger said quietly, "did it take Falcon as well?"

Mouse bit his lip and shook his head. "No, not sorrow." He said nothing else and Tyger understood by his silence that whatever had happened to their sister it was too recent and too painful to talk about. She took a deep breath. "Thank you for telling me the story," she said. Her eyes touched Aliqui's, Kestrel's and then lingered on Mlinz. "It's clear that your love for Mouse saved his life, Mlinz. I am grateful to you for that."

Mlinz could barely look up at her but Tyger thought she saw his dark face flush with pleasure.

"So, how is it, Tyger, that you did not perish with your kin?" Abraham's voice mocked her survival and she felt her anger rising again.

But before she had a chance to react, Iahala took the malice from Abraham's words. "Yes, what miracle of the Earth and Wind made your survival possible?"

Wishing her story were more magical – she liked the sound of a *miracle of Earth and Wind* – she looked at Mouse and said, "No miracle. It was Jarth, the Patriarch. I saw what he and his soldiers were going to do and he promised to spare every Windborn if I gave myself to him." Mouse cried out, but the others were stunned into silence by Tyger's admission. "They said that as long as I did as I was told, they would leave the Village of Wind alone. I don't know how many days I really bought my people. I found out the Patriarch had betrayed me when I arrived at the Village of Wind a dozen or so days ago and found it empty. That same night the reality of the massacre came to me – to several of us – in a dream."

"Ten days," Mouse whispered. "It was ten days after you disappeared. I remember counting them on my fingers."

Tyger looked away and her body became rigid with over-powering emotions. Ten days! Ten days in exchange for six years of pain, humiliation and murder. The truest horror was there, in the burning truth. She had sold her life, and others' lives, for ten days. She pushed her anger down and continued, "For so many years they controlled me because each time I rebelled the threat was there: we'll kill them. We'll kill your people. Your people, the freaks." Her mouth twisted in pain. "Time and time again I brought Originals off the streets and welcomed them into my gang, into the only kind of family an Original is ever allowed. Then I would bring them out into the Wind and wait and watch as my friends died or changed. The Patriarchy made those who survived the Wind their slaves, and I would be thrown back to do it all again."

"You must have been a child. No more than a child...." Iahala's voice was compassionate where Tyger had expected condemnation. Tyger looked at her and could say nothing.

"You gave yourself to save all of us," Mouse sobbed quietly. "You let them take you so we could live. It's not your fault you were deceived. If it weren't for you we all would have been dead." He rose and threw himself into her arms in one fluid motion. Tyger gathered him up, held him tightly.

And as she felt the boy trembling in her arms, she felt the guilt she'd carried for all those years begin to peel away like a garment. Like armor she no longer needed. *Ardyn was right*, she thought. *Perhaps I will find forgiveness here.*

Spider, Fox, Tamarin and Wolf had all once been Originals. Originals who had trusted her only to see friends die and their own bodies change. But they had forgiven her. Forgiven her because she had finally taken a stand against the Patriarchy, the real killer, the real aggressor, and they all believed she would be the one to bring it down.

As the Windriders drew closer to the siblings, gathering around them, murmuring words of support and understanding, the condemnation Tyger had been expecting finally came as Sarah spoke. "Forgiveness comes from the One alone. You can accept Tyger, but you cannot forgive the evil she has brought into the world."

"You mean us?" Spider asked sharply. "Are we the evil?" When Sarah answered with silence, Spider just stared at her. "No, I didn't think so."

Tryl laughed. Sarah shot Tryl a look of hatred, but the cowgirl only grinned. Sarah hissed at them, "The One made this world for Humans and Humans alone. You laugh now but you won't be laughing in Eternal Hell!"

"Humans had their chance and they threw the Earth away!" Jyln shot back.

"All so ignorant! You know nothing of what Humans did!" Sarah retorted. "You'll see! Hell awaits—"

"Who Hell waits for is not for you to say, Sarah," Iahala said calmly. "Your Book also says that only the One can judge." When Sarah only looked away, Iahala turned to Tyger. "What will you do next?"

Tyger shook her head. "I don't know. Everything has happened so quickly. The Windriders and I need time to talk. I need time to think."

Abraham spoke up, a plastic smile on his face. "Well, good luck and may the One be with you. You'll be taking your dear brother with you, no doubt?"

Alarm flashed across Mlinz's features and he leapt to his feet, his mouth open as if he would speak and his eyes on his father. Abraham stared calmly at him, his expression detached, the smile never reaching his eyes.

"Thank you, Abraham," Iahala said. "I'm glad you agree that Tyger and the Windriders need some time here to make a decision. That is very giving of you."

"But—" Abraham started to protest but Iahala cut him off with a wave.

"No need to worry about accommodations. I'll see to all that." She turned her back on him then, effectively cutting Abraham and Sarah out of further discussion. Her eyes twinkled mischievously as she looked at Tyger.

"Thank you, Iahala," Tyger replied. "It will be nice to rest for a while. To choose our path instead of the path choosing us. Nothing would please us more than to stay in Sky."

* * *

"Who are the Windriders?" Tyger asked. A traditional question to begin their night-meet. Iahala had shown them where to go to bathe, where food and drink was stored, and had given them blankets and sleeping mats. Now in their own space, a large chamber filled with stone platforms, nooks and crannies, Tyger's question rang like the first words of a familiar story, bringing them together in this strange new place.

"We're survivors," Tryl said, with a firm nod.

Jyln added, "A circle of survivors."

Spider spoke next. "Warriors. I know each of us doesn't run into battle with a shout, but that's what we are. We protect life."

"We're explorers," Tylon said. "Pioneers."

"We're individuals," Petre offered.

"We are children of the Wind," Tamarin said, grinning.

Fox added, "Keepers of the Wind."

Wolf took those descriptions a step further. "We are the Wind. It runs in our veins, it's laced through our bodies, through every muscle, every sense."

Ardyn spoke one word, "Family."

Tyger looked at each of the Windriders. They had become, over the years, her blood and her kin. She thought of them all as brethren.

"What do you think the Windriders are, Tyger?" Petre asked.

"The Windriders are the Beginning." Tyger looked at each face. They were waiting for her to continue, to explain things to them as she had always done. Taking a deep breath, she said, "Everyone speaks of the End. We measure our existence on the End. Everyone says, after the End, before the End. You say that Mlinz introduced himself as a Sixth Generation Survivor, so even the Humans do this. But why? Why should we give something so evil so much power? Why keep it in our thoughts? I know we can't forget it. We mustn't, or we might let it happen again. But we shouldn't expend so much of ourselves on it. Comparing it to now, before and after. We have to start again.

"What the Patriarchy has done, building their domes and living like scared children, hidden from the New World, from the Wind, that is not starting over. We know enough about the Old World to know that the way the Clones live is a huge regression. All they do is breed! I understand that we must repopulate, but where is the life, the true living? Where are the gentle things?

"When I would go into the Patriarchy Library and hide in the shadows, I would hear the most beautiful things. Poetry, stories, descriptions of people, other cultures, other lives. In that place, it became possible for me to understand the way Humans lived once, and it was wonderful. Before they started to destroy themselves, they had made incredible strides toward a way of being that is nearly forgotten. But I haven't forgotten. It's time for those ideas to come back. Equality. Freedom. Individuality. Not just for Originals, but for Clones, too. We must unite against the Patriarchy. They are the true enemy. They are blood-thirsty. They desecrate the Earth with their domes and slaughter innocent Beasts everyday. They are wrong. Their Beginning is wrong."

Tyger paused then. When she spoke again, her voice carried them into the future. "The Windriders can make a new Beginning. We know enough to make it happen. We have many allies, we just have to know how bring them all together.

"Every new idea needs time and space. This one is going to need lots of both. It's a big goal, but the Windriders have always thought big. We've always been the ones to stand up and make change happen, and this is no different than before. Except this time, we're talking about changing more than just the Industrial District. Much more. I'm talking about gathering strength, returning to New Seattle and changing everything. Not just the city, but all of the Patriarchy! Perhaps even beyond that. It is always best to study the past before planning the future, and so Sky is the perfect place for us to begin."

Tyger watched the Windriders mull over all she'd said. She knew they were interested, could see the excitement shining on their faces. They had escaped to the Wind, they had found Sky, they could rise to this challenge as well.

"Iahala must know and remember so much," Ardyn said, starting the discussion, her eyes resting on Tyger with more than one unspoken question.

"These caverns hold secrets, too," Tylon offered. "The River Sky, the Valley. These stones they call crystals. I know I can find things here to help us... something that could stand up against the Patriarchy."

"And there's no way the Patriarch can find us down here," Petre sighed. "We'll be safe."

"Except for the gruesome-twosome," Spider growled. "Sarah and Abraham don't want us here. That much is clear. They're not as pure and holy as they pretend to be."

Jyln agreed. "But they must have information that will be useful to us. Just how do we get it?"

General conversation began to fill the room, over-lapping, as the

Windriders felt out this new idea, trying it on with words.

"A plan will come to us," Tyger said proudly. "The pieces will fall together like a battle dance. Now I know I've filled your heads with another one of my quests, but there is something else I want us all to do." Her eyes came to rest on Ardyn. "After blood shed and lost souls, we may have found freedom here. For the first time, maybe for the last time in our lives. Let's not forget to enjoy it."

* * *

"Tyger, are you still awake?" Ardyn's voice was a soft whisper. The cavern was dimly lit with crystal lights, the Windriders scattered throughout the room, sleeping on pelts and blankets.

For her place, Tyger had chosen a rock shelf in the wall above Ardyn's head. She leaned over the edge of the shelf and smiled down at her. She slid her body halfway over the edge, dangling and feigning shock. "Who do I remind you of?"

Ardyn threw a balled-up shirt at her. "Yourself?"

"No," Tyger said. "I looked more like this." She mimed struggling with something that wriggled in her hands.

"You're not funny."

"You know I am." Tyger dropped down beside her. She leaned her back against the strangely warm rock wall and stared away into the darkness.

"What are you thinking about?" Ardyn asked after a moment.

"You."

Ardyn's heart sped up.

"You look like Aliqui."

Ardyn's brow creased and her cheeks flushed in the darkness. "Oh...?"

Tyger reached out and touched Ardyn's face as if to confirm her blush. "Same cheek bones and sharp, dark eyes. Almost the same coloring as you, too. Except, you're darker... a richer tone." Tyger's hand wandered up into Ardyn's hair, hearing Ardyn catch her breath. "And Iahala has your hair. Midnight and fine...."

Ardyn looked at Tyger. There was playfulness in her gaze but something else just behind it. Ardyn looked away, steadying her voice. "I might be from the same bloodline originally. The stories say that Clones are just Humans that were changed by the End. Originals are off-spring of Clones, so–"

"Of course, you're more beautiful than either of them."

Ardyn stopped and looked at Tyger again. She titled her head and looked into Tyger's eyes, as if trying to find an answer. "Tyger, what are you doing?"

"Telling you you're more beautiful than any other woman here."

Ardyn blinked once, then again. Around them the large cavern was still and silent; only the faint steady sounds of sleep were discernible. The strange, colored crystal threads that ran through the stone walls of this land glowed faintly, circling the cavern with dim red, blue and green light, casting colors across the Windriders like the blue lumi-lights of the New Seattle streets. Ardyn spoke slowly, changing the subject because she had to. She had to know. "Talk to me about your plan, Tyger." She kept her eyes on the colors laced in the darkness. "There's more to it than what you told us, isn't there?"

Tyger sighed, looking out into the cavern again, her eyes showing her only the darkness. "Why do you want to know?"

"Because I want to know you."

Tyger was silent for a moment. Only one person, long ago, had ever truly wanted to know her. There were too many secrets that no one wanted to hear and too much difference. People loved or hated her, but few dared to know her.

But Tyger knew that Ardyn did not lie. She never had and she never would. She also knew that she could trust Ardyn with her thoughts, thoughts she shared with no one. Tyger knew her words would stay with Ardyn and Ardyn alone.

"Ardyn... I spoke of unity and I believe in it. Clones, Originals, Windborn, P3M, Humans. But I want the Patriarchy to fall. I don't just want Jarth. I want them all. I want every soldier, every scientist. I want them all dead."

Tyger spoke so calmly and she pretended not to feel Ardyn's surprise as she went on. "Jarth grew up among people who were too weak to live in the Wind, and I want him to return to it. He discovered the domes, he kills the Natives – the animals – to feed them, he enslaves the P3M to build them and he deserves to die. He deserves to be left to the Wind like so many Originals that I brought out. Originals that had too much Clone blood and so they tossed with the Dreams, burned with the Fever and died. Died screaming for mercy that could never come as their friends were carted away by the greedy Patriarchy and they were left to die alone."

Tyger's voice became an urgent hush, her emerald eyes burning. "He deserves it! He deserves to suffer just like Sarya did. I want to watch his life leave him. I want to see the fear on his face. The defeat."

"His death won't bring her back," Ardyn said softly. "It won't bring any of them back."

"Don't you think I know that?" Tyger snarled. There was a tense silence for a moment before she continued in a quieter voice, "I know. I can't bring them back, but I can stop him from killing again." Tyger looked at Ardyn and her blazing eyes were still aflame but her words were controlled. "They want to conquer the Wind but the Wind will conquer them instead."

Ardyn brought her hands to Tyger's face. Tyger's skin was as hot as the fire in her eyes. Tyger looked into Ardyn's gaze and saw something she had not seen in a very long time. Something she hadn't seen since she had last held Terri in her arms. Emotion stirred inside her and she struggled to concentrate on Ardyn's words. "Tyger, if you had told the Windriders this, they would have stood beside you just as strongly. You have every right in the world to hate the Patriarchy. Every right to try to bring them down. But instead you talk about saving them. Changing them. What do you really want?"

"I've been killing all my life. Instead of bringing something down, I'd like to build something just once. Even if just for a little while, instead of concentrating on hating Jarth, I want to concentrate on building a world despite him. Perhaps my Windriders will find a way for me to do that."

Ardyn smiled. She let her fingers wander over Tyger's strong features and then down over her broad shoulders and arms. "Your problem is that behind your warrior there is a woman with a mind."

Tyger grinned. She laughed lightly, a bit sadly then leaned over and whispered a *thank you* against Ardyn's ear. With a stretch she rose and climbed back onto the rock shelf where she could stare at the heavy stone ceiling. She laughed again, her voice a smooth rumble through the room. Changing the subject had always been Ardyn's strong suit.

* * *

Several hours later, Tyger still lay wakeful. She knew sleep would elude her this night. Jumping down quietly from her perch, she left the chamber and began to explore Sky.

The stone passage ways were lit by glowing crystals placed at regular intervals in the walls as well as by the dimly glowing threads. She took a turn and then another and eventually wound up in the chamber where the falls fell through.

"I fell through the Sky..." she said to herself, thinking about shooting stars and wondering how it would really feel to fall through all the bronze clouds. She imagined it would be wonderful, but in reality, she knew it wouldn't be much different than being knocked from a Windboard – the fall wasn't much and landing was a pain.

Tyger walked around the misty chamber. There were no bright lights in this room but beneath the streams that ran off from the pool streaks of crystals, like those set in the walls, glistened. She followed one stream and then another until she came to a stream whose bed was not lined with crystal threads. She walked beside it through the huge chamber until it entered a dark passageway that led west from the falls. It wasn't just dark because it was unlit, it was dark in another way. A way that reminded Tyger of the Patriarchy.

Pushing aside her discomfort, Tyger stepped up to the passage. There was magic here. Someone had laid a spell that said *stay away*. A warning to keep people back. Not to protect what was at the end of the tunnel, but to protect those who would go to it. She began to take another step.

"Tyger! Don't!" Tyger spun around. Through the mist Mouse ran to her, grabbing her arm and dragging her away from the tunnel as though he were a much younger child. Tyger let him pull her to a ledge of stone where they sat down. She looked at him with concern. "Why shouldn't I go down there?"

Mouse's eyes were very large as he looked up at her. "That's where Falcon is."

Tyger's brow creased. "What do you mean? I thought Falcon was dead."

"She is. We found some of her clothes there. In the tunnel."

"Start from the beginning, Mouse. Tell me."

Mouse was silent for a moment as if gathering his thoughts. Then he began his tale. "Since before I came to Sky, that passage has been sealed by Iahala's magics. Everyone agrees, even Abraham and Sarah, that there is evil there. Sometimes we hear sounds, deep rumbles from far inside it. Everyone was forbidden to go near it. But Falcon was obsessed with the tunnel. Fascinated.... She told me once that she dreamed about it. Dreamed that at the end of it there was something that was half evil and half good. Almost like the Yin-Yang symbol Aliqui sometimes talks about, but one side was silver and the other side blue.

"She was always trying to convince Iahala to let her explore the tunnel but Iahala always said no. But her obsession got the best of her and Falcon went into the tunnel, right through the magic seal! When Iahala came to see what had happened, she told us that the magic she wields is Earth magic. Forces of nature can pass through Earth magic. Windborn always talk about the Wind in our blood, but that proved it. Our ancestors were the Original babies of Clones. They still had Clone blood. But those of us born changed carry none. We are solely of the Wind and the Wind does not answer to magic."

Mouse searched Tyger's face, wondering how she would take all of this. How much she would understand, how much she was ready to hear. "I wanted so badly to know what had happened to Falcon that Iahala agreed to break the seal. She, Aliqui and Kestrel went into the tunnel. Falcon, she – she always wore black breeches and her silver vest. You remember, don't you?"

Tyger remembered very well the dark breeches that most Windborn wore, she wore them herself to this day. In her mind's eye she could also still see the special silver-colored vest their parents had made for Falcon from the shed hide of a Silver Panther.

Tyger's mother and father had given each of their children special gifts at one time or another. Mouse had been given a bracelet woven of threads of a dozen colors. She noticed he still wore it, though now a small crystal was tucked into the weave. A crystal key? Tyger's gift had been a silver butterfly pendant set with stones. It had been passed down from Tyger's great-great-great-grandmother. Made when the Old World was the only world. But the pendent had been ripped from Tyger's neck when the Patriarch had taken her that first fateful day. She could still see the pendant lying in the gold-white sand, its purple and blue wings shining in the sunlight as she was forced to leave it behind.

Tyger cleared her thoughts with a shake of her head. Mouse's presence in her life was stirring up long-buried memories. "Yes, I remember the vest."

Mouse nodded. "They went into the tunnel and found cloth. Bloody cloth, torn to shreds. Black and silver. There was no body and they think that whatever it was, it – it must have eaten her. Maybe some wild animal who got into Sky somehow and couldn't get back out. But whatever it was, it frightened all of us and Iahala had Aliqui and Kestrel build a wall deeper in, sealing off the passageway completely."

Tears began to spill from Mouse's eyes and Tyger pulled the boy into a protective embrace. "She always talked about you," he said into her chest. "Falcon insisted you were alive. She refused to help carve your name in the Heart Stone with the others who were gone. She just never gave up." He pulled back from her and his eyes searched Tyger's face. "When I lost Falcon, I thought I was the last one. When I saw you walk toward the tunnel, I thought it was calling to you too."

Tyger took Mouse's face in her hands. "The only thing that called me was the Valley and that led me to you. I'll never leave you again. I promise." They rose together then and Mouse seemed to know that Tyger's promises were law. Tyger looked around the misty room, wondering what time it was. It must be near dawn or even later. "You're up too early, little brother. You should get more sleep."

Mouse smiled. "It's almost noon!"

Tyger laughed, surprised.

Mouse wouldn't stop looking at her, his arm wrapped around her. "Will the Windriders sleep all day?"

"Probably." Tyger grinned down at him. "In the city we live

nocturnally, but they'll have to adjust to Sky now. It will take some time."

As the siblings wandered the halls of Sky, more of the lights set in the walls seemed to brighten on their own, perhaps tracking the progress of the sun above the Valley. Yet still this underground world remained quiet.

"Not many people come here," Mouse offered when Tyger asked about the low population of this particular Sky base. "Sarah and Abraham don't want their people near Iahala and the Pagans like to travel mostly. Visitors stay only a short time – things can be very... uncomfortable between Sarah and Iahala especially."

Tyger raised her eyebrows. "I bet."

They continued in silence for a while more but with every new step Tyger began to feel a growing sense of premonition: something was about to be uncovered; something unexpected was about to happen. She searched the shadows, wondering if they were in danger, but then Mouse spoke.

"Tyger," Mouse's whisper was slow and calm, bringing a sharp, sudden chill to Tyger's skin. "Do the Windriders know?"

Tyger stopped walking. They had come to the Gathering Place with its rows and rows of empty benches set in concentric circles. "Do they know what?"

Mouse sat down, his body in shadow. He seemed to reexamine his question for a moment and then, "I remember the Village. I remember the way," he looked up at her, "the way the Elders treated you."

Tyger was as still as stone. Mouse could not tell if she was breathing. "It's my first memory, and so clear. Father holding me. I was always very small. Mother was there. 'This is your big sister,' she told me. 'Tyger. Her name is Tyger.' I remember them saying that a lot. Your name. And the Elders were always angry at them. It wasn't supposed to be your name. It made them... upset."

There was a storm rising up inside of Tyger. A storm of memory. She could feel her heart pounding in every part of her body. She could not speak.

"I remember reaching out to you. Towards your face. The Wind blew your hair back. You always wore it in your eyes. But the Wind blew it back then and they were green. Your eyes were green and even then I knew you were–"

"The One help her if she makes us wait!" Sarah's voice filled the cavern as she and Abraham entered from a passageway far across the room from Tyger and Mouse. Iahala, Aliqui and Kestrel emerged soon after from yet another door. Tyger melted into the shadows, sinking slowly down beside Mouse.

Abraham frowned. "You make us wait and then you don't come alone. We said this meeting was for the leaders of Sky!"

Iahala smiled at the slip. "Am I an official leader now? I thought I was just an Elder." Abraham opened his mouth to speak but Iahala stopped him with a dismissing wave of her hand. "As for Aliqui and Kestrel, my granddaughter is the leader of the Phoenix fighting arts – our soldiers, you might call them – and your daughter is the Lead Flyer, our food gatherers, our guardians. They have the right to be here as much as any of us."

"Fine. You've made your point, Iahala." Sarah motioned absently. "We called you here because after much discussion, Abraham and I have come to believe that the presence of these Windriders is not a good thing. The Land of Sky is meant for Humans and Humans alone."

"What of Mouse?" Aliqui pointed out. "He is of Sky and he is not Human."

Sarah sighed. "Abraham and I think that the Windriders should leave and take Mouse with them."

Kestrel threw her hands in the air. "That's outrageous. That's bigotry, mother, unmitigated bigotry–"

Abraham interrupted her. "It's no such thing! We feel that now that Mouse's people have arrived, they should raise him. We cannot possibly give the boy what he needs to live and excel. It would be best for him this way."

Kestrel glared at her parents. "And what about Mlinz? Will you tell him that Mouse's departure is best for him, too? This is not what's best for Sky; it's what's best for you. You think that removing Mouse will somehow make Mlinz 'pure' again. But it will only make him hate you."

"That's enough, Kestrel," Iahala said sternly. "We are here to discuss options. Keep your temper under control."

"We don't expect you to agree, daughter," Abraham said, his voice almost disinterested. "You embrace anything your brother does that is against our wishes. Nor do we expect you to understand, Aliqui, because of your past... relationship with the dead Windborn woman. But we know what is right. We are thinking only of the boy. It is best to keep children with their own kind. Mlinz's... friendship... with Mouse had no bearing on our decision."

Kestrel opened her mouth to retort again but Iahala silenced her with a look. "Mouse is not a child, Abraham. He is a young man, old enough to make his own decisions. I am sure he will decide wisely when the time comes for him to choose between going with his sister or staying here in Sky." Iahala's face was confident and relaxed, her smile gentle and patient, but beneath her surface calm her mind was racing. There was more to this than they were presenting and yet she was unable to figure out what it was. "We agreed that the Windriders would stay in Sky as our guests. We all agreed," she reminded them, "that Sky offers a safe haven for all travelers –

your missionary friends, your devotees, my Windborn friends. If we are going to discuss changing policy, let us do that after the Windriders depart. It would seem inhospitable while they are our guests, don't you agree?"

"You cannot compare these godless creatures to those doing the One's work," Sarah said, her voice rising.

"In one aspect, they are the same," Iahala insisted, "they are our guests. Despite the fact that I find your friends inconsiderate and narrow-minded, I welcome them into my home. I have done this for years. It is your turn now, Sarah. Doesn't your Book claim that hospitality is one of the most important aspects of a society's success? Wasn't Sodom felled because the inhabitants were inhospitable to strangers?"

"How dare you quote the Book to me!"

"If you are going to live by it, Sarah, you should live by its truths, not just the most convenient interpretation." Iahala rose from the bench on which she'd been sitting. "The Windriders will stay."

"You are a devil woman!" Sarah shouted. "Only you would welcome demons into our very home! Demons from the living Hell! You will be the death of us all!"

Iahala shrugged. "You are entitled to your opinion."

Sarah's fury doubled as she saw that Iahala was perfectly collected. She hissed in a way that Iahala found very unholy, "You have brought children of Hell into our home."

Iahala sighed. Some battles had to be fought over and over again. "The New World is not Hell. Even after all that has happened to her, Mother Earth still lives. Despite our abuse she has given birth to beauty. There are the Great Stones, all the new flora, the marvelous Beasts, the Butterflies."

Sarah barked her disagreement. "Mutants! Distortions of the true miracles of the One. When the One comes again, this world will be burned clean. The flames of the faith shall purify the Earth!"

Iahala shook her head sadly. "Oh, Sarah. It is your belief that sounds like Hell." With that the Wisewoman turned and left.

"Good day, Sarah. Abraham." Aliqui gave them a curt bob of her head then she and Kestrel followed Iahala out.

Abraham went to his wife. He put a hand on her shoulder but Sarah shook it off. "She will not listen, Sarah. Her Pagan ignorance closes her ears."

Sarah said nothing. She was staring after Iahala with hate smoldering in her eyes. When finally she did speak, her words were as dark as the hate she felt. "I told you that if we allowed the Windborn young to stay, more would come! I told you all."

"I remember, Sarah. But you know we couldn't prove it. The people wanted to help. The more we spoke out against the rescue, the more it sounded like prejudice."

Sarah frowned. "It wasn't prejudice, Abraham, and it still isn't. It's the Way. It's the Word. The Book says that when the fourth horsemen rides, he will slaughter one fourth of us by sword, famine, plague and wild beasts. Wild beasts, Abraham!"

"I know, but we haven't seen the coming of the first three riders. And even when we do, the faithful have nothing to fear. The world will end again and be born just as it was before."

"You think being faithful means allowing heralds of Hell into our very home? Give them shelter? Give them food? I think not. This Tyger and her followers must go. And she will take her brother with her. He is the last, and after he is gone, then we can begin the Purification." Sarah turned then and strode from the Gathering Place. Abraham followed in silence.

When the chamber was quiet again, Tyger and Mouse stood from their hiding place. "They are no better than the Clones," Tyger snarled.

Mouse bowed his head, his eyes filled with pain. "They have so much hate inside, Tyger. Abraham and Sarah. So much they think is wrong. Even love. Mlinz has read their Book. He says that it isn't the Book's fault; it's what they make of it. He once told me the story of a terrible city. A city of evil called Sodom. There is an Angel of the One staying at the house of a faithful man, when some men from the city come and demand that the beautiful Angel be given to them so that they can do what they please with the Angel.

"The faithful family helps the Angel escape, and the One tells them all not to look back at the city as they run away from it. The wife does look back and she sees fire and brimstone crushing the entire city and killing everyone, and then the One turned her into a pillar of salt. Sarah and Abraham say the story means all same-gender relationships are evil."

"How can that be?" Tyger asked, confused.

Mouse just smiled a half-smile. "Mlinz thinks the story is about risking your life for your beliefs and protecting what you believe in. He says it means that forcing yourself on another is wrong. But Sarah says that all Angels are men, and for the men of Sodom to want the Angel in any way was perverted and sinful. She says that all same-gender love is a form of violence."

Tyger laughed. "That's ridiculous! What kind of twisted mind came up with that one? Love is love! I wouldn't be with anyone but a woman. A man could never understand me. We may be able to respect each other, be close, but only a woman could be my kindred spirit."

Mouse was not surprised by her words. "What about mother and father? They loved each other."

Tyger ruffled Mouse's hair. "I said *I* would be with no other but a woman, not that a woman being with a man is wrong. I have no right to say where others find love. Only where I find mine."

"Why can't Mlinz's parents believe as you do? They say that even if Mlinz is good and pure of heart, his love for me ruins him."

Tyger took her brother's face in her hands. Her eyes were gentle and firm at the same time. "They're wrong, Mouse. They're both wrong."

* * *

Tyger walked alone now, Mouse having gone to find Mlinz. Her mind raced with uncovered memories that mixed with new questions and concerns. What had she and her Windriders dropped into here in Sky? What turmoil had they caused in coming? And why, why did Mouse have to have those memories of the Elders, her name and her green, green eyes?

Tyger turned a corner and almost collided with Aliqui. "I was just looking for you," they said in unison and had to laugh.

Tyger motioned to Aliqui's ribs. "How are you feeling?"

Aliqui grinned. "Much better, thank you."

Tyger studied her for a moment. "I think you may know why I want to talk to you. But first, I want to ask you a question."

Aliqui nodded once; she knew what the question was.

"You were holding back when you fought me in the Genesis chamber. Did I surprise you that much because I could see your weapon?"

Aliqui did not drop her eyes or smile. She said simply and proudly, "Tyger, in the Land of Sky there are two religions. The worship of the One, and Earth magic. I am a follower of the latter and in my beliefs nothing is held in more reverence than those of this New World. Those who have the Earth and the Wind in their veins. The Great Butterfly, the Native Beasts, the Great Stones, and the Windborn.

"I travel to other Sky bases, because few come here – the tension between my grandmother and Sarah and Abraham keeps most away. I travel and I teach a fighting art called Phoenix to dozens of Pagans each year, and even some One believers. They advance through levels: Warrior, Earth, Water, Air and Fire. A student who has mastered this art can harness the elements of nature. All things and all movements fit into one of these categories and can be counter-acted by the opposite. I have mastered this art. I do not believe I can be bested in fight."

Tyger was fascinated by the conviction in Aliqui's eyes. She had never before heard of a fighting art. Tyger was a street fighter where everything goes. The biggest, strongest and fastest were the winners. Aliqui was Ardyn's build, maybe a few inches shorter, but when she said she could not be beaten, Tyger believed her. "You were shocked because in the middle of the battle you realized I was Windborn, and your belief demands that you...."

Tyger found she could not finish. She was so used to hate. The Patriarchy hated the Windborn, Abraham and Sarah hated the Windborn. But here was a woman, representing hundreds, who honored Tyger's bloodline enough that she would not harm them. Honored them enough that they had taken the Windriders into their home.

Aliqui nodded, as if reading Tyger's thoughts. "So many others despise what you are. What you are capable of. They are jealous because your body can exist in the Wind, live in harmony with the New World.

"But I, and those who worship with me, respect you and yours. When I realized you were Windborn, I still did not know whether or not you were a threat to Sky. I tried to keep you occupied until someone called my grandmother, or until I decided if you were to be trusted."

"And am I?"

Aliqui smiled. "Yes. I trust you."

Tyger could see and almost feel Aliqui's strength and her loyalty to her beliefs. She could feel the respect the woman bore for her, as a Windborn, and something more. Another fascination was laced throughout Aliqui's features and the way she held her body. But Mouse had said it had been only a few days since Falcon had died, and so Tyger asked carefully, "Have you ever taught a Windborn?"

Aliqui looked away. She had known where the conversation would lead. She wasn't nearly healed and wasn't quite ready to talk, but Tyger was Falcon's sister and she had a right to know. And no one could tell her more about Falcon than Aliqui could. "I taught Falcon, and I teach Mouse."

Hearing Falcon's name used in the past tense hurt both of them. But now that Aliqui had said her name, Tyger knew she was willing to talk. She made her voice soft, gentle. "Mouse told me what happened in the tunnel, but I want to know more. I want to know about her, not just her death. Can you do that for me?"

Slowly, after taking one deep breath and than another, Aliqui began. "I was the one who saved her at the Village. I was nineteen years old, she was fifteen. A Windborn adult really, not a child. Unlike Mlinz and Mouse, we didn't get along at first. She didn't get along with anyone. She wanted to go back. She insisted that you were still alive and would return to the Village only to find it empty. Time passed and her spirit never changed. She was full of fire and life. She didn't like being with her own people, they were all too young for her liking, and she didn't like to be with many Humans. I suppose she finally turned to me out of loneliness."

Aliqui smiled a faint smile, her hazel eyes not seeing Tyger but seeing the memories. "I was in the Valley, practicing my defense stance. When I finished, she came up beside me. 'You saved me from dying at the hands of the Patriarchy, but can you save me from dying of boredom?' I laughed. I laughed so hard. I had prayed that she would come to me!

"She had stolen my heart, Tyger. I was enthralled with her. She had a mane of black and silver hair, and eyes to match. She was like the night with streaks of silver star dust. She answered to no one and she believed in nothing... but you."

Tyger closed her eyes, leaning back against the stone wall. Tyger resembled her father more than her mother with orange and red streaked through her black hair. But Falcon and Mouse had grown to look more like their mother with silver and black hair and skin a shade lighter than Tyger's. Falcon's eyes would be black as the night sky, her temperament like their mother's as well – and like Tyger's, too – fiery. Tyger could almost see Falcon, twenty years old, almost twenty-one she would have been.

Aliqui did not see Tyger's musing; she was in her own world as she went on. "She used to have nightmares, horrible nightmares, and she would cry out for you and for her parents. She would wake shaking and I would hold her. She would never tell me what she dreamed, but the words she said in her sleep were terrible enough. Always about steel and blood and tears. There was always the same villain in them. A man, I don't know if he was Human, with blonde hair and beard. She called him many different names, but I remember her trying to warn someone about him and describing his blonde hair."

Tyger went stiff. She was staring at Aliqui with eyes filled with terror but Aliqui was locked in her memories and didn't see her shock. How could Falcon know Christopher Jarth? Hovercraft windshields were one-way glass, no one could see in, and Jarth could never have stepped out of the craft. It was impossible for Falcon to know what the man looked like. Impossible!

Tyger had a fleeting thought of her father then. A flash of memory. He sat near the Heart Stone, chiseling in the latest tale. A young Tyger, not quite five, ran by him, her long hair flying in the Wind. He called to her and braided her hair, twisting it up tight against her head. Tyger had never preferred having her hair out of her face but her father was a quiet, gentle man and she humored him this once.

That day, while she played alone in the Wind, a crazed horse, foam falling from its mouth of sharp teeth, had attacked her. As she scrambled to escape, its claws raked by her head. If her hair had been loose, the claws would have entangled it and brought the child down beneath the beast.

There had been other times as well, times when her father had told the Village gatherers not to go to a certain place, or the children not to play on a specific perch. He had never been able to tell them why, but no on ever doubted him. He had a gift, a connection to those he cared for. Could Falcon

have inherited the same? Tyger had no more time to wonder as Aliqui
continued, tears in her voice if not in her eyes.

"We were together for five years. I was her teacher... her lover. I
taught her the Phoenix art. She learned quickly. It was more than in her
blood; it was her only way to release her tension. To fight her fear." Aliqui
looked at Tyger and Tyger saw the numb shock that still existed in her.
Aliqui was only just realizing that she had lost her love. "I wake up now and
the place beside me is cold. I walk through the caverns and think I'll see her.
Her El Rod still hangs on the wall in our room – just my room now – right
beneath my own. I can't take it down. It's all I have of her."

Tyger reached out her hands and Aliqui took them. They did not
embrace, but stood like that, knowing their shared pain. Tyger guessed that
an El Rod was the crystal weapon Aliqui had fought her with, and Tyger
didn't need to guess how painful it was to have nothing but memories.
Visions of Falcon filled both minds. Aliqui saw her as a woman, tall and
strong, with all her pain hidden behind her fierce pride, and Tyger saw her
as a child carving her favorite thing in the Heart Stone: her sister Tyger.

As Aliqui remembered her lover, her partner, and their time
together, Tyger remembered all the beloved friends she had lost because of
the Patriarchy, she remembered Sarya who was stolen by the Fever... and
Terri that Tyger had left behind. It was the worst kind of pain to lose part of
yourself. To find yourself suddenly incomplete.

"It helps me to know that she was right. That you are alive, Tyger.
Because she loved you, never gave up hope and now I can love you as she
would have. I can know that you were the strength that kept her alive. That
kept her with me."

Tyger looked into Aliqui's hazel gaze and she respected her. She
respected her for being able to share Falcon. "My sister was very lucky to
have you, Aliqui. Mlinz helped Mouse live through that time of loneliness
and I have no doubt that you, not memories of me, were Falcon's strength."
Tyger smiled her bold warrior's smile and Aliqui was not quite surprised at
the love in her eyes. "I would be pleased to call you my friend."

In that moment they saw each other as equals. Despite their
differences – their lives, their warriorhood, their race and breed – they felt a
bond that would never waver.

"Friends, then," Aliqui said, and the oath was sealed.

Tyger walked on down the hall after Aliqui had gone her own way.
Tyger had lost Falcon twice now and she allowed the pain to fall off her and
into the dim passageways around her. Sometimes she didn't know which
tormented her more, life or death. At least Falcon had brought her Aliqui,
and she trusted Iahala's granddaughter in this place where she felt there

were few she could trust.

Tyger turned down another stone tunnel, then another. She could walk all day and all night in these halls, just thinking.

When Falcon had been a child, she had chased after her solemn-eyed older sister and mimicked her walk and talk hoping that someday she would be a tiger too. Tyger could still see her sister in Aliqui's eyes and words, as a child and as the woman the child had become. It was a comfort. A peace.

Tyger grinned and paused. She touched the wall. The streaks of colored crystal were in all the halls, but there was no red streak like in the Windriders' room. There the walls were faintly warm, here the wall was cold. Tyger traced a line of blue crystal about two inches thick like the rest. She looked closely at it and could discern movement within. She was beginning to unravel some of Sky's mysteries. She leaned against the wall and sighed.

When Tyger thought of the Wisewoman and her granddaughter, it was hard to believe how the Windborn children had died of sorrow. The Pagans revered the same sacred things as the Windborn. Tyger had a feeling that the deaths were not from sorrow but from something far more devious. Something far more tangible.

The more she learned about Sarah and Abraham the more she held them in suspicion. Tyger was a grown woman, but what could a child do against one of Sarah's insidious verbal attacks? Her sermons of righteousness and sin. Windborn children did mature quickly in thought and form, but their emotions were often fragile. Their emotions seemed at times to be the only thing that set them apart from the beasts. If emotions were wounded, if thoughts and feelings were discredited, then like an abandoned animal the child might well die.

Tyger felt her claws extend. It was a unforgivable thing to do, to feed on someone's weakness until they broke, but Tyger found she could not put it past Sarah and Abraham if they thought it would clean their home of impurities.

With their mob mentality, the leader-interpreted teachings, the religion of the One and the Patriarchy were quite similar. Just as most soldiers read the morals of their lessons and accepted them without hesitancy, so did these One believers. From what Mouse had told her, Tyger understood that there was one central Book of the One that could be interpreted many ways. But the followers rarely challenged what Sarah and Abraham told them was correct. Tyger wondered how many of them had even read this Book themselves.

Challenging what we are told is essential to life. It is challenge that makes life sweet. Without it, any fool could rule the masses with fear. Old laws would never be changed to fit new times.

Sarah and Abraham closed their eyes to their own hate and bigotry. Their daughter Kestrel had opened her eyes to become Lead Flyer. Perhaps she had seen the truth when her parents had fought the rescue of the Windborn? Tyger felt a rush of anger. If Sarah and Abraham had gotten their way, Mouse would not be alive today.

She thought of Mlinz then. Of the two siblings it was he that Tyger would have expected rebellion from. Mlinz loved Mouse and his love was wrong in his parent's eyes. Yet he had neither forsaken them nor Mouse. It took bravery to do what he was doing. Tyger had no idea how much bravery.

"Tyger." The woman turned to face Mlinz. As if her thoughts had summoned him, he stood just a bit away from her, looking very young in the shadows of the hall. "Can I talk with you?"

Tyger asked him seriously, "I don't know, *can* you?"

The boy paused, and then nodded. He did not step closer to her and Tyger felt the tension between them. If Mlinz's love for Mouse had never caused him undue conflict, than Tyger's arrival and side-choosing certainly had. Now he was watching his feet with his quiet brown eyes and Tyger could almost see the fight going on inside him.

"I suppose by now you know that my parents don't want you here." He didn't look up to see Tyger nod. "I want you to understand that they have their reasons. They think you are an dark omen."

"And I think they're bigots," Tyger said smoothly.

Mlinz looked up. His eyes were at once no longer those of a uncertain child, they were the eyes of a young man who knew what he believed. "They may be, but it's not because they worship the One. The One does not judge. His love is not a biased love."

Tyger saw the passion behind the boy's words. The passion of one who has found his way.

"Mouse and I are in love." Mlinz's voice was modest and proud at the same time. "Our love is beautiful, a part of us, and even though my parents do not see it that way, I know the One does. Mouse and I complete each other. I know we are young, but we are meant to be together."

Tyger went to the boy slowly and put a hand on his shoulder. She heard what he was saying and it made sense to her. "I would never doubt the beauty of your and my brother's relationship. And since you are part of that beauty, and you follow the One, then I must believe that there is some love in the One and some true righteousness." Tyger thought of Abraham and Sarah and then thought of Mlinz. She saw the difference. "I promise I will hold no anger against your god."

Mlinz took a deep breath and uttered a *thank you*. There was a gentle smile on his face as he turned and walked away.

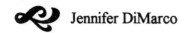 Jennifer DiMarco

"You never cease to amaze me." Ardyn stepped from the shadows.

Tyger smiled at her. "How long have you been standing there?"

Ardyn leaned against the wall and touched the line of crystal Tyger had traced. "Long enough to see the warrior thinking. Not very long."

"Am I close to our room then?" Tyger rested her shoulder against the wall and looked at Ardyn with a grin.

Ardyn nodded, looking at her with a easy smile just a little concerned. "You left early, didn't you? If you couldn't sleep you should have woken me. I would have talked with you."

"Well," Tyger teased, enjoying Ardyn's concern. "I did talk to you for a while, but when you weren't laughing at my jokes I realized you must be asleep."

Ardyn laughed. "I would have liked to talk more, but I guess yesterday's excitement was too exhausting."

Tyger caught her gaze. "So talk to me now."

Ardyn grinned. "Do I have you to myself, or do you have to run off and solve something else?"

Tyger reached forward and slowly brought a lock of hair over Ardyn's shoulder. The silky black strands shone against the woman's white tee-shirt. "Right now I have only one thing on my mind."

* * *

"Sex! Sex is definitely it. Passionate, though. Has to be passionate and in the dark. More mystery."

"No way, battle is much better. Good, clean, fast-paced battle. Life-threatening, blood-pumping excitement. Victory, kicking ass – awesome! Nothing better."

Spider looked at Tryl with one eyebrow raised. "You're nuts! You can say battle is the best pastime when you've got a lover like Jyln sitting right next to you? Your hat's on too tight!"

Tryl threw a half-eaten ration bar at her. Spider dodged. "Oh, sure, throw something at me while you're all the way up there. You wouldn't dare with you were down here with me."

Tryl sneered. She and Jyln sat in a nook high in the stone wall of the Windriders' chamber. Spider stood beneath them, her hands on her hips and challenge in her eyes. "You're on," Tryl laughed, jumping down. The two stood facing each other, all grins and strong muscle. "Okay, it's your challenge, what'll it be?"

Spider took a moment and sized Tryl up. Spider was taller but Tryl was thicker; they were pretty equal. "Wrestling. To the first pin. You think you have a chance?"

Tryl smiled and took off her denim vest. She tossed it aside and was about to toss her hat off too when she stopped and just straightened it instead. "I don't think this'll be so hard. I'll keep my hat on."

Spider gave her a growl through her grin.

"I get the winner," Jyln called from her perch.

The two warriors looked up at her. Jyln lay stretched out across the ledge, one knee raised and a hand on her thigh. Her white-blond hair fell down over her shoulders and her blue-gray eyes blinked with anything but innocence. Spider and Tryl looked back at each other with a bit more determination.

"A battle *for* sex. Now, that's the best," Tryl laughed and Spider grabbed her in a running tackle.

* * *

Tylon and Petre leaned forward together and stared at the glowing crystal set in the wall. They had been walking all through Sky, examining the cloudy shafts that emanated an almost golden light but gave no warmth. Shaking his head Tylon leaned back from it. "Amazing. The colored crystals in the walls, these lights, the weapons, Mlinz's flute – there are so many different kinds and I have a feeling there are a lot more we haven't seen yet."

Petre nodded and looked at his friend. "Mlinz's glider had crystal rods also."

Tylon looked at Petre. He hadn't noticed the rods. After a moment he laughed and wrapped an arm around Petre's shoulders. "My second pair of eyes! What would I do without you?" Petre smiled but then Tylon's gaze became very distant. "Ravyn was always prepared, Petre. When Tyger presented a plan to us, Ravyn would always be able to create new or better weapons, or plans, or something. She was inspired by the warrior in Tyger. I'm not sure what inspires me, but I know what I want. I need to make Tyger – all the Windriders – proud. There's something about these crystals, something incredible. I know I can use them. I just don't know how."

"Yet," Petre caught Tylon's gaze then and Tylon fell silent at the strength of emotion in Petre's solid silver eyes. "I am proud of you already. I was a Patriarchy soldier, but you welcomed me despite. I have no doubt you will make great things with these crystals, but no invention could be greater than your heart."

Tylon stood without words. He had never felt so entirely stunned.

"Hello there, you two! It's Tylon and Petre, right?" Kestrel walked into the cavern carrying a rolled glider over her shoulders. Her voice broke the spell of stillness as she set the glider down in the middle of the room and began to unfold it.

"Yes, Tylon and Petre," Petre confirmed with a smile, unfazed that they had been interrupted. He had already decided he would do all he could to help Tylon with his dream. And Tylon had already decided that making Petre his working partner was the best thing he had ever done.

Kestrel looked up at them and grinned at the curiosity in their eyes. "Interested in Wings?"

Tylon and Petre knelt beside Kestrel, exchanging glances. Tylon said politely, "They're beautiful, but actually we're quite taken by the clear stone called crystal. It's used all over Sky and Petre noticed it in a Wing as well."

Kestrel didn't frown. She liked it when people wanted to learn how to fly, but any kind of curiosity pleased her. "Well, you'll have to talk to Aliqui about other kinds of crystal, but I can tell you everything about the Air rods."

Tylon nodded excitedly, like a child offered a treat, and Petre watched him as Tylon opened all his senses to what Kestrel was showing him. Petre wondered: if Sky began to tumble down around them right now, would Tylon even notice? Grinning, Petre leaned forward to listen to the Human woman.

Kestrel did not continue to unfold the glider, she simply reached into the bundle and slid out a rod three feet long. She held it towards Tylon and, like any inventor who was offered a new marvel, he took it gently into his hands.

Kestrel smiled at him as he touched the surface and studied the shape. The rod glowed with a soft white light. "When the people of Sky first came in contact with the Great Butterfly, they were amazed. Many tried to study them, even to communicate with them, but they had little luck. Then Iahala went to them and without flash or marvel she said that she respected them as great powers and asked them what we could do to help them." Kestrel stroked the fine cloth of the Wing as she continued. "Of all those who had tried to study the Butterfly, I had never given up. They filled my dreams and my waking hours as well. The way they could ride the wildest, most powerful Wind with such easy grace. They were like dreams, forever out of reach and then, with the love of the Earth in her veins, Iahala reached them.

"From that day on I believed in Earth magic, in Iahala. The Butterflies let me study them for days. The way they moved, flew, landed and took off. My parents were furious, of course, but I didn't hear their disagreement. I knew only that I had achieved my dream.

"Then one day, when I was out watching the Butterflies, it came to me. Wings. Humans have been searching for them for centuries, but as I watched the Butterflies I knew how I could do it. I went to Aliqui because she's the Crystal Harvester. She and I worked together.

"It took months for Aliqui, Iahala and me to charge the crystal rods with the element Air, but when it was done, they were lighter than bird's bones and as strong as steel." Kestrel waved her hand proudly over the glider and the rod in Tylon's hands. "And now we have Wings. We can help the Great Butterfly raise their young and we can fly."

Tylon saw the way Kestrel's eyes had grown so bright as she spoke and he thought of Ravyn when she had perfected the Windboard and given it an engine. Ravyn had had that same light in her eyes. That same love. Tylon had no special desire to fly but he knew what victory was. Victory was creating a dream.

A while later Tylon and Petre had gone on their way in search for Aliqui, the Crystal Harvester. Kestrel sat alone in the quiet chamber, carefully constructing her Wing. Slowly she unfolded the sails and then reached for each rod: the sail edges, the abdomen and the thorax. Each piece was named after the corresponding part of a Butterfly because the names from Old World gliders had fallen victims to time. But it didn't matter. In Kestrel's eyes the object before her was not just an incredibly versatile hand-glider, it was a Wing.

As she worked, she sang a soft, wordless tune that repeated itself gently over again. It was one of the songs that Mouse played for the young Butterflies. On his special flute she could not hear it, but he had another that could be heard by Human ears and Kestrel never tired of listening.

She had heard the song played late at night recently, its tune drifting through the stone walls and filling her room. Mouse had been teaching Mlinz how to play for the young because after Falcon had died Mouse had fallen ill and thought his days were numbered. Even sick, the young Windborn had put the life of the Butterflies before his own.

Mouse had recovered almost at once upon Tyger's arrival, but now Mlinz had taken a liking to the music and was playing it for his enjoyment... and probably Mouse's as well.

"Going out flying?"

Kestrel started a little at the low voice. She looked up from her work as Wolf crouched down near her. She smiled and laughed a little at her nervousness. "Actually, this Wing is too small for me. It's Mouse's. But I check all the gliders periodically to make sure they're in good shape."

Wolf nodded, casting a glance at the Sky blue sail with streaks of white. "A lot of responsibility being Lead Flyer."

Kestrel nodded and watched Wolf in silence for a moment. P3M looked almost exactly like Windborn, the only physical difference was the intensity of their eyes. Both had solid eyes with no pupil or sclera, but the eyes of P3M did not burn like Tyger's, Mouse's or Falcon's. Kestrel didn't miss that particular blaze. She found it a bit frightening. She guessed she and Wolf were the same age and height, though Wolf was stocky and thick-muscled where she tended to be slender. His skin was not dark like hers but more of a golden brown. He wore his hair short in uneven layers but instead of looking unkempt Kestrel thought it looked like a pelt. She reached up and touched her own hair, wrapping a dark curl around her finger as she thought. Humans and Windborn... how different were they really?

Wolf looked up at her. He wasn't the kind of man who smiled easily, but there was kindness in his eyes. "I'd like to learn to fly."

Despite her excitement, Kestrel couldn't help her raised eyebrows. Flying a Wing was not easy. It took precision skill and timing. It took grace and genteel talent, things she doubted the burly warrior before her possessed. Unlike ancient hand-gliders, a Wing could maneuver on the very smallest breeze or the most wild Wind for days at a time.

Wolf watched Kestrel in silence, waiting. Kestrel had no way of knowing that in all his life this was the first time Wolf had ever asked for anything. "Flying is very difficult, Wolf, I don't know if–"

Wolf's eyes flashed something she couldn't read and he stood and walked away.

Kestrel jumped to her feet. "Wolf, I didn't mean to–"

But he was already gone. He had expected too much. She was, after all, only Human.

* * *

"Ode to Foxy:
Gentle Foxy, with eyes so brown,
won't you hear the words of this clown?
Your skin is so golden and so fine,
can't you see you were meant to be mine?
To me your beauty cannot be surpassed,
I swear I'm not trying to harass.
My love for you is one of a kind.
Baby, you can wrap me in bandages anytime!"

Fox threw her shoes at Tamarin. They hit him in the chest and he stumbled back, clenching his heart, tumbling onto his sleeping mat.

"You're a real jerk, Tamarin," Fox said through laughter.

Tamarin popped up and grinned at her. "But a jerk who you love and care for, and would love to make–"

"Dream on!" Fox threw a roll of gauze at his head. The boy caught it, kissed it and tossed it back. Fox picked it up with her finger tips and dropped it back into the medical pack she was checking. "Remind me to sterilize that."

Tamarin feigned more chest pains. "Oh, your words bite like rabid Beasts devouring my heart–"

"Shut up, Tamarin, before I bite your blonde head off."

Tamarin stuck his tongue out at Tryl as she hobbled into the chamber, holding her head. "Aw, you're just mad 'cause Spider drop-kicked you across the room!"

Tryl growled at him and sank down beside Fox. "How was I supposed to know she was the Windborn Wonder?"

Tamarin shrugged. "Whenever any of us got sick, she'd always do our work. She's got more than strength, she's got gusto."

Tryl frowned and stayed still while Fox wrapped her head. "Yeah, well, next time I'll be ready. Anyway, I got in a few good punches. She didn't take me down too hard."

Tamarin snorted.

Fox finished with the bandage. "Where is Spider?"

"Off claiming her winnings," Tryl moped.

Tamarin laughed. "Go, Spider! Enjoy that freedom!"

At the mention of her name Spider entered the room with Jyln right behind her. Tryl looked up in surprise. She recovered quickly and sneered at Spider. "What's wrong, couldn't stay in the saddle as long as a cowgirl?"

Spider leaned over until their noses almost touched. "You are a crude, rough-and-tumble punk," she sneered back at her, "and Jyln and I decided we'd rather not do anything without you."

Tryl's sneer turned into a surprised grin that Spider matched. Tryl looked at Jyln and the woman mouthed *I love you* with a wink. She knew Jyl would never leave her out. Tryl jumped to her feet and slapped her leg. "Yee-haa!"

The three walked out together, leaving Tamarin and Fox to laugh.

Back in the corridor, Ardyn looked up, startled by Tyger's sudden silence. "Tyger?" She stopped.

The other woman moved closer to her, her green eyes meeting Ardyn's brown like old friends. Tyger ran her hand through Ardyn's hair. Ardyn closed her eyes and let herself feel only the strength and the gentle certainty in Tyger's touch.

Tyger let her fingers trail down Ardyn's neck, circling to caress her warm cheek as light as feathers or a breeze. Tyger's whisper was barely a breath against Ardyn's lips, "Do you–"

"Whow! Ah, eh, um–"

Tyger and Ardyn jerked away from each other. Tryl stood frozen a few feet down the hall. The cowgirl's eyes were wide with shock and disbelief. She shook her head twice, hard. Jyln and Spider came around the corner, looking from Tryl to Tyger in confusion. Their leader was glaring at Tryl with a certain fire they had never seen before.

"Time to turn around and go the other way, my pals," Tryl said under Tyger's stare. She turned and pushed Jyln and Spider back the way they'd come.

Ardyn looked at Tyger with a grin. The older woman brought her eyes from the retreating three and looked down at Ardyn as the woman began to laugh.

"I fail to see what's so funny," Tyger grumbled trying to force back a grin of her own.

"This is what we get from standing out in the hall." Ardyn laughed harder at Tyger's frown and took her hand. "I thought you were going to kill her right then and there."

Tyger glanced down the hall again. "I still might."

Ardyn reached up and touched Tyger's face. "Don't be angry at Tryl." She caressed Tyger's cheek, her brown eyes soothing and mischievous. "We just need to... be careful."

"Careful, huh?" Tyger smiled, grateful that Ardyn desired privacy as much as she did. Tyger took Ardyn's hand from her face and held it in her own. "Then I better go do some rumor control."

Ardyn grinned, "If that's possible."

Tyger laughed and led the way down the hall. As they turned the last corner towards the Windriders' chamber, Jyln's voice reached them clear and full of concern. "Tryl, sweetheart, were they fighting again? Is that what startled you? Was it real bad like they used to?"

Coming into the room it became immediately clear that Tyger and Ardyn had been the subject of everyone's speculation just seconds before. Tryl looked immediately away from the pair when they entered, but all other eyes flew to them. Tyger strode toward Tryl purposefully, wrapping her arm around Tryl's shoulders. She whispered sweetly, very softly, in Tryl's ear, "You understand, of course, that if you say anything more about what you *think* you saw, I will have to dismember you."

Tryl swallowed hard and nodded. "Got it."

Tyger slapped her on the back. "Good." She looked around and smiled at each of the Windriders. "Good evening, everyone!"

Tylon came into the room followed closely behind by Petre. Both men were talking at the same time. "If we can find Aliqui we can ask her about–"

"Exactly! She must know everything there is to know about–" Both stopped and looked at the gathered Windriders. "Are we having a meeting?" Petre asked Tyger.

Tyger grinned and shook her head. "No, we all just happen to be here. You haven't missed a thing. Right, Tryl?"

The cowgirl nodded her head enthusiastically and Ardyn shot Tyger a smirk.

"Speaking of missing things, I could really use some food." Tamarin moaned, holding his stomach.

"Anything that isn't rock hard will do," Wolf said from a perch in the wall, motioning to a pile of Patriarchy rations. His tone seemed even more solemn then usual.

Tyger nodded. "I'll try to round something up."

"I'll go with you," Ardyn offered.

"I better go too," Tryl stood, giving Tyger a weak sneer, "I mean, you two might start to... fight again."

Tyger smiled at her, but her eyes narrowed. "That won't be necessary."

"What do people eat here, anyway?" Tamarin asked nervously. "Rocks and rivers?"

Fox shrugged, "Sky food will probably be different, but I'm sure it's healthy. Everyone looks well fed."

"And you will be too," Mouse said from the doorway. Tyger turned and smiled at her brother. "Iahala has invited you all to dinner with us. In Sky we eat together three times a day."

"Three times?!" several of the Windriders said at once. In the city they ate once, twice on special occasions.

Mouse smiled, pleased to give this gift. "Iahala said the Windriders are welcome to attend all our meals."

Tyger asked, "Will Abraham and Sarah be there as well?"

Mouse shook his head. "Abraham and Sarah take their meals in their chambers. Communal meals would be with Iahala, Aliqui, Mlinz, Kestrel, myself and the Windriders." Mouse looked up at his sister, pride in his eyes. "If you'll join us."

* * *

"You decided to come, wonderful!" Iahala called as she stood from the head of the table and welcomed them into the dining room. The chamber was small but well lit by glowing crystals set everywhere in the walls. At one end of the room a doorway led into what might be the kitchen and in the middle of the room was a long stone table, surrounded by smaller stone benches.

The table was covered in plates of steaming delicacies. There was a dark stew, sending thick scents of herbs into the air and four different dishes of colorful fruits. There was a rich-looking grain cake glazed with a purple sauce, a tossed salad with orange berries and many a jug of hot, fragrant tea. Tyger realized with some pleasure that the foods here were New World foods, foods gathered from outside the Valley or perhaps foods grown in Sky from New World seeds.

Iahala motioned to Tyger and Ardyn, touching the benches on either side of her. "Come sit beside me. I've been wanting to talk to both of you."

"Thank you for inviting us," Tyger said as she sat and poured herself some tea, Ardyn sinking down just across from her and the other Windriders finding places all around the table near Aliqui, Kestrel, Mlinz and Mouse.

Iahala offered her mug as well as Ardyn's for Tyger to fill. "You traveled very far coming from New Seattle, then the Village of Wind. I do not know what kind of food stuffs the Patriarchy gave you but you can only eat so much Blue Spire and cactus gel. Nourishment is not always easy to find in the Wind."

Tyger agreed, remembering Tryl, intoxicated by too much Blue Spire and snoring loudly. "We survived. That's what's important."

"Yes, that is important." Iahala waited until Tyger and Ardyn had filled their plates then she continued. "The Wind is very magical. The world you come from, Tyger, is full of wonders. So many – some Humans, the Clones surely – think it evil and deadly, but it's often misunderstood. The New World is powerful, but if embraced, it lends its power to anyone." Iahala motioned to the meal before them. "Before the End, Sky was equipped with machines that could take basic compounds and create food of various kinds. But their energy sources were self-contained and did not last more than a hundred years. There was some panic until Humans learned to gather food from the Wind. Until we learned to grow our own edibles by crystal light."

Tyger could feel Iahala's pride in her race. The Humans had done what the Clones had not. "The Elders of my village always said if the Clones had stayed in the Wind longer, instead of running for shelter, they would eventually have adapted. The Wind would have accepted them."

Iahala nodded. "I agree. More Originals would have been born over time." The Wisewoman paused and smiled at Tyger. "I would have liked to meet one of your Elders, Tyger. They must have known so much. Some might even have been as old as I, or older, but their insights would be so different. They were the beginning of the new way of things. They shaped the future with their beliefs."

Tyger was silent in agreement.

"People say that the Wind destroyed the Old World," Iahala said, "but that is as much of a lie as saying that Humans destroyed it. The Wind makes it possible for there to be new life. For there to be a New World. The Wind is birth, not death."

This time Tyger was surprised at Iahala's words. The Humans destroying the Earth was a lie? Who had destroyed it then? Every tale said that it had been their folly. From the Patriarchy to her own village, the legends had been the same. Humans were cowards who hated so much that their hate killed the world and their own people. How could this not be true?

And if it wasn't, what was?

"If it wasn't for the Wind, then the River Sky would not be as powerful as it is," Iahala was saying when Tyger turned her attention to the Wisewoman's words again. "The Wind fills the water and gives it properties no water before the End ever had. The End created many miracles. Neither science nor magic can explain it all."

Ardyn put in, "Yes, I've wondered about that. When I fell through the Sky falls, I took a breath of... water. But I found that I could still breathe. It was amazing. And when I landed in the pool, I felt as if I had just taken a deep breath of clean air."

Iahala smiled. "That is one of the miracles. The forces of the End took the great rivers of the world and destroyed them – all but this one. Once the River Sky was called the Snoqualmie River and was honored for its magic by my ancestors. Snoqualmie means *where miracles happen*. Now, the river spans the entire globe – mostly underground. But there are a few places where it surfaces and is filled with Wind. The Wind strengthens the powers of the river. It makes the water a protector, a sustainer of life. The water filters impurities, lessens poisons in the body. This water-that-is-not-water makes it possible for the Flyers to survive in the New World for long stretches of time because it neutralizes, or at least greatly lessens, the effects of the Wind in Human blood.

"Although some have tried to understand the River Sky and its miraculous properties through scientific study, I choose simply to believe. There is incredible power in belief."

Tyger had to ask, "You say the River keeps out impurities, poisons, and you include the Wind. Is the Wind an impurity then?"

The smallest smile touched Iahala's face. She reached out a hand and placed it on Tyger's. Her palm was warm and her hand, weathered with age, held a solid strength. "Without drinking the River Sky, I could not exist a day in the Wind. My daughter, who died long ago, would have lasted perhaps two days longer than I. Aliqui could live perhaps a little more unprotected. Each generation gets stronger because we are drinking the Sky which carries the Wind and we are eating the foods that come from the Wind. But do not be fooled. We survived the End because we were under the ground, here in the Land of Sky, not because our bodies are stronger than those who perished. At least for now the Wind is still too much for us. But someday we shall be able to walk among the rest of the survivors."

Iahala's words touched Tyger deeply, and she hoped they were truth. She believed Humans would evolve, but she didn't know if they would be accepted. Humans would be considered to be the lowest rung on the evolutionary ladder. Clones, who had once been Humans, ruled now. Originals, those Clone babies born without twins, were closer to being able to survive in the Wind, and were oppressed by the Clones. Windborn represented the final stage in the evolution, able to live completely in the Wind, and the Patriarchy had slaughtered them. How would the Clones treat Humans? Would they be oppressed by the Clones and hunted by the Patriarchy as well? And what of the Great Butterflies? Where did they fit in?

"Iahala, what are the Great Butterflies?" Tyger asked suddenly.

Iahala seemed as if she had been following Tyger's thoughts perfectly in her eyes. "One of the many creatures who survived by changing. The Butterfly was the only winged creature to survive."

"How was that possible? Weren't they unprotected when the End came?"

Iahala took a sip from her tea. "My great-grandfather had a fellowship, a bond, to butterflies. Some cultures called them soulbirds, you know. He could... call them, speak with them. Before the End he sang for them to come to him. He called them with his voice and with his spirit. Several hundred, perhaps several thousand, responded and he brought them into a chamber we now call Skynest. In the walls he had created many nests of flowers grown by crystal light and the butterflies went to them willingly.

"But when the End came it was far more violent then anyone had expected. All of the world seemed to shake and shudder with earthquakes that seemed to express sadness or terror or anger. When the land had finally calmed, my great-grandfather went to Skynest and found that the ceiling had fallen in, opening a passageway to what is now the Valley floor and littering the floor of the chamber with massive standing stones. The butterflies were nowhere to be seen."

Iahala paused here, offering a small, pleased grin. "Years later, more than two hundred years later, the butterflies returned much changed in body and in spirit. The Wind ran in their blood now and the New World was their own."

Tyger looked at Ardyn. The other woman was watching Iahala intently. Tyger wondered if Ardyn also felt the magic in the Great Butterflies – strong magic.

Iahala went on. "The Butterflies are children of the River Sky and of the Wind. They can live in both. Their blood line, like both of yours, carries certain extraordinary gifts."

Tyger and Ardyn looked at each other and then Iahala at the same time. Tyger understood that Clones, Originals and Windborn all had certain abilities that Humans did not, but *extraordinary gifts*?

Iahala explained. "This is the reason I wanted to talk to you. Your blood lines. As you may have guessed, all the humanoid races can be traced back to Humans. Tyger, your blood line is the farthest along in the change. You have a kinship with the Earth and the Wind and all the animal children. At the same time, if you open your senses completely, you should be able to feel certain energies, certain magics."

Tyger remembered Mouse telling her about Falcon's fascination with the sealed tunnel and Tyger's own feelings about it. And there was more. There was the feeling that Iahala herself gave Tyger. A feeling that was not unlike the presence of the Wind. Like all things natural and pure. All things that knew the Way. The Unity.

In one more of the many long buried memories in Tyger's head that Mouse seemed to have uncovered, Tyger remembered her parents talking about the Unity when she was young. It was the union, a connection or kindred, between two Windborn or a Windborn and a Beast. It was also the union between a Windborn and one of the powers: Earth, Wind, Sky or Fire. Tyger had found Unity with the Wind because she could read it and later, with the help of the Windboard, she could fly upon it. Her parents had found Unity with each other. Owl, the village healer, was said to have found Unity with all four of the powers.

Powers, elements, joined in Unity.... Tyger thought about Aliqui's Phoenix art. The Human powers were Earth, Air, Water and Fire. The Windborn had had no water and so they had claimed Sky as an element. But here is this world Sky was water.

Tyger turned her mug in her hands, her thoughts racing. She felt herself being drawn away from this room and the table. Aliqui had said that each element had an opposite that balanced it, counter-acted it. So what was the Patriarchy? What element or power was Jarth and his nation? What was the opposite that could bring him down?

Iahala's voice brought Tyger back from her contemplation. "But the Windborn are not the first to touch the heart of the Elements and the powers that be. There were others before them. Before the End. They were the ones who first lived upon this land that was once called America. They were the true natives to this earth. The first-comers."

Iahala smiled proudly, and her hand fell to Ardyn's. Their skin was the same rich tone. "They were called Indians by those who tried to conquer them but later they were recognized as Native Americans, as the People. Those who first came to know this land. They lived by the Elements and the powers. They were kindred to the animals and knew magic when they felt it." Iahala paused. Looking directly into Ardyn's dark eyes, she said, "I know that in the New World you see only the breed – Human, Clone, Original, Windborn. You are blind to race, which some would say is evolution. But there is strength and pride in knowing your heritage. I am descended from those first-comers and so are you."

Ardyn blinked once, then she looked at Tyger. In a sudden flash of understanding Tyger knew why, despite their differences, they seemed

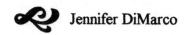

drawn to each other. In a way, they shared a kinship. They both knew power, magic, they both knew this land.

Iahala spoke to them both as if she could read their silent exchange. "Tyger's people are the new natives. But beneath the New World, the Old World still lives. The two worlds are separated by the very strong magics of the Wind and of time. But someday, perhaps, the two will come together."

"Kindred," Ardyn said softly, her brown eyes never leaving Tyger.

"Together, there is nothing a united people cannot accomplish," Iahala finished.

Tyger and Ardyn nodded at the same time, each hearing her words, taking them in, making them her own.

* * *

"Your grandmother seems to have Tyger and Ardyn caught up in quite a conversation," Tylon remarked, looking down the table at the three.

Aliqui chewed a piece of dense bread. "She is very wise. Elders are able to capture your attention with truths that seem more marvelous than myth."

Petre smiled. "How many Elders do you have in Sky?"

Aliqui straightened up a bit, smiling at her grandmother. "In my opinion? Only one."

Tylon shook his head. "I haven't been here very long, but if I had to make a choice between Abraham and Sarah or Iahala, I'll agree with you."

Aliqui grinned, pleased. "So, Kestrel tells me that you wanted to talk to me about my crystals. In all my life I've only known one other to be interested in them. Why are you?"

Tylon shrugged. "We're creators. It's our job to discover and create tools for the Windriders. We've seen what you do with them already: the lights, the weapons, the gliders, but we want to know more."

Petre continued, "Tylon is being polite to include me but I am curious and I have an eye for detail. Though it's Tylon who has an idea in his head about how crystals might help us in the future. He just needs more information to make his idea live."

Aliqui picked up her mug and toasted each of them. "I'll be more than pleased to tell you everything you ever wanted to know about crystals. And trust me, you haven't seen anything yet! Let it never be said that I didn't help bring something to life."

"Discs?! You mean the ones I saw when you all showed up? The ones you were carrying?"

Tryl laughed. "The very ones! They're called Windboards. They slice through the air – silver streaks. Nothing's faster."

Kestrel seemed excited and skeptical at the same time. "I've never thought of anything other than Wings in terms of flying. What are they made of?"

"They're made of Patriarchy steel," Jyln answered. "The boards themselves are just over two feet across, so thin and small that they can be maneuvered with sharp precision." Jyln motioned with one hand as she spoke.

Kestrel frowned. "Steel is too heavy to fly. It would be impossible without a motor. It would have to be steel mixed with Air crystal, like they did before the End."

"Maybe that's what Patriarchy steel is," Spider considered. "It's very light and durable. And all Patriarchy materials come from the ruins of the Old World cities."

Tryl added, "It was Ravyn, a Windrider, who perfected the Windboards. She gave them engines and response modules. But she was working with Patriarchy materials. In all my battles I've seen Windboards crash into brick walls, drop from ten stories up and even collide with motorcycles! They'll chip sometimes, or an attached piece might come off, but they've never cracked or snapped. Never."

Kestrel shook her head in amazement. She spoke quickly, intrigued. "Wings don't cut through the Wind, they ride it. They glide upon it like the Great Butterflies. Mind you, riding the Wind is amazing with its currents and cross-currents, but if the current you need isn't there, you're out of luck! When you ride a Wing, the Wind makes the path, not you.

"The Wings' rods are made of Air crystals and the sails are woven from a plant that grows in the Wind. Sails often get snagged and have to be mended, and, even though it happens rarely, the rods can also break. To fly a Wing is to fly. You must follow the Wind, read it to maneuver and never fight it. Every change in the air presents another path to take. To fly a Wing is to have wings. To be like the Butterflies. No tricks unless the Wind allows. No speed unless you catch a sharp current. If the Wind says slow, you go slow. The way of the Wind is the way of the Wing. That's the first thing new Flyers learn."

Spider, Tryl and Jyln repeated, "The way of the Wind is the way of the Wing."

Kestrel looked up at them. They were looking at her with the same excitement she was showing towards Windboards. "You want to learn to ride Wings?" The three said yes at the same time.

"To be that close to naturally flying must be so beautiful," Jyln mused. "To be able to be part of the Wind that way!"

Kestrel nodded, growing more and more excited at the possibilities. "Oh, it is," she said. Her voice was as far away as her eyes. "It feels so right. Riding the Wind. Knowing it. The Wind tossing your hair or touching your skin is one thing, but flowing, racing, diving along with it is quite another."

"My whole life I've been a Windrider. It would be nice to finally, really ride," Tryl said.

"You can't soar gracefully on a Windboard," Spider joked and the others laughed.

Kestrel took a bite of stew, thinking of Windboards again. "But it must be so grand! I do love the Butterflies; they are my obsessions. I admire and honor them. They are all that is majestic and graceful to me, but to be able to go so fast! To be able to race and speed, to create your own path through the air. Dropping from current to current. It must make you feel so alive!"

"We want to learn to ride Wings; you want to learn to ride a Windboard. We could teach each other. An exchange of learning," Jyln proposed.

Kestrel was about to agree to the plan when from down the table Wolf, who had been listening to their conversation, called out, "Of course, riding a Windboard is very, very difficult. Who knows, you might not be worth training."

Tryl and Jyln looked at Wolf in shock and Spider opened her mouth to rebuke the young man but Kestrel spoke first. "I didn't mean to say that you couldn't learn to fly, Wolf. I was–"

Wolf held up a hand and silenced her. "This matter is between only you and me. If you want to talk to me, talk to *me*. Alone." The young man turned back to his food.

"Come on, then."

Wolf looked up.

Kestrel stood beside him, reaching out a hand. He hesitated and she grinned. "You can finish your meal later. If we need to talk, let's do it now."

Wolf stood without taking her hand but his face was not as closed as it had been a moment ago. Together they walked from the room.

* * *

Tamarin balanced a small green fruit on the tip of his tongue. "Tey, Toxy, took tat te!" he slurred.

Fox turned towards him and squinted her eyes. She smirked at his antics. "Your talent amazes me," she said drolly, then slapped him on the back. He swallowed the fruit whole and launched into a coughing fit. Turning her back on Tamarin, Fox said to Mouse, "So, you take care of the baby Butterflies?"

Mouse nodded. "Not just me, of course. They live in the room we call Skynest. Everyone takes turns tending the flower beds there and handling the Butterflies. They have to be handled or they die, you know, just like real babies."

Fox smiled, almost blushing. "I've always wanted to have a baby."

"Which is where I can help!" Tamarin chimed in.

"In your dreams." Fox elbowed him in the stomach and he slumped over his plate again.

Mouse laughed. "I can bring you to Skynest sometime. It's a wonderful place. The ceiling opens into the Valley. The babies love to meet new people, especially Windborn, and I'm sure that means those who have changed as well. They feel a certain kinship to us. That's why I'm the one who usually brings them out for their daily flight. I take them away from the Valley and find patches of plants that they can eat. They like Golden Leaf and Purple Jewel best.

"I play my flute for them. They like that. It makes them stay together. Naturally, the grown Butterflies each follow the songs of the Great Stones and often they split up, but we teach the young to fly in a flock. There's safety in numbers."

"But one on one is also very important," Tamarin pointed out.

Fox growled at him. She picked up a round, sticky pastry and crammed it in his mouth. "Will you just shut up?" She turned back to Mouse. "Why can't the grown Butterflies take care of their own children?"

Mouse shook his head. "Oh, they can. It's just that the babies can't fly for as long as the adults can. The adults used to carry them on their backs, but birth rate has grown and litters are getting bigger and bigger – too big for all the babies to be carried.

"The Butterflies eat very little so it's easy for them to exist almost anywhere, but they seem to be looking for a home somewhere out in the New World. Because of this searching, the adults sometimes fly miles and miles every day which is too much for the young. So Iahala and all the other Pagans agreed to care for the youngsters until they're old enough to fly by themselves and join the adults in a search for a home."

Mouse paused and grinned. "Sometimes, when I've stayed out late and the babies start to get tired, they all pile on top of my Wing and ride home. It's a great feeling. Like being a parent."

Mlinz, sitting quietly close beside Mouse, spoke up for the first time, a small smile on his face. "I remember once, Mouse had just come in from flying. He had put his Wing away and thought that all the babies had been left in their nests. But when he got to our room and lay down to go to sleep, two of them came dashing out of his hair!"

The three of them laughed and Tamarin joined them, his mouth covered in sticky sweetness. Fox glared at Tamarin. He grinned at her and puckered his lips. She turned away to hide her half-amused grin.

"I could show you Skynest tomorrow if you'd like," Mouse offered.

"That'd be great," Fox said.

"Me, too," Tamarin put in. "I'm great with kids."

"You *are* a kid," Fox pointed out.

"I'm twenty and a half!"

"I rest my case." Tamarin pouted and Fox said, "You know, I wish that for just one minute you'd quit acting like a fool. And then maybe *some people* might find you more tolerable. And the invitation to Skynest, by the way, was not extended to you," she finished haughtily. Turning to Mouse, she smiled, "I'll see you tomorrow." Then she got up abruptly and left the dining hall.

* * *

When the meal was over Aliqui and Kestrel stayed to clean up. Kestrel had returned after her talk with Wolf with a smile on her face. They had worked things out. Some of the Windriders had offered to stay to help, but Aliqui and Kestrel had waved them on. As they scraped uneaten food from the plates to be hauled to the underground gardens for compost and put untouched food away, the two women laughed and talked. It seemed they had always been friends.

"Have you ever seen so many people gobble their dinners so fast? It made me feel good, like we gave them a gift." Kestrel smiled, stacking plates to be washed. After the food composer had stopped working, the kitchen had been completely retrofitted. Like the wash rooms and lavatories scattered through out Sky, the kitchen now had running water powered by their small base generator but it was also equipped with a wide, metal cooking surface, several cold storage units set into the walls and a large dry goods pantry.

Aliqui reached for the dishes. "You would assume that with a leader like Tyger they'd all be rough-spoken warriors."

Kestrel raised her eyebrows and grinned at Aliqui. "Oh, I think there's more to Tyger than that. She does have a temper, but you hear the way she talks? She knows what she's doing. It's a nice mixture – the strength and the smarts."

Aliqui smiled sadly. "She reminds me a lot of Falcon, Kes."

Kestrel went to Aliqui and wrapped her arms around her friend's shoulders. "I'm sorry, Aliqui. I didn't mean to bring up memories."

Aliqui felt her own tears on her cheeks but managed a grin. "It's okay. I just – I miss her. So much has happened, so quickly. It's only been a few days. Sometimes I can't even believe I'm standing here without her. I'm still a little shocked, you know? Maybe more than a little."

Kestrel bowed her head against Aliqui's. They had been through so much together, but not even the death of Aliqui's own parents had hurt her so much. "I'm here for you, Ali. I'm here."

"What in all damnation – Oh, not you too!"

Kestrel and Aliqui moved out of one another's embrace as Sarah and Abraham entered the kitchen, Abraham holding their now-empty dinner plates.

Sarah threw up her hands. "As if being a Pagan witch isn't enough, you have to love women as well? I knew it was bound to happen!"

Color flooded into Kestrel's cheeks. She took a step towards her mother, her fury brimming over. "Oh?! So now the One says that friends cannot touch? Your son has had a male partner for six years but if your daughter chose a woman lover, that would just cinch it all, wouldn't it? That would prove to the world that not even your own children follow your twisted ways! I wish Ali and I were lovers!" Sarah slapped Kestrel so hard that the young woman fell against the wall but Sarah still moved to strike her again. Aliqui placed herself between them, her face, set in anger, still wet with tears. "The people of Sky do not strike their children, Sarah."

Sarah glared at Aliqui but pointed a long accusing finger at Kestrel. "That is not my daughter."

Kestrel stood and looked at her mother in icy contempt. "So it's finally come to this. Finally, I am not your daughter." She stepped close to Sarah and spat, "I rejoice in my disowning!"

Abraham stepped toward his daughter, his eyes filled with pain. Kestrel turned away from them both, gripping the edge of the counter with white-knuckled hands.

Sarah stood for a moment as if frozen, then, "Now you can no longer cause us shame. Your blood is washed from our hands." She turned, her face a mask void of emotion, and left the kitchen.

Abraham stood in stunned silence, caught between his wife's announcement and his daughter's pain. He set the plates carefully on the counter and waited as though willing his daughter to meet his eyes. When it became clear that neither would speak first to the other, Aliqui said, "There is nothing you can do here, Abraham. Your wife has cost you your daughter."

Ignoring Aliqui, he said, "Kestrel, I love you."

Kestrel lifted her head to meet her father's gaze. She swallowed and opened her mouth to reply, but before she could, he continued, "But I love the One more."

* * *

In her chambers, Iahala sat upon her low bed, cradling Kestrel in her arms. The young woman sobbed against her chest, her tears wetting the Wisewoman's robe. Aliqui knelt on the floor beside them, her hand on Kestrel's back, her eyes brimming with sympathetic tears.

Iahala's thoughts were drawn back, back to many years ago when Sarah had given birth to the daughter she had now disowned. It was on that day that Iahala had first glimpsed into the dark heart of Sarah Tarahson. Furious that she was the first Sarah, in a long line of Sarahs, to give birth to a girl child before a boy, Sarah had refused to name the infant. Iahala had coaxed and cajoled, but even as months passed Sarah would not be swayed. In the end, Iahala's heart could simply no longer bear the injustice and she had named the child herself, hoping that, like the bird, Kestrel would find freedom in flight.

Iahala took a deep breath, stroking Kestrel's head of long curls and thinking that even Sarah's son, named at birth by his parents, had taken another name. *Guardian, Mlinz*, Mouse had called the boy when they had first met and since that day Mlinz had never answered to his birth name. Such incredible power lived in a name, power that Sarah could not claim.

"Dear child," Iahala's voice was soothing against Kestrel's ragged pain, "it was not your father's heart talking. No one can love something they have never seen more than their own child. The love of the powers is different from the love we have for each other."

Kestrel shook her head hard. "No, Iahala, he did mean it. He cares more about his Way than his own blood. He would send us away forever if his One told him so. He frightens me. Their hatred frightens me! Their sacred hatred is growing, Iahala, building for some cause."

Iahala pulled Kestrel closer and looked at her granddaughter, Aliqui, over the curve of Kestrel's shoulder. Aliqui climbed onto the bed and encircled both the old woman and her friend with her arms. "Kestrel, we love you. Unconditionally," Aliqui said gently. "You are not alone here. Do not be frightened."

"Kestrel," Iahala took Kestrel's face in her hands. "Listen to Aliqui. She tells you the truth. Neither of us can erase your pain and I will not say to you that what has happened is all for the best. But I can say one thing: nothing would please me more than if I could call you my granddaughter."

Kestrel's eyes widened and she looked from Aliqui to Iahala. Both women smiled at her. After a moment's pause, Kestrel wiped her eyes. Her voice was almost steady when she answered, "It would be a great honor, Grandmother."

* * *

In the cavern the Windriders now called home, Tyger, Spider and Wolf were hard at work creating a suitable workspace for their resident inventor, Tylon.

Tyger met their eyes, then, "One. Two. Three. Lift!" With a collective grunt, the four Windriders hefted a slab of stone off the floor of their chamber and walked it over to the end of the room. They set it down across two other rectangular slabs that would form the table's legs. Tyger shoved the slab experimentally. It didn't budge.

"How's that?" Tyger asked but Tylon was already laying out his tools on his new work table.

"It's perfect," Petre offered from across the room.

Tylon looked up, apologetic. "Yes, perfect."

Tyger smiled. It felt good to make the inventor happy. She didn't want to favor the warriors of her group too much.

All across the room the Windriders were setting out their things and settling in. She surveyed them, feeling a surge of contentment and pride. It already late, probably after midnight, but the Windriders planned to be up with the Sky folk for breakfast tomorrow, so even after sleeping for most of the day, they were settling in again.

"I never thought in a million years that you three could lift–"

"Hear that, everyone?" Spider interrupted. "Tryl admitted she hasn't thought in a million years!"

The room exploded with laughter. Tryl growled and threw an empty flask at Spider. Tyger laughed with them as she went to join Ardyn and Petre who were taking turns trying to remember bits of poetry. She sank down beside Ardyn as Petre recited.

"I walk the shores barefoot
picking up the empty shells
of my childhood.
Gentle swirls and curls
homes of tiny secrets
living legends
eternal stories.
The waves I hear
are only
my own heartbeat." Petre sighed. "I always liked that one, but I never quite understood it. The sound of waves in a shell, maybe like the voices in our memories. But even our memories are shaped by what we know and who we are."

"Tyger brought us a lot of poems from the Patriarchy's library but I always liked poems about the moon," Ardyn mused, leaning back against her rolled pelt. "The moon and the night. I guess I really am an Original at heart."

Tyger grinned at her. "Nocturnal child."

Ardyn recited,

"Our eyes met in a crowd.
We danced for as long as we dared.
The smile on her lips, so slight
the sparkle in her eyes

laced with mystery
was a promise all too familiar.
She whispered words
I was never meant to catch
only guess.
My imagination conquers for me
images.
A slow, cold chill
runs down my spine but
my cheeks flush hot
my heart beats fast.
She comes to my side
for just a moment unnoticed
close enough to feel her warmth
yet far enough for the crowd to ignore.
She brushes a lock of hair from my cheek
her touch lingers.
Again her promise lies
behind her action.
I touch her hand.
We go our separate ways
to wait all day for night to come
for darkness to descend
and embrace us."

Glancing over at Tyger, Ardyn's eyes blazed suggestively, but Tyger only met her gaze with a faint smile. Tyger had never brought that poem back from the library.

Petre missed the exchange. "It's amazing that you can memorize like that."

Ardyn gave him a grin. "It's a gift."

"One of many," Tyger murmured.

"Petre! Uh, help!" Tylon was stretched across his new table as over an ever-growing pile of tools, a bag of tiny nails split and spilled everywhere. "Please!"

Petre gave Ardyn and Tyger a shrug. "I'm needed." He stood then called to Tylon, "I told you to double bag!"

Tyger looked at Ardyn more directly now and Ardyn feigned innocence. Tyger reached forward and brushed a lock of hair from Ardyn's cheek. "I never knew you were a poet."

Ardyn grinned. "I have a few hidden talents."

Tyger didn't reply for a moment. Then she asked, "Did you write that poem for Sarya?"

Ardyn shook her head. "No, I wrote it for you."

Across the room, Tryl and Jyln were recounting one of their favorite battles to Spider. "Then out of nowhere rides this massive Wheeler, right? And he careens into the street and pulls his gun. Then Jyln swoops down and–"

Jyln interrupted, "And I circle around him, trying to take his attention from Tryl because she's trying to get Tylon's foot free from the rubble and then–"

Tryl cut back in. "Tyger shows up! She takes one look around, counts the seven Wheelers and goes all out. She starts charging 'em and knocking 'em from the bikes and just going crazy. Ardyn catches on and leaves me with Tylon 'cause I just about have his foot free and she starts charging the bikers too!"

"Then Ravyn comes around the bend," Jyln continues, "with Byn and Sarya. By now we're scaring the Wheelers off because there's too many of us. They wind up running. And from those two bikes that got left behind, Ravyn devises the first Windboard engine!"

"The Wheels..." Spider shook her head with a smile. "Even when I was still in New Seattle they were butting heads with us. Tyger was the biggest, baddest thing on those streets. That pissed everybody off – gangs and gang leaders."

"And the Patriarch!" Tryl added.

Spider's eyes were distant for a moment, then she grinned. "I would have loved to fight along side you two." Jyln and Tryl smiled. Spider went on. "When I first became a Windrider, I was the only girl and the group was huge. Lion and Fox came later, but it was still hard to be accepted by the boys. Tyger was a woman, but to the boys she was a legend first. It would have been great to fight alongside women warriors and not have to prove myself to the guys."

"Like Tylon. Before Petre he was the only guy." Tryl handed a flask of water to Spider and continued, "I already miss it. Fighting, I mean. I thought I'd like peace, but it makes me tense. I know it hasn't been very long since we clashed with the Patriarchy, but I want some action." Tryl slapped her leg, laughing. "I want to deal some damage, you know?"

Jyln kissed Tryl on the cheek. "Well, I don't miss wrapping your broken bones. You can get rid of your extra energy tomorrow when Kestrel takes us out flying."

"Hey," Spider frowned, "I was complaining too."

Jyln kissed Spider on the cheek with a playful sigh. "I can't believe I have two of you to put up with."

"Fox, are you letting me beat you? I've never seen you play so badly," Wolf observed, staring at Fox's last toss of small colored stones.

Fox looked up at Wolf and frowned. "I'm just distracted that's all." She motioned with her eyes to Tamarin who was sitting across the way, his chin in his hands, watching her. "He's so annoying, Wolf. He follows me everywhere. He compares me to flowers, sings me songs, and at dinner he tried to cut my fruit into bite-sized pieces for me! I just can't stand it."

Wolf shrugged. "Maybe he's really in love."

"Oh, please." Fox rolled her eyes. "I'm just a challenge to him. He only wants me because I keep saying no. Everyone knows about his reputation with women." She paused and then added, "You know, if he quit acting like such a jerk, I might even give him half a chance. But no, Wind forbid he act serious for once."

"Give him a break, Fox. People can change." Fox gave Wolf a skeptical glance but shrugged. Wolf called over to his brother. "Hey, Tam, you wanna play?"

The other young man shook his head. "I have a headache."

Wolf looked suspiciously over at Fox. "I hit him in the head," she admitted. "He offered to make babies with me."

Wolf stopped himself from chuckling and caught Fox's gaze. "You know, maybe you hurt his feelings. You might want to apologize."

Fox flushed with anger. "He's the one who should apologize. It's his own fault. If he didn't insist on making stupid comments all the time I wouldn't be tempted to smack him." Wolf just stared at her. Finally she backed down and said, "All right. But if he calls me 'foxy' one more time, I'm going to knock his head clear off his shoulders." She turned toward Tamarin and said, "Come over and play Toss-stones with us. If you can mind your manners, that is."

Tamarin grinned and jumped up to join them. As he crossed the open space between them, Wolf called to Tyger, "Hey, when are we going to have a night-meet?"

Tyger, who had been sitting very close to Ardyn, jumped back in surprise. Although it was nice having all the Windriders together again, she could have done with a little more privacy. She growled good-naturedly at Wolf and said, "Welcome to your new home, Windriders. Now – go to sleep!"

* * *

As the Windriders settled down for the night in another part of Sky, Sarah stalked back and forth across the floor in the chambers she shared with her husband. Her voice rose and fell in anger and frustration as she paced. "Sometimes I wonder why the One gave us such sorrows. We are good people! We follow His Word and read the Book. Yet such evil, evil things He has sent us!"

Abraham watched his wife from the edge of their bed. "Tyger and the Windriders have caused unrest among all our people."

Sarah stopped pacing and marched over to her husband. "Tyger is a true demon! But I wasn't talking about that, I was talking about our children!"

Abraham's eyes opened wide. "Oh, Sarah, you can't be serious! To call them evil–"

"Is to be kind!" The woman returned, cutting him off savagely. She stopped then and looked at him. The man had lowered his head, his brow creased with turmoil. She went to him and wrapped her arms around him. Taking a slow breath and choosing her words carefully, she said, "Abraham, I know you have doubts, but you must listen to what you know is true. We stayed at this Sky base to keep an eye on Iahala, despite the fact that our people, our strength, are elsewhere. You must be strong in your faith, Abraham. We have kept that witch in check, but surrounded by her evil we must be sure to keep to the righteous path. Without you, we cannot begin the Purification. Without you, the Way of the One can never be."

Abraham sighed. "But are we not a family, Sarah? Are we not the parents of our children?"

"Yes, we are a family. We are a large family – all the Believers are our children." Sarah's voice was sure and calm. "We must not favor some children over others. We must not fail them all, Abraham. The One tests us even now and we must not fail." Abraham looked away. She gripped him more tightly. "Oh, Abraham. I know you. I can see through you even as the One can. You must understand that disowning her was inevitable. She would never have seen our Way. Never. It is Mlinz we must try to reach. We must get him to give up this foul love of his and embrace the love of the One. Maybe tonight the One will send me another dream. Perhaps He will tell me when the Purification should begin."

Sarah backed away then, kneeling down beside Abraham. Slowly, she reached under the bed frame and drew out a small vial. She held the small glass container up to her eyes, watching the continually swirling, blue liquid that filled it.

Abraham looked over at her, stared with no expression at the vial. "Oh, Sarah, must we?"

Sarah gave him a stern glance and removed the vial's cap. She handed the open cylinder to Abraham. "You know it isn't really a choice. It will settle you. Calm you. Calm both of us."

Abraham looked down into the spinning blueness. "Sarah," he whispered, staring down at the vial. "Did you see her eyes? That Windborn, Tyger. Her eyes were full of love. Full of joy to see her brother."

"Do not be swayed, Abraham."

"Her love for him is so deep. And her pain... her pain because she has lost her sister, it's so evident. Perhaps... perhaps we shouldn't have, perhaps it was wrong—"

"No–!" Sarah tried to stop his words, but Abraham continued to speak almost as though she were not there.

"Perhaps, we have misunderstood the One." He took the vial, staring at the blueness. "And now we are being punished. Our plan to be rid of Falcon has failed–"

"There has been no failure!" Sarah insisted. "Falcon is gone and the tunnel is properly sealed."

Abraham tilted the vial back and forth, watching the liquid churn. "But because of the accident we were infected as well. Is it destroying us? Are we losing sight of the One? We both know that once you're infected, you begin to question the truth. You can no longer distinguish between reality and non-reality. Are we losing sight of the Way? Sarah, I–"

"Enough!" Her voice was a sharp slap. He fell completely silent. She continued in a hiss of impatient anger. "Those facts only concern those in withdrawal! Those who do not have a consistent dose, not us! Speak no more of this foolishness, man! I know the truth, the One and the Way – and so do you. As long as demons and those who support them are allowed to live, the world will always be twisted and wrong. Decent folk, One Believers, will never rise to greatness. Is this what you want, Abraham? Is it? Do you want demons and witches to rule the earth?!"

Abraham shook his head, taking in a slow breath. "No, Sarah. You're right. The One made only Humans in his image. All others are distortions of the truth."

Sarah took a deep breath and relaxed. The crisis had passed. "Here." She touched his hand holding the vial. "Drink. This is the last we will have for a while but the Users will arrive with more long before withdrawal begins."

Abraham sighed again. He closed his eyes and swallowed half of the vial's contents. Sarah swallowed the other half. They both sat for a frozen moment with their eyes closed, feeling the drug fill their bodies with swirling sensations. Then Sarah tucked the empty vial away.

After a moment, she picked up the thread of their conversation from where it had been broken a few minutes before, dreaming of the days to come and the promise those days held. "Once the Purification is over then we'll be rid of all the demon-blooded and the Pagan trash. We can start over. Start anew. We'll have other children–"

"Mother, Father...?"

Sarah and Abraham looked up as one. Mlinz stood in the doorway of their room. He was carrying tea for both of them and had his Book tucked under his arm. His face was very pale. Sarah forced a smile and stood, wondering how much he had heard. "Come in, Son. How long have you been waiting?" She took a step towards him, but something, everything, in her face frightened him.

The tea tray dropped from his hands; the mugs shattered on the stone floor. Clutching his Book, Mlinz turned and ran down the hall, leaving his parents to wonder just how much he knew.

* * *

Back in his room, Mlinz knelt beside his bed. Still trembling from the encounter with his parents, he tried to focus his mind through prayer as if that could erase the menacing look he'd seen on his mother's face when she had beckoned him into the room. Was it just his imagination or had she meant to hurt him? And what had they been talking about when he'd come in? It must have been important or they wouldn't have looked so upset at his arrival.

In the darkness of his room, Mlinz squeezed his eyes shut, willing the images to fade. "Great One, Creator and Sustainer, Salvation and Truth," he prayed, "I call to You now with a voice full of fear. You know what I have heard. You know what has scared me. I will never ask for my own safety, but I ask now that You please protect the Windriders, the Pagans and," his voice caught in his throat for a moment. "And Mouse, my beloved. I ask this and nothing else. You are the All Knowing and the Righteous. I know that any ill is not from Your hands but from those who twist Your Word to fit themselves. Let Your Will be done. In the Name of the One, Amen."

There was a sound in the darkness and Mlinz turned, fear twisting his stomach. A shadow stood in the doorway. For one moment, he fought the urge to run, but then the shadow shifted and became Mouse's familiar form. Mlinz rose from his knees and Mouse came to him in silence. For a long moment, they embraced without speaking. "Are you okay?" Mouse asked.

Mlinz nodded wordlessly. He had already promised himself that he would not endanger Mouse. If he told anyone about his fears, it would be someone far stronger than either of them. It would be a warrior.

* * *

The leader of the Windriders was dreaming. In her dream, she heard the sound of someone singing. No, not someone. Something – a Great

Stone. Elusive and beautiful, the melody wove around Tyger, tugging at her, beckoning.

Within the dream, Tyger woke and sat up slowly. She could still hear the song in her mind. Then, she heard it throughout the room. Was it Mouse's flute? The tune sounded too alive, too natural yet subtly different from the true songs of the Great Stones.

Tyger looked around the dimly lit chamber, trying to isolate the music. As her gaze swept past the doorway, a flock of adult Butterflies moved past. Their leader froze just outside the threshold to the chamber where the Windriders slept peacefully, its antennae twitching and its eyes searching the darkness.

Tyger watched in silence as the Butterfly cocked its head and alighted in the hall. It seemed to Tyger as though there was an innate intelligence in the Butterfly's gaze, as though it were looking for something or someone. She sat, stunned, and watched the gold and blue Butterfly begin to metamorphose, a subtle shifting of its face, but she could not place why the Butterfly seemed so familiar to her.

It took two steps into the chamber. The rest of the flock fluttered almost impatiently at the door. Its antennae flickered wildly and then, as if finally locating what it had searched for, the creature turned directly toward Ardyn.

From her nook in the wall, Tyger looked down at the sleeping woman as the Butterfly came closer. Tyger called Ardyn's name but her voice was drowned out by a sharp and sudden shriek that shattered the stillness. Suddenly the room was full of adult Butterflies and the light crystals which were scattered about the room exploded in flashes of light. In the midst of the chaos, the eyes of the Windborn Tyger and the once-black, now suddenly blue eyes of the Butterfly met and held. Tyger sucked in an abrupt breath. She *knew* this creature.

Again, Tyger opened her mouth to speak but there came a tremendous roar and the stone walls of the chamber came crashing in, changing to liquid silver as they reached the stone floor. Tyger was swept from her sleeping place, caught in a swirling vortex of hot silver. Fragmented images flashed in her mind: a dismembered Butterfly's wing, a glass vial filled with swirling blue, a Windborn Elder's angry face... a lock of Ardyn's hair–

Tyger woke up.

Startled, the leader of the Windriders sat up suddenly, breathing hard. Her heart pounded in her chest and sweat covered her torso in a fine sheen. She looked around the chamber in alarm, eyes searching for the Butterfly. But everything was dark and quiet. The only sounds were the familiar sleeping sounds of her Windriders.

She turned, letting her legs hang over the edge of her perch while she took several deep breaths to clear her head. The images of the dream bothered her, but the absence of certain facts bothered her even more. Tyger gazed down at Ardyn, enjoying the way her body reacted to Ardyn's with respect and need.

The dream was spurred by being in this new strange place, by her desire for Ardyn. This she knew. But why a nightmare? Why Butterflies?

Before Sarya had died she had wished to be a Butterfly. And Tyger could see gentle, soft-spoken Sarya becoming a small, peaceful Old World butterfly, but not a Butterfly like those here in Sky. These creatures were large, powerful, majestic. They were living myth. That was not the way Tyger saw Sarya.

Tyger stared into the shadows of the chamber. What she felt for Ardyn was nothing like what she had felt for Sarya. But what did that really matter? The simple truth was that since the End, death had become a huge part of life. No matter what the culture, it seemed to Tyger that little time was given to grief, to mourning. Be that wrong or right, it was the way of this New World.

On the day she had buried Sarya beneath the golden sand, she had in some ways buried her sorrow. It had been so few days since that silent funeral, a few dozen maybe? But she had been allowed to mourn Sarya far more than many of her friends who had died in the Wind, and though she and Sarya had been lovers, was the difference so great? Why did she dream of Butterflies with Sarya's blue eyes? Why did she tangle all of these images together?

Someday she would have to sort out all the muddled feelings that spilled around in her head, but for now she was content to be where and who she was. Content to let each day bring her what it would.

She opened her eyes and looked down at Ardyn once more. Two memories filled her mind. She saw Ardyn on the cliff face looking at the gold and blue Butterfly with longing. Then Tyger remembered Iahala saying that she and Ardyn could feel magic when it happened. As she was starting to put these two thoughts together, she was interrupted by a sound. As in her dream, it was a song that resembled the song of a Great Stone. A song coming from very near by.

Feeling as though she had fallen back into her dream, Tyger turned toward the door. She saw a bright colored wing tip at the doorway's edge followed by a large gold and blue wing. A head appeared, large eyes searching the darkness of the Windriders' chamber and coming to rest on sleeping Ardyn.

Tyger felt a shout rip from her throat as she dropped from her perch, landing protectively between Ardyn and the Butterfly. As the

Windriders woke, the Butterfly's wing and head were followed by its body. Someone took the cover off a light crystal and the room was cast into light and shadow. The Gold One stood in the doorway with the flock close behind. The Gold One looked into the room, its antennae twitching and its head cocked, but it came no farther. All the Windriders were awake now, all eyes were fixed on the creature in the doorway. In the expectant silence, the Gold One opened its mouth.

Tyger braced herself for its horrible cry, but the sound it made was joyous and gentle, almost a coo. Without more to say, the Butterfly moved calmly on, singing songs with its flock and fluttering down the hall.

The Windriders turned slowly to face Tyger where she crouched defensively before Ardyn. Tryl cleared her throat, breaking the strained silence. "Kestrel mentioned that the adult Butterflies can be real trouble-makers down here in Sky. Guess that one was just curious, eh?"

Ardyn reached out a hand and touched Tyger's face, bringing Tyger's eyes to her own. She asked gently, mischievously, "Did you think it was going to eat me?"

Tyger blinked twice, looking down into Ardyn's rich brown eyes and seeing the hint of a smile. Despite themselves the Windriders began to laugh and soon Tyger couldn't help but join them.

* * *

When the Windriders came into the dining hall, breakfast was just ending and Iahala looked up from the table she was helping to clear. "Windriders! Up so early?"

A fresh burst of laughter erupted from the group. Tyger wrapped her arm around Ardyn's shoulders and smiled over at Iahala. "I woke everyone. One of your Great Butterflies flew into my dreams, and then into our chamber. It was just a bit unsettling."

"Unsettling, nothing!" Aliqui waved her hand over the mess on the table. "We were just eating peacefully when the entire flock descended on us. They slurped up our food, danced on the table and flew on to wreak more havoc. Leaving us to clean up the mess."

"They're celebrating something," Kestrel added. "I just wish they'd do it less destructively." She bent over and picked up a broken plate.

"Oh, it wasn't so bad," Mouse teased. "They're just full of energy."

Aliqui gestured to her clothes which were spattered with food, "Speak for yourself, Mouse. At least you had the good sense to dive under the table."

Mouse grinned sheepishly, and, silent as usual, Mlinz smiled at him. Turning to the Windriders Mouse explained, "Even though we call the full-grown Butterflies adults, they're still very playful. I'm glad something has made them happy."

Iahala patted the boy on the shoulder. "Well, as long as there's no more singing we'll be fine."

"Singing?" Tyger asked, feeling a sudden twist of remembered fear from her dream.

Aliqui explained. "When the adults sing in the caverns the sound gets amplified because of the way the caves are built. This weakens the crystals." Aliqui turned then to Iahala. "But you're disrupted by them the most, Grandmother. They're always coming to talk to you and can't get any work done."

"What can I say?" Iahala raised her hands in surrender. "Maybe now that they know where the Windriders are living, they'll talk to them instead." Iahala looked concerned, turning to Tyger and the others. "That is, if they didn't scare you too badly."

"Tyger? Scared?" Tryl said and the Windriders laughed as if that was the most ridiculous thing they'd ever heard.

"Hey, show some respect." Tyger gave Tryl a playful shove and a growl. "As you see, Iahala, my Windriders have an exaggerated appreciation for me." She winked back at Tryl. "But I don't mind."

"Well." Iahala smiled. "Since no one's scared, perhaps some breakfast then." Amid cheers from Tamarin and Tryl, Iahala led the Windriders to the pantry where they could choose foods to break their fast that didn't have Butterfly footprints all over them. After they had all done a little snacking, Iahala asked what they planned to do with the day. All of the Windriders started talking at once until Tyger shrugged. "Each of us has developed appetites for certain Sky trades as well as Sky meals."

With that the Windriders began breaking off into groups, following Mouse and Mlinz, Kestrel or Aliqui. It wasn't long before Tyger and Ardyn were left alone with the Wisewoman

Iahala reached out her hands. "I better hurry before someone returns and claims you two."

Ardyn smiled and took Iahala's hand but Tyger hesitated. "Can I catch up with you in a bit? I won't be able to concentrate until I... check in with everyone. I don't want them to feel disconnected from me or that I'm no available to them. This is a very new and different place for all of us."

Iahala nodded once. "I understand. Of course." But Ardyn frowned. "Tyger, don't you think they can take care of themselves?"

Tyger straightened her shoulders, looking down the long halls where the Windriders had gone. "Whether they can take care of themselves or not really isn't the issue. I'm their leader. They are my responsibility." Turning toward Ardyn she smiled. "Remember, no matter what magics Iahala weaves for you, you can't do anything without me. I'm your other half."

With a nod to the Wisewoman, Tyger strode after Kestrel and her excited new students.

Tyger caught up to and followed the five of them out into the Valley. It was a beautiful day and the Windriders circled around Kestrel almost nervously before settling down in the soft grass for their first lesson in the art of flight. Tyger sat a little ways from them, listening with half an ear and watching the multitude of tiny flowers that covered the landscape as they turned their white and yellow faces toward the warm sun above.

"The first thing you have to learn is the parts of the Wing. They're very easy because they correspond to the parts of a Great Butterfly." Kestrel looked up from her glider at Wolf, Tryl, Jyln and Spider. They all had the same looks of confusion on their faces.

Kestrel smirked, remembering that they would have no idea what she was talking about. "I'm sorry. I'm used to students who have studied the Butterflies. Let's start with the basics." Looking right at Wolf she continued, "I'm sure you can all handle it." She turned from them and gestured to her Wing which sat nearby already assembled. "Each Wing has a name. Mine is called Swallowtail. Flying a Wing is about knowing the Wind, something you are all familiar with. But knowing the Wing's parts is just as important." Kestrel rose from her kneeling position and walked to her glider. It was braced on its steering bar with its nose angled up. She touched each part, never knowing that once they had been called sail, kingpost, noseplate, crossbar and keel.

"The cloth is called the wing. The wing catches the Wind. Each wing has two front edges that angle back into wingtips and then dip inward and meet at a point in the middle of the back called the tail. They form almost a triangle but with one side of the triangle scalloped."

The Windriders nodded as Kestrel traced the basic shape of the Wing with her hands.

"See this rod that sticks up in the middle of the wing? It continues down through the cloth and attaches to the top of the rider brace which is also the control bar. The flyer rides secured in the brace and eases the control bar forward and back to maneuver the Wing. The rod that sticks up and passes through to the control bar is called the antenna. It's the antenna that feels the changes in the Wind and tells you they're coming. These four cables up top, the ones that go from the antennae to the front tip, both wing tips and the tail, can feel the Wind, even the slightest current. And these cables beneath the sail," she continued, pointing, "run from the bottom of the wing tips to the ends of the control bar and then back to under the tail. These are also part of the detection system. All of these cables help the antenna rod tell you about the Wind."

Kestrel moved around to the front of the Wing to continue her lecture. The others followed her. "This plate on the front tip of the sails is called the head, because we're always told to think first and that way you remember to always keep the head piece facing the way you are going. If you feel the Wind change and your head piece isn't pointed the way you're headed, fix it, quick!

"For instance, if you were headed due west and your antenna told you a strong current was coming from the south, you shift your weight on the control bar and move your head piece into the north so that southern currents will get behind you and push you forward instead of hitting you from the side and maybe sending you tumbling. Or, maneuver away from that southern current all together if you can! The Wings are at the mercy of the Wind sometimes and you have to remember that.

"Then, we have the thorax. The thorax is the rod that runs across the back of the wing from wing tip to wing tip, and the abdomen is the rod that goes from head to tail. The antenna rod passes through the center of both these rods where they cross each other. Think of it this way: the thorax and the abdomen are the bones, the cloth is the skin and the cables the nerves of your Wing.

"As for basic flight knowledge, it's important to know that it's the act of falling that actually keeps you flying. The Wind gives you lift and the weight of your body gives you drag – resistance – and you can fly. Air over your wings and air resistance beneath them are the two most important aspects of flight."

Kestrel stood up straight and crossed her arms. "Okay. Do you want me to go over anything again?"

"So, to take off you have to drop in order to cause enough resistance below, right?" Tryl asked.

Before Kestrel could answer, Jyln asked, "The way the control bar is set up you must be able to just slightly shift your weight to make very dramatic moves. Is that correct?"

"What you're saying," Spider put in quickly, "is that unlike a Windboard, a Wing would be completely at the mercy of things like convection currents. Is the Wing strong enough to deal with, say, the power of a rotor column?"

But it was Wolf's question which got her first response. "Your glider has about an eighteen-foot span?" When Kestrel nodded, he continued, "Eighteen feet of lift would be able to handle, what, a hundred-eighty, hundred-ninety pounds of drag?" Again Kestrel nodded. "But you don't weigh more than... one-thirty, one-forty," Wolf guessed. "Why not go smaller?"

Kestrel grinned at them. "I should have known you would catch on fast." They grinned back at her. Kestrel said to Wolf, "As Lead Flyer, I like to have a little bit of extra power in my Wing just in case I wind up carrying something extra or helping someone. But the larger the size of the Wing, the harder it is to control,"

"More pull than drag." Wolf nodded.

"Right. But I've been flying for so long that I can counter the difficulty with skill."

"I would never doubt that," Wolf added factually.

Kestrel put her hands on her hips. "I can see that we're ready to move past the basics." She turned toward Tyger, "Are you to blame for their incredible curiosity and their knowledge of flying?"

Tyger shook her head and started to protest, but was shouted down by a chorus of enthusiastic affirmations.

Seeing that they were in good hands with Kestrel and each seemed content for the moment, Tyger rose from where she'd been sitting. Tryl broke away from the others and came toward her. She stood just looking at Tyger for a moment. "You seen what's been up with us?" the cowgirl finally asked.

Tyger nodded, "You know I'm all-seeing."

Tryl grinned. "I never thought I'd ever be interested in anyone other than Jyl. But Spider is different. It doesn't matter to her that we love each other... more. I mean, it didn't stop her from letting us know she was attracted – to both of us. She isn't interested in coming between us."

Tyger looked over at Spider. "It's the difference between having a lover and a partner. Since I've known her, Spider has always preferred lovers. She's very intense, and I think it'll be a long time before she finds someone to match her intensity. Until then she won't choose a partner. But that doesn't mean she won't want to connect in the meantime."

Tryl seemed to think about that, pondering it. "I guess I never think about stuff like that. I've never been with anyone but Jyl, never wanted to be with anyone else." Tryl cast Tyger a sly smile. "I mean, if you've got the best, why look at the rest?"

"Well, just be careful," Tyger offered. "The eyes of the One are everywhere!"

Tryl feigned fear. "Oh, evil, evil! If I'm going to be damned for love, then you might as well haul me off to Hell now, 'cause I ain't stopping!"

Tyger laughed, Tryl returning to her lessons while Tyger turned away, her thoughts on the One. It did seem very strange that the One taught that loving someone of your own gender was wrong. She had never heard of something so pointless and narrow-minded before. Maybe, she mused, it was just Sarah and Abraham who were wrong. Their interpretation simply had to be incorrect because if they were right, a very large portion of the population was damned!

Tyger didn't know how things were done in other domes, but in the domes of the Patriarchy men and women were separated. Women were encouraged to choose female partners with whom to raise their litters of children and if soldiers ever found love, then it would have to be with another male soldier as they had no contact with Clone females. They gave their Seed at the Life Center and continued with their duties of protecting the Patriarchy's reign, maintaining the cities and keeping the slave sites in order.

She wondered whether or not anyone had heard of this Book in the domes and if they had, what was thought of it. She imagined it had been banned – after all, something like that would undermine the entire structure of the domes' social order.

But aside from that, it just didn't make sense. Had reproduction always been so end-all-be-all that the Book had condemned all other forms of sex? Dismissing it from her mind, Tyger walked toward Mouse and Mlinz who were standing with Fox and Tamarin. Fox cast Tyger a glance and motioned with her head to Tamarin who was hovering nearby. Tyger almost laughed at the strained look on Fox's face but she only shrugged.

"How are things going over here?" Tyger asked as she joined the group, wrapping her arm around her brother's shoulders. Mouse smiled up at her. "I was just about to call the little ones. Fox and Tamarin were going to play with them a bit while Mlinz and I readied my Wing for flight."

Tyger nodded. She glanced at Mlinz. It was obvious that something was troubling him, but before she had a chance to ask him, Tamarin said, "Hey, Tyger, you know what? Foxy –" he broke off suddenly and sent an apologetic glance toward Fox, "I mean, Fox apologized to me and my headache disappeared! That's why I'm here too."

Fox just grumbled in reply, but Tyger could see she was secretly pleased to have the young man's company. Then Mouse cleared his throat and brought his flute to his lips. He began to play a tune Tyger had once heard from a Great Stone near their village.

As the melody flowed out of the instrument and was carried away on the gentle breeze, Mlinz said, "The young Butterflies like to dance. They like it best when you dance with them. Some of them like to climb in your hair or have their wings stroked but don't worry, they'll let you know if they want more attention."

"How will they let us know?" Fox asked. Mlinz smiled a small smile and had no time to answer as the young Butterflies arrived. They came rushing out of the Sky falls across the Valley, their wings tucked until they hit the air and then they dove into loops and swirls. They filled the air like shooting jewels, darting over Kestrel and her students and dashing across the Valley to circle Mouse, swaying and dipping to his tune. They sang in response to his music.

Suddenly, Mouse tossed the flute to Tamarin with a wink. The little ones rushed to the new musician, hovering about him, waiting for a song. Tamarin looked to Fox and was surprised to find that she was smiling at him. She said, "They're beautiful, aren't they? Like a storm of a million colors. They're watching you so intently."

"I really like them, Fox," Tamarin admitted seriously. "There's something about them. Something incredible—" he broke off, as if suddenly aware that he had revealed something of his true self to her. When he gained enough courage he looked at her and she met his gaze steadily.

"Come on, Tam," she whispered. "Play for them."

The sound he made on the unfamiliar instrument was the most ridiculous sound anyone had ever heard and everyone struggled not to burst into laughter. But the Butterflies loved it and began to dance. Tamarin cast another glance at Fox and she urged him on. Tamarin tried again, blowing softer, steady. The Butterflies began to sing, continuing to spin and dive around them. Fox came to stand beside Tamarin, laughing as Tamarin's playful notes delighted the young creatures. Tamarin began to skip, moving around, a smile in his eyes as the Butterflies and Fox followed him off into the Valley. Tyger watched them go and a slow smile spread across her face. Fox was falling for Tamarin's charm.

Tyger turned to Mouse. "You've done a good thing here today, Mouse. And you may have found someone to take care of the Butterflies for you."

"I think you're right," he mused. "I'll have to find a Wing they can both ride at the same time."

Tyger laughed. "Do the young have to be taken out of the Valley?"

"Not every day."

Tyger took her arm from Mouse's shoulders and met Mlinz's gaze over his head. "Well, then, it looks like you just got a day off. Why don't you put the Wing away. This is a very big Valley. Find a private patch of sunlight and bask. There's been a lot of excitement since we arrived. Enjoy some time alone."

Mouse looked at Mlinz. Mlinz looked slightly stunned. Tyger realized that no one had probably ever talked to them as a couple before. After a moment, Mlinz reached out and took Mouse's hand in his own. "I think I'd like that," Mlinz said, surprising them both with his tender agreement. He looked up at Tyger. "It's important to spend time in the light with someone you love, isn't it? To come out of the shadows and the underground?"

Tyger looked deeply into the young man's troubled brown eyes. "Yes, it is," she said. "Very important."

After some searching, Tyger found Tylon and Petre with Aliqui back down in Sky in a large room not far from the Windriders' chamber. From floor to ceiling the room was filled with mounds and clusters of crystals in every color and shape imaginable. Silently, Tyger moved to join them.

After sitting in the Gathering Place and just talking about crystals for a long time, Aliqui had finally brought them here to this chamber of crystalline. Tylon stood with his eyes wide and his jaw slack in wonder. His pale blue eyes reflected the glory and the colors about him. He looked to Aliqui, but the words would not, could not come.

Standing behind him, Petre finally spoke. "It's beautiful."

Tylon turned and took Petre's hand. Petre had found just the right words. "It is," Tylon agreed. "It really is."

Petre seemed to fall into the dreamy look in Tylon's eyes and was glad when Aliqui spoke and Tylon turned to face her because then Petre could hide his blush.

"This is the Crystal Garden. This is where the crystals that become our El Rods and our lights are grown."

Tylon began to walk around, peering closer at the mounds of stone covered with clusters of colored crystals. He seemed to forget that he was holding onto Petre's hand and he dragged Petre behind him unconsciously. Petre didn't mind, that much at least was obvious. Aliqui couldn't help but cast Tyger a knowing glance behind the backs of the two young men. Tyger responded with a nod and a grin.

"Aliqui," Petre said, "I heard your grandmother say that she was Native American. I'm not sure how bloodlines within the same race work. I mean, in our culture there is no designation made by color of skin, only by breed. But with Humans, how is it that you are slightly lighter of skin and hair than your grandmother if you are the same line?"

The Patriarchy had starved Petre of knowledge about people just as it had denied Tylon the knowledge of science. Aliqui smiled at Petre's curiosity, so different from Tylon's yet equally as undeterred. "Within the Human breed, there are a multitude of races, called nationalities. Now, nations are clusters of domes, but before the End nations were often very large sections of land governed by one leader. Before the End, our racial differences were the cause of a lot of bigotry, but in the Land of Sky, probably because so few Humans did survive, we have been able to see beyond that. Pagan and One believers alike.

"My father was light of skin and hair like Sarah but my mother, my grandmother's daughter, was dark. I am a little of each of my parents." Aliqui paused. When Falcon had been here and someone had asked about her mixed origin, she would laugh and say that another thing she had inherited from her vivacious, French father was her skill as a passionate lover. Then she would turn to Falcon and wink. But today, without Falcon, the joke was hollow and useless. Today, she not only missed Falcon terribly but her parents as well.

Tyger touched Aliqui's shoulder and the woman emerged from her dark thoughts.

Focused on the crystals, Tylon asked, "There are mounds for different kinds of crystals, I'm guessing. This mound of red crystals is fire crystals, right? The blue are water, the white are air, the green, earth. But what are these clear crystals? You mentioned once that you 'charge' them. What does that mean?"

Aliqui came forward and reached for one of the clear crystals. It slid easily from the cluster of others leaving behind a hole in the stone mound. She took her El Rod from her belt. "You see, my El Rod is actually four crystals bound together. When someone is initiated into the Phoenix fighting art, he or she is given a single crystal devoid of energy, devoid of any color like this clear one. The crystal is then brought here and taken to the Earth mound where it is charged with Earth energy. It becomes the weapon for the initiates training in Earth which is level one.

"To charge the crystal, it's slipped into the desired stone. Years ago, my grandmother magically and physically created conductors of energy within each mound. The initiate asks the power of Earth to fill the crystal and tells Earth what she or he will use the crystal for. The second level of study is Water, then Air and then Fire. When each level is achieved, the warrior receives and charges a new crystal. There are four levels, just as there are four elements and when each of those elements are mastered, the four crystals are bound together to make an El Rod." Aliqui paused and gestured to some of the other stone spaces that were covered with crystals of mixed colors or changing colors.

"Some of these are my grandmother's projects," she explained, "but most are for Phoenix practitioners. Maybe a few new students will arrive from other Sky bases while you're here. They come and go every now and then. It takes a long time for a crystal to charge, but once it's complete, it never has to be recharged."

Aliqui replaced the clear crystal and continued. "Before the End, science made crystals more receptive for this kind of use. Once, they just cast rainbows on the walls, but now they have become objects that harness the power they once only symbolized. They have brought magic into our world in a way that allows it to be utilized."

She paused again and pointed to the darkness in the nooks and crannies of the cavern's ceiling. Tylon, Petre and Tyger all peered up after her. "Crystals shed light on a mysterious world but they still grow in the shadows." She gestured to the far end of the room where there were two more mounds of stone. One was empty; the other was packed with many crystals, all glowing faintly. Walking over to this mound, she removed one of the crystals and said, "All crystals start out with the same neutrality. They are all open eyes and we choose what we want them to see – what we want them to become."

She held the crystal up towards the ceiling, the shaft lying flat against her palm. "You have to concentrate to use most crystals, be in touch with its power. But with this light crystal, for example, or with the dark crystals that my grandmother sometimes grows, there is an activation word which allows them to work unattended. We call it a command word, but it only works with the light and dark crystals, not the El Rods."

Aliqui spoke a word that was more just a sound and the crystal in her hand began to glow brightly. Its color changed from white to gold and then a slender shaft of light shone from the end. Holding it up in her hand, she brushed the light across the ceiling, dispelling the shadows and revealing the crystals growing in the darkness above. A mist ebbed around them, hugging the ceiling, and now it seemed to thicken, cloaking the young clusters and shading them from the light. Aliqui moved the light away. "You shouldn't do that for long; light stunts their growth. Once those are mature, they'll be moved into the mounds with the others, but for now there they stay in the mist and grow."

"You do with magic what we do with technology," Tylon said. Aliqui looked at him questioningly. He reached into the pouch at his belt and extracted his Energy Cylinder.

Tyger stepped toward him. "Tylon, we agreed not to use the E.C. out of battle."

Tylon met his leader's gaze evenly, asking her permission. "I'll be careful." She hesitated but nodded once.

Tylon took the palm-length steel shaft in his hand and, pointing it away from them, he flipped his wrist. The glowing blue beam shimmered as it emerged. His was fashioned like a sword.

Aliqui looked from the intriguing weapon to Tylon's face. "You don't have to concentrate to keep it engaged?" Her voice was surprised, but not impressed. She was about to continue, but the expression on his face stopped her.

Tyger stepped in and took the weapon gently from Tylon's hand. She flicked it off and said, "Once, E.C. had hollow cores, but now it's filled with a kind of living organism which will consume any organic matter it touches. It's what the domes are made of. What we stole to escape." She handed the disengaged weapon back to Tylon. The color had finally returned to his face.

"I'm sorry," he said to Tyger, his voice very small. "I didn't think it would bring back so many bad memories."

Petre put his arm around the other man's shoulders. Tylon smiled weakly at him and then, as if physically shaking off the past, he turned back to Aliqui. He smiled, encouraging her to continue.

Aliqui looked at Tyger who nodded. "We use crystals for more than just El Rods and lights," she began, moving them toward another part of the cavern and pausing before a smooth wall. She touched a slightly discolored patch on the stone and the next moment the wall was sliding away. Aliqui turned and gestured for them to enter. "This is the Hidden Garden. Iahala's garden of magical crystals and gems. Each batch grows from a different sculpture that resembles some of the most prominent of the Great Stones," She walked into the room and the young men followed her.

Tyger lingered at the threshold to the garden, eyes flicking over the massive stone sculptures – all covered in clusters of crystal – which were enfolded by a blue mist snaking delicately across the floor and rising in tendrils toward the ceiling.

Petre still had his arm about Tylon's shoulders and the inventor seemed calmer. There were good reasons behind her instructions to keep the dangerous E.C. hidden – but bringing up bad memories wasn't something she had thought to worry about.

As if he heard Tyger silently calling his name, Petre turned and looked at her over Tylon's shoulder. Petre smiled at her, assuring her that he had everything under control. Her gaze thanked him and she turned from the Hidden Garden, her thoughts turning towards finding Ardyn and Iahala.

Tyger left behind the crystal-lit land of Sky and returned to the Valley above, pleased to be back in the breeze and sunlight. Kestrel, Mouse or Mlinz had left the door beside the falls open and again she wondered about their keys. Allowing herself a moment's rest, Tyger sat down on the soft gold-white sand beside the pool. She watched the reflection of the bronze sky in the blue tinted water then lay back, gazing up at the streaks of clouds moving quickly across the heavens.

Tyger tried to imagine what a solid blue sky would look like but couldn't. The sky without bronze was like a cactus with green skin instead of blue or a lion without talons, a horse without claws. She smiled and decided to let the Old World alone and enjoy the New.

From somewhere across the Valley, Tyger heard the sound of a flute drifting across the rich-scented grass. Looking for the source of the music, she saw Tamarin and Fox some distance away surrounded by

Butterflies who danced and sang in response to his inspired flute playing.

The song was soothing and Tyger eased back again, closing her eyes. The music brought colors into her mind, a vibrant and lively kaleidoscope. The sun felt especially warm and healing after being underground. She had become accustomed to its brilliant rays when the Windriders had escaped from their nocturnal life in New Seattle. It reminded her of her childhood.

Tyger let her mind wander as the music changed, letting her thoughts change with each new tune. When the song was fast, she saw herself on her Windboard, cutting through the Currents of a narrow alley. She was jumping and leaping, striking and parrying as she remembered the excitement of battle without the gruesome attachments.

As the music grew even faster, she was speeding beneath the Skyway, away from the Patriarchy, racing to catch up with the wild herd and draw them away from the Patriarch's trap, swooping down on the Retrieval Squad, crashing through the window of the Hovercraft to rescue Ardyn....

The notes changed again to something slow almost sensuous and Tyger, drifting towards sleep, found her memories following suit. The tune became a suggestion and Tyger was immersed in a whisper between lovers, a strong hand taking her own, words spoken as a promise, and two women moving closer together. Two women standing, the New Seattle Currents blowing their hair together – tiger-striped and auburn. She fell asleep then in the soft grass, old, old memories coming to the surface as she dreamed.

Tyger felt soft lips brush her own. For a moment, she thought she was still dreaming, but she wasn't. She opened her eyes to find Ardyn kneeling beside her. Ardyn kissed her again, more deeply this time, and Tyger had no time to wonder who she had been dreaming about. Slowly Ardyn drew away and Tyger sat up. There was the faintest smile on Ardyn's lips as Tyger touched her own as if to keep the kiss there.

"Iahala wants to talk with you. She's been calling but you'd fallen asleep." Ardyn grinned. "I decided to come wake you."

Tyger returned her grin and warm gaze. "Thank you."

Ardyn leaned forward and touched her lips to Tyger's cheek, feeling the warrior's face flush. "You're welcome."

Tyger stood and began to walk across the Valley towards the seated Elder. Ardyn called after her, "Later you'll have to tell me who you were dreaming about. The smile on your face looked very pleased!"

Tyger cast her a glance that was full of mischief but when she turned away, Tyger put her hand to her head as if that would somehow help her remember the dream more clearly. Her senses were still reeling with visions conjured by more than just Ardyn's unexpected touch. Her mind was filled with visions, memories, as elusive as shadows. Memories of a woman... not Sarya, not Ardyn.... Who had she dreamed about? Tyger shook her head. The woman's face was so close, but she couldn't quite place it. With a shrug, she let the dream slide away, trusting her unconscious to prompt her once it had put all the pieces together.

* * *

Iahala sat at one end of the Valley, her legs crossed upon the soft grass and her brown eyes closed. Her robe, a mix of earth tones, was adorned with a stripe of River Sky blue spiraling from neck to hem. In her hands she held the pale wood talking stick. Tyger had noticed it at Iahala's belt before but she had never had a chance to really look at it.

The sound of Tamarin's flute and the sounds of the other Windriders' voices did not reach them here as the faint Wind blew them further out into the Valley. Tyger found the silence seemed to hold a living presence of its own.

As Tyger approached, she realized that the Elder sat near a hole in the Valley floor. Curious, Tyger went to the edge and peered over. The drop was a good hundred feet, maybe two. A handfull of young Butterflies whizzed up the hole and raced past her. She stumbled back and heard Iahala's low laugh. "Careful, Windborn, the seal over that opening keeps Humans from falling into Skynest, but not your kind."

Tyger expelled her breath and shook her head, sitting down beside the Wisewoman. "I was born in a world of Wind and Great Stones. I grew up with steel and concrete, and now I'm surrounded by magic. What else will life hand me?"

Iahala smiled gently, her eyes full of possibilities. "Adventure."

Tyger laughed. "I thought you'd say something more–"

"'There will come the Tiger, the Magic, the Butterfly and the Fourth Power, which is too great to be known,'" Iahala's voice was deep and sonorous. "'Then the child of the Wind who is beast and warrior, who left her world and embraced the steel, shall rise and drink the red-silver wine that unites the world as one.'" Iahala looked at Tyger. The Windborn's eyes were locked onto her face. Iahala clutched the talking stick more tightly in her aged hands, keeping the symbols hidden. "'The warrior child who is woman and native shall turn the tides of the rising Wind until the New World becomes the Old World and the Old becomes the New.'"

A long silence followed as the two stared at each other. Tyger found her voice first and said, "The Patriarch always said I was a legend, but I'm not. I'm just a woman. Just a normal person."

"Legends are full of 'normal' people, Tyger. And you are a legend, whether you like it or not. You have always been more than just a child. Just a woman. Just a warrior." Iahala gestured to Ardyn, who lay a distance away near the Falls, her hands linked behind her head. "She talked about you.

Ardyn believes you are more than just a warrior. I believe it, too. I see the way you touch the lives of those around you. You are strong and bold, but you are not directionless. You have a goal. You have knowledge."

Tyger lowered her head as shame touched her. "Wise One, if only you knew better some of the evil I have done you would not make me a legend. You would not make up stories about what I will do."

Iahala slowly reached out one hand and covered Tyger's curled fist. "I did not create the legend, Tyger. Those words I spoke have been handed down for generations. They were the last words spoken by the Riddler. After the Test. They were the words that ended one world and began another. I do not make up stories about you. Only you can make this story."

Tyger shivered as though a cold hand had just taken her by the back of the neck. The words that ended the world. Ended the world. She shook herself as if to dispel the chill and looking up into the old woman's eyes said, "Tell me. Tell me how the world ended."

Iahala looked at Tyger for a long moment. "I've spent most of my life trying to decipher the legend," she said at last. "Many long and silent nights I wondered whether the End could have been avoided if another answer had been given. I never imagined that the words of the Riddler would come true in my lifetime, but your arrival has changed everything. You need to know the whole story, Tyger, so that you may understand your place in it." She paused for a moment then and looked down at the talking stick in her hands. Turning it over and over for a moment, she seemed to be considering where to begin and how to tell this tale. This was no casual telling. This was the epic story of the Earth. Of the Humanrace that was now so much more. How much would Tyger really understand?

Iahala pushed her concerns away. She would tell the whole tale. Let the passion of her words, if not the meaning, fill this young warrior beside her.

Iahala lifted her dark eyes to Tyger's face and began to speak. "I am 136 years old, Tyger of the Windriders. It has been 296 years since the End of the Old World. I am a Fourth Generation Survivor. My great-grandparents were First Generation. They saw the End. And through HashiSekai technology, through the IkioiHashi implant..." Iahala moved her hair back from her ear and Tyger stared, shocked, bewildered, at the crystal-like disc that sat just below the Wisewoman's chestnut skin. "I see the End as they did. I know the history of all our people."

Iahala paused a long time. Tyger could not stop herself from staring at the strange, shimmering disc. Finally she looked away, back to meet Iahala's gaze. "Please," she said, her voice betraying her confusion and her wonder. "Tell me everything."

Iahala continued. "Once, long, long ago, the world was green and blue. The Earth was clean, fresh with towering trees, rolling meadows and rivers that ran clear and strong, meeting oceans deeper than a lover's passionate gaze. The world was young, beautiful and untouched. There were many religions practiced and many ways of worship. But Humans came into power and knowledge, and unlike other animals, who adapted to their environment, Humans changed the environment to suit their selfish needs. They covered the grass with gray stone and silver steel. They bled the rivers dry and vomited filth and corruption into the pristine waters of the native seas.

"They were weak. They needed the Earth's life-force to sustain them. The fossil fuels, the raw materials. They destroyed the forests even after they learned trees provided the very oxygen they craved, required to survive. When the waters were black and the skies impenetrable darkness, they abandoned the world in search of new places to destroy.

"And Humans, Tyger, were experts of destruction. Late in the high-tech age discoveries in uniquatum physics, robotics, genetics and neuroschematics, cognitive exploration, came so quickly and changed their world so completely that Human societies struggled to keep up with the overwhelming scientific knowledge that was pouring almost daily out of the research facilities. They lost their faith in magic – in the idea of something larger and wiser than they. After all, they could manipulate the very genes that made them what they were. They saw themselves as Gods.

"They abandoned the idea of family. They slaughtered each other by the tens of thousands. Communities, which had once been the very foundation of the Humans' lives, were shattered into divided sects and states that claimed they were their own countries. The different religious practices, which had often been a source of hatred and contention, became a sword by which many died. The Christian religions, in an effort to preserve their faith, merged together to form one religion, and even though lipservice was given to their unity, they were deeply divided within. Over time not even their joint strength could stop their own corruption. The One believers of today do not follow the teachings of the man Jesus... it is hard to know what they follow. All over the world, communities, religions, countries were corrupted by the segregation and bigotry inherent in their own laws. It was no surprise that since these entities were being destroyed from within, alliances between entities crumbled and fell.

"That is not to say that there were not many wondrous discoveries during this time. Archaeological evidence proved the theory of evolution and other studies proved the existence of a great creator. These both became mutually inclusive studies and were accepted as scientific fact. Virtual reality and essence study – the study of the elemental powers inherent in everything – were in wide use. But despite these marvelous achievements,

wars were still fought over land and ideas as if it were somehow possible to
prove something by killing all those who were opposed. Perhaps you have
heard of the Mutant Rebellion, the Lavender Inquisition, the Pride Wars, the
Age of Demons? We came to rely upon our technologies so much that we
lost our own Humanity. Even with all our new toys and powers we turned to
such basic instincts. Humans became unable to see past each other's
differences to our similarities and that had catastrophic results." Iahala took
a deep, sharp breath. "But I'm going too fast... there is so much more I
know."

So far, Tyger had understood most of what Iahala was saying. But
then the Wisewoman seemed to fall into the trance of her own words and her
story took a bizarre and barely comprehensible turn. It was as if Iahala had
tapped into a deep source within her brain, accessing facts, truths that Tyger
barely grasped. She could only sit, listening, as the downfall of the world
spilled out into her lap.

"Japan bridged the hardware/wetware divide late in the twenty-
second century and the world changed. Rumor said that they had had the
technology for a decade or more but had waited to reveal it to the world until
they had 'perfected' it. They named their creation IkioiHashi, Mighty
Bridge. Only about an inch in circumference, the crystalline disc was placed
behind the ear, usually just into the hairline of a user and held in place for
thirty days with a semi-permanent adhesive. After a month, several thousand
microscopic cyberorganic filaments had grown from the disc in through the
skin and bone to wind themselves around and through the user's brain.
Properly equipped with this interface, all a user had to do to enter the system
was insert the cellular jack to achieve a wireless satellite connection to the
fully interactive online world, HashiSekai, BridgeWorld. The jack, a
slender, short cylinder made of the same crystalline material as the disc, was
pushed through the disc's paper-thin center, a quarter inch into the user's
head where the end was nestled at the center of the filaments. Connection
was severed when the jack was removed. It all seemed so simple.

"The twenty-second and twenty-third centuries were known as the
era of the Mega Corporation. Huge conglomerates with enough employees
and enough money to shape their industries and the needs of that industry.
Until IkioiHashi, the American government had been resistant to any
research that combined the human body with computers, but the U.S.A. and
Japan waged a colder cold war than the U.S. had ever waged with Russia.
After the Japanese introduced the IkioiHashi, an explosion of cybergenetic
experiments began in the United States because the president could no
longer afford to tell the Mega Corps *no* if the U.S. wanted to keep pace with
Japan. Saying no simply wasn't an option anymore. Of course, the Mega
Corps used humans in their experiments because animals were much more

expensive – they were far rarer than humans – and human weren't protected by as many laws. There were a lot of hungry people then in the United States. They sold themselves to the Mega Corps quite willingly in exchange for food, homes and entertainment. It couldn't be called slavery if you sold yourself into it, right? A generation, perhaps two, were spent fighting the efforts for and against human experiments. The great media pun: *Guerrilla tactics used to save human lives.* It was the experiments though – for good or for bad – that began the alterations of DNA in so many people which allowed the End, the Wind, to create Clones from Humans. Originals from Clones... Windborn from Originals.

"At first only government officials of various nations had access to HashiSekai. But that didn't last. Several nations offered crippled versions to the general public for commercial entertainment purposes. After locking away some of the more powerful aspects and tools of the HashiSekai system with passwords and codes, an amazing new toy was presented to amuse the masses. Much like the first online 'world' which presented a system of words and previously loaded graphics, the HashiSekai system had wide appeal. The difference that drew not just many people, but almost all people to HashiSekai was that unlike its predecessor this world was not limited to an exchange of words. Users appeared online in 'physical form' able to see, smell, hear, taste and touch – to experience this system like a second world without so many of the real world's dangers. It offered another existence and sometimes a better one. It wasn't just a place to exchange words and ideas, it was its own reality. Users had form, substance. They could come together, organize, experiment, explore and implement – all online. These weren't just clubs gathering anymore, these were communities, cities, countries of like-minded activists. The possibilities were as infinite as the imagination, which was why the government locks didn't last long. Soon, sooner than anyone expected, the general populous had complete and unregulated access to what was quickly becoming a preferred new world. Living in the real world was increasingly difficult with the problems and traumas that came with an planet over-populated with irresponsible people. Turning to the stars was just too expensive. But turning to HashiSekai was only a one-time payment of an average month's paycheck and an additional average day's wages for each month of use thereafter. Thousands of banks were willing to offer loans. Anything to get people off the streets, out of trouble and into their own minds where they couldn't hurt themselves or anyone else.

"For a long time users were enthralled by the magic of the system and content to pay the fees. They were required to enter HashiSekai through a system provider, an authorized gateway, but they didn't seem to mind. It was a marvelous system and such an incredible rush to experience! Eventually, however, users began to dislike the gateways. Entering directly into the main system proved more attractive to many, freeing them from the monthly payment and from the rules enforced by programmed limitations that surrounded you like a bubble whenever you used an official gateway. It was illegal to enter the system directly, but it was impossible to track a user not entering through a gate and the booster device that allowed unregulated access cost only the price of a few years online.

"It took even longer, the middle of the twenty-fourth century, for the booster to become wide spread, but even before it had, special interest groups began to claim territories on the system. Territories were the programs that made up the virtual world. A program might create a small area like a room or a house, or many programs could be linked together to create a city. To claim territories for themselves, groups would build defensives surrounding the territories they wanted. Passwords, puzzles and labyrinths were defensives that could consist of 'physical' obstacles, word and number games. Groups also began to build roadways, links, from one space to another, charging tolls for passage. The HashiSekai system designers tried to remove the groups and their defenses from the system but found they could not. HashiSekai was designed to adapt to the users, to be malleable, to allow individual expression. They could neither flush out these groups nor stop their growth. Instead they simply programmed more areas for legal users to use – and subsequently steal – and they placed more of their own counter-defensives online.

"The system guards were nicknamed Tag-alongs because when they discovered a user not traceable to a legal gateway they simply stuck to the user, interfering with programming, movement and all other activities. For a good while this seemed to slow down the illegal activities on the system but not forever. Programs were created and sold that would create Tag-along killers. Some were serious like the ReProgrammer which infected a Tag-along and rewrote its purpose. Others were just as useful but humorous like the nicknamed BBGun program which would effectively shoot holes into the Tag-along program until nothing was left of it. Responding to the eventual destruction of their guards, the system designers hired real life users to take the place of the Tag-alongs. This proved to be the first step in a very deadly game. When using the system, the human brain became just another program... a program that could be destroyed and manipulated just like the Tag-alongs. But those practices took another generation to perfect.

"Conciseness downloading was discovered by the masses several generations after IkioiHashi was first introduced. Slowly the information emerged that before the public had had mass access to HashiSekai, officials and leaders of hundreds of Mega Corps and political organizations around the globe had escaped the violence of their real lives to exist full-time in the virtual world. Buried deep, deep in the system and surrounded with self-propagating defense systems that had once seemed infallible, officials that found real life too dangerous had chosen to have their entire consciousness, every memory, every thought in their brain, downloaded onto the system allowing their physical body to die while their consciousness, embodied within their new virtual form, would write its own program called 'life.' From their virtual mansions these leaders continued to run their companies, their countries, their lives. But once these VIPs were discovered, their defensives penetrated, their consciousness could be kidnapped and ransomed just as effectively as their flesh and blood bodies might have been. And something more. Copies of a consciousness could be made and a clone of the VIP formed. A perfect twin to help predict future decisions.

"At the same time, life expectancy was up, almost doubled. An average human might live a highly productive and quality life to one hundred-sixty with a little help from science. Women were having children into their sixties or later, waiting as long as they could so they could gather as much information and life experience as possible. Experience that was copied and downloaded into their child's brain. Why spend years trying to instill your beliefs and values into your off-spring when you could do it at birth? Why send them to elementary school, high school, college when you could just download everything you had learned and how you had learned it? Commercial companies offered a whole line of programs promising straight 'A' brilliance in every subject from reading to quantum physics. Of course, sometimes it wouldn't work. Sometimes a child's brain simply could not handle the stress of the direct hardware/wetware connection. But wasn't death a legitimate risk for perfection?

"There were no more national secrets. Secrets could not be kept. Increasingly more and more was done online – business as well as mundane aspects of standard existence, like seeing your doctor or ordering products. With a professional hacker to uncover their online persona, government officials could be tracked down after logging on no matter where their physical bodies might be. Once discovered, anyone online could be downloaded, and their knowledge sold to the highest bidder. When connected to the system compliments of the hardware/wetware bridge, a user's brain was connected to the system, and everyone knows that a bridge goes two ways, brain to system and system to brain. The IkioiHashi acted like a brain stem, converting thoughts, brain waves, into commands for movement or speech so that the user could command their projected online form, like he or she did his or her own body. But the IkioiHashi also allowed connection from the system to the brain so that information, feelings, senses could be remembered, felt, processed. It was this connection that allowed other users access to another person's brain – a consciousness full of memories, strategies, plans and more. A consciousness could simply be copied, searched for pertinent information – so much of a consciousness was mundane – and sold to those who disagreed with the downloaded plans or philosophies so that counter-measures could be launched. A Democratic interest group could track down a Republican candidate, copy his or her consciousness, find out future plans and tricks, and prevent or prepare for them all – and the Republican candidate would be none the wiser.

"By the end of the twenty-fourth century big and little wars were being fought on every front across the virtual world. Animal rights groups attacked company officials where animal testing was done – and those who supported animal testing attacked the activists. Rival publishing houses scanned the brains of the editors to find out what forth-coming trends they planned to follow. The religious far-right sent programs into the brains of gay users that would create depression and remind them, subliminally, to repent. Sports coaches scanned the competitors' players looking for weaknesses. Everyone was out to forward their own agenda. More extremist groups decided they weren't satisfied with just making copies of a consciousness. They created programs that would make them a copy and then wipe the brain clean – forced comas. They created programs that would make their copy and then detonate a neural explosion within the brain causing heart attacks, strokes, seizures or death.

"Understandably, this wracked every nation, shaking multiple facets of various cultures to the bone. And as time passed and users got better and better, the havoc crossed national boundaries. International alliances began to weaken as spies on every side revealed and stole disturbing bits of truth. Some governments panicked and tried to revert to the primitive combinations of telephone, email and post, but they were even less secure. It became impossible to protect the most valuable resource in the world – information.

"Disease ran rampant like never before after years of precious control as warring nations raided vaccine storage felicities for Cancer A4 through X19 and HIV1 through 8. The skies, the seas and even underground wars were waged with weapons that were terrifying combinations of man and machine. Some dared to say that the wars were what saved us all, because despite the deaths, the population continued to grow and our natural resources were soon depleted. Massive solar energy projects failed because they were both incredibly expensive and incredibly labor intensive. We turned fully to nuclear fusion just in time for the fusion wars to begin. We lost entire cities in overnight raids. Wars went on and on, claiming almost the entire twenty-fifth century, causing set-back after set-back as nations were constantly forced to rebuild.

"So the governments fought each other and they fought their own people. The real life race wars began, the religion wars, the environment wars, and the virtual wars continued to expand and claim more lives. In America and in many other nations, martial law was declared but the people only rebelled stronger. For once in history the people had as much power as their leaders. The cities – both real and virtual – stood so tall they began to scrape the heavens but the moral fabric of our civilization was like a cloth ready to be yanked out from beneath us – ready to fell everything that stood too high. We had entered the cybernetic age when even the soul could be digitized. Extreme measures and counter-measures were expected daily, hourly occurrences. We had entered the ultimate game of chess locked in violent and never-ending stalemate. It didn't really surprise anyone when China destroyed all of its communications satellites, severed its telecommunications wires and closed its borders. The HashiSekai system was cellular. Without the satellites and without the wires, the system was dead to China. No more virtual reality wars, no more stolen secrets, no more high-tech rebellion. One by one other nations followed suit. They all wondered why they hadn't thought of it first.

"By the year 2510 we had a planet without international communication and with very little national communication as well. Without the virtual world to bring them together, many of the rebellious and disgruntled groups began to fall apart. In an attempt to rebuild, again America declared martial law and states closed their borders. This time they met with only scattered resistance. Terrorist acts continued but they were more random, less organized.

"The fusion wars had created fall-out aplenty and time to study radiation first hand. One of the first things discovered through this research was the semi-organic, superconductive crystal-like material with which the Japanese had created the IkioiHashi. Speculation was made that perhaps Japan had had the material in their possession since 1945 when Nagasaki and Hiroshima were first bombed but other rumors said that the world governments had known of the crystal for centuries and simply chose now to reveal it to the public. Incredibly light but infinitely strong, the crystals were superdurable conductors of energy that could be recharged over and over again. Perhaps more amazing was the crystals' seemingly uncanny ability to adopt the attributes of the substance around it. When nine parts crystal were mixed with one part steel, for instance, the result was an amazingly light, exceptionally strong steel. The new material was put into wide spread use.

"The other shocking discovery was that of the Chaos Cells. Dubbed chemically-organic and, some argued, sentient, the Cells' existence consisted of constant movement as they split in two, consumed one another, split again, consumed again and so on. As they consumed they cast off (and sometimes ate) a pliable skin that would encase them within it, protecting them from any casual interference but allowing organic objects to be pressed through the skin... and be consumed. To survive at this incredible split-and-consume rate for any extended period of time, the Cells needed to have access to a special mix – fibrinogen, water, oxygen, amino acids, iron – that basically added up to blood. Luckily, researchers found a way to synthesize the mix, though, again, there were dark rumors. After much study the Cells were employed to create domes around first just the centers of the cities, but soon over more and more land. This was the government's answer to the radical pollution problem and it seemed to work.

"By this point some of the groups that had been powerful in HashiSekai were reorganizing, quietly. One of these was a group of environmentalists that began to do their own research on the crystals and the Cells. The crystals they accepted and adapted to their own needs but the Cells worried them. They were concerned about a possible poisonous fall-out or by-product from the Cells themselves but the government would not heed or aid them. Finding themselves ignored, these activists began to develop, of course, counter-measures. Mother Trees, they named them. Trees made by a combination of nature, the crystals and science that grew faster, larger and, most importantly, harder than any other tree on the planet. These trees literally grew too fast and too hard to be cut down or removed by the government and they served the double purpose of bringing much needed oxygen to the atmosphere and hindering the thus-far unchecked creation of the Cell-skinned domes.

"Across the globe, even without contact, nations were moving along similar paths at various rates. The next major development was the race to claim the moon. The leaders of so many countries were not willing to try to rebuild their shattered societies; they wanted to start with a clean slate. But there is only one moon, as you know, and none of the nations wanted to share. This wasn't to be like Earth where so many nations shared a single space. The moon had to be all or nothing. So the wars in orbit began. And when any nation set down on the moon, tried to begin building, the fighting picked up on the surface.

"The majority of the Earth was beginning to recover, to heal, but the governments kept pushing for the stars. They seemed to forget about the huge population that needed them. Instead of changing, they fled the scene of destruction, leaving behind what they saw as an empty shell that had only once been a beautiful Earth. Perhaps they felt betrayed, as if Mother Earth had a duty to last forever, but more likely these government teams were too busy rubbing their hands together in demented delight, imagining wealth and riches that would come from the rape and pillage of other planets. But numerous attempts to terra-form Mars, to build stations in space and on the Moon failed. It began to seem hopeless; no nation would let another succeed, so raids and warring continued in space and on Earth as well. The star wars continued through-out the twenty-sixth century.

"Meanwhile, on the surface of the Earth, in America especially, people began to divide into two categories that became all encompassing. There were those who supported space exploration and those who wanted to salvage the Earth. As time passed the groups became divided along many lines, including religion, use of force and even quality of life and lifestyle. The two groups were called many things including Patriots and Rebels, Escapists and Fighters, and even One believers and Pagans.

"It wasn't until the very end of the twenty-sixth century that any nation achieved interstellar travel, centuries later than scientists had predicted hundreds of years before. The moon, Mars, our whole solar system was announced too small to share but the universe itself seemed just big enough. We were a divided and wounded people, had been now for centuries. It had taken us a very long time to gain this accomplishment of star travel but when we did, it was still a bone of contention among many. By the time the ships started to return – some of them had been in space for generations – almost all the world was domed. We were a planet peppered with round bubbles, fueled by the energy of the Cells and run by computers. Between the domes stood the towering, rock-hard Mother Trees, visible even from space. The ships began to return in the early twenty-eighth century."

It was here that Iahala paused again as if the flood of memories threatened to overwhelm her. Tyger watched her, watched the sunlight catch the edge of the IkioiHashi disc, knowing that she had just heard the genesis of the crystals, of the Mother Trees that had become the Great Stones, of the Cells and Domes and so much more that her head was reeling. But Iahala recovered and continued, for the story was not yet done.

"Humans.... So many of the nations sent ships into space, ready to find planets they could colonize. Places where they could build more advanced domes that were completely self-contained. Ready to conquer – to find, destroy and move in. But every ship returned without alien-life contact... or so they thought. Shortly after the ships began to return to Earth, things started to go wrong. At first, nothing was thought of it and incidents were blamed on computer error, changing weather patterns, human fallibility. Systems were failing. Not just in America, but everywhere. Because the ships had not been prepared to deal with aliens that were not flesh and blood. Alien forms that could infect the computers of the starships without detection. Ships that were then connected to the giant computers of each nation. The computers that handled everything from turning on the power in someone's house, to maintaining the life-support in the domes.

"By the time they understood what was happening and gave these malfunctions a name – the Virus – it was too late. Global communication had been severed so long ago and the United States, the last country to be infected by the Virus, had no idea that the End was coming so quickly and with so much power. By the time the various governments realized that there was no way to purge their systems, the Riddler – the most heinous form of global destruction – was already loose upon the Earth.

"The Riddler appeared in the United States on August 14, 2702, three-hundred eighty-five days after it had first been unknowingly downloaded from starship computer banks into the computer systems of Reunited Russia and Japan. Four-hundred and seventy days before the End.

"All life support, food distribution and control systems failed. There were riots everywhere as nation after nation of people panicked in the wake of something they were at a loss to understand. How could technology fail them? How could their bright and shiny machines suddenly stop working, turning against them? And then they saw the Riddler for the first time. The Humans saw the ambassador of their destruction for the first time. On a billion view screens and holo-projectors across an almost devastated world, the Riddler appeared in a vast wash of blues and greens, an ever-moving matrix that could control every function in the entire system. Some thought it almost beautiful, and like many viruses, it was beautiful in its own complex and sinister way.

"In a hundred languages, a thousand dialects, it spoke to the nations of the world. 'I am here to test you. I have explored your technology and found it primitive and self-consuming. The only way to save yourselves is to prove your worth.' And then it posed the first question. 'Why are you here?'

"Every nation received this question and every nation was given a certain amount of time to answer it – sometimes hours, minutes or days. This question that philosophers have asked since Humans first began to examine their place in the grand design. What could we answer? The Riddler was testing our souls. We were so cut off from ourselves and each other, that the United States could not provide the Riddler with an answer within the time allotted. The punishment for this failure was the slaughter of millions as the Riddler detonated our own bombs.

"The second question came then, in the wake of this destruction and a mounting fear. 'What is courage?' And although the officials bickered among themselves, an answer was given to the Riddler, an answer provided by a child of an official who had lost her twin in the bombing. It was amazing that they listened to her, that they gave value to a child when they rarely had before. She said, 'Courage is living even when you don't want to.' The Riddler seemed to accept her answer and returned control of life support to the individual domes."

Iahala stopped and let the gravity and scope of her words sink in. Tyger, struggling to fit this new information into what she already understood about the world and its history, gazed at Iahala with an increasing uneasiness. "I know how this story will end," she said softly. "And it doesn't make it any easier to hear."

"You have seen the result," Iahala agreed. "But by knowing the reasons you may understand what the future holds for you."

Tyger nodded. She gestured for the old woman to continue.

"In the United States, government officials began scouring the population for great thinkers – philosophers and spiritual leaders to help them answer the Riddler's questions. If an individual provided an answer that the Riddler accepted, the person and his or her family was granted shelter in deep underground caverns which were protected from the growing chaos above. But these caverns were little more than prisons and the great thinkers were little more than slaves used and then discarded by the government as Humans had once used the earth. The government wanted to make sure they could always reach these people who pleased the Riddler. There was no choice – you gave answers to the Riddler to help save your people, and when you gave an answer, you were sent underground.

"It was horrible at first, for these Answerers, living so far beneath the Earth they knew. Wondering whether or not our combined intelligence would defeat this enemy. My great-grandmother was one of these people. And the underground world was called Sky because that was what the Answerers missed the most.

"My ancestor was a member of an environmental group, one of the groups that had created the Mother Trees that became the Great Stones. She answered the question, 'What is the Earth?' She said, 'The Earth is a living power who remembers and gives birth and death both. The Earth is home.' The government didn't much like her answer, but they had a feeling that the Riddler would. They were right.

"My great-grandmother, accompanied by her companion, my great-grandfather, had not been in Sky long when a man and a woman were brought to Sky and proclaimed leaders. They were public figures, leaders of a religious movement that had risen and been crushed a dozen times. Their sect had condemned thousands to death with words and even more with laws and their own fists. They had each answered a question of the Riddler. The couple were named Abraham and Sarah Tarahson, leaders of a powerful group of One believers. They were the great-great-grandparents of the Abraham and Sarah you know today. The Abraham and Sarah who carry the memories of their ancestors just as I carry mine.

"The man's question had been 'What is faith?' He answered, 'Faith is believing in what you cannot see and cannot understand.' The woman's question was 'What is love?' Her answer was longer, much more dangerous. 'Love is the love of the One. The One God. Love is embodied in the bond between a man and a woman.' After the government submitted these answers to the Riddler, the Riddler disappeared from the computer screens it had inhabited for four hundred and seventy days. And so, these two great Answerers were sent to Sky as heroes... just in case the Riddler returned.

"The government hoped that these two answers had vanquished the Riddler at last. But that was not the case. The Riddler had not left, but was busy compiling all the answers from all the nations. And when the computations were complete, the Riddler decided the fate of all of Humankind. The United States had in fact been last to finish the questions and our final answers – Abraham and Sarah's answers – had spelled everyone's doom.

"You see, Tyger," Iahala explained, "What Sarah forgot, or perhaps never knew, was that love cannot be defined by such narrow terms. She dismissed the love we have for the animals we share our lives and our Earth with, the love we bear for our countries, the love some of us showered on the Earth herself. She announced that there was only one god. She claimed that love can only exist between men and women, ignoring the love between two women, two men, even a parent and child. Those omissions cost billions of lives. Yes, there had been other unsatisfactory answers. But the Riddler had allowed for just so many of these and hers put Humankind over this limit.

"When the Riddler returned, it announced that if we believed we were the only living creatures in the universe who mattered, that our god had created us and only us, that love was defined in such elitist terms, then we must be destroyed. Our narrow-mindedness and self-importance must be stopped before we expanded into and corrupted other parts of the universe. So, on December 5, 2703, the Riddler Ended the world. With our own bombs, our own chemicals, our own twisted tools of destruction, the world was changed forever. Humanity had failed.

"But you cannot blame the Humans alone for the End, although it was our own arrogance that brought us to the brink of complete annihilation. Because even though we had stockpiled our weapons and polluted our Earth, there was still hope. There was still a chance for us, as a species, to change. But when the Riddler posed those questions, that test, we were not prepared. We had not evolved or grown into a people who embraced these truths. In the face of this challenge, our demise was less our own fault and more simply inevitable." Iahala bowed her head as if remembering that day, and maybe, through the IkioiHashi, she did. That day when all the hopes and dreams of countless billions were destroyed by an intelligence that could see what they could not – or would not – see. Their own ignorance.

Tyger took a deep breath. She wasn't sure what she believed. Was it Humans who had Ended their own time or something else, some alien life? Did it really matter now who was to blame? Now that the choices had been made and the Old World was dead beneath the New? Tyger felt as if this tale was within her now, a stone to be carried around with other stones that made up the history of this world, her world.

When Iahala spoke again, her voice startled Tyger. It was different, gentler, filled with the power of hope.

"The Riddler was a power greater than us and it intervened when we tried to expand beyond our single Earth. It told us, before it brought destruction down upon our heads, a destruction we had earned, that there was still hope. That as an united people we would rise again." Iahala brought her face up and looked at Tyger. "The Riddler said that someday a child of the Wind would come and unite us. This child would be both wounded by life and wrapped in an armor of strength because of it. She would lead followers more diverse than ever seen before and her eyes would burn the color of the Earth... like no other Windborn before her. And we would be given another chance.

"If we used this chance to overcome our ignorance and embrace our differences instead of using them as weapons, if we ever sought our place in the universe again, perhaps this time we would not be denied." At long last, Iahala's hands relaxed their clenched grip on the talking stick with its hidden symbols. She met Tyger's fierce gaze with an expression of unconcealed joy. "So much depends on you and your Windriders that not even legend speaks it all. Whether you like it or not, your place in this history has already been determined. The warrior that was foretold to us has come. You are that warrior, Tyger. You are that child of the Wind."

Tyger said nothing. Iahala waited, barely knowing how overwhelming this influx of information must be. Tyger's solid green eyes were fixed on some point in the distance as though the images from Iahala's memories were blending and churning with her own recollections, her own dreams, her own fears.

Mouse's words came back to her, his calm, soft whisper, "Do the Windriders know?" *Do the Windrider's know who you are? Do you?* Then she was swept still further back in time....

She remembered an overheard argument between her parents and the Village Elders. The word *kokopelli* repeated again and again. The knowledge, as a child, that her parents were keeping from her some secret. Yes, some identity. In the Village her green eyes had been an uncomfortable mark of distinction that she never understood; she'd tried to cover with her wild striped hair.

Was she to accept, that, like her birth itself, her differences and her path were preordained? She was born of the Wind and the Wind is a powerful thing. Hadn't she always known she was destined for something? Hadn't her parents and the Elders and all the other Windborn always known? Despite her parents' attempts to shelter her, despite Jarth's cruel betrayal – his slaughter of her people – despite the terrible decisions she'd had to make, she knew that she must do... something.

Her gaze refocused slowly on Iahala's still form. The old woman seemed almost frail at that moment, as if this telling had drawn something vital out of her. For a moment, the Windborn and the Human stared at each other without speaking. Finally Tyger said, "If legends are made of struggle and challenge, then perhaps I am a legend."

Iahala looked as deeply as she could into Tyger's green eyes. She seemed satisfied at what she saw there. "You will do what must be done."

Tyger knew it wasn't a question. She nodded her head. "I always have."

* * *

Across the width of the Valley, Ardyn watched Tyger and Iahala finally fall silent. Though Ardyn could not hear them, she could tell that for a long time Tyger had been listening to Iahala with rapt attention. Ardyn's curiosity pulled at her. She wanted to go to them, to be part of this obviously fascinating conversation but respect for her leader and the Wisewoman held her back. She would get the information out of Tyger soon enough... somehow.

A smile crossed her face as it occurred to her that there had been a time when she would have glared at Tyger from afar, in fervent belief that whatever Tyger was doing, it had to be wrong. But everything was different now and she marveled at how much her feelings for the Windrider's leader had changed.

Leaning back on her hands, the soft Valley breeze in her hair, Ardyn closed her eyes and thought of Tyger. Whatever Tyger was, or could be, here in Ardyn's mind, she had become a woman first. What did others see? A beast, as Ardyn had once seen? Just a warrior, hardened by life and by battle? Ardyn saw more than these – the unconscious habit Tyger had of running her hand through her hair, the way she sat at night-meet with one knee raised and one arm resting across it, or the way her eyes became a deeper green when she was lost in thought. Her gentleness with Mouse, her quick, deep laughter, her passion for life and those she loved. These aspects spoke of something deeper than warrior.

Ardyn opened her eyes. She looked again at Tyger leaning back from Iahala, both of them lost in their own deep thoughts. What had they been talking about? She sighed. Probably mysteries and magics. She let her gaze move to the other activities in the Valley. Mouse and Mlinz sat together, talking in the sun. Fox and Tamarin were lying in the grass, the flock of small Butterflies swirling above them. Kestrel was standing with Wolf, Tryl, Jyln and Spider talking about her Wing, Swallowtail. The glider reminded Ardyn of the gold Butterfly and her thoughts meandered, strangely, to memories of Sarya.

A woman whose delicate build had hidden a fierce and beautiful spirit, Sarya had been three years Ardyn's junior. Ardyn had loved her. And so had Tyger. But it was Tyger Sarya had taken as her partner. Their rivalry for Sarya's affection had driven them apart and, finally, drawn them together. It had taken Sarya's death for them to see past their anger.

They had had one night together – Ardyn and Sarya – one memorable night when Sarya had welcomed Ardyn to her bed and allowed Ardyn to make love to her. In the sweet aftermath of that union, Sarya had extracted a promise that Ardyn had been bound to keep – to make peace with Tyger.

At first, she didn't even want to consider it, but bit by bit, she had allowed herself to see something in Tyger other than what she hated. She had come to respect Tyger even as Ardyn's love for Sarya had deepened. But all that had changed when they escaped to the Wind.

Sarya had fallen victim to the Fever of Phase Two, dying in the arms of the two who had fought to own her. A shiver run through her body as Ardyn remembered Sarya's dying wish to become a butterfly. There was something about the Gold One that reminded Ardyn somehow of Sarya, but what it was exactly, she couldn't say.

As if beckoned by her thoughts, the entire adult flock of Butterflies burst with a splash of water from the Sky falls. Beneath the huge expanse of their color-drenched wings, Ardyn felt suddenly very small. The sun shone through those wings casting colored light on the ground and making the patterns on each wing blaze. They circled, led by the Gold One. Ardyn looked hard at it again, trying to discover why it was linked with Sarya in her mind.

She contemplated the Butterfly's face. The eyes were full of intelligence, almost superiority. They hinted at an intimate knowledge of the powers of magic. They were solid eyes like Tyger's, but instead of green, they were black and round. The black-skinned face, as well as the Butterfly's black body, looked as tough as leather but as smooth as silk. There were high, pronounced cheek bones and defined brow line. The thin lips, the small nose, looked almost....

Ardyn paused as two other Butterflies flew up beside the Gold One. As she gazed at them, she began to notice subtle differences in their individual characteristics. The other Butterflies also had large eyes, but the knowledge behind their gazes was not the same. The Gold One seemed to carry a secret. The faces of the others were smoother and fuller, their bones not as pronounced. Their noses were just two small holes in the center of the face and their mouths weren't much more.

Ardyn stared. The Gold One looked down and met her gaze. She had been wrong. Its eyes were not black like the others, but a dark blue. Ardyn froze. The great creature continued to look at her with an expression of puzzled recognition on its not-quite-humanoid, not-quite-Butterfly features.

She watched in stunned stillness as the Gold One opened its mouth, but instead of singing, it moved its lips as if trying to pronounce a word. Her name? Then the Gold One's antennae twitched and it burst away with speed Ardyn didn't know it possessed. Ardyn began instant pursuit. Following after the Gold One, Ardyn was running straight for Tyger and Iahala.

The Butterfly reached them first and the two stood. It stopped, hovering in front of Tyger. Looking at her. Ardyn thought she saw one of the Gold One's skinny black legs stretch out and touch Tyger's face, but then its antennae twitched again and it dove away, down into Skynest, the rest of the flock pouring in after it.

When Ardyn reached the two women, Iahala was frowning and peering down into Skynest. "A reminder that life continues...." she murmured to herself, a bemused look on her face.

Tyger turned toward Ardyn. "That Butterfly–" Ardyn began.

Tyger cut her off before she could continue. "Yes, it does remind me of her."

"I want to get a closer look," Ardyn added, but Tyger didn't appear to be listening. Ardyn paused and stepped closer to her. "Tyger? Are you all right?"

"Fine." Tyger met her gaze briefly. "I have a lot to think about. Iahala would bring you to Skynest, if you like. I could catch up with you later."

Ardyn could almost see words and pictures spinning across Tyger's face and body. She had never seen Tyger so distant. "I should stay with you," she said softly. "You may need me."

Tyger smiled, wholly present for a moment. "You know I do my best thinking alone."

Ardyn wanted to protest, but Iahala took her arm. "Would you come with me, Ardyn? The behavior of the Butterflies puzzles me."

Ardyn nodded, moving away with Iahala even as Tyger's gaze became distant again. What had happened here? Ardyn pulled her thoughts from Tyger with conscious effort as Iahala went on.

"I have never seen the Gold One so interested in strangers. The singing means they are celebrating something, but what? I think it would be best for all if we find out." She lead Ardyn across the Valley toward the entrance to Sky. "If only we could just glide down into Skynest like the flock!" she teased, but Ardyn could tell Iahala, too, had her mind on many things.

Ardyn glanced back over her shoulder for one last look at Tyger. The Windborn was standing very still, her head tilted toward the sky. But Ardyn knew Tyger wasn't looking at the clouds, she was lost inside her thoughts. Somewhere only she could go. Until Tyger had thought things through she would say nothing about her troubles, puzzles or ideas. For now it was best to leave her alone.

Looking back at the Wisewoman, Ardyn asked, "Iahala, what is the Gold One?"

Iahala smiled, reaching out with her crystal pendent to open the door into Sky. "The Great Butterflies are reflections of our dreams, and the Gold One is their elusive leader. I will tell you what I know but it is only a small part of all they are." Then it was Iahala who looked back towards Tyger. "Sometimes I wish I knew more... about so much."

They descended together then, into Sky, making their way toward Skynest where the mysteries of the Gold One would begin to be revealed.

* * *

A strong breeze passed over them, stirring the Valley grass in long waves and Kestrel decided it was time. They followed her to one side of the Valley, stopping to peer up the jagged cliff face. "You see that platform jutting out about eighty feet up?"

The four Windriders did. It was just large enough for maybe two Wings to stand side by side. Tryl whistled. "That's up there."

"It sure is," Kestrel agreed. "It's where I train all new Flyers. It's a good take off point, just high enough to be a challenge. There's your way up." She pointed to a ladder-like path of hand- and foot-holds etched into the stone, rising to the platform. "I'll meet you there."

With that Kestrel lifted her Wing off the ground, moving away from the cliff, and then raised it off the ground, holding it level at her waist. She winked at Wolf, drew back and raced forwards the wall. At the last moment she brought the head of the Wing almost straight up, vertical with the cliff, and with a jerk she kicked her feet into the back harness and the glider was snatched up into the air. She caught a thermal column beneath her sails and, the green-blue cloth shimmering like a million waves, like the Valley grass beneath her, she rose up, off the ground, drifting slowly skyward. This was the power of a Wing.

"Anyone ever beat you there?" Tryl called up to her.

Kestrel pretended not to hear. Only Aliqui's Falcon had ever made that climb so fast. In her silence, the four Windriders threw themselves into their task, Tryl and Spider betting who would reach the platform first.

Kestrel alighted upon the ledge, her Wing taking up about half of it. Just a short time later, Wolf's wild head of salt-and-pepper hair appeared above the platform's edge. He pulled himself over, breathing heavily. Jyln came next, followed by Tryl and Spider... not necessarily in that order. Kestrel smiled at her Windrider pupils. Her eyes lingered a moment on Wolf. His sun-golden body was covered with a sheen of sweat. He saw her watching him and met her gaze, his face bright with exhilaration, his eyes very deep. Kestrel turned away.

"Don't rise outside the Valley. Don't force a dip or dive, just glide. Sometimes there are rotors over toward the west end, so stay away from there. If you fly over the falls, you'll drop some in the convection current, but don't worry, just gain altitude slowly like we talked about. When you're returning, keep your feet in the harness until you're fully above the platform and only follow the main air streams, the ones the sails tell you about, not the antenna quivers."

Tryl chuckled. "Well, that's a lot we can't do. Is there anything we can?"

Kestrel smiled. "Yes," She looked out over the green Valley. "You can fly." They all fell silent, imagining. "All right, who's first?"

Tryl, Spider and Jyln all chimed together like excited children and Wolf fell totally silent. So it was Wolf that Kestrel chose. She reached forward and took his hand, much to his surprise. "Wolf, you first. Than Tryl, Jyln and Spider."

"Hey, I'm last?" Spider half-joked.

Kestrel smiled at her. "Least reluctant goes last so you'll have time to get reluctant. That way you'll be just nervous enough not to pull anything reckless."

Spider grumbled, but did not object further.

Kestrel looked at Wolf, her simple Human eyes meeting his fiery ones and they both knew the sudden nervousness he was feeling was a fear of heights. She didn't say anything, but her eyes told him that she knew. He only nodded silently at her and they walked together to where Swallowtail waited. Wolf reached out and touched the Wing hesitantly. After a moment, Kestrel said softly, "My first time, I was so afraid I could barely climb up here. Then, before I took off..." her voice was a whisper, like a breeze, against his skin. "I just closed my eyes."

Wolf looked at her and Kestrel watched conflict flash across his face. She guessed that the strong Windborn had never closed his eyes in fear in all his life.

"Go for it, Wolf!" Tryl urged.

Wolf did not move.

Kestrel said even softer, "If you don't want to, it's–"

Wolf lifted the Wing and attached the front harness, gripping the control bar firmly with both hands.

"All right!" Spider cheered.

Kestrel walked about the Wing making last minute checks. She stole glances at Wolf, thinking, for a moment, about his youth, about the youth of all the Windriders that sometimes showed through their tough exteriors. They were all about her age, though they had seen and lived through so much more. "When the next steady breeze rolls by, you'll feel the antenna shudder. If the shudder vibrates all the way through the brace and the control bar, you'll hear the sails moving as well, and that's when it's time. Listen to your sails." She paused. The young man looked at her. "I created the Wing, Wolf, and you control your courage. Nothing can go wrong." Wolf nodded. Kestrel continued. "At the height of the breeze run towards the edge as fast as you can, keeping Swallowtail's head up. Just before you reach the edge, push out, kick your legs up into the back harness and then pull back on the control bar. From there, it's all reading the Wind."

Wolf grinned and Kestrel saw how his anxiety had fallen away as they moved into familiar territory. "That part will come naturally."

Kestrel smiled. "I may be able to fly with the Wind, but you have it within you. That's the true union. I envy you."

Wolf, caught off guard by her words, was still searching for a way to respond when the control bar shook as the cables tugged and the antenna shuddered. The sails mimicked the rolling tides and suddenly Wolf was running towards the edge.

At the last minute he pushed out, tucking his legs up and pulling back on the control bar just as the currents caught his sails. The ground slide away from his feet and then suddenly the wolf was flying.

Once the Windriders had thought that the Valley had no Wind but it did. The Wind blew in the Valley, but not the same Wind that roared over the New World. Here the Wind mixed with the spray of the Sky falls, and was filtered by the breath of the green grass. Here the Wind smelled like the Old World and felt gentler, softer. A Wind that Humans and Windborn alike could live in and could fly.

Wolf felt this new Wind on his body and on the Wing and seemed to ride it effortlessly. Below him, he saw the beauty of the Valley and if he rose equal with the Valley rim he could see the New World of white-gold sand, Great Stone and a slowly setting sun. He was gliding between two worlds and the feeling was indescribable.

From the cliff face, Kestrel watched Wolf circle and soar as he and Swallowtail moved, following the currents. She remembered the excitement of her first flight, the pure rush of adrenaline, the unbelievable grace of flight. Looking at her three other pupils she knew this day would lead to something great.

* * *

Far below Wolf on the Valley floor, Fox laughed and twirled again with the young Butterflies. Two alighted in her red- and gold-striped locks and clung to her as she danced. Through her joy and her laughter she knew many things at once: the fading sunlight, the soft green earth, the flowers, the Valley and the falls. She knew the Butterflies, their colors, and the music of the flute.

But above and beyond all this, she knew Tamarin. The impish and playful young man who had been her friend and a major cause of annoyance for the past six years. She knew him now as she had never known him before, and she loved him.

"Fox, look!" He ran up next to her, spinning with her in the cloud of babies. For just a moment he stopped playing his music and pointed. Two especially small Butterflies were twirling together in the air, their tiny wings extended as wide as they would go and their feet linked between them as if they were holding hands.

Tamarin began to play again, taking to the instrument as naturally as the Wind takes to the Great Stones. Moved by the beauty of the melody, Fox began to sing, simple notes that matched and melded with Tamarin's and as the melodies intertwined, she laid her hand on his arm, then shoulder, then back, dancing around him, touching him with honesty, in love, for the first time.

Tamarin had closed his eyes, his cheeks flushed as he continued to play. Fox whispered against his ear, "Your music is beautiful." It was the first compliment she had ever given him. Tamarin lowered the flute and turned his head. Fox thought that his lips brushed her ear but she couldn't be sure.

"Not as beautiful as you," he said softly and for a split second his smile and his eyes held a gentle tenderness that captivated Fox and touched her heart, but then he raised the flute and began to play once more and all there was to know was the sunlight, the soft earth, the falls and their music.

* * *

Mouse sat down beside Mlinz, handing him the small blue flowers he had picked. He smiled across the Valley at his sister, Tyger. It was so wonderful to just be able to look up and have her there. She hadn't changed so much in his eyes, taller surely, fiercer, but still the same. "I thought I was all alone," he said, a breeze teasing his feathery hair. "But now, I feel like I've finally come home again. All my memories are alive in her eyes.

"I remember the Village story-teller trying to describe the green of the Old World," he continued. "We children just didn't understand. Finally he pointed at Tyger and said the Earth had once been the color of her eyes. Then we understood. The richness, the intensity. She was the only one in our Village with green eyes. I don't remember much more than that, but I do remember how others saw her. There's something... magical about Tyger. Ever since that day the story-teller pointed to her, I've thought of Tyger as carrying a bit of the Old World inside of her, maybe waiting to be reborn."

Mouse leaned against the smooth boulder at their backs, the last of the sun catching the tiny crystal Mlinz had given him. A symbol of their bond.

Mlinz reached out slowly and touched the crystal that was woven into the bracelet Mouse wore. With his fingertips, Mlinz traced the translucent clouds trapped within it. "It must be wonderful to have at least some good memories of your family."

Mouse looked at Mlinz. His partner's face was solemn, his eyes deep and full of shadows. The sun on Mlinz's skin made it look like polished ebony. He was deep in troubled thought, and Mouse wanted to help him, if only Mlinz would let him. "Would you like to talk about last night?" Mouse asked finally.

Mlinz shook his head. But his hand reached out and clasped Mouse's to him, as if he was afraid someone was trying to take Mouse away. "It's nothing really," he said, but Mouse was not convinced.

"When you want to talk, I'm here, Mlinz–" Mouse leaned forward to touch his lips to Mlinz's cheek. The other boy jerked away. Their hands remained linked, now even tighter, but Mlinz had severed all other physical contact. Mouse frowned. "It's your parents," he said, recognizing these familiar signs. This struggle Mlinz fought for as long as they had loved each other.

Mlinz looked away. He knew that if Kestrel had been sitting next to him a lecture would have already begun. She would argue that he couldn't possibly love their parents as well as the One that condemned his love for Mouse. She would insist he could not live a double life with so many conflicting views and someday he must choose. Choose between belief and love. But his bold sister was not near him now. Only Mouse was here and Mouse was never critical in the way Kestrel felt entitled to be. Mouse had lost too much in his past to be critical of the present, any present.

Slowly, Mouse reached out again and stroked Mlinz's hair and then his cheek. He gently squeezed the hand that held his in some desperate plea. "No matter what happens I will always love you, Mlinz. Until the sun turns black and the End comes again, I will love you, no matter who you are or what you believe."

A tear slid down Mlinz's face. He would go to his parents and somehow, some way, he would convince them that their evil Purification was not right and could never be the will of the One. Because the One had brought Mouse into his life and could never be part of evil.

He must make his parents listen because Kestrel was right. Mlinz was a coward. He could never choose between belief and love.

* * *

Tylon, Petre and Aliqui stood in the Hidden Garden. The stone sculptures stood like dancing trees caught in time and movement, blossoming crystals of every size and color. Mist the color of the River Sky dripped slowly off the stone trees and pooled through out the secret room, creating an atmosphere of peace. For over an hour, Aliqui had allowed them to explore the Garden, marveling at all they found there.

She showed them crystals that would one day be able to create shields of protection and crystals of healing, strength and tranquillity. Crystals for dream-interpretation, wisdom and many, many more, each with its own powers. But of them all the most powerful were the Spirit Crystals. These were the finest: strong and pure enough to house a spirit in transition that needed a safe place to wait before choosing its next life.

Aliqui was telling them more about the Spirit Crystals when the singing began. The song was joyous and familiar. She turned toward the sound and was shocked to see the hidden door to the Garden open.

"Who–" she took a step forward as the door way was filled with the colors of the Great Butterflies. Singing, they flooded the room, perching everywhere, their wings moving with their song, their antennae twitching in the blue roiling mist.

"How did they open the door?" Petre asked quietly but Aliqui could only shake her head and stare at the Gold One.

The Butterfly leader sat on the top of a stone tree, the highest point in the room. Its skin was no longer midnight black, but growing lighter and its eyes were a deep blue, more intelligent than Aliqui had ever seen them. Its face... was almost Human.

The music continued to build and, for a moment, Aliqui and the two Windriders were entranced by the sounds and sights around her. But then the moment passed and the sound began to grate on Aliqui's nerves. Instead of moving toward a harmonious conclusion, it continued to build toward a frenzied climax. Aliqui saw Petre and Tylon cover their ears and she grit her teeth. Then, suddenly, the crystals began to tremble. First only the smallest of the crystals moved, then those a little larger and then a few more and so on. Aliqui stood frozen, feeling anger rise with her confusion. What were the Butterflies doing?!

Aliqui's gaze shot to the Spirit Crystals. The precious handful grew delicately from the very stone tree the Gold One sat upon. The crystals were shaking visibly, as if at any moment they would to fly apart with the strain.

"You'll ruin them!" she yelled up at the Gold One. But the leader only stared down at her. She advanced towards the Gold One, climbing up into the stone tree. "Why are you doing this? We need these crystals to help lost spirits. Why don't you want us to do that?!"

Aliqui was screaming now but she was barely heard above the rising song. Like the crystals, her body was shaking as if she would explode as she moved ever closer to the Gold One.

"Aliqui, don't–" Petre moved toward her but Tylon held him back. They knew so little about this culture.

Everything seemed to happen at once. As one, the Spirit Crystals shattered, spitting a hundred fragments like broken glass into the air. Aliqui leapt from the stone trees, landed beside Tylon and Petre who had dove to the ground. Crystal after crystal was breaking now, the sound like hard rain on the stone. Then the song ended.

In the hideous silence that followed, Aliqui struggled to her feet. Tylon and Petre followed suit. The Gold One continued to stare impassively down at them. Without caring if the Windriders followed her, Aliqui turned and ran. Her feet crunched over crystal shards and then she was out of the Hidden Garden, out of the Elemental Garden, into the long corridors of Sky, her voice raised to a shout, calling for her grandmother.

* * *

Almost half a mile of twisting corridors away from the crystal gardens, Iahala slid open a stone door. "Welcome to Skynest," she said with a smile.

Ardyn stepped into the room with its circle of standing stones, feeling the raw sensation of power that flooded into her body. Her eyes took in the stone walls peppered with small nests, the darkening of the bronze sky high above. She felt as if she were seeing the world through the eyes of magic, seeing the world for the first time.

She could feel the pulse of the living stone about her – its veins of crystal full of hot and cold color. She heard the breath of the sky, the Wind forever rolling, urging the clouds this way and that. The rich, strong smell of the green Valley.

Above all, almost like a taste in her mouth or a second skin, was the magic in this place. It came to her, embraced her and surrounded her like a long awaited friend. It was outside and within all at once. Gentle and powerful, overwhelming and subtle. Loving and relentless.

This place, Skynest, was alive.

Iahala's soft cry broke Ardyn's thoughts. The Elder was staring at the small woven blanket in the center of the circle of standing stones and at her wooden bowl filled with salt, water and a little clay. But there should have been something else in this bowl as well. The Spirit Crystal was gone.

"The adult Butterflies must have flown back out into the Valley before we got here. Since they are not able to open doors themselves, that is the only place they could have gone... surely. But they–" Iahala's voice stumbled. "They have taken something of mine with them."

Ardyn went to the Wisewoman's side. Iahala was looking around the ground, around the base of the standing stones and then she began to check each of the many nest nooks. She explained, her voice becoming more and more concerned, "When an innocent dies, one who has lived with balance, the soul of that innocent has the power to call to me. If I hear the call, I welcome the spirit out of that waiting place between lives and give the spirit a safe haven inside a Spirit Crystal. Each Spirit Crystal takes long days to prepare for the arrival of an innocent, and once the innocent enters the crystal, their spirit may stay there until ready to choose a new life."

Iahala paused and straightened up from the nests she'd bent to peer into. "When the Windriders arrived, I left a Spirit Crystal here. A spirit was near but hadn't yet entered the crystal, as I was called away from the spell to welcome it. If the spirit was strong enough to enter without my spell... or if someone else...." Iahala's face paled. "I can no longer feel the spirit near. If it is within the crystal...."

Ardyn placed a hand on Iahala shoulder. "What? What would happen?"

Iahala shook her head. "I am not completely sure. This has never happened before. Only I can touch a Spirit Crystal once it is full. If someone else does, the spirit is drawn from the crystal into the body of the other."

For the second time that day, Ardyn felt a cold shiver run through her. "But wouldn't there already be a spirit in that body?"

Iahala nodded gravely. "Yes. The two souls would battle for possession of the physical form. Eventually, one would relent to the other."

"And if one didn't?" Ardyn asked in a whisper.

"The rules of nature would be broken. The world would witness something it has never seen before."

"Maybe someone took the crystal before the spirit was inside and the spirit just left this place on its own." But even as Ardyn said these words she somehow knew they weren't true.

Iahala knew it too. She brushed her hands against the sides of her robes. She glanced around the room as if hoping the crystal would suddenly appear, but her mind was already moving ahead to what she must do. "We must go to Aliqui. If another Spirit Crystal is full grown, we can try reclaim the misplaced soul."

As they turned to go, there was a sudden commotion at the door. Aliqui, followed by Tylon and Petre, burst into the room.

"Grandmother–" Aliqui tried to speak but the flock of adult Butterflies pushed past her into Skynest.

Iahala gasped. The Gold One flashed above the circle of stones and threw wide its sunshine wings. For a moment, the whole room was filled with the golden power of the swarm leader. Ardyn stood completely transfixed by the Gold One's clearly blue-eyed gaze. Then her eyes were blind to the world as images flashed through her head and she could do nothing to stop them.

Ardyn saw golden wings against a bronze sky. She saw the Wind as a living creature. She saw a crystal and knew it to be the missing crystal. She heard the beautiful and haunting song of the Butterflies. Then Ardyn saw the faces of their new friends – Iahala, Aliqui, Kestrel, Mlinz – then walls of stone streaked with colors. Suddenly Tyger was there, before her mind's eye, the warrior laughing, her face turned toward the sun. Then she saw Tyger's tears, felt an unfathomable sadness and re-experienced the dance of love-making, of touching Sarya, the only woman she had ever lain with. Suddenly, the images were gone and Ardyn felt her knees grow weak. As the Butterflies soared up and out of Skynest toward the sky, Ardyn felt as though they took all her strength with them and she collapsed to the cool stone floor.

As the blackness that swirled at the edges of her vision cleared slowly, Ardyn felt Tylon and Petre kneeling beside her, their arms wrapped around her. She heard Aliqui's voice, "They sent her visions." Iahala agreed, "Yes, truth visions."

Ardyn brought her head up. She looked skyward and her heart yearned for something she could not quite name.

As if from far away, Ardyn heard Iahala say, "It has begun. It has finally begun."

* * *

Tyger of the Windriders stood in the Valley of Sky, her face raised to the evening sky and her green eyes closed. She held her body straight, her arms at her sides and her feet slightly apart. Her fiery mane of black-striped hair just barely touched her strong bare shoulders and her leather breeches and boots were worn from travel.

When she was a child, she had ridden on the back of a wild horse and fought the dangerous Flesheater plant for its healing blood. She had braved the Patriarchy, conquered the harsh streets of the Industrial District, ridden a Windboard and led the Windriders to freedom. She had seen battle, played traitor and rebel as well as trusted friend and passionate lover.

She had escaped to the Wind.

The Great Butterflies soared out from Skynest and the Gold One brushed Tyger with its wings as it flew by, but Tyger did not acknowledge its passing. Despite everything and perhaps because of everything, Iahala's tale had confirmed one thing: she must leave this Valley. She must go back to New Seattle. In all her life, with all she had seen and everyone she had met, at this moment she knew only one certainty. Tyger was thinking of evil.

* * *

Part Two

Within a dome of living cells lay the city of New Seattle, where life and the miniature world were divided in half by culture and prejudice. Surrounded by a high, spiked wall, a silver steel complex sprawled, dwarfed by the tower at its center. In this tower, upon the top-most floor whose walls were made of black glass, there stood a steel desk with eight deep claw marks across the surface where some beast had been dragged away from murder. And, behind this desk, sat evil.

Just as Tyger stood, at this very moment, in the Valley of Sky, staring up at nothingness, Christopher Jarth sat here, in New Seattle, staring at nothingness. His close-cropped blonde hair and short, meticulous beard gave his already severe face a sinister look. He had small, dark blue eyes, sharp eyebrows, taut jaw and brow. His angular body matched the harsh look of his face, giving the cold impression of the killer he could be. He wore crisp black fatigues with the marks of a General. But there was more to him than that. Much more.

Jarth was not just another high-ranking military man. He was law-maker, magistrate, senate and congress. Christopher Jarth ruled New Seattle and forty-nine other domes, all under his command and his command alone. Subject to his whim, his power, his politics.

He thought about his slaves, the misbegotten prodigies of the Tiger – those Originals that the Tiger had brought, long ago, from New Seattle into the Wind. Yes, four of them had escaped – with the Tiger? – some time ago, but he still held others. Six groups of four. Still his. They had completed six more domes in the last few days. Six towering steel skeletons, rising over a mile of barren land, boasting huge circulation fans, fire extinguishing systems, decontamination systems and so on – everything his perfect self-contained worlds needed, all delivered by his slave freaks. But the six new dome shells just sat, letting the Wind howl through their beams and spin their fans. He had not yet expanded into them, had not begun to move his citizens in or even grow the domes' skins. The six separate work groups had not yet been reassigned. Nothing was happening on schedule.

Normally, this would have bothered Jarth to no end. He would have been rabid with anger that those six slave groups were living easily, free from any tasks. He found comfort only in the truth that he had not sent squads out to deliver rations to the slaves in the past twelve days.

On another day, Jarth would taken pleasure in the fact of their starvation, but today, even that small victory seemed hollow. Once, Jarth's kingdom of domes had been third in the population race – a race which guaranteed his power, his security, his might. Third place, for just a short time... but no longer. He had lost five Originals who had called themselves the Windriders. He had lost ten of his own soldiers who had tried to stop the Windriders' escape. Then there were those four slaves and, of course, the

Tiger. Five, ten, four, one. Twenty down. Just twenty and the Patriarchy had fallen from third to what? Sixth? Tenth? It was hard to comprehend the cruel irony of it all.

Oh, and those ten hadn't been just any soldiers. They had been his best. Three had been his pride and joy. Colonel Gerald Sart: loyal, vengeful Sart. Jarth's second in command. His envoy to the Tiger. The man who was the leader of the P3M project, the project that assured more Wind-metamorphosed slaves were made from Originals. The man who had headed Jarth's Retrieval Squad, making sure those metamorphosed freaks didn't just escape to the Wind and disappear....

Then there had been Sergeant Matthew Marcs – young, blood-thirsty – he'd used his brawn in any way the great Patriarch told him to, including torture, and maybe even murder.

All the soldiers who'd gone on the mission with Sart to re-capture the Tiger and her Windriders had died. Good men. Strong sergeants who had gained favor with their willingness to obey and their sharp minds – despite their admittedly weak Clone blood. A blood that Jarth shared and that boiled now.

His fist clenched around the small black tape recorder on his desk. No, in truth, not all the soldiers had died. One had not. The third of his three favorites. He pushed the *play* command for the twentieth time that day and the two-hundredth time in the past twelve days, since the recording had been found among the ruins of the Retrieval Squad, since Hell had begun.

The recording played, crackling from exposure to the Wind. "Colonel Gerald Sart, born 0266 AE, litter number 089.3. Reporting 0296 AE. Last report. Coordinates four miles from the future dome sight #393. Ten miles from New Seattle, dome #342. Mission Objective: Against orders and without making Patriarch contact, the Tiger took her Windriders and escaped to the Wind. Under the order of General Jarth, I led a Retrieval Squad to bring the traitor and her followers home to dome #342.

"Mission Outcome: Failure. The Tiger has destroyed us."

Jarth could not stop the agony of the shudder that tore through his body. Sart's voice broke and stumbled, because of many days' sand and Wind damage or because of the man's own pain, it was hard to tell. But beneath Sart's obvious physical trauma, there was something else. The soldier's voice was emotionless. The voice of someone already dead.

"It was my hope – my plan – to capture and torture the Windrider known as Ardyn, filed as Original 445.2, in hopes that the Tiger and her other followers would surrender to save her. Instead they attacked with – with death-weapons, and we fell. It was my fault. All of this: the ruined Hovercraft, the lost lives, every–"

Jarth hit the fast-forward button. He was tired of Sart recounting his failure, blubbering over his useless existence.

The entire silver and black room, from the steel floor to the tinted glass walls that looked out over the city, hummed with the snapping whirl of the recorder. Jarth's face was as austere as the steel and as cold as the glass. New Seattle and everyone in it were his. Everyone in all the domes, from 342 to 392 and the surrounding building sites, was his. He told himself this, trying to reassure himself, trying to ease the maddening doom that was falling upon him like a hungry animal. Like a starved tiger.

He pushed *play*.

"Eight died. Seven by the strange death-weapon. It resembles the Windriders' Energy Cylinder which, until now, inflicted, at worst, third degree burns. This new weapon," there was a pause on the tape as though Sart was fighting with the demons of memory, "literally consumes the victim. The seven men who fell to it are... *gone*. Only Sergeant Marcs' body remains. He was slaughtered by the Tiger when she found him interrogating Original 445.2. I – I can smell his corpse from where I sit, rotting... but the others, their bodies no longer exist.

"One soldier survived," Sart continued, and only here did an edge of fury creep into his defeated voice. This was the part of the tape that enraged Jarth the most and he cranked the volume of the tinny speakers as if increasing the volume would also increase his rage and bring him strength. "One soldier went completely unscathed. From the beginning, a traitor among the higher ranks has been suspected. This is the only way I can explain how the Tiger was able to slip by our sensors, enter and escape the compound and other privileged security areas. I have no idea how long the Tiger and the traitor had been forging their relationship, but it was clearly a strong one. The boy, one of the favored soldiers, left with the Windriders as one of their own.

"His name is Sergeant Petre Tarrl."

The growing fury that had threatened to consume Jarth since he'd first heard the tape finally broke free. Jarth bolted from his chair and hurled the tape machine against the far wall of his office. It struck the black glass with a dull *crack* and fell into pieces across the silver steel floor.

"Tyger!" he screamed into the darkness beyond his windows, his fists clenched into white-knuckled balls, blood trickling down his palms. He had had her under his powerful fists for so long. So long! She never knew, never guessed that he had destroyed her village of freaks. She had worked for him. Lived for him. She had been his slave. His property.

Jarth stormed over to one of the small cacti he kept at each corner of his octagonal room and crushed it with his foot. The ceramic pot filled with plastic pebbles burst under the impact; the fragile plant collapsed, a pile of thick skin and a tangle of spines. But this didn't help. This was not the feeling Jarth longed for. It was nothing like the hot gore he craved. She had been his. His!

Now all his best were gone. He had no elite warriors left to fight his battles, no exceptionally strong bodies to be controlled by his stronger mind. The rest of his soldiers, all seven thousand five hundred of them, were exactly what their breed implied: Clones. They didn't have the zest or the courage to do his bidding. And what was it? What did the mighty ruler of the Patriarchy want, to appease his wrath and humiliation?

Jarth stared out into the city. It was dark with night and so the Central District, where his Clone citizens lived, was unlit, but the Industrial District was peppered with hundreds of the blue-purple lumi-lights. The Industrial District, the home of his Originals, and once the home of Tyger. Jarth had killed her family, electrocuted her entire bloodline with a glorious death-weapon made by his weak-bodied, strong-minded scientists, but there had to be others. Others she cared about. Tyger had known Originals other than the Windriders. Surely she had a few friends still living in the Industrial District. He smiled sadistically, slowly. Maybe someone more then a friend?

Not long after the Windriders had first escaped the dome, population and radiation scales had showed the re-entry of two others. If the Wind was too strong for them, perhaps some of Tyger's followers had returned. Yes, Jarth nodded to himself, finally he was thinking clearly again. He already had all the bait he needed to lure the Tiger back.

Jarth wanted them all. Any of Tyger's lovers, any friends, any allies, the two that had returned. He wanted them all, and Jarth was used to getting everything he wanted. He would take them alive out into the Wind and bind them to his once great squad of now downed Hovercraft, and then, at the place where all his best fell, where Sart committed suicide in agony and Petre Tarrl betrayed him, he would slowly strip off their skin – the skins of Tyger's last loved ones! – and beat them until Tyger, wherever in all Hell and the Wind she was, heard their screams and came to save them. Only to die with them.

Jarth became very still. He wasn't thinking clearly, was he? He must not allow his rage to cloud his vision. He must harness this energy. He must use his mind, the mind that built him this empire. To drag Tyger's loved ones out into the Wind might bring her into his hands, but it would also drop his population even further.

He looked down at the gelatinous innards of the synthetic cactus. He must be patient. He stared back out at the city, at those unsuspecting streets where the Originals played their gang games. A plan would come to him. A plan that would satisfy his need for blood, fulfill his desire for revenge, all without damaging his kingdom. He would not let Tyger possess him so much that he wounded himself. He would not play into her claws like prey. He was the hunter, not the hunted.

Survival was of the utmost importance. It had been that way since the End and would continue to be so, long after today and long after tomorrow. He would strike back at the Tiger. She would fall. The Patriarchy would rise to the top again, and he would be its proud leader. He alone would rule this world power.

He would scour through the personnel files, check every databank and find a new second in command, a new soldier as loyal as Sart and as fierce as Marcs... but not so surprising as Tarrl. He would find the best. Those men he had lost, what were they really? Just numbers. Just characteristics to duplicate. They had not been his friends, his confidants or companions. They could be replaced, where he could not. He was Christopher Jarth. He was the Patriarch.

His eyes wandered to his desk where an altered E.C. sat, the only item, other than the recorder, that had been recovered from the wreckage of the Retrieval Squad. A slim, steel shaft filled with death. For his new module soldier, he would have a new weapon. He touched the lasergun at his belt. Like all others, it could only stun. He grinned. His scientists, though very resourceful, were about to be given their greatest challenge. He would ensure that his new colonel would not just have a new weapon but the deadliest weapon ever made.

Jarth turned back to the glass wall and stared out over his capital. His first world. Yes, a plan would come and once more he would tame the Tiger and own the Wind.

* * *

Caught.

The boy screamed as he was hit with the shimmering silver web and thrown against the wall. The edges of the web struck the brick and the tips shot into the stone, pinning him just above the ground. Below him, the battle for survival raged on. As it had always been, the two rival gangs fought over food, drink, weapons and ammunition – everything an Original needed to stay alive. Once these items had been provided by the Patriarchy on a regular basis, but no longer. Once battles had been fought over which gangs got the best materials, not over who got anything at all. But times had changed.

The dark intersection of Jefferson and Terry, shadowed by the ominous Ramp, was lit by only one lumi-light casting a feeble blue-lavender glow. Through the pooling colored light, five Spiders fought against a new gang, Speed, represented by ten warriors on silver-striped skates.

There was a tumble of bodies for a moment as the two groups clashed, grappling over two bags of food. They were out-numbered but also far more experienced fighters, so soon the Spiders gained possession of the bags. Threads shot out from the Spiders' wrist mounts, hitting the roof edge of a nearby building and sticking there. A moment later, they swung away, taking the food with them.

Ten heads jerked in amazement. Where had they gone?! A lanky boy in skates beat his fists against each other. He screamed after the Spiders. "The Windriders go and so does our food! The Steel is punishing us!"

He dodged a bolt of Thread shot out of the darkness above. Dirty and thin, he wore a loin cloth; aleather ammunition belt was buckled across his emaciated chest. They were all starving. All the Originals. He shouted again, "You Spiders were their allies. You must know where they went."

Another skate-wearing young man yelled towards the Spiders. "Bring the Windriders back and we make the Steel happy. Happy Steel means food again!" He flung out a skinny arm and pulled the trigger of his crossbow. A bolt flew and a Spider, dangling somewhere above him, dropped to avoid it.

The woman hit the pavement in a crouch. She too was thinner than she usually was, but her body was still strong. Joanna, second in command of the Spiders, had long, crisp black curls that fell like a cloak over her nearly bare, dark-skinned shoulders. The patchy light played across her black and gold cover-alls, her golden-brown eyes sharp as she taunted the rival gang members, "Can't take it, eh? I knew you Speed punks wouldn't last. I've seen a hundred gangs try and fail, but you're the sorriest excuse for warriors I've ever seen!"

Most of the Speed warriors hung back, knowing Joanna's strength, but the two angry boys dove at her. She rolled aside, evading them. "What's wrong, Speeders? Can't keep up?" One moment she was dark shape upon the street, then her Thread flashed out and she was gone. The Speeders looked about wildly. Where would the attack come from next?

On a rooftop just above the deserted intersection of Jefferson and Terry, the five Spider warriors paused to catch their breath and check their weapons. Dresses alike in black and gold cover-alls and black boots, they still looked so different. Curn, burly and pale-skinned, stoically watched the nervous skaters five stories below them. Belle, slight, with jet-black, Thread-straight hair, was checking over her Thread mount. Jamie, long of limb, blue-eyed, blond-haired, was standing very still, just waiting. Darja, his skin as dark as Joanna's but his black hair as straight as Belle's, was surveying the surrounding streets.

Joanna looked over her team. She couldn't see much in the darkness, but nothing seemed serious. All of them nursed a few scrapes and purple bruises, not much more. Their Threads were saving them from most of the hand-to-hand. Thank Ravyn for that.

Threads came from a steel cylinder that looked a lot like the E.C.s the Windriders had once used on these streets, and, like the E.C.s, Ravyn had created Threads years ago. But instead of a limited fighting beam of blue energy, these cylinders shot rays of strong silver thread that could adhere to any nonliving substance. Unlike the Speeders' crossbows that came from the Patriarchy "toy" bins and shot hard rubber bolts, the Thread was used only by the Spiders. Threads allowed the Spiders to swing through the streets of New Seattle using stealth instead of brawn to overpower their enemies.

"I think they have another bag," Curn commented. "Do we let them keep it?"

Belle made a sound of disbelief. "It's survival of the fittest," she said.

Joanna agreed. "They keep it if we can't take it."

Belle stepped up onto the roof ledge. One of the leather straps holding her Thread cylinder on her wristband was close to breaking. She couldn't swing from her Thread safely now but she could still use it to fire. Without another word, she whistled to Curn because he wouldn't be able to see her wink. He affixed his Thread to the ledge and dropped over the side. Belle snapped a web cap over her Thread cylinder.

"Be right back," she laughed and jumped off for Curn to catch.

Darja and Jamie followed their example and doubled up on one Thread. Quick Jamie would guide the Thread while sharp-eyed Darja shot at the racing Speeders.

Joanna slung the two bags of rations across her back, anchoring her own Thread into the ledge. "Can't miss all the fun," she murmured and drop over the edge after them.

Joanna immediately spotted the third bag. Belle, her legs wrapped around Curn's waist, her hair like a wave of shadow behind her, was shooting silver webs from her Thread, pinning the scattering warriors to the street. Darja and Jamie and were swinging and firing randomly, keeping the Speeders guessing. Joanna flipped her Thread off, free-fell, shot the Thread out again. From her new anchor a few stories closer to the street, she was able to maneuver a dive toward the last bag of rations. She missed and a chunk of broken concrete whizzed past her head.

So.... Joanna wasn't really stunned. Leave it to the Speeders to break the rules of the streets and start using weapons that could maim. She gave a sharp whistle to the other Spiders that said, let's end this. Then she dropped into the middle of the Speeders.

Since the Windriders' departure, the Spiders had emerged as the new Industrial District leaders in New Seattle – the gang most often challenged and most often victorious. But Speed had risen from the misfits and the rubble, a new gang at the bottom of the heap, looked down upon even by the Rollers, who were not that far from the bottom themselves. Speed had little in the way of clothing or weapons, but they did have their skates, single-bladed with five wheels in a row that ran from toe to heel and Joanna had assumed these skates were Speeds' only asset. But now she saw differently. They also had a strong leader.

Joanna threw another one of the warriors that dove at her as the other Spiders dropped down beside her. For a moment she thought it would be a free-for-all, but then a young voice commanded the Speeders back.

With unevenly cropped blond hair and a lanky build, she was younger than any of the Spiders there, maybe seventeen or eighteen, but she stood boldly and the Speeders listened to her, backing away from the Spiders. Perhaps Speed would make it after all. If any Original survived this time.

The girl squared her shoulders, straightening the two ammo belts the crossed her bare chest. She wiped blood from her nose from where a bolt of Thread had probably hit her and sneered at Joanna. Not a good sign. Joanna tensed.

"Decided to play it fair, did ya?" She twirled a three-foot pipe in her hands, shifting back and forth on her skates. Joanna and the other Spiders did not reply or move. Joanna knew their unwavering stares would unnerve the other gang more than anything else. The girl broke the uncomfortable silence, hoping to goad them. "Who taught you all to fight like that? Just tear through, blast a few web-things and fly away?"

Joanna didn't move or speak but she could feel the other Spider's stirring behind her.

The girl spat on the ground at Joanna's feet. "Probably your leader, right? Everyone knows Terri's a coward."

Anger flashed across Joanna's face. Twenty-four days ago, Joanna had brought Terri a letter from Tyger announcing the Windriders' departure. Reading that letter broke something in Terri that had not mended. Joanna couldn't stop herself from taking a step towards the girl, from uttering the low, sharp words that spilled from her mouth. "Terri has fought harder and fiercer that anyone else on these streets now. She's only changed since–"

But the girl was laughing now, trying to impress her warriors, no doubt, that she had pushed past the Spider's control. Trying to break the spell of fear the Spider held over her fighters. Most times the hot stares of the Spiders could scare the wise away. It was terrifying to meet gazes with your enemy, to see they were no different from you. But Speed was far from wise. Joanna growled at the insults in the girl's eyes but she only laughed more.

"Growling at me now? Maybe Terri wasn't your teacher. Maybe it was the legendary Tyger, hm? The wild beast! Was she a coward too?"

The young woman was thrown to the ground but it was not Joanna who had reached her first.

From the high shadows of the towering Ramp, three figures dove down like birds of prey. Two rode the Currents on the slick silver discs called Windboards and one swung from a Thread. They were all Spiders. They had all once been Windriders.

It was Terri who leapt from her Windboard with a holler, her teeth bared, knocking the girl-leader to the street. One kick and the girl's pipe went spinning away, another and the crossbow at her belt snapped. Spiders were known for their fighting skills and it was Terri who taught them. Spiders moved like the night because of her, and no one moved like Terri.

The rest of the gang members stood as if frozen, watching the duel between their leaders. The girl had finally climbed to her feet, delivering several stiff punches. Terri blocked them with open palms, slapping them away until she had a clean shot, snapping the blonde's head back with a direct jab.

Terri was as strong and fit as one could be in these hard times, for she knew how to sustain on nothing. But her body showed the hardship of pain and it was that pain that came rushing forward now empowered by her anger.

She took hold of the girl's crossed ammo belts with one hand and back-handed her with the other. The Speed leader dropped suddenly down, wedging her feet into Terri's gut and flipping her head-over-heels. Terri rolled with the throw and wound up in a crouch, waiting for the girl's next move.

The Speeder was staring at Terri as though she seemed to see the Spider for the first time. In that hesitancy, Terri stood up. She was five foot nine – not too tall for an Original – with a mass of auburn hair cut short on top, thick muscles moving beneath her cocoa-colored skin covered only with cover-alls and boots. She stood with her feet apart, her hands slightly open and her pale green eyes blazing.

In that moment the young leader of Speed knew that no matter what she did, she could not win. And she was right. But she was also a leader and she knew what she must do. She threw herself at Terri with screaming curses and flying fists. Terri caught her twice in the head with quick jabs and then knocked her legs out from under her with a simple, sweeping kick.

The girl went down and Terri dropped onto her back, pinning her shoulders. Terri grabbed hold of her short hair and turned her head. Her voice, once smooth as honey, was harsh from lack of use. "Listen to me, girl. Tyger was the bravest warrior who ever walked these streets. She fought with the best and felled anyone who stood against her. You aren't worthy enough to say her name."

The Speeder coughed, and whether in her own bravery or her own stupidity, she spoke, her voice breathless. "It's her fault. We're dying and it's her fault! She could be long dead! But if the Patriarchy, if the Steel didn't have her corpse as proof, we'd all be starved forever! She wasn't even one of us. An animal, a freak! Her fault–"

Terri hauled the girl to her feet, her lips turned back in anger and her eyes filled with unshed tears. She pushed the Speeder away before she could see them. It was a hard shove that made her stagger on her skates.

"Take your fools," Terri's anger was brimming on every slow word, "and leave."

"No." The word was cold and came before the Speeders could move. Terri looked at Byn, who stood hovering on her own Windboard, big Howl crouched beside her, baring his canine teeth. They exchanged glances and Terri was not upset that the child had spoken. Byn too had a right. Terri did not rule her Spiders, she simply led them.

Byn stared down at the Speed leader. The Speeder was perhaps three years younger than Terri but that was still seven years older than ten-year-old Byn. But no matter. Byn had known Tyger, followed her, trusted her and escaped with her to the Wind. And when Byn began to die of the Fever, it had been Tyger who had carried her back. Byn knew things and had seen things that no child should have lived through and right now made her no child. No one insulted Tyger, her Tyger. "No one calls Tyger a coward and walks away."

Byn looked to Ravyn. The intense, dark-haired, dark-eyed woman

had also been close to Tyger. One of Tyger's own. She had created the E.C.,
the Thread, the Windboard and last, a death-weapon, the ultimate cultural
taboo, all for Tyger and the Windriders.

On her Thread, Ravyn slowly lowered herself to the ground before
the Speeder. She looked into the eyes that had never before seen the woman
she had called *coward* and *freak*, and they did not waver. But neither did
Ravyn's. These were hard streets and this was how they were lived. Without
words Ravyn brought her staff up, then brought one metal tip down. It struck
the Speeder's knee and she crumbled to the ground with a sharp groan.

The other Speeders emerged from their frozen shock all at once and
rushed forward to help their leader. Ravyn watched and was not untouched
by the brutality of the scene. The streets had always been harsh but now they
were harsher and this only proved it.

Ravyn reached to her belt and flung her first aid pouch at one boy.
"It's not permanent. Take her to your homebase. Care for her. Next time
she'll think before she calls blame." All the Speeders were listening to her.
Ravyn was respected for her words and ideas. "Remember that fault lays
only one place. On the Steel."

No one spoke. There was nothing more to say. That was the only
answer. They could do nothing now but wait and see, and try to survive.

* * *

High above the rest of the Industrial District, the eight Spiders
came home. Their base was on the twenty-eighth floor of a ruined
warehouse, with only one way in or out: a portal in the outside wall that
could only be reached by Thread or Windboard.

Joanna swung in first, landing in the middle of the brightly lit floor
with Ravyn alighting right beside her.

"Terri's back!" Joanna called to the sixty other Spiders who
lounged in the large space. She half expected a cheer to rise from the group,
but was met instead with confused stares.

"We can see that," someone said, as Terri expertly guided her
Windboard through the narrow opening. "She comes and goes all the time.
So what?" There was some laughter.

Joanna's brow furrowed. Had no one else seen the change? Terri
had seemed weighed down by the world, cut off from everyone, retiring
earlier and earlier each dawn and always alone. Had no one else noticed how
different, how without fire, Terri had been until tonight on the streets?
Joanna turned to Terri. The other woman smiled grimly. There was a
darkness in her eyes and a heaviness about her. Her strength seemed hidden
again as though her anger had sapped her energy instead of burning her
pure, healing her.

"I never left, Joanna." Terri spoke tightly but without anger.

Then Terri pitched her voice so all could hear her. "We fought with Speed," she said, then shook her head. "Things fare worse and worse on the streets. Once Spiders only intervened to save other's lives. Now we fight to protect our own. But nothing has changed among us. We are still the Spiders. We still respect the honor of our name and the names of our allies. We fight to protect. Strength through protection. Never forget who you are." Terri walked away without saying more, crossing the wide warehouse space and disappearing into her private room.

Joanna stared after Terri as the Spiders crowded around Jamie and Darja, who were doling out what little food they'd found. It came out to about a ration bar each.

Joanna took a deep breath. She had also felt the pain the Windriders' departure had caused. But Joanna's beloved, her Ravyn, had returned to her. Terri's extreme grief baffled Joanna. Terri and Tyger had been friends – as much as the gruff Windborn leader had ever let anyone be her friend. But in this world, friends were lost. It was a fact of life.

Why was Terri so profoundly affected? Why did she hide her feelings from the Spiders?

It was true that very few of them knew the truth. Only Terri, Ravyn, Byn and the Eyes – Belle, Curn, Darja, Jamie and Joanna – knew that Tyger and the others had escaped to the Wind. Before the Windriders had gone, though, the Eyes had spied on the Patriarchy for Tyger in exchange for supplies. It seemed normal that some things stay secret. But why should Terri pretend? She couldn't possibly be fooling everyone.

"I never thought I'd strike to defend Tyger's honor," Ravyn remarked, pulling Joanna out of her thoughts. Joanna took her eyes from Terri's closed door and sighed. She went to Ravyn's work table against one wall. Byn was seated on the table's edge, swinging her legs a little, while Howl chewed on one of her boot laces.

"Someone has to," Byn said.

Ravyn smiled up at her partner and wrapped her arm around Joanna. With her head she gestured toward Byn. "How is it we're raising a warrior?"

Byn laughed and, before Joanna could answer, said, "Ravyn! Before your leg was maimed, you slashed and swung with the rest of them whenever you could – Tryl and Jyln used to tell me stories about you. And Joanna is a warrior. Not the kind of warrior like we had in the Windriders, but she's a warrior. A protector."

"A protector and a warrior aren't exactly the same thing, Byn," Ravyn said. "A warrior is someone like Tryl or Jyln, or Tyger. They live for battle, for the thrill. A protector fights only when there are no other choices. Terri made a good point tonight. Even though the streets are changing doesn't mean we have to."

Byn cocked her head. "The Spiders looked like warriors tonight. Terri fought like a warrior against that Speeder."

Joanna nodded. "You're right, Byn. But we were fighting for honor tonight. To teach that new gang a lesson. You know how that can be. But it doesn't have to change you in your heart."

Byn made a disapproving face and scratched Howl's furry head. "If you want to survive when your world changes, you change too. Tyger taught the Windriders that."

"But the Spider's aren't the Windriders, Byn," Joanna reminded her. "Terri tells us that instead of change we can stay the same but with more certainty."

Ravyn looked at Byn. Like most Original children, Byn was growing up too fast. She accepted these streets as the only way, the warrior's path as the only path. "You'll always be a Windrider at heart, won't you?"

Byn smiled at her adopted parents. That was how she saw them. How she loved them.

"I love the Spiders and Terri, but if I could have beaten the Fever, if I could have changed with the Wind..." She paused, seeking understanding in the two women who watched her. "I was a Windrider first before I was anything and if things had been different...." Byn bit her lip and looked away, ashamed to be fighting tears.

"You'd still be one." Ravyn finished for her.

Joanna walked around the table and knelt down by Howl, taking Byn's hands. She looked up at the little girl. "I hope you'll accept us as a close second choice."

After a moment Byn nodded and slid off the table, wrapping her arms around Joanna's neck. Joanna could feel Ravyn smiling at them and without much warning, she found herself thinking of Tyger. Once, Joanna had hated her. Hated her for the power she had over her Windriders, and for taking Ravyn away. But now Joanna felt differently, for it had been that same warrior who had seen Ravyn's pain and sent her back. It had been that same warrior who had given them Byn. It was hard to hate Tyger now.

* * *

In the darkness of her chamber, Terri's thoughts were not broken by the sounds of laughter and conversation that drifted from the room beyond her door.

Turning slowly toward her pelts, she saw a figure lying there with one knee raised, one arm resting on that knee. "Tyger?" she asked without thinking.

The dark-haired visitor groaned and shook her head in dismay. She wore black and gold cover-alls, shirtless beneath, and her full breasts threatened to spill warmly from behind the metallic bib. The woman moved so that her face was illuminated by the single lumi-lantern and Terri saw it was Sandra. "Tyger's gone, Terri. But I'm still here." She let one hand fall, brushing over the bib of her cover-alls invitingly. "You seem pretty obsessed with her. You two have something going none of us knew about?"

The growing revulsion Terri felt turned easily into anger, but she managed to control her voice as she held out a hand to the other woman. "Let me help you up, Sandra."

Sandra did not move. "You don't want me to go. Not really."

Terri's face remained emotionless. "Yes, really I do."

Sandra stared at her a moment more and then sighed and stood without taking her hand. They stood for a moment eye to eye. "You better snap out of this soon, leader, or more than just me and your second in command are going to notice."

Terri looked into Sandra's blue eyes. They were light and clear, surrounded by soft white and centered with a deep black pupil that was wide in the dark room. They could have been the eyes of any Original and that was not what Terri wanted. "Good-bye, Sandra."

The woman snorted. "I brought you some food. It's beside your pelt." She spun on her heel and walked away.

Terri listened to Sandra's boots on the floor and did not turn when they paused before the door. "I know what's has gotten into you," she said. "The Wind. The wild Wind." Then she added, her voice quiet and concerned, "I just hope it doesn't drive you mad."

Terri closed her eyes as she heard the door open and close. She stood for a while, still and silent. Then she left her room, sliding into the patchy light of the large communal living space. She moved quietly through the half-shadows, not really seeing or hearing anyone. At the outside door she slipped through, onto the platform that jutted like a miniature Ramp from the side of the building. Finally she was alone.

Terri looked out over the city, her people's half – the Originals' half – and counted the lumi-lights for a while. But as she knew they would, her eyes came to rest on the Windriders' old homebase, many blocks away near the west wall of the dome. She wondered who lived there now or if it was empty; empty and cold as a corpse.

Unbidden, a conversation she'd had with Tyger, on this very platform, rose again in her mind.

"If you can't talk to me, then who can you talk to?" Terri had asked.

"No one," Tyger replied. "No one." At the time Terri had thought it a lie.

Terri had asked her, "You could never hurt someone you love, could you?" Tyger hadn't answered.

Terri, leader of the Spiders, closed her light green eyes and touched her lips in memory. She saw for a moment two women's long hair – tiger-striped and auburn – mixing together in the Currents. She had no way of knowing that miles, worlds away, Tyger, lying by the Sky falls, had been haunted with this very same memory. A tear slid down her cheek. Terri felt the Currents toss her hair and she wished they were the Wind. The Wind that would drive her mad... and set her free.

* * *

"Tell me a story!" Byn plopped down beside her four friends and they quickly complied.

"It was late at night, over on Union street, where all the rubble is stuck with glass shards, you know? We were all racing, just having fun, and then we turned into this alley and–"

Jamie interrupted Belle and took up the story. "There were the Wheels terrorizing a bunch of Rollers! The Rollers were really new back then, like Speed and the Climbers are now, but they were real arrogant. They might have even started it all–"

"But anyway," Curn cut in with impatience. "Back to the action. So the Rollers had freaked when things got too heavy and grabbed up some glass shards, right? And the Wheels were circling them on their motorcycles. Whoever started it didn't matter much anymore because the Wheelers were pissed and weren't going to let even one of the skateboarders get away.

"So we knew this battle – the Wheelers, who had been around longer than the Windriders even, against the newcomers who were pissing their pants and waving glass – was going to be bad. Real bad." Curn smiled and winked. "Unless, of course, we Spiders intervened."

Darja took over with factual pride. "So we dove in, dizzying the Wheels with our swinging and flying bolts. Terri was with us five and she took a bullet for Joanna but kept on fighting.

"The Wheels began to draw back, but to our dismay, the Rollers retreated along beside them! To them, the Wheels had been a known danger, but the elusive Spiders – even when we fought on their side – terrified them!"

Byn laughed despite herself. She laughed so hard that she collapsed against Belle, tears leaking out of her eyes. They all sat around Belle's piles of pelts, in one corner of the warehouse. Byn loved it when the four told her their stories. They were so funny! Her favorite was when they used to all go out and knock skateboards out from under Rollers with their Threads. Their collection of gathered prizes was mounted on the wall behind them.

Byn stroked Howl's big head that lay on her legs. She smiled at the

Spiders, wiping her eyes. "I think you guys have to learn the difference between being heroes and being intrusive."

Jamie frowned. "Now that's not true. Terri taught us to intervene whenever the battle is set for death."

Byn slapped her thigh, careful not to hit Howl. "Intervene and intrude are darn close! Tyger taught us that when a battle looks rough, leave it be. More bodies just makes it worse. Help if you're asked. Help if it's your ally. Otherwise, help yourself and get the hell home!"

They all laughed, knowing very well that though Tyger preached that belief to her followers, there hadn't been a battle she'd ever happened upon that she hadn't become a part of. Curn stood and reached down with his strong hands, scooping Byn up and flipping her onto his shoulder. "You saying that you Windriders are better than all of us Spiders, huh?"

Curn began bouncing her up and down, and through laughter, Byn managed, "You said it, Curny, not me!"

"Curny!" The big warrior repeated, shooting Belle a glance to which the woman shrugged innocence and batted her eyes. Curn laughed, shaking his head. "Byn, you spend too much time with Belle. We'll talk later about what that'll do to you–"

"Turn me into a contented guy?!" Byn squealed.

To that Curn had no retort as he, Darja and Jamie blushed. Holding Byn to his shoulder with one hand, Curn flung the other out. His Thread flew sure and steady, grabbing a beam high in the ceiling.

"I'll show you who's better, little Windrider!" Curn said with a smile as he had so many times before. Then he retracted his Thread, speeding up the silver string, Byn holding tight and shrieking in excitement, as Curn flipped and twirled and pretended to free-fall.

Ravyn and Joanna were her parents and every Spider was Byn's brother or sister. Whatever Byn called herself, she was loved by her new family and she loved them back, no matter who she missed.

* * *

"...now if I..." Ravyn muttered to herself as she leaned closer over her work table, peering at the collection of small metal shapes before her. She wore simple glasses, her black bangs hanging over one eye. They needed to be cut. She brushed them back and sighed.

Finally, the warehouse was quiet and dark; only her work area was lit by a lumi-lantern. The others were sleeping and through the shuttered door that closed out the rest of the world – doors that she herself had designed – only the faintest shafts of daylight showed through. It was dawn; the Clones were rising and the Originals were falling back into the shadows.

"Why do I have this feeling that you aren't coming to bed any time soon?" Joanna asked softly, coming up behind Ravyn and encircling her in her arms.

"I have a lot of work to do."

Joanna nuzzled against her partner's neck, breathing softly next to her ear. Ravyn hummed her approval but didn't stop examining her collection. Joanna sighed. "Well, if there's no way to get you to quit, can I help you along? Maybe even get you in bed before dusk?"

"Two minds are always better than one," Ravyn said. Joanna grinned at the unexpected invitation. Usually, Ravyn shooed Joanna away from her work table. Shooed everyone away, in fact. "I asked Belle how the new Thread webs were going," Ravyn continued. "She said not so well. It takes time to change the tip piece and then someone else has to carry the person using the web-shooter. Doesn't seem worth it."

"I disagree. The webs pin opponents without hurting them too badly. It gets them out of the way. They hold for about five, sometimes ten minutes. That's long enough to win a battle, gloat a while and go."

Ravyn chuckled. "Still, it could be better...."

Joanna hugged her closer and bowed her head to Ravyn's shoulder. "You're always making things better. Nothing is ever good enough for you."

Ravyn turned from the table and kissed her, taking her by surprise. When she drew back, Joanna asked, "What was that for?"

"For making everything better that I can't."

"I never thought I'd hear you say you can't do something."

Ravyn shook her head, remembering the first time she had said she couldn't – said *no*, in fact – to Tyger's request for a death-weapon, but eventually she had gone ahead and done it. This *can't* was different though. "Did you know," Ravyn began, her voice becoming distant, "that Tylon was in love with me?"

Joanna met her eyes and nodded, a little confused. "Yes. From the first time I saw him look at you. It was pretty obvious."

"You help me see things like that. His feelings weren't obvious to me. I didn't really know until I was leaving him. Leaving him and all the rest of the Windriders. I never meant to hurt him."

Joanna let her gaze drift to Terri's door. She knew how painful it could be when someone you cared about was hurting.

"Jo," Ravyn gently interrupted her thoughts. "You need to let Terri take care of herself. Whatever she's going through, she needs to battle through it and come to the end on her own. She's a strong woman. Whatever it is, it won't break her."

Before Joanna could reply, one of the shutter doors opened slightly and Terri slipped inside. Her hair was wild from the last of the Currents and as she stepped away into the room, she wiped her eyes with her hand.

"She goes out on the ledge every night," Joanna said. "She used to go out there... with Tyger. To see her off. They'd talk sometimes, I guess, alone." Her thoughts drifted back and her eyes grew distant. Then she shook her head and added, "I don't like to see her this way." Joanna looked at a nearby corner where Byn had fallen asleep next to Belle, curled up with Howl. "I think I know why some people will never be anything but Windriders. Tyger, she has a kind of fire. It can burn or purify. Take or grant. Byn will always ride her Windboard, enjoy battle and live fast. And even though you use a Thread now, and you've always really believed in our ways, there will forever be that difference in you that says she has touched you. That fire."

Ravyn was silent and Joanna looked towards Terri's room. "And whether Terri leads us now or not, maybe she'll always still be part Windrider. Maybe all Windrider." Joanna paused and once again Ravyn felt her arms tighten around her. "I don't know what I'd do if Terri disappeared. She is my first leader and I owe a lot to her. When I almost lost you it nearly killed me. I never want to feel loss like that again. But when I look at Terri, I see past the mask she wears for everyone. There's something...." But then words failed her.

Ravyn drew Joanna close and kissed her gently. She reached around Joanna and switched off the lantern. Work would wait. Now was time to be with her lover.

* * *

In the darkness of her room, Terri lay on her pelt and stared at the ceiling. At that moment, nothing existed for her except the memory playing like an old movie inside her head...

"I've seen you watching me," Terri whispered. She smiled slightly when Tyger's face registered her shock. But then something slid into place behind Tyger's eyes, they narrowed; when Terri didn't speak into the growing silence, Tyger said, slowly, "You're very beautiful."

Terri could still hear those words echo in her head and they were as erotic and provocative now as they had been to her fifteen-year-old ears then. She wished now she'd responded in words to Tyger, but at the time it was all she could do to laugh it off. No one had ever been that direct with her before and it both intrigued and frightened her.

Terri had been curious that night. Curious about the strong warrior with her not-Original body, her strange accented speech and mysterious secrets. Her solid eyes. Her passion. Curious about the young woman who had simply appeared in the Industrial District.

Terri had joined the fiery-haired stranger's gang of Windboard riding hellions and had quickly grown to love Tyger like everyone else. They had been the first... batch... of Windriders. Terri, Paula, Leah, Han, Jin,

Jillein, Kenni, Brian, Marken, Fey and Cam among others. Twenty in all.

Then it had happened. It was a special night, their first battle – a victory against the Wheels. In the heady aftermath of the fight, back at homebase, the Windriders began pairing up, needing to work off the lingering adrenaline rush, wanting to feel connected to their sister and brother warriors in a new way. To celebrate their idea of victory that had become reality.

Tyger, however, had retreated to her quarters alone. She had not been approached by anyone. Terri followed her, silently, her heart pounding, pausing in shadow to watch her leader disrobe.

When Tyger turned and found her watching, she did not seem surprised.

"I've seen you watching me," Terri whispered, but already she was moving out of the shadows, pressing her body against Tyger's, running her hands over her broad shoulders, across her chest.

Tyger has seemed suspicious at first. Was this pity? Was this curiosity? She answered simply, "You're very beautiful."

Terri kissed her then, hard as she could, shaking with passion and some fear, as Tyger's strong arms encircled her.

"What do you want, Terri?" Tyger's voice had been ragged and her body had begun to move against hers. Terri had raised her face to Tyger's, her lips parted and wet from their kiss. "I want you," Terri said. "I want you."

Terri had never known if she had been Tyger's first, but she had wanted more than anything to be her last. She had fallen in love with her so deeply, so completely. And for a while it seemed that nothing could part them.

Until Tyger had taken those first Windriders and disappeared from New Seattle, leaving Terri behind. When Tyger reappeared, alone, she was changed. She had begun the transformation from the young woman Terri loved to the hardened warrior she became. The warrior who had left the streets again and again, taking new groups of Windriders with her. The warrior who sent Terri away, to the building Terri still called home and later sent her the young fighters who had become the first Spiders. The warrior who had left the city yet again, twenty-four days ago, after staying for so long, and had said her first and last good-bye not in person, but with a letter:

"My dear Terri,

"Tomorrow night I leave New Seattle, as I have three times before. The Windriders are going with me. My goal is to reach the village of my birth.

"It is no easier now to write these words than it would have been five years ago, the first time I left and you stayed behind. It is no easier now to tell you I'm leaving than it was to send you away from me. I can't say why I'm so willing to risk everything, everyone but you. I don't know. Maybe I never will.

"I know you don't understand. I'm sorry. I wish I could have spoken these words to you myself, but I know I never would have been able. I know this time I'm doing the right thing but that doesn't make the danger any less.

"Terri, the other times I left, we both knew I would return to the city, alone. This time none of us will return."

And to the leader of the Spiders, those words were worse than the silence all the times before. Before there had been the fear for Tyger's safety and the questions surrounding her journey, but Terri had always known Tyger would return and begin to build the Windriders again. She had wondered what happened to the others... but not too hard.

It was too difficult for Terri to believe that this time there would be no return for Tyger. Ravyn had returned, Byn had returned, but Tyger would not. She knew that Byn and Ravyn knew the secret. They knew where all the Windriders before them had disappeared to. But Terri saw something in their eyes that told her she did not want to share this knowledge. She did not want to know. It was one more terrible secret. One more horror in a world where horror was a way of life.

Trembling, fighting tears, Terri spoke aloud to the apparition of Tyger that haunted her, waking and sleeping. She longed for peace, for solace. She longed for Tyger. But Tyger was gone and as much as Terri hated to admit it, Sandra was right. It was time to move on. Closing her eyes against the tidal wave of memory, she whispered harshly in the darkness, "Goddamn you, Tyger. Goddamn you to hell." And then later, more softly, she chanted, "I hate you," over and over as if willing herself to believe it.

When dusk came and the Spiders rose to greet the new night, Terri rose with them, but she was not free.

* * *

Darkness is the absence of light. Where there is light there can be no darkness and where there is darkness there can live no light. This is not enough to describe the night, shadows and pitch of the Below. This was more than a lack of brightness, this was a total absence of color, tone or gradations of grayness. There was only black. To close one's eyes provided more light than to look upon this absolute nothingness.

There was no sound. No faint murmur, no tiny throb. No sight, no sound, only darkness as complete as a thing could be. Whole and full while at the same time being empty and shallow.

Through this unfathomable darkness, something moved. It moved with steady certainty, brave and sure. It kept in contact with one wall of stone at all times, following its curves and turns ever westward. The cold stone, with its various textures, was a welcome reality to the creature who traveled the Below.

In such a stark, vacant void, it would be easy to lose one's mind. And sometimes, when her mind spun or swam for no reason she could name, she thought losing her mind wouldn't be so bad. But she did not. She held onto one image to keep her sane and one oath to keep her moving. The vision of a child, running as fast as her sixteen-year-old legs could carry her – which was not fast enough – the Wind gushing her tiger-striped hair back in waves as the Hovercraft scooped her up and carried her away. And the oath? That she herself was terror incarnate and would wreak bloody havoc in exacting her revenge.

She was a figure of black moving through the same. Her eyes closed and each of her senses heightened. Everything there was to know of this place, this creature knew. But above all other knowledge, in this place of nothingness and silence, she knew the sharp smell of silver steel and Clone blood. She knew the searing stench of laser burns, lumi-lanterns, soldiers and hot death and this was how she moved west – using the stench of the Patriarchy as her guide. West towards New Seattle. Towards the Patriarch.

* * *

Part Three

Darkness. Like being swallowed by a black beast. A thick, heavy void where light and color were consumed and digested with the poisonous juices of shadow. It was a living, breathing presence with eyes of midnight and teeth of black steel that saw all and knew all. It moved, it pulsed and it was. And its existence was neither all good nor all evil, it simply was. Monstrous, the darkness moved forward without ever abandoning the conquered lands it left behind. When it conquered, it consumed. It had a goal. It knew where it wanted to go, what it wanted to do and how.

Tyger looked ahead of the darkness then and saw its destination. Silver steel loomed close, bright with the sharp sounds of life and death; the Patriarchy waited in its pulsating dome, unaware of the beast who stalked it. For the merest moment Tyger felt pity, even pain, for the blind silver. The poor cold steel that could so easily become a corpse. Then the blackness descended and washed over the silver like scorched molten lava. Spears of steel pierced the beast and both were dying, and Tyger pitied neither one.

The leader of the Windriders awoke from her dream and was glad that both the black and the silver had been destroyed. It seemed best that way. It seemed safer. And then the dream's power left her and she was part of reality again, a leader looking out over her sleeping gang.

Things were quiet and peaceful and Tyger found her eyes touching each of her followers with thankfulness. They were safe here, away from consuming beasts, away from the silver steel. They had time to enjoy life. Her gaze came to rest on Ardyn. She forced herself not to reach out and touch her, least she wake her from the quiet beauty that was hers in sleep.

They had talked late into the night again. Events were unfolding in Sky that none of them had control over or fully understood. It both unsettled and fascinated Tyger. As she gazed down on the sleeping woman, her thoughts turned. No longer did she wonder what lay between her and her destiny, but she wondered what lay between the two of them. Ardyn was turned on her stomach, her dark hair falling over her bare chestnut shoulders like strands of black silk, a little blanket pulled half way up her back. One hand rested on the pelt beside her face, fingers entwined in the thick fur. A wave of warm desire washed through Tyger. But was there more than just that simple need? Did she feel something deeper? Did she need to? There was a longing, yes, but that had been there for some time now, unnamed and still so. A longing like sharp fire in her dream beside the falls. Was it a longing for Ardyn? Or who?

Tyger's thoughts were broken by the sound of Petre crying out in his sleep. "Wait. Don't let him win. Don't let go...." His voice sounded thin and plaintive. He woke with a start and sat up, an image of crying faces fading before his open eyes. As Tyger watched, he stared at his hands, as if wondering what he could do. Then, at a loss, he turned and sadly examined the distance between his pelt and Tylon's and the expression of love and longing on his face spoke volumes. Ravyn had never known Tylon loved her, and he had seemed, then, content to be in her presence if he could not have her love. But when Ravyn had returned to New Seattle to save Byn's life, a part of Tylon went with her. He hadn't been the same since then and Tyger saw him closing himself off from the others, turning a blind eye to Petre's affection.

Petre lifted his eyes from Tylon and, as if he could feel her watching him, sought Tyger's face in the gray darkness. Their eyes met. Petre's gaze drifted from Tyger to Ardyn's sleeping form and he raised his eyebrows in question. Tyger said nothing, neither accepted nor denied his assumption. Before either of them could speak, there was a sudden noise in the corridor that quickly exploded into shouts, curses and screaming.

No amount of time in Sky could dull the sharply honed warrior training in any of the Windriders. They were awake and on their feet almost before the first shouts died away, hands scrabbling for weapons in backpacks and tucked under pelts. Tyger leapt down from her perch, shouting at Tryl and Jyln as she moved toward the door, "Put the blasted E.C. away! We don't want death here! Dig out the old weapons, for Wind's sake!" But a moment later she countered that order as her ears took in the sounds of chaos outside.

Tyger pounded down the hallway, following the noise of battle, the Windriders not far behind her. In the room where the falls crashed down, the room called Genesis, she found the struggle already in progress.

At first, Tyger had assumed the commotion was a result of the growing tension between the Pagans and the One believers. She guessed they had finally given into their rage at the others' stubbornness and engaged in physical combat. Because of these thoughts she was unprepared for what she saw. Tyger took in the conflict in one sweeping glance.

Iahala, Aliqui and Kestrel stood in the middle of the room; Mouse and Mlinz were off to one side. Aliqui and Kestrel were circling a band of five Humans dressed in rags. The intruders' eyes held wild fire, flames of insanity. The women's El Rods glowed red-hot, but they were clearly wary of the weapons the others held – weapons shaped not too unlike handguns, but larger. It was clear to Tyger, seeing the wary concentration in the warriors' eyes, that these weapons weren't the Patriarchy's weak toys that shot rubber bullets. These shot death.

Clutched between the grimy hands of two of the invaders was a quivering adult purple Butterfly. It was wounded. Holes in its wings leaked bright blue blood, and it struggled against the intruders' crushing grip on its wings. Tyger saw the swarm in the shadows of the chamber, led by the Gold One, moving closer and closer to the enemies, ready to brave even a shower of metal bullets to save their kindred. All about Mouse and Mlinz, the babies were flapping wildly, called to the battle by the purple Butterfly's cry for help, but too afraid and too young to do anything about it. Tyger looked from the Gold One to Kestrel and Aliqui and knew this would be a suicide battle. A battle she must stop.

"Give us River Sky, and we leave! We give back this one!" The biggest man among the strangers yelled to Iahala, throwing her five large, empty water skins. He was waving his semi-automatic weapon erratically. Iahala said nothing. There was fury and disgust in her eyes.

"Now!" The man screamed and he pulled his trigger. Bullets rang off the stone wall across from where the intruders stood, sounding like bolts of thunder and death. Tyger dove to the ground. She heard her brother cry out as handfuls of young Butterflies were picked from the air by the metal rain.

At that moment, the Windriders entered the room. As Tyger rose from the ground, Tryl, Jyln, Ardyn and Tylon stepped forward, blazing E.C.s alive in their hands. Circling to the side, the other Windriders held Patriarchy crossbows and rifles. The leader of the strangers turned away from Iahala and as his crazed eyes fell upon Tyger he cried, "Monster women! This New World has made monster women." He licked his lips. "I'll take you as well as the Sky."

"I don't know who you are," Tyger began, her voice becoming the growl of her battle fury, a deep thick rumble. She sank into a low crouch, her emerald eyes boring into him. "But I don't care. You bring death here and so death shall carry you out."

"Come on then," he sneered, spittle dripping from his mouth. "Dead or alive, I'll have you dead or alive."

Tyger extended her claws and drew back her lips to show her sharp teeth, every muscle tight and ready to spring.

And then the man pulled his trigger again, his aim dead center, but Tyger was no longer there. She had leapt into the mist of Genesis. He screamed in frustration, a scream joined by four other voices – his companions – as they were pelted with hard rubber crossbow bolts and bullets.

Tyger dove in front of the leader as around her, the Windriders bearing E.C., Aliqui and Kestrel moved in to engage the other Humans. Even as Tyger delivered her first blow, she took a chance. The Humans holding the purple Butterfly were not letting go, rather they were crushing it tighter, shooting their guns this way and that as the Butterfly cried out against its abuse. Tyger could not get to the Butterfly physically... but perhaps she needn't need to.

Friend.... she sent her thoughts out into the room, directed them as best she could to the Butterfly. *Friend,* she sent again even as she caught her opponent and threw him back against the wall. She couldn't tell if her attempt at this bond was working. *You must throw your wings wide with all of your strength and then become small as you can and drop away from them!*

Great Wind, what was she trying to do here?! She doubted for a moment, catching her charging enemy and tossing him over her shoulder. Then her mind seemed to explode with colors and symbols and emotions. The bronze sky, the sunshine, the pain, the fear, bright blue, bright green, the bronze sky again and more fear.

Escape! Tyger cried out to the Butterfly and then she cried it aloud, "Escape!"

But in that moment when the Butterfly's mind touched hers, Tyger's concentration was lost and the Human screamed, cracking his metal gun against the side of her head. She tasted blood and water as she pushed herself out of a small stream of River Sky.

"Mine!" barked the Human as he dove at her before she could rise, but she roared and slashed, opening the man's face in a gush of hot blood. His hands came up and he discharged his weapon. Tyger could feel bullets whizzing by her face and then her world exploded, this time not with the colors of the Butterfly, but with pain.

Her eyes were blind for a moment as her mind registered the sizzling holes in her arm and hand. The pain was excruciating, more intense than anything she'd ever felt before and it knocked the breath from her lungs and the strength from her body. Her head spun and she feared she would–

Stand up! It was a purple fire, raging through her head, burning away the pain for just a moment. *Stand up!* It wasn't really words she was hearing, just the feeling, the command, and Tyger stood.

She could not make her left arm move so with her right she slashed at the man again. As blood washed over Tyger's face and splattered across her breasts and shoulders, one part of her knew she had torn out the man's throat. The other part of her reached out toward the Butterfly and it followed her instructions immediately.

Despite its pain it threw wide its wings, splattering her captors with spurts of its bright blood. The two Humans were thrown off balance and the Butterfly folded in on itself, dropping low and then bracing its feet against the wall at its back. It thrust itself away from them, more hurtling than flying straight at Tyger. It stuck to her back, lighter than she had ever imagined it could be, as she leapt into the mist, evading the two enraged Humans.

It was at that same moment that Ardyn struck once, then again and one of the would-be captors fell. Ardyn's E.C. was deadly life in her hand, living death. It was clear from the expression on her face that she felt no remorse to see the stranger's life end with the agony of being eaten from the inside out.

Tryl had killed before with her E.C., had killed Patriarchy soldiers who had oppressed her kind all her life, but now, fighting a man she did not know, she found it was not too difficult to take another life. She just thought of those large, purple wings, bleeding. One hard, clean strike from the blazing blue shaft and the consuming cells encased in the E.C. found their way into the Human's body. He screamed once and was gone.

Jyln and Tylon fought not far from them. Jyln's opponent mistook .her slenderness for weakness and that was his fatal mistake. Her lightning-quick movements brought her within striking distance and when his gun discharged for the last time, she struck it aside and the bullet intended for her embedded itself in his leg instead. One quick stroke with her E.C. and he fell.

Not unlike Tryl, Tylon was brought to battle fury at the sight of the wounded Butterfly throwing itself at the wounded Tyger for safety. At first he did not hesitate to strike out at his opponent. But when he saw behind the lunacy in the stranger's eyes, saw that this intruder was no more than a boy, he hesitated. And it cost him.

The Human boy, sensing a split-second advantage, did not hesitate to shoot Tylon, once then twice with his smaller handgun. Tylon felt his shoulder explode with a fiery pain and his arm flung out, his fingers gripping his E.C. almost numb. The Human staggered back but not fast enough. The E.C. caught him in a clean swipe and its deadly contents spilled out in his face. Both fighters fell to the floor in agony, but soon the Human's body was gone.

The chamber was suddenly still. All that was left of the strange Humans was the bloody body of their leader and their weapons, which even now Aliqui and Kestrel were gathering to destroy. Blood slicked the stone floor, washing away in some of the streams, and most of it was the blood of the Windriders. Iahala came forward.

From the ground where she sat, Tyger looked up at Iahala, the purple Butterfly still wrapped across her back, and the Windriders clustered protectively about her. Tyger's face was pale; she had difficulty speaking. Jyln had made a tourniquet for Tyger but her arm lay paralyzed, her breeches dark red with her own blood. How much blood could a Windborn lose? How much time did she have?

"Wisewoman." Tyger's vision swam but she made her voice work, made herself look up towards Iahala. Vaguely she felt Tryl and Ardyn kneeling beside her, holding her. She thought Mouse was near her as well, but it was getting difficult to grasp the reality around her. "We know that to kill these strangers, we made ourselves killers. But when the choice is the death of those we love and the death of strangers, we choose to be killers rather than mourners."

Iahala sank down before Tyger. "Tyger, child of the Wind and leader of the Windriders, if you ever hear me say anything, hear me now. You have done no evil here today." And in her voice Tyger heard the voices of a hundred others, of every one of the Windborn who had died in the nets of the Patriarchy, of every Original she had taken to die or be changed in the Wind and given to Jarth. Tyger heard Iahala's words and wept silently. Moved by her grief, her pain and Iahala's understanding, the Windriders cried with her.

Before Iahala could say or do more, the Gold One came forward. Iahala stood and moved back. The Gold One took her place, standing before Tyger. It seemed to motion to Mlinz who came and place the dead young Butterflies between them. Then Mlinz moved away and the adult flock came forward from the mist and began to sing. Tyger heard the song as though it came on soft waves, lulling her into a place of peace. It was a song like sleep and tears, for here, upon the cold stone, lay twenty dead children. They lay like scattered petals of broken flowers.

Tyger felt her pain ebbed away and did not know that Tylon and the Butterfly felt the same. Her head cleared a little, just enough for her to see.

The Gold One looked to the fallen body of the man leader and flung its wings wide. They were huge wings, much, much larger than the purple Butterfly's and they seemed almost to glow, to blaze with power. If there had been a touch of magic in this room a moment before, there was a world of magic now. The swarm leader's blue eyes met the opening staring eyes of the dead man and the song of the swarm rose like a tidal wave. For a moment reality was gone and the stone all about them shimmered like the pouring falls. The song changed from crying to screaming and then the dead man moved and groaned and stood. The Gold One had brought his soul back to his broken body, dragged it back from wherever it had been.

He was not healed – his throat was still torn away – so he could say no words but he was alive. He looked at all those who stared at him and knew not why they watched him with such great fear, and then he saw the Gold One and he looked into the blue eyes that had suddenly turned the color of hate. He tried to scream for it was not enough that he perish, he must die twice and be destroyed.

The Gold One opened its mouth. For a moment Tyger thought she heard it speak, but then the Human man burst into flames and burned while everyone watched, frozen. And when his body turned black and fell to ashes, the Gold One ate the ashes so not even his charred remains would return to the Earth, and the fire of the Butterfly had already eaten his soul. Only the

Gold One knew that a pouch of vials filled with a blue swirling drug had perished with the man. Vials that now would never be delivered.

Then the song changed and the Gold One turned to Tyger. The Windriders and Mouse moved away from their leader as if on command. Tyger felt the purple Butterfly let go of her, standing on shaky legs.

Again the Gold One spread wide its wings but this time it was not to destroy. The song was soothing and calm now, the sound of healing. The purple one slowly opened its bullet-riddled wings and one by one the young Butterflies who had lain lifeless upon the stone ground rose magically into the air and covered each of the holes, melting into the wounded wings and making them whole once more. Those young Butterflies would feel the Wind again after all.

The purple Butterfly began to sing with the rest, joyously moving its wings as it joined the large ring of the swarm. The Gold One turned toward Tylon. He stood and came forward but then turned away, not out of fear – he felt unworthy. But before he could move, the Gold One touched his mind and gave him a vision.

He saw himself in a hall of silver and red. He wore a jacket like the ones worn by the people of Sky, full of swirling colors. But this jacket glowed brightly with an aura of power. The right arm of the jacket shone red, the left green, the front white and the back bright blue There were others with him, but he could not see who they were. In his hand was a weapon that looked like a E.C. but was not. When it fired, it shot a glowing net, not a bolt of death.

Before he could understand the vision's meaning, he found himself suddenly back again in the chamber called Genesis. He heard two metallic *pings* against the stone and looked down to see the two bullets that had dropped from his healed shoulder.

"Thank you," he whispered, his voice husky with awe.

The Gold One only turned back to Tyger as Tylon stepped aside. Tyger felt no pain now, only a warm tingling, the living sensation of bones and muscles mending. She wanted to say something, wanted to express in words all that was in her heart, to connect with the startling intelligence and the somehow familiar presence in the wise eyes of this powerful leader, but words failed her. So, slowly, Tyger stood and then, for the first time in her life, she went down on one knee in respect.

If the Gold One understood the importance of this gesture, it did not acknowledge it. Instead, it sank down beside Tyger and for a moment, they were equals, despite their differences. Then the Butterfly reached out and touched Tyger's mind.

In her vision, Tyger flew over the New World. She rose above the Valley and then over the site of her village. She saw the Patriarchy's cluster of domes including dome #342, and she saw other domes, belonging to other nations, not too far from the Patriarchy. Something was swirling in the Wind above the domes, something dark with malice seemed to be rising, bleeding off them, entering the atmosphere, mixing with the Wind.

The vision changed. She saw six half-constructed domes. Six sites where P3M were enslaved. Enslaved because of her. For a moment, Tyger's pain at being reminded of all she longed to forget nearly overwhelmed her. What she had done that the Gold One would cause her this pain? But then Tyger understood what the Gold One was showing her. She realized that the Patriarchy was angry, preoccupied and had abandoned the P3M. They had little food and less water. The P3M had no way of knowing that should they escape from the sites, their freedom was assured. Jarth wasn't monitoring the cameras that spied on them and no soldiers lurked, hidden in Hovercraft to catch run-aways. But that did not address the more immediate problems of food and water. Tyger knew the slaves had to be saved or they would die. They had to be freed.

Tyger's gaze re-focused as her mind turned from the images in the vision to the now-familiar surroundings of Sky. There was an urgency in her now. She felt strong. She knew what had to be done. She forgot about the bleeding domes.

The Gold One and Tyger stood. Tyger saw how gracefully the Gold One stood on two legs. The Gold One looked down. On the floor lay the last of the slain Butterfly children. As Tyger watched, it lifted from the ground. It was beautiful, with shimmering, fiery wings that were striped with midnight black, colors identical to Tyger's mane. It came closer to her, hovered before her heart and then, pressing itself against her, it became a part of her.

Tyger looked down at the tiger-striped, Butterfly-shaped mark over her heart. The blood from the battle was suddenly gone and there, rising and falling with her breath, was the perfect imprint of the young Butterfly. Slowly she raised her hand and touched the mark. It was soft, part of her skin, part of her. When she looked up, the swarm was gone. Her gaze took in those about her. Her Windriders stood in silent awe, but they didn't seemed surprised that the Gold One had bestowed this gift on their leader. A gift with a hidden meaning.

Tyger looked to the people of Sky, to her new friends. Aliqui's gaze was far away even though her eyes were on Tyger's face. Instinctively, Tyger knew she was thinking Falcon, perhaps wishing she were here. Kestrel's brown eyes were fixed upon the Butterfly mark. After a moment, her eyes lifted and she smiled at Tyger.

But when Tyger looked to Mlinz, she saw something below his expression that she couldn't quite read. He was troubled by something but she couldn't see what. Mouse stood beside him now, proudly beaming up at Tyger, his face almost obscured by the hovering cloud of the small Butterflies.

Lastly, Tyger looked at Iahala and found the Wisewoman was watching her. The old woman's expression was a mixture of wisdom, relief and, like Mlinz, a knowledge of something yet to be revealed.

Iahala spoke, "If there were any doubts of your intentions before, your actions today, and those of your Windriders, have spoken clearly of your courage and honor. Let me be the first to say that it would be a great pleasure if you and your Windriders would stay with us indefinitely. There is so very much we can teach each other."

"Wise One," Tyger said softly, moving across the stone floor to where Iahala stood, reaching her hands out and grasping Iahala's. "The Gold One has given me a vision that I cannot ignore. There is much to think about, and for once, I do not want to do my thinking alone."

Tyger paused and looked back at her Windriders, and then her gaze lingered on Mouse. "The Windriders may not be in Sky for much longer. I would like all of our new friends to help us decide which course of action is best." The tone of her voice hinted at the severity of what she had seen and the importance of the decision ahead. "There are those who will die if we do not act quickly. And I will not stand aside and let loved ones die." She gestured to all of those gathered. "Come. Let me tell you what I have seen."

They gathered in the Windriders' chambers. Tyger spared no moment and told them all about the abandoned slave sites she had seen in her vision. She paused a moment before continuing, her eyes touching the faces of those before her. Then she explained why she must do something for these P3M. Why more than just saving lives was at sake.

"They are my friends," she said and her eyes touched Tamarin, Fox and Wolf but rested on Spider. They had once been slaves as well, and Spider had not wholly forgiven Tyger for the Windborn's role in that evil.

"The Patriarch took me from my village with the promise that as long as I did as I was told, he would let my people live. One of the many tasks I had to perform to ensure the safety of my village was to pretend to escape from New Seattle when the Wind was in Phase Three – the stage of metamorphosis. I was instructed to take my gang with me – those who were my followers at the time – and expose them to the Wind.

"The Patriarchy knew that some would change and some would die. Those who changed, who were now able to survive in the Wind, were taken and enslaved by the Patriarchy, forced to construct the inner metalworks of the domes – the circulation fans, climate controls, other various systems and, of course, the huge metal frames of the domes themselves. The Patriarchy's soldiers, the Clones, they couldn't do this kind of work even if they wanted to. They can't survive in the Wind long enough to build the structures, and many of them lack in mental abilities as well.

"I cannot tell you how this enslaving of those who had trusted me horrified and haunted me. There was nothing I could imagine that would be worse." She paused here for a moment and then said, "Except the murder of my family and the destruction of my village. It was a terrible price to pay, this balance of two evils. I tried to rationalize it, believing that the freedom of the many Windborn might somehow justify the enslaving of a few handfuls of Originals. It was my dream to preserve the Windborn bloodline. To protect my home and my people." Tyger glanced again at Spider. She knew there was no way to make Spider understand just how devastating the decision had been. Each time Tyger had taken her followers to be exposed still haunted her. Each life lost to the Wind. Each life given over to slavery. The faces of the living and the dead troubled her dreams and had turned her into someone she had come to despise.

If she looked to Spider for understanding, she found herself unable to read the expression in the other's eyes, eyes that had once been a smooth gray and were now solid silver. She pulled her gaze away and continued, "But I know now I was wrong. Wrong to trust the Patriarchy. Wrong to betray the Windriders. All those years I believed Jarth's lies. And when I discovered the truth – that he had destroyed my village despite his promises – I knew I could no longer deny the evil of what I had done. It was time to make amends. I have yet to pay penance for my deeds, but there is no doubt within me that someday I shall. The world is a circle, and everything comes back to you." After a moment, she went on, her voice stronger now than it had been a moment before. "Spider, Fox, Tamarin and Wolf are with me now because I proved that my loyalties had changed. They chose to follow me and escape the Patriarchy despite the fact that the Patriarchy promised them food, drink and shelter, while I could promise nothing. Nothing but freedom."

This time when Tyger looked to Spider, she saw the other woman acknowledge the courage it had taken for Tyger to admit her mistake and change her life.

"Now," Tyger said, turning back to the others, "I have another opportunity to help those I left behind. I have the faith of these Windriders who stand here. I have a place which offers food and shelter – the land of Sky. I have something, some home to offer the other P3M. I can offer myself, my own life.

"But life is ebbing from those who are still enslaved. The Gold One has shown me that our escape and the destruction of the Retrieval Squad has enraged Jarth to the point where he is no longer rational. He has abandoned the slave sites and left them without supplies – without food and water. If we don't do something soon, they will die."

A loud rumble of anger erupted as Tyger finished speaking and she spoke into their anger, linking them together through their rage at Jarth and their desire to help. "We must go for them. We must ride out and bring them to safety. If Jarth comes with more soldiers, they will have to be killed. Because it is time for all of our people, all of our friends who have shared the name Windrider, to be free."

There was cheering then, followed by shouts of "When do we leave?" and "I'm ready right now!" To Tyger's surprise, Spider's voice rose in Tyger's praise, her eyes burning with a warrior's pride and a belief in Tyger that the Windborn hadn't thought she'd ever see again.

In the midst of the chaos, Tyger's gaze was drawn to Mouse. Tears ran freely down his face and she moved toward him, one hand outstretched. "Mouse?"

He turned to run from the room, but the Gold One stood suddenly in the doorway, blocking his way. She touched him and he turned into her arms. "But you've only just arrived..." he managed.

"It's all right–" she began, but fell silent as the tumult around her quieted suddenly and all eyes turned toward the Gold One whose presence commanded attention.

It stood on its two bottom legs, its four other arms spread wide like its wings, and once more Tyger marveled at the creature's once-black eyes that were now such a deep, familiar blue.

Then the Gold One spoke. In all the years of the Great Butterflies' evolution, no one had ever witnessed anything as spectacular as what had transpired earlier in the chamber of Genesis. But that glorious show of death and rebirth seemed somehow less impossible because of this moment. The moment when the Gold One used their language for the first time. "No." It's voice was androgynous, a perfect blend of gender, wisdom and power.

The shape of the Gold One's mouth seemed to make speech difficult, but it had accomplished what it set out to do – it had their attention. It continued now, speaking into the minds of all of those gathered. *Tyger must not go. She must not yet leave Sky. It is not time for her questions to be answered.*

Tyger, confused and angry, opened her mouth to reply. But before she could say anything, the Gold One's gaze swung around and locked into hers and she knew that this was the way it must be. This was the way of destiny and fate, and there was no point arguing fate. But that did not mean she would abandon this mission.

"Gold One," she said, "we must do something. I will not stand by and let them starve. I put them where they are, it only seems right that I get them out."

Again, the Gold One filled their minds with its voice. *You did not bring them where they are. Destiny has brought them there. They are strengthened by their lives, strengthened for their fate. You will not be the one to free them. They do not call to you. To save them is not how you will do your penance.*

Then, its message delivered, the Gold One turned and left in a swirl of golden wings. And those who were gathered there clustered around Tyger, looking at her and at each other.

Something in Tyger still felt unsettled. She wanted badly to go, to act against the Silver Steel she hated. She felt that desire burn inside her like a flame that threaten to consume. She felt tempted to ignore the Gold One's words, to proceed as she had planned. But even as she thought these words, she heard the Gold One's voice in her mind alone: *If you want to drink the silver wine, you must wait until it's poured.*

And in that moment between understanding and action, Tyger heard the voices of her friends rise around her. "Tyger, we're the ones." It was Wolf. Wolf and Spider. Tryl and Jyln. Tyger looked at their faces and knew it was true. It was in their eyes.

"We might call ourselves Windborn," Spider said slowly. "But we aren't really. And we aren't some code, P3M, that the Patriarchy assigned to us either. We're something else all together. Something that doesn't have a name yet. The others, still at the dome sites, they're our kin. Our only kin. We have to be the ones to go."

"It's hard to leave you," Tryl's voice was restrained. "I've always stood with you, Tyger. You've been my leader since the beginning and we've gone into every battle as a team." Tryl looked away and there was sadness as well as strength in her words. "But when you told us about your vision, I knew I had to go, with or without you. I felt pulled to this." Tryl looked back at Tyger and the emotion in the warrior's eyes was simple conviction. "Let me do this for you now. In your name."

Tyger reached out and gave Tryl's shoulder a hard squeeze. It said everything that she could not convey through words. Into the silence that fell, Jyln spoke. "I have always defended life. Even on the battlefield I've prevented bloodshed, but I've spilled blood as well. I know what it is to respect life, to honor it above all else, and this is why I have to go. It's one thing to live in slavery. It's another to die in it."

Jyln and Tyger looked at each other. The beautiful warrior gazed into the solid eyes of the Windborn who had many times been called a beast. "You were the one who taught me that, Tyger. Because of you, we will be victorious in this."

It was then that Tyger the warrior, the tough-shelled leader, took each of the four volunteers into her arms. After a moment, she drew back from them and cleared her throat. She grinned and looked at Spider, who was even more controlled in her emotions than Tyger. "I'd always do anything for a courageous warrior," Tyger joked. She expected Spider to grin back at her, but the woman wiped her eyes with the back of her hand and Tyger thought she saw tears.

"We'll try to be that, Tyger," Spider said when she had found her voice again. "Be courageous."

Mouse touched Tyger's arm. "You've been adventuring for so long, Tyger. You haven't had a chance to find a home since you left the Village. Stop being a warrior for a little bit and let Sky be your home."

Wolf assured her, "You can trust us, Tyger."

Finally Tyger nodded. She looked at the four. She must choose a team leader. "Tryl, you've been my second in command for a very long time; Wolf, you have good instinct and natural wisdom; Spider, you're sharp, in both thought and action, and that gets you out when you're deep in trouble, but Jyln, you're fast and quick-witted and that keeps you out of trouble in the first place. How in the Wind am I supposed to choose? Who will lead you?"

"I'd like to lead them, Tyger," someone said. Tyger turned toward the speaker. She was not surprised, ultimately, to see it was Petre. "Because of my time in the Patriarchy, I'm the only one among us who knows exactly where the sites are. Let me use something of what I learned to aid those the Patriarchy has harmed."

There was something else Petre wasn't saying and Tyger instantly thought of his nightmare early this morning. What had he called out? "Don't let him win"? "Don't let go"? Had he dreamed of the P3M?

"Any Clone who can survive the Wind is a good man," Wolf said.

Even though everyone seemed to agree that Petre was the best choice, there was one among them who did not wholly support his choice. Petre looked at him then, but Tylon only turned away.

Tyger spoke, "Petre, you were my friend among my enemies and the only one who knew all my faults and still stood with me. Once I said you were a good soldier and a better man, but it makes me proud to say that now you are a strong Windrider as well."

"Thank you." Petre's voice was tender and proud.

"I would like to join the Rescue Squad as well," Kestrel said suddenly, naming the team.

Mlinz shouted in response, jumping to his feet. "No!"

Kestrel turned to her brother. She was clearly stunned; perhaps he was stunned by his own protest. Kestrel put her hands on his shoulders. It was the first time they had touched in years. "Mlinz," she spoke softly, as if they were alone. "I am an excellent Flyer and fighter. I can bring water from the Sky to keep the Wind from my blood." She paused and her voice became very gentle. "I need you to love me enough to know I'll return to you, because I love you enough to know you'll be waiting for me."

Mlinz's eyes filled with tears. His throat worked as he tried to speak and the silence between them deepened. Finally he said, "I love you, Kestrel."

"And I love you, my brother." They stared at each other for a long moment, letting the deeper bond of blood build a bridge between their two philosophies of living. Then Kestrel squeezed his shoulders once and turned away. "We can take the Wings," she said. "They can carry more weight then the Windboards and easily be rigged to carry more than two people. It's one thing to find the Valley once, but to find it again is another matter. The Rescue Squad will need help. Help I can give."

Tyger nodded. It was all decided. The gathering broke up and everyone set about the tasks that would help prepare the Rescue Squad for their departure.

* * *

Before great danger there should always come great beauty. In the Old World they had waved flags, sang songs and held parades before going off to war. In the New World there were battle cries, gang calls and shows of skill. In the Valley there was birth, rebirth and life.

It was less than twenty-four hours since the battle in the Genesis chamber. After much activity and frantic but careful preparation, that time had come. Iahala, the Wisewoman of Sky and the leader of the Pagans, stood atop the boulder beside the falls and raised her arms. Tyger, Ardyn, Tylon, Fox, Tamarin, Mlinz and Aliqui sat on the grass beside the white-gold sand. Mouse and Kestrel stood on either side of the pool. All were listening.

Iahala began. "Great Mother Earth, hear us today as we welcome new life unto you, first life of us all. Father Time, hear us today as we begin again. Brother Sky, hear us as we reach to you with new hands and Sister Moon, now unseen, but always near, guide us as you have since the Creation."

Mouse began to play his flute and the music was rich and full, an intricate maze of complex patterns and rhythms. The music continued as Iahala spoke again, her eyes drifting to the powerful falls, to the ribbon of blue touched with white clouds. "Great Falls, chosen of the Snoqualmie tribe of the Old World, honored by us in turn, life-bringer, protector, welcome today and be womb for the birth of those who shall fly the sky, your namesake, for the cause of freedom. You whose soul's name is and shall forever be, Snoqualmie, the place where miracles happen."

As Iahala's words faded, Kestrel began to sing. She asked the Earth to give strength, Time to give speed, the Sky to give peace and the Moon to give magic. Silently, the others joined her in her prayer.

As the music floated on the air, weaving magical protection, seeping into every living thing it touched, the members of the Rescue Squad began to arrive. Petre emerged first, from behind the falls, gliding upon the sails of his Wing, which glowed orange and black in the soft light. His Wing was called Monarch. Tryl followed him, launching from the stone ledge behind the falls and swooping through its gentle spray, lifting on the thermal current and then dropping gracefully down into the gathering. Her Wing's name was Heliconian, its sails a creamy gold that blended into fire-orange and were edged in black.

After her was Jyln. Jyln's Wing had sails as white as clouds with eyes like an Original's – gold iris and black pupils – at its tips. The Wing's name was Sulphur. Spider followed Jyln on a Wing named Satyr, Spider's tall body encased in powerful wings the color of silver stone veined with bronze.

Wolf arrived last, demonstrating his quick mastery of the new skill. His stocky body was borne on a Wing whose sails were of the deepest bronze and red, with shimmering waves of silver, a Wing called Metalmark.

As he settled to the ground beside his companions, Iahala chanted, "By the powers of Earth and Time, Sky and Moon, and by the elements which wrought the Wings, it is done."

The gathering replied, "Blessed be. So mote it be. It is done."

Thus the birth of five new Flyers was complete. Blessed by the powers they were born, reborn, and made anew. To start a quest was to begin again and such beginnings should always begin at the place where miracles happen.

They were well prepared, but despite this a healthy sense of danger lingered. They went to face the evils of the Patriarchy, whether directly or indirectly. There was no way of knowing the price of this quest. Would they succeed? Would they return...?

Tyger came to where Tryl, Jyln and Spider stood before their Wings, noting their travel gear and the Windboards strapped beneath the gliders. "My three women warriors," Tyger grinned. "All leaving. Who will I talk exploits with?"

"You were never one to brag, Tyger," Spider chided. Tyger acknowledged her words. They clasped hands.

"You may never completely forgive me, Spider, for all I've done. But I'm glad you came with us, sharp words and all. I had forgotten what it was like to have someone around who had more of a temper than I." Tyger paused. "I'm also glad you're going. You and Wolf..." Tyger's voice fell into silence and the two women stared at each other for a moment. Then Tyger said, "You'll make sure this is done right." Spider nodded.

Tyger embraced the others in turn, speaking softly, reminding them of where they had been and where they were going.

While Tyger spoke with Jyln and Tryl, Wolf stood slightly apart from the rest. Tamarin approached his brother, Fox a step or two behind. The brothers had never been separated before and it felt strange, as though Wolf was taking something of Tamarin with him and leaving part of himself behind as well.

Wolf looked at his brother, recognizing how much he had changed. Much of his flippant attitude was gone, replaced by new respect for others. There were actually tears in his Tamarin's eyes.

Wolf drew that taller man into a bone-crushing embrace. "I will return to you," he said quietly.

When Tamarin drew away, his face hardened for a moment. "If the soldiers show up it'll be the first chance any of us P3M," he spat the term with contempt, "will have for revenge. Be careful. But," he let a sudden and fierce grin steal across his face, "be sure to slam a few of the steel-suckers for me!"

They laughed together, and Wolf promised he would.

Petre walked over to Tylon because the other young man would not come to him. The inventor sat on a small rock, his eyes on the grass and Petre paused where he stood before he spoke.

Petre had been struggling with feelings since the first time he took Tylon's hand and Tylon welcomed him to the Windriders, despite his Clone body and the horrible Skin suit he'd had to wear. Finding himself in such close proximity to someone he cared deeply for had taken a lot of getting used to, especially when that affection was not returned. In the Patriarchy Clones did not love. Clones gave Seed, patrolled, learned, and then, eventually, died a good soldier. Now, he felt something new, something different and those feelings battled with the knowledge that Tylon had loved Ravyn and that maybe he still did.

"Tylon." When Tylon looked up and met Petre's eyes, what Petre saw was not the anger or disgust he had expected. After all, he hadn't known if Tylon would even consider loving another man. What he did see was confusion and sadness and it made Petre's heart ache.

"I loved Ravyn," Tylon said slowly, "but she never knew. It wasn't her fault. She was just never intuitive that way. But I let myself grow closer and closer to her and then she left me. I told her how I felt, but still she left me.

"So I closed myself off. And then, when Aliqui was showing us the crystals, I saw you watching me and I saw her look at you. She knew. She knew what I didn't." Tylon paused. He looked at the ground and then his eyes came back to rest on Petre's face. "I don't know how I feel about this,

Petre. I care about you. But I'm not sure I love you the way you want me to.
I have a lot of feelings, all mixed together, and I don't like that. There are
more women than men among Originals. I've never had another male
friend. Other than Mlinz and Mouse, I've just never heard of men being...."

"I've never known two men to share love either," Petre said when
Tylon's voice fell silent. "But the idea doesn't bother me. Maybe some
soldiers did, I just didn't see it. Then again, I never knew a Clone could
change with the Wind either. Maybe I'm just destined to be the first at
everything." Petre swallowed hard. "But you're a man of facts and familiar
theories. I can see that this bothers you. Which is one of the reasons why I'm
leaving."

Petre turned away then, but Tylon caught his hand. Petre could feel
Tylon move close behind him, their bodies almost touching, Tylon's breath
warm against the back of his neck. When he spoke, Tylon's voice was
almost a whisper. "Ravyn left me. Do you have to, too?"

"I am not Ravyn," Petre said evenly, for a second time. Then Petre
turned around slowly to face him again. He looked at him for a long
moment, his expression one of tightly controlled pain.

"I told you once I didn't want Ravyn," Tylon said. "And that's still
true. I don't know... who I want."

"It seems you have a lot a thinking to do," Petre said quietly. "And
so do I. Maybe it would be best for you not to want anyone for a while. I want
to go on this mission. I know my blood may still be Clone blood, but I want
to live in this body, out there, in the Wind, just because I can. I think I've
dreamed the faces of the P3M. I think I'm meant to go to them. I think I can
help. But I have lived for the conglomerate all my life, doing whatever
would please the Patriarchy, and now that I'm free, I've grown selfish. " He
paused and then added, "If you tell me to stay, Tylon, I will."

They stood in silence for a long moment. Finally Tylon shook his
head. "I can't give you what you want because I don't know what I want. I
thought I didn't have to know, but I do."

"Yes," Petre said simply. "You do."

Tylon nodded, looking at Petre, wishing he could just fall into his
hazel eyes. Wishing it were all that easy. Petre smiled at him, gently, and
turned away.

Nearby, Kestrel and Aliqui smiled and embraced. "You teach these
Windriders the right way to fly, Kes. They need a little grace worked into
their rough hides."

Kestrel nodded but asked seriously, "You'll be all right, without me
around?"

Aliqui took a deep breath. She hadn't been able to keep Falcon out
of her head all day. She wasn't surprised that Kestrel could tell. "I'll try,"

she answered honestly.

"I always knew you'd fly away from me some day." Mlinz joined them, Mouse close behind.

Kestrel took her brother into her arms. "I don't know what's come over you, Mlinz... or what's come over me, for that matter. I haven't been a sister to you in a long time but I won't hurt you again. I don't believe how you believe, but I will never hate you because of it."

"It is time!" From the center of the folk, Iahala called to them all. "The Wind is rising, and I have gifts for our adventurers."

Everyone gathered about the Wisewoman, and the six who were the Rescue Squad came to stand directly before her. Iahala went to Petre first. She reached into a pouch at her waist and drew out a headband made of soft cloth, colored with swirls of blue, green, purple and red. She tied the band in place across Petre's brow and then stood looking at him for a long time. Finally she asked him, "What did you dream?"

Petre spoke softly. "I have seen the faces of these P3M. In my dreams more than once and before that, on the walls of this Valley. Their cheeks are stained with tears and always it is night. At first they only cried, 'Who?' because they did not know who would come for them. But soon they called a name. My name. And I am sure now that they wait for me."

Petre did not understand the tears that fell suddenly from Iahala's eyes. She only looked at him in silence and then nodded once. She moved to the others, giving each one a headband like Petre's, made of soft Sky cloth and washed in the River. Iahala came to Kestrel last and smiled at her with pride.

"Daughter!" A shrill voice cut into the warm air. Everyone turned to see Abraham and Sarah approaching. They looked strange in the sunlight, as if they belonged in the darkness of the underground. "If you put on that Pagan band, you will no longer be a child of the One!"

Kestrel shook her head in utter disbelief. "I ceased being a child of the One when I felt your hate, and I ceased listening to your words when you struck me." She looked into Iahala's eyes and nodded, standing very still as Iahala fastened the cloth around her head.

When she had finished, Iahala turned to the new arrivals, meeting Sarah's furious gaze with one of quiet calm. "You disowned this child, and I have taken her in. Kestrel has been named my granddaughter."

"Evil witch!" Sarah screamed and she threw herself forward. But before Sarah could touch the Wisewoman, Tyger had stepped between them. In one smooth motion, she spun Sarah, pinning her arms behind her back. The woman struggled, screeching like a demon. "How dare you!"

Tyger let her go suddenly and the force of Sarah's struggling carried her forward onto the ground. She lay sprawled only long enough to hit the grass with her fists, then she was on her feet again, opening her mouth to spit more vile words. But Tyger cut her off, the warrior's voice rising up powerful and commanding. "In my Village we did not attack our Elders and we never struck our children. It amazes me that you call Windborn animals, and yet you behave like the worst rabid beasts. Now take your man and your One and go. You are not welcome here."

Sarah's eyes swept over the gathering and settled on Mlinz. "Come, boy. I want you with me!"

Unsteadily, Mlinz stood from where he sat beside Mouse. Mouse made to catch his hand but did not. As Mlinz passed Tyger, he spun toward her for a moment. His voice was a harsh whisper, full of terror. "Don't let him walk alone." Then he turned away quickly.

Tyger took a step toward the boy but Sarah grabbed him. He turned slowly in his mother's arms, his face toward the Windriders. Tears streamed from his eyes. He looked at Mouse. "I'll protect you–"

"Isaac! Stop talking nonsense," Sarah scolded with a hiss. Mlinz' face went blank. His body became almost limp.

Tyger couldn't sort out what was happening. What bizarreness was this? Mlinz looked suddenly half-dead and Mouse had leapt to his feet. Tyger looked to Iahala for answers, but the other woman's gaze was riveted on Sarah's face.

Abraham stepped beside his wife then and took Mlinz's hand. The boy, held between his parents, was like a rag doll, simply moving with them, utterly defeated. They spun him around, led him away, back toward the door into Sky. As soon as they were gone, the gathering erupted in confusion.

Tyger took control quickly. She motioned Aliqui to her side. "Will you go after them? Watch them?" The other woman nodded. Tyger motioned to Tamarin and Fox. "If they split up, each of you follow one. Be discreet. Don't let them see you."

Tyger turned. "Tylon." The man was standing as soon as she said his name. "Go to our room. Watch our things. The weapons especially."

"Hold down homebase," he grunted.

At Tyger's grim nod, he glanced quickly back to Petre. Their eyes met, then Tylon slipped away, moving with Aliqui and the others through the door into Sky.

Tyger looked over at Ardyn. The woman sat upon the grass, thirteen-year-old Mouse gathered in her arms like a terrified child. Gently she rocked him, tried to comfort him. The two women exchanged glances and both heard the words again.

"'Don't let him walk alone,'" Ardyn repeated. "What did Mlinz think would happen?"

"I don't know," Tyger growled, "but I'm going to find out."

Tyger turned at last to the Rescue Squad. They were silent as they waited for her to speak. "The journey you have before you is one of the most important any of us could ever take. It looks as if we will be having our own conflicts here, but you six must keep your minds on your task. Each of you was called to this quest. You are going to see the wilds of this New World like never before. Be careful and be brave.

"Our thoughts will be with you. Don't forget how much each of you means to us and how evil the Patriarchy is. Most of all, remember: you're Windriders. You do not hate without reason and you never kill unless you must. Stand by each other and beware of the Silver Steel."

They all looked at Tyger for a few heartbeats, then turned and picked up their Wings. As a strong breeze raced across the Valley floor, they ran toward the cliff wall. A few minutes later, they were hovering above the Valley, Petre and Kestrel flying together in the lead. Tyger raised her hand to them. They caught the Wind and were gone in a flash of color and speed and magic.

Iahala met Tyger's eyes and the two leaders shared a moment of silence. There was more than just conflict that awaited them... much more. And they both knew it.

* * *

Tyger carried Mouse easily as she walked beside Iahala and Ardyn down the winding corridor that descended into Sky.

"They preach love and redemption, but they harbor such hate and damnation," Iahala mused. The sound of their footfalls echoed in the stone hallway. "They say we are all children of the One, but they close us out. I have been trying for a long time to decipher their beliefs. But much of it is still beyond my understanding." Iahala's voice was almost pained. "I feel we're on the brink of something terrible. Something that Mlinz knows, but will not share."

"Mlinz says he worships the One, yet I see no hate in him," Tyger commented. "And he loves Mouse too deeply to have accepted his parents' teachings. He told me once that his One is not their One. I believe him." Tyger paused and stroked her brother's back. "You're right. There's something else going on here. There's more to Sarah's madness than just her beliefs."

Iahala nodded. "Sarah knows that it was her ancestor's answer to the Riddler that brought about the End. I have to believe that affects her. But I don't know how much. Or what this means within the context of her fanaticism.

"For that is what this is, Tyger," Iahala continued. "Not insanity, but religious zeal. And it is far more deadly. It warps interpretation of signs and symbols. It demands a search for a deity, instead the recognition of the simple magic which is everywhere, at every moment. Yet to recognize this magical world would belie their beliefs – make their faith a non-reality.

"So the choice to choose a different path is closed to Sarah and Abraham because they *are* fanatics. The world must adhere to their code, to their religion, or they must force it to. And force it they will. They will do it in such a rational and sane way that we are baffled by them. For the good of their divine souls and in the name of their One, they will twist and bend every nuance to destroy whatever – or whoever – they perceive to challenge their beliefs. Their 'sanity,' Tyger, is far more dangerous than any madness could ever be. I have lived here with them for many years and this, I know."

They walked in silence for a while and then Ardyn mentioned, "Mouse told me that when he went to his room last night, Mlinz was terrified but would say nothing about it." Ardyn glanced at the boy now, asleep in his emotional exhaustion. "Mouse was convinced it had something to do with Sarah and Abraham."

"But if that's true," Tyger frowned, "why did Mlinz go to them?"

"Most likely," Iahala murmured, "he thinks can change their minds. He knows they won't listen to anyone else who talks peace."

"He's right." Tyger rumbled, flexing her claws. "And even if they listened to me, I wouldn't be talking much." Then she shook her head. "Sky is a beautiful place. I don't want to be a part of its downfall."

"Your actions will not destroy Sky, Tyger," Iahala assured her. "But you may well be its savior."

* * *

Tamarin and Fox were waiting with Tylon in the Windrider's chamber. Tyger placed Mouse down on Ardyn's pelt and turned to them. "Tell me."

"I don't think he's in immediate danger," Tamarin began but when Tyger looked doubtful, Fox continued. "Mlinz seemed to be holding his own. We followed them undetected to Sarah and Abraham's rooms. Aliqui didn't think they'd be splitting up any time soon, so she sent us back to you. She's still near them."

"Well." Tyger took a deep breath. "We'll just have to wait and see. I hope Mlinz is strong enough to stand up to his parents."

Tamarin gave her a pleased grin. "He was giving them major grief while we were listening. Whatever shocked him before wore off!"

"Or he fought it off." Tyger glanced quickly at Iahala. The Wisewoman just looked back her, silently agreeing.

"I want to go to Mlinz." Everyone turned as Mouse spoke, pushing himself up from sleep.

Tyger went to him. "I don't think that would be wise, Mouse. Fox and Tamarin tell me he seems to be doing fine. I think we should trust whatever plan he may have."

Mouse stared at her. He stood. "I'm going to my room. I want to be near him and he's everywhere there."

Tyger was silent as Mouse walked out. Then, without hesitating, she motioned for Tamarin and Fox to follow him. "Be respectful." They nodded and slipped out the door.

Tyger turned to Iahala. "There is a lot I'd like you to tell me. About the Humans we fought in Genesis. Why they wanted water from the Sky. And who is Isaac?"

Iahala studied Tyger's face. "I don't know what to tell you." Tyger raised her eyebrows. Iahala explained, "Yes, I know some truths, but nothing makes sense to me right now. I must think on it." Iahala reached out a hand to Tylon. "Right now I would like to take Petre's friend to the Crystal Garden. I think he wants to see the crystals again."

Leaning, lost in thought, against his work table, Tylon looked up in some surprise. "I-I would like to go back." Struggle was evident on his face and Tyger knew it would be best to keep him occupied.

"We'll talk later then." Tyger and Iahala exchanged agreement and the Wisewoman led Tylon away.

"You save Iahala from Sarah's attack, dispatch half the gang to the New World, the other half throughout Sky... what else can you do?"

Tyger looked up at Ardyn. The woman sat on Tyger's pelt, one knee up, one leg dangling over the ledge. Tyger asked, "What else do you want me to do?"

"Don't you thrive in time of danger?" Ardyn's voice was low and warm as she stretched her legs out along Tyger's pelt, leaning back against the wall of the nook. Tyger's eyes wandered over the woman's body.

"There's probably something I should be doing," Tyger admitted but she was already crossing the room toward her.

"There is," Ardyn slid back on the pelt, into shadow, propping her head up on one hand and stroking the thick fur of the pelt with the other.

"Timing is everything with you, eh?" Tyger jumped, grabbing the ledge and lifting herself over. The nook was set about ten feet up the wall. "I'm surprised you could get up here."

Ardyn said nothing. She reached for Tyger, her eyes smoldering and her hands hot. Their lips met and parted. Tyger took the woman into her arms, drawing her closer.

Ardyn made a sound deep in her throat as Tyger's hands moved across her and grasped her shoulders. There was a sudden burning sensation down her back, painful, but at the same time sharp with pleasure. Tyger pulled away and Ardyn saw her hesitate. "Tyger, I don't care if Sky is crumbling down around us, if you say another word, I'll kill you." She could feel Tyger's heart pounding under her hand, felt the skin hot under her touch. Felt her own heart racing to match Tyger's.

Tyger's thoughts whirled for a moment. They were in the middle of dangerous times, unsteady politics. What the two of them felt for each other was a fierce passion, not a love between life-partners. But even as these thoughts surfaced, desire burned them away.

Ardyn slid her hands behind Tyger's neck and brought Tyger against her. Their lips touched again, but this time Ardyn traced Tyger's mouth with the tip of her tongue. Tyger shuddered. Her eyes closed. Ardyn kissed the soft lids, kissed a long wet line to the nape of her neck.

Tyger's mind filled with visions that swirled like flames and filled her blood. Her hands moved down Ardyn's back and pulled her up tee-shirt. It was then she realized that her claws were extended. Alarmed, she tried to draw back but with a soft moan Ardyn held her tighter.

Tyger looked at her with shocked apology. "Great Wind, Ardyn, you must be..." Tyger looked over the other woman's shoulder. The back of Ardyn's white tee-shirt was stained with blood where Tyger had held her. Ardyn kissed Tyger before she could say more, but now the Windborn held her clawed hands away from Ardyn. Ardyn drew away just enough to speak, her voice husky with her need, her body trembling, shaking. "Do I have to tell you to hold me?"

With a deep breath, Tyger brought Ardyn closer, and Ardyn muffled a cry against Tyger's neck. "Sweet Ardyn." Tyger's breath was hot as it slid across Ardyn's ear. Ardyn could almost hear Tyger's heated grin. "I don't seem to be able to retract my claws...." She pressed her lips to Ardyn's neck, softly moving her sharp teeth over the smooth skin. "I want you," Tyger whispered. "But I can't hold you like this. I won't hurt you."

Ardyn caught her breath. "Tyger, please. Don't stop!"

"I won't," Tyger assured her. "Let me feel you beneath me... beneath my body, beneath my mouth. Would you like that, sweet Ardyn?"

Ardyn responded with a deep moan, as Tyger pressed her down into the pelts, feeling the damp heat against her belly when Tyger straddled her waist. Ardyn closed her eyes as Tyger bent to kiss her neck and then her cloth-covered shoulders, as she was enveloped by the rich scent of the Wind. Ardyn reached up, touched Tyger's face with her fingers. The dark skin seemed polished, it was so fine, the cheeks burning to the touch.

The Windborn turned her head and the tip of her cat's rough tongue traced Ardyn's palm. Ardyn shivered, teasing. "By the powers, Tyger, how do you make love to a woman?" Tyger looked up, meeting Ardyn's eyes and her lingering smile. She knew what she meant. "Very carefully," she replied. "And very gently."

Ardyn held her gaze as Tyger felt Ardyn's hands move from her face, over her shoulders and bare breasts, and then continuing down to the waistband of her breeches. "And how does a woman get to make love to you?" This question was quite different, one that Tyger had no answer for, for things had never been that way.

There had been only one person that she had trusted that much, wanted that badly. It had been long before Sarya, very long before now. She tried not to think of her now, pushed those memories back because they hurt too much.

Ardyn felt the hesitation in Tyger's body and saw the restrained desire in her brilliant green eyes. She smiled gently, daringly. She understood Tyger's silence. "That will have to change." She touched Tyger's face, where her eyes were so distant, to see if Tyger had heard her. Ardyn watched as Tyger returned to herself and smiled back at her.

"I told you I couldn't concentrate around you." Tyger's voice was deep.

Ardyn grinned. "You're above me, I thought it would different." Tyger bent down and kissed her again. When she began to draw away, Ardyn held her in place. "Tyger, I don't want to wait much longer. My patience is growing thin. I watch you, the way your skin shines like ebony in these shadows, the way the lights play along your body..." Ardyn ran a hand lightly over Tyger's breasts. "You have so many fine features. We have to find a place we can be alone." Ardyn's fingers slid through Tyger's hair.

Tyger laughed softly. "A chamber with three other people not private enough for you?"

Ardyn drew Tyger down on her, her lips warm against her ear. "Tyger, my leader, you don't seem to understand." She paused, taking a deep, slow breath that made Tyger hold her closer. "We have to be alone because I am going to touch you, and when I do, I want to hear you roar." And for a moment Tyger didn't have the breath to tell her that this tiger didn't roar, because she knew, if Ardyn touched her, she would roar and much more as well.

* * *

In the Crystal Garden, Tylon knelt on the floor by the mounds of stones covered with crystals. Etched around each stone's base were various symbols and words. He reached out and touched them. Iahala watched.

"Those are runes," Iahala said, coming to stand near where he knelt. "They're a very ancient language. I could teach you if you'd like."

"I would," Tylon said and he gave her a sudden grin. Iahala smiled back at him.

As Tylon moved from mound to mound, Iahala followed, watching his face. "The first group of runes comprises the spell that calls to the powers to fill the mounds. It is like a prayer. If the mound did not call the powers, the crystals could not be charged. The second group of symbols," she pointed to the runes that made up a second row, "form the six symbols of power: the pentagram, the compass-cross, the moon, the rune for strength, the rune for protection, and the sign of the element called upon to fill the mound."

"So there's magic here?" he asked, waving his hand over the crystals that stood from holes in the stone mound.

"Yes. You do not feel it?"

Tylon shook his head.

"Do not be concerned. You do not need to feel magic to work with the crystals." Tylon looked relieved and she continued. "There is magic within each crystal, of course, but there is also magic that passes between the crystals. This magic is called wild magic, because it is uncontained. It goes where it pleases." She held her hand above the crystals, feeling it tingle and grow warmer. Though Tylon would never be able to feel this, she felt certain that he was destined to create something to do with crystal magic. In her mind an image repeated itself. Something made of green earth magic, red fire magic, blue water magic and white air magic.

"How do you control magic?" he asked.

"You don't," Iahala answered honestly. "Magic belongs to itself. You can ask things of it. You can gather it, contain it for a time and form it, but ultimately, it will only do what it wants, what it does naturally."

"Can I tell you something?"

"Of course," Iahala said.

"I had a vision. In it there was a jacket covered in magic, with power. It seemed natural to me that I should wear the jacket, that it was meant to be worn, but it doesn't seem to make sense...." his voice trailed off for a moment and then questions began to tumble out of his mouth. "You said you can contain magic, is that the same thing as adhering it? What's the difference between containing magic and charging something with magic? What can you charge?"

"Tylon," she laughed, raising a hand for him to slow down. "I am an old woman! One question at a time!"

Tylon blushed and apologized.

Iahala went to the mound of Light Crystals and gestured for him to join her. "You can contain magic for only a short amount of time. Like a captured animal, you must be able to care for it or it will die. Never let magic die, Tylon." She looked at him to see if he was listening. He was. Intently. She continued. "To contain magic, you must create borders in which to hold it. Borders can be made of crystal, runes or anything that is bespelled, instructed to be a border, a guardian."

As she talked, Iahala was rearranging the Light Crystals into a circle. "With this circle, I create a border. And all the wild magic that was floating between these crystals is pretty much held in one place, here at the center of the circle. It's not completely contained, of course. But for that to happen, there would have to be no space at all between the crystals. If this was a complete border, the magic would stay within it. Then whatever the border was adhered to, whatever the border was built on and connected to, then the magic would adhere to that as well. In this way, the magic is contained.

"This is different from charging. Charging is conjuring magic for a specific task. Imbuing an object or item with certain powers. In that case, the practitioner calls magic to fill an object with enough power necessary to undertake that task."

Iahala glanced at Tylon again. His eyes had a far away look in them and there was an expression of pain on his face. She stopped speaking and touched his arm gently. "Tylon," she said. He jumped a little at the sound of his name.

"I'm sorry," he said, his face flushed with embarrassment. "I was just thinking that Petre should be here... to help me unravel this mystery and then ..." he trailed off.

"I understand," she said. Before the silence could turn awkward, she offered, "Shall we check on the Hidden Garden?"

He nodded, clearly grateful for a new task to focus on. He followed Iahala to the hidden doorway. Iahala placed her hand on the bare stone, and the wall slid away. She and Aliqui had returned late the night of the Gold One's destructive visit. Iahala had been shocked at the damage at first, as she helped Aliqui gather up the shattered crystals. But still, the bareness of the Garden now was stunning. So few crystals had survived.

Iahala motioned to the pile of bags and baskets filled with the broken crystals. "I may never know why the Gold One did this. The crystals are utterly crushed. I never knew there was a power on Earth that could do that."

"Crystals don't break?" Tylon asked.

Iahala opened the lid on one of the baskets. She reached in, then raised her hand, letting a fine, sparkling powder fall from between her fingers. "This is not just broken, Tylon. This is crystal dust."

Tylon stared at the stuff. "But how did the Butterflies get in here in the first place? Aliqui had closed the door behind us!"

"And how did they move through the Skynest door to here? I can only say that the Gold One now opens our doors. I don't pretend to understand. The Gold One is changing, and Butterfly magic is.... Instead of knowing more about them each day, sometimes I feel I know less. Theirs is a wild magic, no doubt."

Tylon knelt down and began running his hands through the

powder. It was both sharp and soft.

Iahala walked around the Garden, looking up at the mostly bare stone trees. "In all my life I have never seen the Butterflies destroy anything. Nor have I seen such a metamorphosis as I see on the face of the Gold One. I have never witnessed such magic as I saw in the Genesis chamber... and, until now, I have never lost a spirit that called to me."

Tylon looked up at her. She stood behind the cluster of stone trees, her body framed by the stone branches.

"There is some connection," she whispered. "And there is where our answers lay."

* * *

"Sit down, child. For the sake of the One, standing like that makes me think you're trying to be superior!"

His mother's eyes bore into him and Mlinz sat. But he did not take the offered seat beside her.

They were in his parents' chambers at the small reading table where the family had once gathered nightly to read from the Book and share their love. But that love had never gone out to Kestrel. Even when she was a child, before she became fascinated with things they disapproved of. They had never even named her. Why hadn't Mlinz ever thought about this before? Why hadn't he seen how wrong it was?

Mlinz thought of his sister now, and in his mind's eye he saw her flying herself farther and farther away with the five Windriders. He hoped they were safe. He hoped he would see her again.

Mlinz knew he could never have gone off into such danger, even though he had once to save the Windborn children. But something had been different about that time; something had called to him just as this time, Kestrel was called. He and Kestrel had always been so different, since the very beginning. Since his parents had named him Isaac.

"Isaac." His mother's voice broke into his thoughts and he turned his head reluctantly to face her. "Why must you insist on associating with the Pagans? You know how much that displeases your father and me."

Mlinz saw her deep eyes sparkling, and suddenly he understood what was happening. His mother had had another vision and, as always, Abraham was following her without question. That's why they were calling him by his birth-name. That's why they were suddenly asserting themselves in his life.

Mlinz looked at Abraham, as dark as Sarah was fair. He ached for him, for the gentle father, the kind man who continually fell under his mother's harsh influence. There had been a time when Sarah and Abraham had shared all their responsibilities and decisions, but over the years, she seemed to grow stronger as if she sapped his strength. And now there was something haunting about his silence. Something permanent and final.

Mlinz felt fear grip him. Once he had believed Sarah's visions did come from the One. But when she claimed that the One told her to let the Windborn children die, he had simply known she was mistaken. And if the visions didn't come from the One, then where did they come from?

"Why are you calling me Isaac again?" he asked, keeping his voice neutral. But it shook just a little anyway, and she smiled as though this was a victory in and of itself. He felt very small under Sarah's watching eyes but he wanted to hear her explanation.

"It is time to reclaim your given name. You have played games too long." Sarah's smile grew. "The time of your calling has come."

Mlinz, once Isaac, felt colder then he had ever felt before. He wished Mouse were here with him. It was as if the power of Hell had turned to ice and entered his veins. He thought he heard someone laughing and the sound frightened him. He offered up a prayer to the One, to his One.

When Mlinz looked up, he realized it was Sarah who was laughing. "Dear One, boy! It's not as if I've named your death!"

Again there was that glimmer in her eyes, and Mlinz sank back in his seat. He knew the Book better than she imagined he did. And if he knew anything, he knew that she had indeed named his death – and most probably the deaths of others as well.

"You know how your father and I have been very unhappy with the arrival of that pack of animals – those Windriders."

Mlinz felt anger surge inside him. But he stayed calm and reminded himself that the One was with him.

His lack of reaction seemed to incense her and Sarah's eyes narrowed. "We feel that their like were never meant to dwell in the beauty of Sky. Of course, no Wind-changed things or Pagans were either, for that matter. Only the children of the One."

"Children of who, Mother?" Mlinz found his voice as he felt a sudden strength in his anger. It was an anger that had listened to her hatred for so long and her condemnation in the name of the One – a One which she desecrated each time she opened her mouth with such prejudice. "Children of my One? Or the power you worship?" His meaning was clear. He was accusing her of following the Dark.

But it was not Sarah who reacted. It was Abraham. The man moved with a furious speed that made him seem as if possessed. He grabbed Mlinz by the front of his shirt and lifted him from his chair, shaking him so hard that he felt as though his teeth would come loose.

"Isaac never would have spoken to his parents so!"

Mlinz held himself as loosely as he could. In a moment his father stopped shaking him. Mlinz looked into his father's face, searching for answers. Something was wrong. Something was terribly wrong. Never had his father been like this. Mlinz saw pain in Abraham's eyes. Pain and something more. Remorse. Struggle? But if his father didn't want to be doing this, then why was he?

Sarah rose from her chair. She stood before her boy, beside her husband and said, "Isaac, beloved, I hear you."

Mlinz looked into her eyes and knew she was lying. Yes, Sarah heard his voice, but she did not hear his words. Suddenly, images began to take shape inside his head and he began to understand everything. His parents. His place in the family. His own fear that had made him seem a coward. His desire to try and find a balance between the impulsive, impetuous Kestrel and what he had perceived as his stoic, long-suffering parents. But he knew now that he had been wrong all this time. And so had Kestrel. She had called him a coward, but he wasn't. He was just waiting for something to crystallize inside him, something to happen that would help this chaos all make sense.

And that moment was before him now. He saw his sister and her brave defiance. He saw Mouse and felt the boy's gentle love for him. He saw Tyger.

Tyger had defended herself against Sarah's verbal onslaught from the very first day, something few save Iahala had ever dared. He saw Tyger's face, remembered the wisdom and pain in her solid eyes, remembered her gentle with Mouse, bold and brave fighting the five Users in the Genesis chamber. Tyger said what she believed. She stood up for what she felt was right and did not lie in order to make others feel better. She was used to being a leader and her word was law. She was practically a stranger to compromise. But at the same time she listened to her followers.

Tyger would never let an insult slide past her without responding to it – even if she did nothing more than acknowledge the depths to which the speaker had sunk. But Mlinz – he had been willing to overlook so much. So many slights and insults. So many hurts and false promises.

Why was he so reluctant to push away what he knew was false and embrace what he knew in his heart to be true? There was no reason. There was no reason to hide any longer. And as this became stunningly clear, Mlinz sent a silent prayer to the One, thanking the One for bringing Tyger to him.

Sarah spoke again. He looked at her as if with new eyes. "You think I do not follow the One," she said, "because you disagree with the way I see things. But your perception of what is good and what is evil has been twisted because of the time you spend with the Pagans and your... friend." Sarah's mouth twisted. She would not speak Mouse's name.

"But I have been given a vision," she continued. "The One has sent me a plan. Soon all of those who are not his children will be sent away and your understanding of right and wrong will return."

Sarah absently touched the cross that hung in the hollow of her throat. It was the symbol of suffering but also of rebirth. Mlinz thought of Mouse who had watched his entire village die. He thought of the Wing ritual he had witnessed today and knew that his mother knew nothing of either suffering or rebirth.

"The One will cleanse all of Sky for us, Isaac. The word will go out to all our followers, all over Sky, all over the world, after we have begun the cleansing here. All those who believe in the One will be His hands. And when it is complete, we will give Him thanks...."

Sarah droned on, and Mlinz was stunned. She was revealing her plan! So confident was she in his loyalty. His thoughts spun. It became clear to him that if he was to live, he had to get out of this room.

"All this time," he said suddenly, letting his body slump as if in acquiescence to her wishes. "Mother... I've been so confused."

His mother scrutinized him carefully. He held his breath for one heartbeat, his eyes dropped to the floor in a gesture of defeat. Would it work? Would she believe him? The silence lengthened. Finally, his father spoke. "Yes, Isaac," he said, his voice full of sudden hope in his son's redemption. "They blinded you."

"They blinded me!" Mlinz let his anger at his parents put the passion into his voice. "They lied to me all these years, just to make me see what they wanted me to see and nothing else!"

"Yes," his parents agreed in unison, their faces suddenly flushed with imagined victory.

"It was all for their own purposes!" Mlinz began to cry, but the tears were not for himself. They were for the family he had once known. For no matter what his parents were, they were his only parents and now he had lost them to their hatred forever. "They were using me as if I was no one – not even a person with feelings and thoughts of my own!"

"My son!" Abraham cried, and swept Mlinz up into his arms. "I always knew you would come to see the truth." He was crying now too, and seeing his father's tears and knowing what was to come made Mlinz cry harder. He allowed himself to be held, allowed himself this one moment of grief for the life he was about to leave behind.

Abraham released his son slowly and Mlinz sank back into his chair. He was beginning to feel exhausted and hoped this would all be over soon. But when he looked at his mother, he saw that she would not be so quick to embrace his sudden transformation.

From the depths of his memory, Mlinz called up the love he'd once borne her. A love both unconditional and unquestioning. He let it fill him, let it spill out like the tears which stained his face. Reaching out he cried, "Oh, Mother! You are the only one I can trust. You will show me the way."

For a moment, he could feel Sarah's hesitation, but then, she too, was fooled and she embraced her only son. As he let himself be rocked in her arms, Mlinz realized this was the first time in his life he had ever lied. It was more difficult than he had imagined it would be. And far more painful.

After a time, Mlinz drew back slightly, wiping away his tears. "I'm going to go right now and get my things from my old room!" he said. "Is it all right that I move in here with you, Mother?"

"Of course, Isaac," she said after only a moment. If she had any doubts at all, they were fading quickly. "We are your parents. We want you to be with us."

Mlinz nodded. They did love him. That much was true. But if this was their kind of love, it wasn't something he wanted. He got up slowly, pausing at the doorway. He looked back at them and smiled. Then, he slipped into the shadows just beyond the door and waited for a moment. Just around the corner of the hall, Aliqui watched him in shock. She motioned to him but he did not see her.

Just as Mlinz had expected, Sarah and Abraham began to speak as soon as they thought he was out of earshot. Aliqui would not be able to hear their lowered voices, but he could make out every word.

"I think that was wise," Abraham said so softly. "Letting him go. He would have mistrusted us had we made him stay. He will not betray us."

"No, he won't. He has the fear of damnation in him," Sarah agreed. "We've bought ourselves time. I'm sure he suspects nothing ill. And time is what we need."

There was a pause. Then Abraham's voice again. "Why haven't they returned?" His voice was raw, almost a harsh whisper. "They must know our need.... They live with it themselves."

"They know nothing, Abraham. They've lost their minds to the Drug. They are called Users for a reason, you know."

"Then we are dead," he said, his voice fearful and hollow at the same time. "Soon we shall leave this earth and stand with the One."

Mlinz heard Sarah blow out an exasperated sigh. "It amazes me, at times, how witless you are! We will not die and face the One because of the Drug!"

"Don't be a fool, Sarah. We'll die soon if we don't get more. And what if they don't return?"

"They will return." Sarah's voice was venomous.

There was a long silence. Standing in shock, Mlinz thought about the miles of corridors and the tons of rock between his parents' room and the Genesis chamber. They had no idea that the Users had come and gone. Then

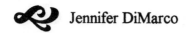

finally Abraham's voice floated out over the distance between them. It sounded plaintive, frightened. "What's happening to us, Sarah?"

"Nothing!" Her voice was steely. Mlinz could almost see her expression. Rigidly held control that never wavered.

Abraham must have begun to pace; his footfalls were nervous slaps against the stone floor. "The Users need water from the River Sky – here at the strongest source. We paid them with dozens of flasks full, and they agreed to infect Falcon with their Drug–"

"Abraham! Say no more!"

He ignored her. "But they are a crazed people. When we followed Falcon into the west tunnel to ensure she had not evaded them, the Users were still there, angry, confused, they infected us all–"

"By the Might of the One! I pray you, go no further!" There were sounds of a scuffle. Sarah called out softly in frustration. "You tell me this story again and again, even in your sleep you torture me with it! Don't you think I know it? I *was* there. Are you losing your mind so soon?!"

"Sarah." Abraham's voice was little more than a gasp beneath harsh breathing. "Please! By now, without regular doses of the Drug, even a Windborn like Falcon must surely be dead. How long can we possibly have if the Users do not return and bring us more?"

"I told them to come only to our chambers. To avoid the Genesis, lest they be spotted. I told them as long as they gave us vials of the Drug, we would supply them with Sky water!"

"But they are mad! All mad! How do we know they'll do as you say–"

"Abraham! Do not abandon the cause now! Do not turn from the One! The One needs you – I need you!"

Silence fell between them again. Mlinz heard a chair scrape against the floor and his father's voice came again, muffled this time. "I will never turn from you or the One, woman. Even as I feel the Drug churning within me, I shall not be led astray."

"The Users will come soon, Abraham. Any day now. Then we will have more than enough time to begin the Purification and to bless its beginning with holy blood." She paused. "I feel the churning too. But I believe. You must believe, Abraham. The One will guide us. No matter what this comes to... we must complete the offering. It is the Way." Sarah had no way of knowing that the Users had fallen. No way of knowing that no more Drug would ever come to Sky.

"I do believe," Abraham said. "I have faith."

"Today," she answered him, "we start it all. It's always better to chisel away at your enemy instead of throwing yourself against solid stone."

"The Purification is the only way," Abraham murmured in absent-minded agreement.

"Come," Sarah said. There were sounds of movement within the chamber. "We must catch ourselves a tiger!"

And with that, fearing he would be caught, Mlinz sprang from his hiding place and almost collided with Aliqui. He gasped, but she pulled him into the shadows, covering his mouth with her hand just as Sarah and Abraham passed by.

"Tyger," Mlinz breathed, fear gripping him. "We must find Tyger!"

Aliqui read the terror on his face. "Follow me!" And together they ran down another long hallway, hoping to reach the Windriders' chamber before the two One believers. But they did not know that only Ardyn waited there. Tyger had gone off in search of Iahala, with questions she wanted answered, and Sarah and Abraham would find Tyger first.

* * *

Tyger turned right and then left and then right again, a grin on her face. Some things could not wait. She had to ask Iahala about the Human invaders, and she had a few questions about Sarah and Abraham. After that, she wondered if she should ask for a private room. How she would explain the request she wasn't sure, but she was certain that she found Ardyn's bold sensuality refreshing. It would be a shame to let it go to waste. But whether or not they found a private space, Tyger had already decided she would not allow Ardyn to make love to her. Things simply did not work that way.

As her mind lingered on Ardyn, a vision came unexpectedly. It was not the vision of the Gold One, but a vision of flames being tossed like hair by the Wind. It was the image she had first seen when she lay by the falls and it had appeared again when she had held Ardyn close. Desire rose like fire in her blood and she felt as if she were melting into hot, rich cream. She almost turned back for the Windriders' room then, the longing touched her so deeply, but two figures stepped into the corridor before her and her desire was instantly extinguished, replaced with anger and distrust. She froze.

Sarah and Abraham smiled at her. Their expressions were tight, their skin clammy in the faint light.

"Tyger," Sarah said.

"You're calling me Tyger?" Her voice and her emerald eyes held the cool fire of pre-battle fury and the two flinched at her growl. "Not *demon*? Not *beast* or *thing*? *Freak* is usually a favorite." Tyger's hands curled at her sides, her claws not yet visible. She was calm and flippant. She did not fear them.

"We have not come to make peace with you, Windborn." Sarah snarled her words into a slur against Tyger's race as if it was evil incarnate.

"Then you've come to apologize for insulting my brother? For attacking the Wise One? For–"

"Yes! She is why we come! Not for you or your cause!" Sarah spat, silencing Tyger. "The one you call 'wise.' The one you and yours support and empower. We come for her. To show you that the Pagan way is not what it seems to be."

Tyger looked steadily at the two, letting them see her for what she really was – not a beast, but a woman with experience and intelligence. Sarah's gaze faltered, as if she had seen something she would not accept. "So, you intend to discredit them. You want to take my strength and the strength of my Windriders away from Iahala and her Pagans. You think then it will be easier then to defeat her."

Sarah's face was a mask of forced casualness. Beside her, Abraham cleared his throat, his voice almost calm as he asked, "You won't come with us willingly, then?"

"If I don't come willingly, then I don't come at all. And why would I?" Tyger put her hands on her hips. "You'd have quite a challenge ahead of you. Do you need a challenge? I believe in the magics I have seen here. No matter what you try, you will fail."

"Then the least you can do is grant us a moment of your time if even to rejoice in our failure. Just a moment, so that we might understand each other better." Sarah's voice was smooth and persuasive.

Tyger was not taken in by their pretense, but she was curious. When Sarah motioned for her to follow them, she did, wondering where Mlinz was, wondering where they would take her.

They walked deeper and deeper into the winding corridors of Sky, the corridor sloping downward, first slightly, then dramatically. Tyger noticed that the stripes of colored crystal set in the walls were more abundant, growing thicker the further down they walked. Finally, the hallway ended at a stone wall. Abraham placed his hand against the wall, and a small panel, like a chip of stone, slid aside to show a digital reader with a small speaker, not unlike one she had seen in the Patriarch's compound, though clearly more advanced.

The multi-color lines of crystal from both sides of the hallway all appeared to converge somewhere behind the reader. Tyger peered a little closer and saw that in addition to the scanner and speaker there was a key pad numbered one to one hundred and several colored lights. Abraham passed his hand beneath the scanner and Tyger saw that he wore a ring set with a bit of crystal.

The speaker spit a response back into the hallway. "Welcome, Abraham Tarahson. May the One be shining on you today. Do you wish to enter the Core?" Tyger couldn't tell if the computer's voice was meant to be male or female. Perhaps it was both.

"I do," Abraham answered.

"Will you be entering alone, Abraham Tarahson?"

Sarah answered for him. "No, computer, I'll be entering with him." Sarah passed her crystal-ringed finger under the scanner.

"Welcome, Sarah Tarahson. May the One be shining on you today. Are there any others?"

"One other," Abraham said.

"Please present Microcrys Identification."

"She has none," Sarah said haughtily.

The computer didn't respond immediately. Lights blinked and flashed as its circuits completed its thinking process. Then the voice spoke again, "Should I register this visitor as a charge of Abraham Tarahson and Sarah Tarahson?"

Sarah nodded, which looked foolish. As if suddenly remembering the computer couldn't see her, she said, "Yes, a charge. Her name is Tyger."

"Last name, please."

Sarah laughed. "Just call her Tyger of the Windriders."

The computer paused again, then, "Proper greeting?"

Sarah opened her mouth but before she could speak, Tyger stepped forward and said, "The same greeting as the Wisewoman Iahala, please."

The computer analyzed the voice and the information given. "Tyger o'th' Windriders is already a registered charge of Iahala Snoqualmie. Shall I grant Tyger o'th' Windriders Tarahson access as well?"

Sarah and Abraham spun to look at Tyger. "She's already brought you here?!" Sarah demanded.

Tyger was amused by their distress but found no reason to lie. "No, but obviously she had planned to."

Sarah and Abraham looked at each other, but then Sarah muttered, "It doesn't matter," and to the computer, "Yes. Register Tyger as ours as well."

The computer blinked a few lights. "Thank you. Welcome, Tyger o'th' Windriders. May magic and the powers that be stand with you today. Are there any others to enter the Core?"

"No," Sarah replied tightly.

The computer didn't react to her tone of voice but merely continued with, "Thank you. Welcome and enjoy."

The wall before them shimmered into silver opacity and then part of it disappeared, allowing entrance. Tyger followed Sarah and Abraham through and could not contain her shock. The entire room, floor, ceiling, all four walls, were made of colored crystal lines. It was as if the space, perhaps thirty feet square, was insulated with the skinny pipes or strings of crystals, each glowing, pulsing with light. Tyger felt as if she were standing in a box woven of colored reeds. When the door solidified behind them, only it was gray stone.

"Welcome to the Core, Tyger o'th' Windriders," Sarah said, staring at her with open victory. "Welcome to the heart of Sky's... magic." Tyger looked at Sarah in silence. Sarah raised an eyebrow at her. She waved one hand at the surrounding room. "Is this too strange for you? To stand amid all this moving color?" Sarah raised her voice, directing it into the room rather than at Tyger. "Chair, style B." Out of nowhere a chair materialized. It had a steel frame, a padded seat, back- and arm-rests. Sarah pushed it towards Tyger; it rolled forward on small wheels and Tyger stopped it before it bumped against her legs.

"I think I'd rather stand." Tyger was unable to completely remove her shock from her voice.

"Why did I know you'd say that?" Sarah teased. "Fine, then, suit yourself." She looked at Abraham, who stepped a little away from her, giving commands to the computer just under his breath. As Sarah spoke, images appeared in the air above and behind her. A corridor from Sky, the Genesis chamber, an aerial of the Valley itself as seen from high up one of the walls, different kinds of crystals, charts showing molecular breakdowns of crystals... and several other images that Tyger couldn't place, that she assumed were from other Sky bases.

"The crystal lines that run through all of Sky are hollow cylinders that carry Microcrys energy," Sarah explained. "Microcrys energy is a pure form of energy, practically alive really, that is powered in part by different chemical reactions and by the falls. The Core is the computer that controls this energy. All over the world, underground bases that are part of Sky have similar units. All of the Units are linked together so we can communicate with one another without having to travel.

"The system is really quite simple." Sarah smiled. "You should be able to understand it." She didn't see Tyger's claws sink into the back of the chair that she gripped – it certainly felt like a real thing! "Blue lines control our water system, red our heat, green the stability of Sky's construction and white is our life support. Other colors control combinations of systems or less important systems. And, of course, the crystals have natural attributes that can be adapted and harnessed. But there's no magic, just electronic pulses that tell panels and computers and mechanisms inside the walls what to do and when.

"Even the mysterious El Rods, that Aliqui and her folks fight with, even those are just small conductors of Microcrys energy."

Tyger stared up at a huge schematic of the Land of Sky. The picture showed Sky as a massive criss-crossing network of color-coded crystal lines whose encrypted messages ran the entirety of Sky. "What about the Crystal

Garden?" Tyger asked in a neutral tone. She knew the Crystal Garden was a public place open to all but she purposely did not mention the other Garden, hidden behind the walls.

"You mean here?" Sarah smirked and nodded to Abraham. He said, "Show coordinates 568H through K in transparent contour with visible Microcrys pathways."

Tyger didn't quite understand the command but the second he stopped speaking, another image appeared in the air. It was indeed the Crystal Garden, the walls and stone mounds shown light gray and transparent and Tyger could clearly see the lines of crystals that filled the insides of each mound. Green lines filled what she assumed was the Earth mound, red lines filled the fire mound, and so on. Even yellow lines filled the mounds of light crystals and stretched up to the ceiling where other light crystals "grew."

"You see, no magic," Sarah said.

Tyger looked at her. The image of the Crystal Garden showed the open space and the stone trees of the Hidden Garden as well. Sarah and Abraham must have noticed it before. Did they think it was just a room of Pagan sculptures? No lacy crystal lines reached there. "What about the Great Butterflies?"

Sarah laughed, "What of them?" Her disbelief answered Tyger's question. The Great Butterflies had truly been born of the Wind and did not represent scientific tampering.

Tyger rested both hands on the back of the chair, still intrigued by its existence. She asked her last question. "And the River Sky? Does it carry magic?"

Sarah exchanged a glance with Abraham. It was as if they had been waiting for this question. "Sky has power, yes. When so many rivers and oceans were swallowed by the End, it has survived. It spans the globe now. Somewhere, perhaps, there is an undiscovered spring that it flows from, or an ocean it is filling. It isn't known. We do know that drinking it keeps the Wind from entering our bodies, and it can be taken into the lungs like air. Some say that the End made the Sky what it is. Some say magic, some say the One. But many others say science." Sarah paused then. Her silence toyed at Tyger's nerves. She wanted these answers now! Sarah made a saddened face that was almost comical, it was so patronizing. "The River Sky has brought us almost as much bloodshed and fear as it has life, Tyger. One has to stop and wonder which is better. So much evil...."

Tyger could hear the sick humor in the woman's voice. Of course the life the River Sky gave its people was worth any trouble it brought. Without it, the Humans would all be dead. But her sadistic tone suggested that to Tyger and her kind the Sky was not worth its existence. But what had

Sky done to Tyger?

Sarah waited, hoping Tyger would ask about those evils, but the warrior only said, "Continue," her voice curt and abrupt.

Sarah frowned, clearly annoyed with Tyger's tone. She sighed loudly. "Fine." She rolled her eyes. "There is a group, a gang you might say, who inhabit some of the tunnels between Sky bases. They are called Users. They are Humans like us but addicted to a drug that has never been named; for both Pagans and One believers know that to give a name to something is to give it power. So we call it simply the Drug. Someone only has to try it once. After that, there is no stopping. The Users travel the tunnels and call no place home. When their children are born they inject the Drug as their first gift. It is said to grant the Users wonderful dreams of the Old World and that is all they want. But it also causes madness. Irrational fury." Sarah paused for a moment before she dropped the last piece of information into Tyger's lap like a stone. "The main ingredient of the Drug is water from the River Sky."

Tyger found that hard to believe. How could something that healed and protected also ravage the body? But she herself had heard the Users scream for Sky. What was the truth? She shook her head. "There will always be those who abuse magic for their own selfish proposes."

Sarah's face flushed with anger. "Abuse magic, yes, of course! There will always be the evil ones, won't there? Evil in black and silver garb?"

Tyger's hands suddenly clenched the chair so tightly she felt her claws sink past the padding and touch the hard steel; she felt her blood throb over her taut tendons. Tyger did not move or speak and Sarah stepped closer to her. "Iahala wouldn't bring you here, Tyger. Iahala won't come here. She believes that knowledge gathered through technology is wrong. So only Abraham and I know the reason there is 'evil magic' in the west tunnel. The tunnel where the River runs most fitfully and mixes with chemical compounds in the stone floor to form a kind of gel. A gel that every month is gathered by the soldiers of the Patriarchy, in their black and silver fatigues. Gathered to make into food and drink. Perhaps you thought the Patriarchy made their rations solely from the plants they brought in from the Wind? Water, even as thick as the gel might be, is needed for life. The soldiers have even learned to take Microcrys crystals from the walls to use as the cores for their laserguns. Yes, the west tunnel is their supply lace. We let them find it a long time ago.

"It is important, for reasons you needn't know, that Iahala not know of our association with the Patriarchy. It would sit badly with her 'magics.' The Patriarchy, the Silver Steel, as you call it, does not know the Land of Sky is here. They have never tried to go farther than their tunnel and the narrow-minded fools probably never will."

An image appeared in the room. It was a rough map of the world like the Patriarchy kept on their library wall. And like that library map, their were lights where each dome stood and flashing numbers listing thousands of city populations.

Sarah smiled up at the map. "Someday, when we are ready, we will contact them. And then we will conquer them. Their evil way – illicit sex, drugs, tolerance – shall fall to the ways of the One. All this will happen just as soon as they attain Number One status in the world order. And then what will happen, Tyger? Then your enemy will fall and in their place a nation of the One will rise."

And Users acted irrationally? Tyger just stared at Sarah. To tell Tyger of her plans was ridiculous, but Sarah's eyes blazed wild with righteous conviction and Tyger knew Sarah didn't care who knew their plans now. It made no difference; with the power of technology behind them, she could not be stopped. At least, that's what she thought. Sarah was absolutely convinced of the rightness of her plan and the certainty of the its success. Tyger was not surprised that it was all about power and dominance. Perhaps it always was.

Sarah's voice turned darker still. "The Silver Steel's hate for Windborn was very convenient to keeping the Land of Sky a secret. When a certain Windborn, with far too much bravery, quested into the west tunnel, she terrified a group of soldiers gathering crystals and gel. They thought she was a wandering... freak." Tyger's eyes blazed into Sarah but Sarah only shrugged. "So they slaughtered her."

Tyger's breath came fast and Sarah was suddenly laughing. "And Iahala says a dark beast killed her. Indeed! The soldiers tore her limb from limb, I'm sure, too afraid to even tell their leader. Afterwards, they built a steel wall to stop any more freaks from crossing into their territory. Of course the wall helps us as well, for now none of them will discover us before we are ready. So now we wait. Either for New Seattle to rank first in the population race or for Christopher Jarth's demise. It doesn't matter. When that time comes, we will give word to our own warriors, and the One will rule the greatest nation in the world. With no Windborn and no Pagans and no magic. It will be our own Apocalypse. Our own Revelation. The End of the End and the start of the True Beginning."

Tyger sat very still. If Sarah was telling her the truth, once more it all came back to the Patriarchy. The Silver Steel. Of course Sarah and Abraham had stood against saving the Village of Wind. The best interest of the Patriarchy was also their own, and they wanted all those who were different from themselves destroyed.

Unknowing allies as well as worst enemies, Tyger mused. She

wondered if this was what her dream had meant. The dream of the black beast descending on the silver Patriarchy. The One's followers would wait for Jarth to do all the dirty work and then they would take over and rule supreme.

If that happened, Tyger couldn't even begin to fathom what would become of New Seattle – to all the Patriarchy's domes. What would become of the Clones and, more importantly, all the Originals? Could the One Believers really conquer New Seattle? Could they defeat the steel Patriarchy? Tyger remembered the weapons of the Users – the showering bullets – and her question was answered. All Human weapons were death-weapons.

Yet out of all these questions, one fact remained. And this knowledge burned brightly within her, burned with a raging hatred. Once again, Jarth had killed her kin. Once again, his mindless soldiers had killed out of hate and fear. She could only believe Sarah's story. What reason did she have to doubt it? The Steel had killed Falcon. She allowed her fury to show on her face.

"Leave me," Tyger growled.

And they did. They left her there not because they knew, in rage, that she could kill them in a moment. Nor did they depart because they could see her claws buried into the holo-generated chair. Sarah and Abraham left with faces triumphant, their thoughts transparent as glass. They believed that they had completely discredited Iahala and turned Tyger's hate away from them and back to the Patriarchy, which would, in turn, make her departure to avenge Falcon's death a foregone conclusion. But most of all they left because, although Tyger had the strategical skills of a warrior, they still thought her incapable of the intelligence required to use the computers of the Core.

They were so wrong.

As soon as the wall had closed again, sealing her away from the One believers, Tyger sent the chair spinning across the room. She paced, tight and fast and then looked up into the empty air where Abraham's images had disappeared upon his departure.

"Core, do I have access to information stored by Sarah and Abraham Tarahson and Iahala Snoqualmie?"

The computer's androgynous voice filled the glowing room. "Yes. Tyger o'th' Windriders, as a registered charge of Abraham Tarahson and Sarah Tarahson and Iahala Snoqualmie, has complete access to all text, sound, image and program files stored within the Core."

Tyger felt like laughing out loud. "How do I access this information?"

"With proper commands."

Tyger paced. "Show me the place Iahala Snoqualmie calls Skynest."

"Skynest is registered at coordinates 910B through E. Is this the image you would like to view?"

"Sure."

"Not an acknowledged reply. Skynest is registered at coordinates 910B through E. Is this the image you would like to view?"

Tyger narrowed her eyes. "Yes."

"How should the image be displayed?"

Maybe this wasn't going to be possible. Then Tyger remembered. "Show coordinates 910B through E in transparent contour with visible Microcrys pathways."

The image appeared about three feet in front of Tyger at eye level. She studied it. No crystal line came up through the standing stones or into the young Butterflies' nests. The only crystals shown were green for structural stability.

She took a shot in the dark. "What is the current inventory in the Armory of the One?"

"At which Sky base?"

Tyger took a deep breath. "All bases."

The computer began a very long list of weapons Tyger could barely pronounce, never mind comprehend, even as it flashed various pictures of the myriad equipment of war.

When it was finally done she began asking for every map she could think of and was only partially surprised to discover that some of the map images were marked with the Patriarch's stamp of ownership. The Core was pulling information directly out of the Patriarchy's computer banks.

"Make me a copy of the map to the Underground," Tyger requested, looking closely at the mazeworks of tunnels that stretched, just as Sarah had said, from Sky all the way to New Seattle and exploded into a million pathways beneath the city.

A duplicate of the image appeared next to the first. "Copy made," said the computer.

Tyger sighed. "Create a copy of the map of the Underground that I can take with me when I leave the Core."

There was a pause and then, "Does Tyger o'th' Windriders require a hardcopy?"

"Yes."

Again, an image appeared in the air before Tyger but it took twice as long to materialize, sparkling like tiny bits of crystal coming together. When the image was finally readable, black lines on thin off-white cloth, it dropped to the ground and Tyger retrieved it.

"Thank you–" The door opened with a whirring sound and Tyger spun. "Clear images!" she barked but the computer was speaking already.

"Welcome to the Core, Aliqui Snoqualmie, Mlinz o'th' Windriders and Ardyn o'th' Windriders."

Tyger let out a breath. The door closed behind the three. "You're not easy to find," Ardyn teased, looking around the room in wonder. Mlinz stepped up to Tyger. He looked different somehow, more sure of himself. "They are no longer my parents," he declared.

She embraced him proudly and he flushed. "You gave me the courage to face the truth, Tyger."

"It was within you all along, Mlinz," she responded gently. Then she turned to Aliqui. "How did you find me?"

"We heard Sarah and Abraham gloating. I was stunned they left you alone here." Aliqui's eyes scanned the images that were still floating in the air. "I think they'd be stunned too."

"Let's share what we know," Mlinz offered and he told Tyger everything he'd heard his parents say. He lowered his voice when he shared that Falcon may have been infected with the Drug. He could feel Aliqui's pain like fire that burned beside him and when he looked at her, her eyes would not meet his. Mlinz looked at Tyger, telling her with his gaze how bad Drug infection could be. How by now, Falcon would be losing her self-control, her judgment, herself.

Tyger showed them her maps and spoke of Sarah and Abraham's ultimate plan, then, carefully, she looked at Aliqui. "Whether or not Falcon was infected with the Drug may be a moot point. Sarah and Abraham claim that they saw her killed by Patriarchy soldiers." Tyger paused. "It makes sense."

Aliqui just gazed at Tyger. She had nothing to say.

Mlinz was nodding his head. "They want to cleanse their kingdom before taking over another. I think I could continue to pretend to go along with them. To find out everything – when, where, how, what."

Tyger disagreed. "I'm afraid for you now, Mlinz. I'm not certain they will protect even you. And if they discovered your pretense?"

"But there's so much we still don't know. Even with you registered as their charge here in the Core, you won't be able to access everything, Tyger. And there are sure to be things they don't even record," he insisted.

"Let him go," Aliqui offered, "I'll keep close to him. Tamarin and Fox can spell me. One of us will sleep, one will watch Mlinz, one will watch Mouse. They'll never be alone."

Tyger was still skeptical, but she finally agreed. "One condition, Mlinz. If you feel it's getting too dangerous, call out to Aliqui, or get out of there. Take refuge with the Windriders for good."

"Agreed," Mlinz said. He beamed at her and she knew she'd done the right thing. Mlinz took off his Microcrys Identification pendant and showed Tyger how to use it to enter the Core as his guest or to open doors around Sky. "You must not leave, Tyger. Going after Jarth is exactly what they want. With you absent from Sky, we'll be hard pressed to stand against them. It would take days for other Pagan allies to arrive and you frighten them. We need that right now."

Tyger squeezed his shoulder. "I have to go after Jarth, Mlinz, but I can promise that I won't leave Sky until I know you're safe. Not until all my questions have been answered."

The four of them left the Core together. They walked together for a while and then Aliqui and Mlinz took one corridor and Ardyn and Tyger took another. Winding their way back to the Windriders' chamber, they walked in silence. At one point Ardyn slipped her hand into Tyger's but Tyger barely noticed, her mind was so full of spinning thoughts.

She knew what she had to do. After sorting through all the new information she'd gathered in the past few hours, she had to create a plan that would result in the failure of the One believer's plan. Then, she would find, in herself, the difference between her own past of murder and betrayal and the murderous actions of the Patriarch's soldiers. They had both completed tasks in the name of Christopher Jarth. She needed to justify killing Jarth's soldiers while allowing herself to live. Because, for taking Falcon's life, she would kill them.

When all her mental sorting was done, she would go to Iahala for the other side of this tale. What was magic and what role did Microcrys play in it?

But she had to act quickly. For soon her fury at Jarth would boil over and she would revisit the faces of all her dead kindred – of her sister whom she loved most of all – using their deaths as the fuel that would make her rage burn higher and higher. When that happened, Tyger o'th' Windriders would do just as Sarah wanted. She would let her fury consume her. She would leave the Land of Sky, cross the distance that separated her from Jarth, and, without a second thought, she would tear him limb from limb.

* * *

Part Four

"Nobody wants a warrior with a conscience," Spider teased Wolf. They were flying steadily west towards what Petre knew was the closest of the slave sites that lay between the Valley and New Seattle.

There was little air turbulence today and flying was smooth enough for conversation. Without any Great Stones nearby, the Wind was almost silent as it carried them along in a tight cluster. And because they were a group of many differing views, they had made their way into a debate. A debate which Spider continued by saying, "People want a hero who craves action. One who jumps in with both feet and claws her way out! Not someone who stops, waits, looks around, thinks about the ramifications of it all and then–"

"Heroes die fast," Kestrel called over. "They're gone quickly because they don't think, and they go mad because they become just like those they kill."

Spider snorted. "You would take his side, Kestrel."

Wolf smiled and Kestrel winked at him. It was apparent to everyone that they made a good team – Wolf and Kestrel most of all. Kestrel liked Wolf's intensity, and Wolf was beginning to like just about everything that had to do with Kestrel.

"Tyger has a conscience," Jyln noted. "And she's still a powerful warrior."

"Don't anybody knock Tyger or I'll bust your Wing over your clogged up head!" Tryl shouted, half-seriously.

Spider laughed at her. "I didn't mean like Tyger, you protector-extraordinaire! She's been a warrior too long not to have a conscience, but she can still raise hell. Great Wind, it was good seeing her fight again. Makes your blood boil!"

Tryl let out a whoop of approval, throwing her Wing into a sharp, playful dip.

A little ahead of the rest of the Flyers, Petre flew his orange and black Monarch in silence. He could just hear the others. He thought about their words and decided that no matter what, people always wanted to cheer for the flawless beast. A hero with no emotions and a sharp, quick weapon. Tyger was neither flawless nor all beast, but she was close enough to both that everyone loved her.

Tylon, on the other hand, was a different story....

Petre smiled at the memory of Tylon's face. It swam before him in such loving detail that Petre almost felt Tylon's presence. Tylon, Petre knew, would never be a warrior, nor would people follow and love him for his marvelous strength, but it didn't matter to Petre. Petre loved him despite everything – despite Tylon's reservations, despite Tylon's conflicted feelings. Petre loved him truly, deeply. Just the fact that he could love

Jennifer DiMarco

210

someone so unconditionally – requited or unrequited – was a gift that some never received and he felt lucky to have it.

Petre's thoughts drifted as he watched the gold-white sand passing below them. The sun was very bright after so many days in the Land of Sky, and it was nice to feel its warmth again. Here and there he saw a giant cactus boasting huge flowers. But as he looked more closely at the landscape below, Petre saw something strange. Something that didn't belong. He shifted his weight and hovered, peering down at what looked like a huge mesh screen that had slid back to uncover a deep hole in the ground. Its design was unfamiliar to him. It was not Wind-made or Patriarchy-made. He called out, "Kestrel?" She answered with a scream.

Bullets thundered randomly down at them, speeding out of the glare of the sun. Six women on gliders carrying semi-automatic machine guns flew straight at them.

"It's the Flock!" Kestrel shouted. Petre noted she was bleeding in several places. "Their guns aren't very efficient – lucky for us!" She was shaking trickles of blood from her eyes.

"How do we fight them?" Petre asked her.

Kestrel shook her head. "We don't!"

"They'll just come after us again, won't they?" Petre's thoughts were racing. "We have to knock them from the sky!"

Kestrel just looked at him for a heartbeat and then, "All right. Let's try it!"

With a sharp movement Kestrel dove, flipping her Wing upside-down. When she righted herself, she had completely changed direction and was racing after the enemy team that had swooped past them. Maneuvering on the slightest stream of Wind, Wings were far more agile than gliders had ever been. The others copied Kestrel's move and followed after her.

"They came from that hole?" Petre shouted.

"Yes," she acknowledged. Kestrel drew her El Rod, motioning for the others to do the same. She squinted at the quickly retreating Flock as they pushed to catch up. "It's a special ventilation screen for the Land of Sky that draws air in without sucking up sand. It also filters the Wind. There aren't too many ways to get above-land from Sky and the Flock knew they wouldn't be welcome to use the Valley. They must have opened the vent to get out."

"Where the fuck do they get their weapons?" Spider and Tryl barked at the same time. Everyone was nursing small wounds from the erratic firing.

"Old World," Kestrel answered. "Iahala says that long before the Years of Glory and before the Closing when nations sealed their borders everyone had them."

They were close now, riding almost right on top of the Flock. More bullets shot upward, but none found their mark. The Flock's members were at a disadvantage – they had to turn awkwardly to shoot and they had not expected pursuit. Kestrel maneuvered the Flyers into the Flock's blind spot.

"What are they?" Jyln asked peering down. The sails of the Flock's Wings appeared to be painted gold-white like the sand, blending the Wings into the landscape. But where the paint had peeled or the sails were torn, it was clear that the Wings had once been brightly colored like their own.

"They're Users," Kestrel said, clenching her teeth and waiting for the Wind to be right. "Humans who are addicted to the Drug. It was Users you killed at the Genesis chamber, a Sky Squad. The Flock is a User Cell Squad." Petre could guess what Kestrel meant for he knew of cells, one kind at least, and they were as deadly as Kestrel's voice suggested. The Dome Cells. The Eaters. But what could these Humans want with the River Sky and Cells? What bizarre concoction was that?

"Those Wings?" Wolf began.

Kestrel glanced over at him. "They got them by killing Flyers."

Then the Wind changed. Kestrel dove and they followed her lead. They came in fast. Had Tyger been there, she would have been able to see Kestrel's El Rod blazing red as the woman soared low over one of the Flock glider and severed the left wing cable. The cable snapped in two with a sharp *twang* and Kestrel pulled Swallowtail up with all her strength, flipping upside down so the Flock could not easily take aim on her from below. She shot away on the Wind. In her haste to break clear of the Flock's formation, she did not see the crippled glider drop from the sky, carrying its rider down with it, nor did she recognize that the felled Wing had once been Falcon's.

Wolf growled and began his attack run. With his El Rod, he struck the antenna on one Flock glider. The crystal pole that controlled the glider's top cables cracked in half and the glider plummeted to the earth. He pulled Metalmark upward, following Kestrel. A handfull of bullets exploded through one corner of his left sail, but Metalmark only shuddered and raced away.

Spider and Tryl dove in unison; Jyln was just a Wing length ahead of them, already slashing at a glider below her. Tryl swung her El Rod's blue whip down and made a clean slash, taking off a half of a Flock glider's sail. Spider sliced through the center line of another glider with her red sword beam, and both women spun away from the bullets and curses that followed.

The last of the Flock flipped her glider over to face the last of the Flyers, these Wing-riders from Sky, the ex-soldier named Petre. Without hesitation, he struck and shattered her bottom antenna before the woman had even completed her turn.

Crystal shards flew into the Wind as the entire control bar triangle fell free from the demolished post that had secured it to the glider. The flyer dangled by her back harness for a moment before the glider stalled and went down. Just before she was out of reach, she threw her catch-hook with its attached safety line. The steel hook buried into one edge of the Monarch's sail, and the Wing dipped violently.

Petre's El Rod flew from his hand. The woman's hook tore the sail off his glider as it seated itself, the User dangling, dragging behind him in the Wind. She began to jerk the line, jolting Petre's glider and then catching it off-balance. Monarch began to spiral downward. Petre grabbed for his Windboard that was bound to his crossbar. He missed and reached for it again. His hand found its familiar shape and he ripped it free, leaping from the Wing and onto the board. A moment later the Wing crashed with the sound of breaking crystal and breaking bones.

Petre landed off-balance on the Windboard. He fell to his knees but managed to stay on. Riding low and fast he caught up with the other six. For a moment, they stared at each other – and at Petre in particular – in silence. Then Jyln began to shout high and joyous sounds of victory. Tryl, then Spider, then Wolf and Kestrel joined her. It was their first battle as a team. And if any of them had had any doubts before, they doubted no longer. Petre deserved to be their leader.

* * *

 Part Five

It was night when she appeared in New Seattle and the dome wall never moved. She let in no Wind and set off no alarm. She penetrated the unpenetratable city. In the place called the Central District, the streets were silent, empty and devoid of light. She was the dark, so she moved as the dark. She had forgotten what light truly was; it had become as faint a dream as love or goodness. But the blackness here was not the same. The void of the Underground had been far beyond this deep shade of the midnight streets; it had been like walking through nothingness. Like walking through Hell.

She paused before a silver steel wall twenty feet high. She knew that fifty paces on the other side was the service entrance for the patrolmen of the Patriarchy. She looked at the spikes atop the wall, knew they were twelve inches high, saw the Patriarchy's lazy cameras photographing the night. It was exactly as she'd seen it in the Core. Exactly as she knew it would be. Except that somehow, those hovering images in the Core had seemed more real. Larger than life, exciting in their newness. Now the tall silver wall was just there. An obstacle between her and her destiny.

She vaulted over the wall during the split second when one camera scanned right and the other scanned left. One hand slipped between two spikes and as she pushed off, one of the laces on her black leather vest snagged and snapped. She touched the ground twenty feet down on the other side and cursed herself for a long moment, her emotions raging, her senses churning. How could she have been so foolish?! She had practiced that vault a million times in the Core and had she ever broken a lacing? No. Until now she had made the leap perfectly. How could she have let this happen? She looked up and she knew. It had been that first sight of the Tower as she came over the wall. A momentary pause as she registered her final destination. And so, in imperfection, she had left behind a record of her passage. So be it. For there was nothing to be done about it now.

The sight of the Tower utterly mesmerized her. Unlike the wall, it was much more awe-inspiring in real life. Solid steel, a structure without windows until the top floor. And then it was as if the designers had decided to make up for all the windows they hadn't installed by encasing the entire top floor in glass. One man's office. A solitary place from which to view this world. And below that glass-encased vantage point, located on the floor below, was the private residence of Christopher Jarth, leader of all the Patriarchy, born in the year 0255 AE, killed 0296 AE. Today.

She walked through the court yard of the Patriarchy, past the red lumi-lights that swept back and forth but never touched her. New Seattle housed no one like her, but once it had. She had not come from the Wind, but she was of the Wind. She had been too long in the dark to think of herself by name, too long with the maddening, unexplainable churning

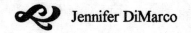

within her skull, but she was someone. Someone indeed.

She was the bringer of death to Christopher Jarth.

Her name was Falcon.

* * *

Christopher Jarth had just heard good news when the alarm went off. It was an alarm he had never heard in all his years as ruler, except in his nightmares.

The Patriarchy was under attack.

Jarth staggered once when he heard it, falling against the glass window behind his desk. The banner of the Patriarchy swayed above his head, and he knew it as a bad sign. He stood beside his chair for a moment, envisioning hoards of Windborn pouring into the city, waving their clawed hands and screaming, led, of course, by Tyger, fiercest of them all.

Jarth's mind turned from the terrible fantasy back to the present reality. He believed there had been a mistake. He pulled out his desk chair and sat down, pulling his computer console toward him as if it could reassure him that his place in the world was safe. Rubbing his fingers across his forehead, he cursed the headache that had dogged him for days. He hadn't been able to get rid of it and the siren's wail was making it worse.

He checked the essentials first. There had been no opening in the dome wall, and even if there had been a malfunction there, all the freaks had been slaughtered when he had destroyed the Village of Wind.

He checked the population readings at the slave sites. Nothing had changed. None had escaped or died, so it couldn't be the P3M. That left only the possibility of the Originals rising up. He laughed at that. They were surely so weak from hunger they wouldn't even be able to get off their pelts, let alone scale his walls! The P3M at least had stores of extra food; the Originals wouldn't last much longer. Jarth knew that soon he would have to restock the ration bins lest his population status become endangered, but he was still a little bit too angry to give the order.

Gathering his strength, his taut face bearing a tight frown, he pushed the button on the intercom. "Wenright! What the hell is going on down there? Did you fools blow a circuit?"

Wenright, Jarth's lead scientist, had recently been made a Colonel. Today, Jarth had promoted him to second-in-command when Wenright had brought the news that the Skins definitely worked. Jarth grinned helplessly just thinking of it. Oh, life was bright for the Patriarchy! However, the steady scream of the klaxons wasn't helping his damned headache. And where the hell was Wenright?

Wenright answered after a moment and Jarth's blood went cold. The scientist was breathing heavily. "General, this is... no mistake! Someone has entered the building... by destroying the identification scanners. Every soldier on the grounds is trying to find the intruder... so far all we have is a trail of broken scanners."

Jarth felt all the blood rush from his face. It was one person then. One. He remembered. He could see her as clearly as if she stood before him now. Running straight at him. His soldiers grabbing her at the last moment. Her claws sinking into the steel top of his desk. Jarth touched the eight long gouges. *Dead*, he thought, *we are all dead.* Once again his mind wandered and he tore it back. What was wrong with him? He blamed his damned headache and jabbed at the intercom.

"Pull in the patrolmen, damn it! This is no game here! If we have an intruder I want the bastard caught!" It must be an Original, Jarth screamed at himself. The dome hadn't opened to allow the Tiger in. But what Original would be stupid enough to come into the Patriarchy? How had it even gotten this far? He had cameras mounted on the twenty-foot, spiked walls, for god's sake. The cameras. He swung to his computer again. Nothing. Every camera was operable.

"Yes, Sir, General. I'm going to send you a squad of men."

"What are you talking about, Wenright?!" Jarth barked.

The answer came hesitantly. "The trail of the intruder is leading to you, General. Whoever it is has already reached the tenth floor of the Tower."

Jarth's blood ran cold. The Tiger was coming to collect her dues. "Damn you, Wenright!" Jarth growled. "Sart never would have let this happen." He could almost see the scientist shrivel on the other end of the connection. But it was true. Sart had always been at Jarth's side. He would have never let something evil come this far into the silver steel of Jarth's kingdom.

"But, General, you wanted me to stay here in the lab, to work on the new Skins, to finish the–"

"Don't give me excuses. You're a Colonel now as well as a scientist! Start proving it! Get your ass up here. Now!" Jarth cut the connection with such force that he actually disconnected the line from the jack in his desk. But he wouldn't realize that until it was too late. He was breathing erratically, his small fearful eyes darting around the room.

He turned suddenly and straightened his banner, smoothing out the black cloth with the Patriarchy's symbol: the halved circle with the words, *Allegiance Divided*, above it and their dome number, 342, below. Of all the banners in all his offices in each one of his many domes, he loved this one the best. His first. He would have thought that this was the banner he would want to be buried with, but he never thought about death that way. It was treason. The Patriarchy was nothing without him.

Jarth looked out over the Industrial District. It was *their* time now. The Originals. Night was their time. Which of them had the bravery – no, the idiocy – to attack him? He had no doubt it would be one of Tyger's so-called gang. An ally perhaps, or a one-time lover. Either way, it didn't matter. He would kill the intruder. And he would enjoy doing it.

Up until this morning, population had been the most important thing to Christopher Jarth because it resulted in power, security, and pride. But now Jarth had new plans. Wonderful plans.

Every soldier born to the Patriarchy was fitted at birth with a biological statistics monitor chip. This tiny implant, set close to the heart, could report the health of a soldier anywhere within a Patriarchy dome or Hovercraft. Wenright had amplified the reader to scan out into the Wind one hundred miles in every direction and he had received a reading from Sergeant Petre Tarrl's bio-stat chip. A very alive Sergeant Tarrl. Tarrl alive meant the Skin suit had worked. Jarth knew there was no possible way someone could exist encased in a Skin for very long. Clearly Tarrl had taken it off but was still living. Wenright was looking into the ramifications of that. Wenright believed that long term exposure to the alien substance of the Skin might actually affect the body permanently. If that was so, many new doors had just opened for Christopher Jarth.

Jarth would encase hundreds of his soldiers in Skins and send them out into the Wind to build domes, thus eliminating his need for P3M slaves. The soldiers would then feed Original males to the Cells of each new dome and breed with the Original females. Population would drop for a while but soon it would more than triple. Soldiers would work harder than slaves ever did because his soldiers were loyal as dogs. And by offering them an opportunity to choose a mate? Well, that just about guaranteed that the new domes would go up faster than Jarth could decide where to put them.

Jarth grinned. Within his domed cities where Originals and Clones were separated, the union between a soldier and an Original would be declared a disgusting taboo at best, lead to an all out revolution at worse. But who would know what type of twisted games went on out in the Wind at the building sites? The rules were different in the Wind. Jarth had calculated that in less than a year his nation would be ranked the most powerful in the world. The Patriarchy would rule supreme and all other nations across the globe would have no choice then but to recognized his greatness. "And there's nothing you can do about it," he said to the darkness of the city, but he meant his words to travel far beyond New Seattle. Far out into the Wind. "Poor Tyger," he crooned. "There is nothing you can do." And then he laughed.

Behind Jarth, the elevator opened, and he turned. "It's about time, Wenright–"

She leapt from the elevator's box and touched the ground only once before she reached him. Jarth screamed. It had claws and fangs and it was Windborn.

Her hands closed around his neck and her knee slammed up into his ribs. He struggled against his attacker and against the excruciating pain.

Falcon loosed her choke-hold on his neck and he wrenched away from her. Her fist, meant for his face, crashed through the supposedly shatterproof glass behind them. She screamed in frustration, her arm torn and bleeding. The pain only enraged her further and she threw him aside.

Jarth hit the glass wall and slid down. He gasped for breath through his bruised throat, focused his eyes on the Windborn. She was like stone or steel. Unlike Tyger, she had no soft curves, no gentle features. She was all angles and plains, sharp and harsh.

Falcon turned on him. Stood facing him for a moment. Her arm dripped blood onto the silver floor and in the red lumi-light, Jarth saw that her eyes, like everything else about her, were black and silver. She was the colors of his Patriarchy. Jarth looked away.

She fell upon him then, hauled him up by his hair. As she slammed him against the wall, the glass shook behind him, and Jarth suddenly knew how very far a fall fifty stories would be.

"Look at me," she growled, an inch off his face. Her voice was deep and raspy from lack of use. He tried not to look but found himself unable to resist the power of her eyes. "I am Falcon of the Village of Wind. Child of Hawk and Robin, sister of Mouse... and Tyger."

Jarth's eyes widened.

She smiled, pure malice, revealing sharp teeth. "That's right, Christopher Jarth." She pronounced his name with the same thick accent Tyger had had when she had first come to him. "Look at me and see your death."

He looked. She was as tall as he, black hair streaked with silver that fell in a dark wave to her waist. It was thick, like fur. Her features were sharp, knifelike. Even her eyebrows and the shape of her eyes were severe. Her skin tone matched Tyger's and they also shared a preference for that same stance: feet apart, braced, knees almost imperceivably bent. Falcon's shoulders were broad and corded with muscle. It was clear from her strength and her anger that she had not spent the last six years since the Village fell in destitute wandering.

Her clothes – breeches, boots, vest – all black leather with silver studs, terrified Jarth, who thought it cruelly ironic that his death would come dressed in his own colors. His colors made hers.

And as his gaze traveled the length of Falcon's body, Jarth saw the pendant that hung about her neck, resting against her breast bone. The delicate butterfly with wings of swirling purple and blue. So much like the Industrial District's lumi-lights. Looking closer, Jarth realized that this butterfly was not the delicate creature portrayed in the history vids, but something else entirely. The butterfly's wings were lined in a bright silver that could slice through the Wind and strip flesh from bones when it passed.

Jarth had seen it before... and then he remembered.

The child Tyger had worn it on the day he took her. It had fallen into the sand as she struggled with his soldiers. She'd looked at it with such longing. There had actually been tears in her eyes. He had laughed at her.

But he wasn't laughing now. Before he could stop himself he blurted, "My god, you really are her sister."

She hit him. Her claws tore through his cheek and he crumpled to the floor, blood seeping over the fingers he pressed to his mauled face. Falcon kicked him in the head with her booted foot. Hard, but not too hard. This would be long and bloody, just like the deaths of her people who had thrashed in agony, bubbling at the mouth, within Jarth's electrical net.

She reached down and lifted his one hundred-eighty pound frame with ease and threw him against his desk. He crashed against the steel, rolled over the top and, reaching for something to stop his fall, tore his banner from the wall. Lying on the floor between the wall and the desk, Jarth knew that if he didn't act fact, he wouldn't be able to act at all. Reaching for the laser at his belt, he steeled himself for another attack. He was leader of the Patriarchy, and he would not be killed by a freak!

But Falcon reached him before his hand had even touched his holster and yanked him upright. She held the front of his shirt with one hand, the hand that seemed little more than shredded skin, shredded muscles and veins on bone. She spat in his face. "This is for everything you did to my people." She cocked her fist and release it, shattering his nose. "This is for the nightmares you gave to the survivors." Her claws tore his other cheek.

"This is for all the changed-ones you made your slaves, who cry in the night when no one can see them." She knocked out three teeth and then paused. There was no skin left unbloodied on his face. But he was still with her; he was still conscious. She had to be careful. None of her wounds thus far would kill him. "But know, Christopher Jarth, leader of this thing called the Patriarchy, that I do not come to kill you because of any of them. I give you this pain for them, but your death will come as retribution for another."

Jarth looked at her through the blood in his eyes. His blonde beard was a sticky red. He struggled to speak around the missing teeth. "Who?"

"For the child you took before the nets fell. The one child who meant so much to my people, whose disappearance you knew would gather all of us together in grief. All the Windborn together where you could drop your death from the skies. For the woman-child, who, after your killing was done, must have suffered and died by your hands." She reached down and crushed both of his hands in her undamaged fist. He screamed as bones cracked and broke. He screamed but he heard the words she spoke. "I kill you for my sister. For Tyger!" She pulled back his head to expose his soft neck. Tears mingled with the blood on her face. Her lips peeled back from her sharp Windborn teeth. She would rip his throat out. "For Tyger," she said again, but softly, as though Tyger's spirit might hear her, wherever it may be.

But she froze when she heard a voice behind her. "Tyger lives."

Jarth watched Falcon's eyes flash with unexpected confusion. She hesitated. The elevator doors had opened and four soldiers had entered the room followed by a scrawny man in a long silver lab coat. The soldiers leveled their lasers at Falcon. She let Jarth drop to the floor, turning to face the new-comers as Jarth moved away from her with the last of his strength.

"I tell you truth," the man in the lab coat said. "Your sister is alive."

Falcon glared at him. "If you lie and I have postponed my rightful kill for you, old man, you will fall right after your leader does."

Beneath his white hair, the dark eyes of Jay Oppenheimer Wenright were fearful. He looked down at his leader, crumpled on the floor and covered in blood. When he spoke again, his voice trembled slightly. "It is no lie. Tyger lives. She has escaped New Seattle and returned to the Wind."

Falcon's black eyes bore into Wenright's. From his vantage point on the floor, Jarth could tell she was weighing this new information and hope surged through him. He struggled to his feet, wiping at the blood flowing from his mouth with the back of his hand, wincing at the pain, wondering how many bones in that hand were broken. He spat onto the floor. "But we can find her again," he said, gambling, guessing, hoping.

Falcon turned to face Jarth. Her face was expressionless and it was clear to him that she was still prepared to kill him if he did not provide her with some concrete proof. And quickly.

Jarth staggered to his desk. He made his right hand work despite the pain, lifted the torn banner from the floor. He placed it carefully on his desk and sank into the chair. He felt suddenly light-headed and fought to stay conscious. He looked at Falcon, standing no more than five feet from him. "She came to *us*, Falcon. The Patriarchy does not go looking for children."

Falcon's eyes narrowed and he knew he had hooked his fish. But he must proceed cautiously. He'd been able to lie to Tyger because some part of her had wanted to believe that what he'd said was true – that her people had still lived. Falcon was different. He knew she would kill him if he lied to her. If she realized his words were lies. "We found your village and thought to destroy it," Jarth said, measuring each word. "But your sister begged us to spare her. She said she would do anything we asked."

"She wanted you to spare her? Her, above all the others?"

Jarth nodded and regretted it instantly when his vision darkened suddenly. He took a deep breath and willed himself to concentrate. "So we took her and slaughtered your village. She wanted to be spared. We can always use... workers. There was nothing for her out there. She had no other life to go back to. She had left them." Jarth almost smiled. Everything he was saying was true. It was only part of the larger truth. But Falcon could not have known that. He wiped absently at the blood on his face, the pain in his hands jolting him. "She could tell the Wind's Phases, we couldn't. The Fever, the Dreams and the Change. She told us those. She told us everything about the Wind. And she helped us solve our greatest problem.

"New Seattle needed to expand, but Clones cannot live in the Wind. So Tyger agreed to help us. In the Industrial District, we have a breed called the–"

Falcon sneered at him. "I know how your city works, Jarth. And I am not interested in your dreams of grandeur. Tell me what I want to hear or I will kill you now."

One of the guards moved, but before he could fire his weapon, Falcon crossed the distance between them and with a swift spinning kick, sent the soldier crashing to the floor. She wrenched the weapon out of his hand. "Do not insult me with weapons that only stun!" She pointed the laser weapon at the other soldiers. She shot one. He fell, unconscious. The other two stood still as stone. Falcon put the barrel of the captured laser against Wenright's head. Then she swung the barrel toward Jarth. "We have wasted enough time, Christopher Jarth."

Jarth's vision blurred. He swallowed past the lump in his throat. Then he said, "She took gangs of Originals out into the Wind for us. Those who died, died. Those who lived became our slaves."

There was a long, deadly silence. Falcon knew of the P3M. She knew someone had to have brought them into the Wind during the right Phase to be changed. Finally Falcon spoke. "She did this so she could live?"

"She did whatever I asked."

Falcon stared at him. "I have thought I would be the avenger for a dead child. The child you used to fell my village. I thought surely you knew who she was to us. Our only green-eyed child. But of course you could not know. You were, you are, ignorant."

Then Falcon's expression changed. It was as if her swirling thoughts overpowered her. Rage flooded her features. She looked suddenly, totally, terrifying and, Jarth thought, not totally sane. The churning in her skull exploded behind her eyes like spinning blue fire. "I cannot believe Tyger sold herself to you. I cannot believe she lived when we were all to die!" Falcon was almost screaming now and for a split-second Jarth thought his ploy had failed. But as she continued to rage, he realized that she did believe him. Her rage was not for him. It was for Tyger. "She lived to be a murderer, that she might be spared? Stealing life from Originals as you stole life from my people!" Falcon's voice rose to a shrill cry, piercing and painful. Then she fell into abrupt stillness and her expression became thoughtful. Still holding the laser pointed at Jarth's chest, she added, "That does not sound like my sister."

Silence again. Jarth felt cold and he knew he could be close to passing out. When Falcon spoke, her voice sounded very far away. "I did not know her as well as I thought," she said. Her eyes met his and he saw that she was again calm. "I believe you, Christopher Jarth. You are an evil man, but I believe you in this. I always knew my sister would grow up to become an extreme. Every Windborn knew this. But no one guessed she would take the path that would betray us." She paused again. She stared down the nose of the laser at him. "Hear me in this, Clone. Unlike Tyger, I will not be controlled by you. And if I discover you have lied, I will tear off your head and eat your black heart."

Jarth could not stop the rampant shivers that swelled through his body. He managed, slowly, "I have not lied to you, Falcon of the Village of Wind."

Falcon lowered the laser. "You say she has escaped to the Wind. Took the life you gave her – living when she should have died – and it wasn't enough. I can see you feel betrayed by her. But nothing she could have done to you will ever make amends for what you did to the Windborn. Do you understand that?"

He nodded cautiously.

"Have you suffered for what you did to my people, Christopher Jarth?"

The leader of the Patriarchy met Falcon's eyes. "I have," he said.

"You will suffer more," she said, flashing a lunatic smile. "But not today. First, she must die."

Jarth closed his eyes. He had never imagined this confrontation. Had never imaged this outcome. A surge of adrenaline shot through him at the thought of what would come next. Falcon could bring down what a squadron of soldiers could not. She could catch the Tiger. He knew this and he loved her for it.

"How do I find her, Christopher Jarth?"

"I had planned to send two under-cover soldiers into the Industrial District where they would find Originals who knew the Tiger and discover where she went."

Falcon laughed at him. "Send Clones into the Industrial District? Are you stupid as well as foul?"

Jarth choked back his anger. "They would be disguised." He motioned and the two soldiers that remained conscious came forward. They were identical. From their belts they took intricate masks of black leather –

each strange, haunting and different. When they put them on, they appeared less similar on the whole.

Falcon was not impressed. "I wasn't talking about a disguise, great leader of the Patriarchy. I was talking about endurance. But that aside, you know as well as I do that the Originals can barely feed themselves right now. They will not welcome two additional mouths."

Jarth stared silently up at her. How did she know so much?! "I will return their support, and I'm sure my two Sergeants can handle–"

Falcon spun and threw herself at the two men. Her claws tore through one man's uniform shirt and the other's cap. She turned even as she struck and delivered one kick and then another. They tried to block her onslaught, but it was hopeless. She slipped easily inside their defenses. Both were still standing, however, and she stopped short of felling them.

"They might do," she admitted. Jarth noted that she was not winded. "Give them to me. I assume no Originals know that Tyger worked for you. They all just adore her, I'm sure. The brave, bold Windborn." She spit. "I'm sure they love her as much as you despise her."

"She ruled," he said simply.

"She was born for it." After a pause, Falcon continued, "No Original who was loyal to her will ever tell a stranger where she has gone. But kindred? One of like blood?" Falcon squinted her eyes. "That will work."

Jarth nodded. She was right. He figured she often was.

Her tone became factual. "I will need attention." She raised her arm and gave him a smirk. "And so will you. You look half-dead." She laughed at him. He failed to find her joke amusing and gave her a tight-lipped smile. A few minutes more, he told himself. Only a few minutes more. "Have the two soldiers dressed like me. We should look like we wear like gang colors. We leave tonight. Have you any other gifts?"

Jarth motioned to Wenright. The scientist looked at Jarth, perhaps considering how much longer Jarth would stay conscious, the he took a package wrapped in soft cloth from his coat and handed it to Falcon. Falcon slid the cloth away, pulling the slick black laser from its holster. Jarth was pleased that Wenright had brought it. He said, "It fires explosive bullets filled with Cells. Made from the core of the Tiger's own weapon. Fitting, yes?"

"Eaten from the inside out," Falcon murmured, "like you have done to me, dear sister." She attached the holster to her belt. Crossing to Jarth's desk, she leaned over the scarred metal and met his eyes squarely. The butterfly pendent between her breasts swayed as if in flight. "Know, Christopher Jarth, that I do not work for you. This death is for my people. I will use you as you used her, and I will kill her, have no doubt. After that, I

disappear. If you ever get in my way or anger me again, I will kill you
without hesitation." She paused and smiled. Jarth knew he would never get
used to her icy grin. "When I am done with her, is there anything you
want?"

"I want her dead, nothing more."

But Falcon pressed him. "Are you sure?"

Jarth knew she would not ask again. He took a deep breath. He
dreamed. "Her head," he said. "I want the head of the Tiger to mount on my
wall."

Falcon looked at him for a long time and then smiled again. This
time there was even more ice in her gaze. "The Wind gives and it takes
away, Christopher Jarth, but I think her head is something it will give you."

With that she turned on her heel and left. Just before he slipped
from consciousness, Jarth found himself wondering what the Wind would
take away.

* * *

"Have I told you lately how incredible you are?" Joanna whispered into Ravyn's ear.

Ravyn smiled and buried her face in her lover's hair. "Yes, but you can tell me again." They lay alone in their private room, one of only two rooms that were closed off from the Spiders' large open space. The pelts were soft on their bare skin and they were quietly dozing off to sleep.

"You're incredible." Joanna murmured against the nape of Ravyn's neck and kissed her. It was the first time in a long while that they had gotten in bed before dawn, and it wasn't very far from that. It felt wonderful to have a few extra minutes alone, time to just–

"Ravyn! Joanna!" Byn burst into the room, Howl bouncing beside her. By the light of the lumi-lantern, the child's eyes were full of excitement. "The Patriarchy is filling up the ration bins! All of them! Right to the top! Terri wants us all to go down right away! Everyone's getting ready now."

Ravyn and Joanna exchanged glances. Why was the Patriarch reinstating his support?

Byn dropped down between them, shaking them. "Don't you understand? This means that Tyger's back! She's come back and the Patriarch isn't mad anymore, so the soldiers are bringing us food!"

The two women sat up slowly. Ravyn reached out and took the child's hands. Joanna gazed gently at the girl as Ravyn spoke. "Byn, the Patriarchy could be celebrating because they've killed her." Byn opened her mouth but no words came out. Ravyn continued slowly, "But if she has come back, that means this last escape was no different than all the times before. The other Windriders will be slaves and Tyger will be coming back for more."

"Ravyn," Byn gasped, "You don't believe that, do you?"

Ravyn squeezed her hands. "Don't misunderstand me, Byn. I love Tyger. She was our leader. Much more to you than that. But I need you to promise me that if she has come back, without the other Windriders, you'll stay here with me, with the Spiders."

Byn sat frozen for a long moment. Then she bowed her head and cried as they both held her. "I promise," she said through tears. "I promise."

* * *

Terri was the first of the Spiders to land near the Marion Street ration bin. They called them ration bins but they held much more than food; they also stocked clothes, weapons, ammunition and raw materials including leather and metal. Some of the larger, more prominent gangs had their own bins. The Wheels, who hadn't been seen on the streets in weeks, had one and the Spiders had one. Even the new gangs knew the pecking order. She didn't expect there would be any trouble.

"All right." Terri started pointing as Spiders dropped down from

Threads all around her. "Curn, Darja, Jamie, you three go on up and start tossing things down to us." The three young men nodded, starting to climb the story-high bin.

"Terri, don't be sexist," Belle teased.

Terri smiled at her, the first smile she had mustered in many days. "Go on up with them, Belle. Joanna, I want a guard hanging from those shadows."

Using her Thread, Belle climbed the bin to catch up with her lovers, and Joanna met Terri's eyes. Terri was still smiling but there was a caution in her green gaze. Terri saw the question forming on Joanna lips – why did they need a guard now? – but she raised a hand to forestall it. "Don't question me, Jo, just trust me."

Joanna nodded. She shot her Thread, pulling her body into the shadows just to the left of the group. She had a clear view of the street. Watching her, Terri realized Joanna was irked by her command. That was what Joanna had hated about Tyger's followers. No questions, just trust.

The four bin-climbers let out a shout at the treasures they found once inside. A moment later, items began to arc out of the steel box to be caught by the waiting Spiders, or bounce off the ground. There were leathers – breeches, boots, jackets – bolts of cloth, scrap metal for Threads, and lots of food and flasks of drink. The Spiders gathered up as much as they possibly could, stuffing back-packs, pouches and filling arms. Then they swung away, back to homebase where it would all be divided and life would be good again.

As the crowd of Spiders thinned, Byn approached Terri. She watched her for a time, watched the way her eyes darted at every sound, watched the way her body was tense, almost quivering. There was something in the air. Something not right. Byn could feel it and she looked to Terri for confirmation. "Terri," Byn asked softly, "is she back?"

Surprised by Byn's question, Terri looked at the little girl. She knelt down beside her – just the way Tyger had done – and saw the tears start in Byn's eyes. She searched Byn's face for a moment before she said gently, "Of everyone who would know, Byn, it would be you."

Byn nodded. "That's what I thought you'd say. But you also feel her here, like I do." Byn reached out and touched Terri's heart.

The leader took a deep breath. She looked away for a moment before she could meet Byn's eyes again. Terri's auburn hair blew in the Currents. It was almost daybreak. "No, Byn," she said finally, "I don't think she's back."

"Do you think she ever will?" Byn was almost whispering.

Terri thought about Tyger's last letter. *I will never return.* Never, ever. "I hope so," she whispered.

"That ration bin was so full...! Why, I haven't been in something that full since Belle's pelt last night!"

Belle elbowed Curn where he stood beside her. He just laughed. Most of the Spiders had already gone home; the only ones left were Terri, the four bin-climbers, Ravyn and Byn, and Joanna, who was still up on watch.

Terri shook her head. "Something has made the Patriarch very happy and I don't know if I want to know what it is."

"Well, I don't care." Curn bit into a mashed ball of sweets. "I'm a simple man and I don't look at gifts too closely. We've got food and more. That's what counts."

"I'll agree with that 'simple man,' part," Belle commented. Darja and Jamie laughed. "We're going to head back, Terri, all right?"

Terri didn't answer right away. Then she turned to them as if she hadn't heard. "What? Right, yes. Go on ahead. We'll catch up."

Belle exchanged looks with Ravyn, who shrugged, agreeing that Terri seemed elsewhere. "We'll be along soon," Ravyn said, her eyes saying what her voice did not – she'd keep an eye on Terri.

"Well, come along then, my boys," Belle wriggled her eyebrows at Curn, Darja and Jamie as her Thread shot out. "Time we go celebrate!" In a moment more the four were gone.

The sun was rising outside the dome and the Currents had stopped. The Industrial District's lumi-lights blinked off and across the city in Central the Clones' day was just beginning.

Terri stared down the same street that Joanna was watching from above. Her eyes narrowed in the brightening light. It was time to go home, but still Terri did not move.

"Terri?" Ravyn reached out and put a hand on her shoulder. "What–" Her eyes tried to find what Terri was so intent upon.

Before she could make the discovery, Joanna landed among them and pointed. Her voice was tight. "There. Near the shadows. Two men. They're wearing masks over their faces and they're," she paused and looked at Terri, then at Byn and Ravyn. "wearing black and silver. They don't look armed, there's just something about them." Joanna paused, searching for an explanation. "They move with identical rhythm."

"Something's wrong," Terri growled, watching as the two figures moved out into the light, openly making their approach. There was a feeling or scent in the air that she could not place.

"Yes, much is wrong. Tyger of the Windriders has left the city, and I have been trying for six long years to find her."

She appeared as if from nowhere, her strong, tall body walking before the two men. They were all dressed alike, in black leather with silver studs – breeches, boots and vests with no shirts. The men's faces were hidden by animal-like masks. From the woman's throat, a butterfly pedant caught and reflected the first light of day. Her left arm was wrapped in thick leather from wrist to elbow, hiding the cast beneath. She smiled at them, but it was not a smile of kindness or greeting. Her smile was cold. "My name is Falcon of the Village of Wind. Some call me the Butterfly." She stopped just before them, standing boldly. Her stance was neither friendly nor threatening. It was unreadable. She extended her right hand toward the Spiders.

Terri looked into the black-silver eyes, the solid Windborn eyes, and she knew instantly that Falcon was Tyger's sister. Falcon's eyes had the same multitude of secrets, the same depth. Not the same secrets, though, Terri realized, for Tyger's secrets were like shadows and Falcon's burned like flames.

Terri did not take Falcon's hand even though part of her wanted to. "I am Terri, leader of the Spiders. Allies of the Windriders. You speak the truth. You have come too late for Tyger."

Falcon looked at Terri, caught her eyes like wild things and held them. There was something in Terri's voice that seemed to intrigue her, something about the way she said Tyger's name. It was as though Falcon could read everything inside her head and her heart. Falcon's excitement at that moment was real enough and her eyes flashed. "You... knew... her, then? We were just ready to give up! We've been searching the city for someone who knew her."

"You mean you've searched the Industrial District?" Joanna's face was hard. Her anger carefully held in check. She did not trust this stranger. Her champions were strange, her voice insincere.

Falcon waited a beat before she answered Joanna, as if scrutinizing Joanna, and when she did answer her voice was low and slightly menacing. "No, I mean the entire city. I searched the Central District as well. Even the Patriarch's compound. I didn't know where Tyger might be and I have come so far."

"From the Village of Wind?" Ravyn asked.

Falcon turned to Ravyn, her mouth open to speak. But when she looked into Ravyn's eyes, and then into Byn's, her expression changed from bravado to curiosity. "How is it," her voice demanded an answer, "that your eyes have seen the Wind?"

If Ravyn was surprised by the question, Falcon could not have read it on her face. She answered simply, "We were Windriders. We went out with Tyger. She spoke of you. Of Falcon, her younger sister. She thought you were dead." Ravyn paused, her voice tinged with suspicion she could not help. "How is it that you've been searching for her? How did you survive the massacre of your village?"

"How do you know about that?" Falcon's eyes narrowed. When Ravyn didn't reply, she shrugged and added as if it were of no consequence, "I was one of the children rescued by... friends.

"Duke, Liege and I," she continued, motioning to the men behind her with an absent wave of her hand. "We came into the city by secret means. I have known for some time that Tyger was taken by the Patriarchy. I saw her stolen." Falcon's hand touched the butterfly.

Byn pointed at the pendant. "She told us about that too. The pendant. She said she lost it in the sand. It meant a lot to her."

Falcon nodded carefully. And Terri, watching her, knew there was more to this story than she was letting on. There was something special about that pendant. It had been intended for Tyger, but now Falcon had it. That meant something, she was sure of it. But what?

It was Byn who asked what they all were wondering. "Why do you wear the colors of the Steel?"

"They are the colors of power," Duke answered.

"Silence!" Falcon hissed, shooting the man a raw glance full of fury. She looked back at Byn, the residue of her anger still on her face; the girl took a stumbling step away from her, reaching for Ravyn's hand. "Forgive me." Falcon took a deep, slow breath. "You have seen through their disguises, no doubt." The two men gave startled grunts.

"They're soldiers, aren't they?" Joanna demanded.

Falcon shook her head. "No, but they are Clones." The men fidgeted, looking at each other. Falcon looked back at them again, and they fell still. "They are Clones from another nation, not so powerful as the Patriarchy. I found them abandoned in the Wind. They follow my word now." Falcon looked directly at Joanna, pinning her, daring her to argue. "I would never bring the Patriarchy into the Industrial District. You should know that."

Joanna did not respond. Falcon's story did not settle their fears and suspicions of her power and her strange champions. Joanna, Ravyn and Byn continued to watch her warily. She was like a wild thing, like chaos.

Falcon pretended to appear insulted as she looked from face to face. "What have I done?" she asked with mock tenderness.

Joanna stepped instinctively between Falcon and Ravyn and Byn, not afraid to let her distrust show on her face. "Terri, I think we should–" Joanna looked at her leader and could say no more.

Terri was staring at Falcon. Her thoughts were racing. Ravyn and Byn had tasted the Wind and had lived with Tyger for many years. They knew the power of a Windborn and what it felt like. But Terri had loved

Tyger, had held her in her arms, felt her passion. She possessed their insights and something more. She could look into Windborn eyes and tell whether the soul was at peace or in flames. She saw flames in Falcon's eyes.

But she also saw her body. So like Tyger in form and attitude and mannerism. So much like Tyger had been when Terri had first met her. If Falcon was truly Tyger's sister, how much malice could she possibly hold? Could there be such a thing as an evil Windborn? Before Terri could convince herself that there was good and evil in any breed, she found Falcon looking at her. Terri swore she saw tears in the solid eyes.

"You understand, don't you, Terri?" Falcon took a step towards her, slowly, carefully. "I just want to find her. Tyger's everything to me. Surely you understand that?" Her black eyes, streaked with silver, were beseeching.

Terri was holding her breath. There was nothing wrong with anything that Falcon had said. She had searched the Patriarchy, for Wind's sake, trying to find her long-lost sister! But there *was* something wrong here. Terri could feel the others' eyes on her. Their uneasiness was palpable. Yes, there was something about Falcon that was not quite right... but she had traveled so far, seen her people die, and there was so much Falcon could offer them.

It was as if Falcon could read Terri's thoughts on her face. Terri's indecision, her mind screaming at her to get away, her heart willing to risk everything for the possibility that Falcon might be able to find Tyger. And if Terri could help Falcon find her, then Terri would make Falcon take her to Tyger. Terri would be with Tyger again.

Blinded by this desire, Terri did not see the smirk that played about Falcon's lips as she appraised Terri's long auburn hair and athletic body. A body that held skill and power. A body with green eyes. Falcon knew that Terri would give her what she needed or Falcon would indeed take her... though not to Tyger. Terri didn't see the arrogance in Falcon's expression, the plan that was already forming in Falcon's mind – how one Windborn might look so much like another when the candlelight fell in just the right way... how secrets can be shared, or stolen, under the guise of passion. By the time Falcon uttered, "Terri, please help me." Terri had already made up her mind.

"Come." Terri forced herself not to fall into Falcon's gaze. "We'll go back to Spider homebase. Today we'll feast on what the Patriarchy has given us. Then we'll sleep. When night falls again, we will talk about Tyger."

Terri turned away to ready her Windboard, missing the impatience that flashed through Falcon's eyes. When she turned back, Falcon simply grinned in acquiescence.

Below Terri's feet, the Windboard's engine sputtered in the morning stillness and rose up off the ground. Falcon stepped up, pressing her body against Terri's back, wrapping her arms around the Original's hips.

"I hope it isn't far," she said in a voice that implied the opposite. Terri took a shaky breath and urged the board away.

Left behind, the three other Spiders stood silently, watching the two masked Clones. Duke spoke. "Falcon gets angry if we aren't near."

"I bet she does," Joanna snorted.

"Is it true you got into the Patriarch's compound?" Ravyn asked.

Duke took a deep breath, his eyes angry behind his leather mask. "It was not as easy as she made it seem."

Joanna and Ravyn exchanged glances. Joanna glanced after Terri and Falcon. "Let's get going." Byn took Ravyn's Thread and Ravyn took Byn's Windboard. The two parents did not want their daughter carrying one of these men. Joanna held onto Liege awkwardly and Ravyn had Duke sit. And then the five were moving through the streets, trying to out-race the day.

But Duke and Liege, Sergeant Maurer and Sergeant Hayes, did not mind the light, nor did they mind playing subordinate. For Jarth had taken them aside before they went out, taken them where Falcon could not hear, and given them gifts she would not see. Gifts that shot bullets of death. His command stayed sharp in their minds for his words were law and made everything else worth while.

"After the Tiger falls, crush Falcon," Jarth had said. "I want you to crush the Butterfly."

* * *

Part Six

"I'll be right back," Mlinz said brightly. He waved to his parents as he left their room to get their breakfasts.

"Don't forget to get yourself something, Isaac," his mother called tenderly.

"Oh, I won't," he added, then ran down the hall. He only had a little time or his parents would become suspicious. Mlinz ducked into Windriders' chamber and searched the darkness.

"Mouse?" he whispered. A light went on in answer. The other young man sat up from his new pelt, wiping his eyes.

"Mlinz? Is that you?" Mouse's sleepy voice was full of such hope the Mlinz ran to him instead of answering. He sank down beside his partner.

"I miss sleeping next to you," Mouse said softly.

"I miss you too. I miss you so much, love."

They fell silent then, savoring their stolen time together.

Across the room, hidden by the shadows, Tylon watched them. He could feel their love for each other like a presence in the room. He realized, suddenly, sharply, that he had been wrong to let Petre go. What difference did gender really make? Wasn't love, love?

* * *

Back in their room, a room they hardly ever left now, Sarah and Abraham sat at their table and looked at each other in silence. They had tried to get Tyger to leave. It hadn't worked. They blamed Iahala. She still had too much power. They must strike at her directly. At her heart.

But even with their plans spinning around them and their son playing into their hands, when they spoke, it was of something else entirely.

"I checked the Genesis chamber. Nothing," Abraham rasped.

Sarah nodded. "It was a long shot at best, that the veil might have dropped, gone unnoticed."

"When Isaac spoke of the battle, of the murders..." Abraham shuddered. "No User will come here now. They'll settle for River water from one of the streams, even though it isn't as pure as the Falls. They'll never come to us. Deliver to us...."

"We'll just have to try to stay in control. Stay on the Path." Sarah spoke tightly, fidgeting. The churning within her was growing.

Abraham looked fearful but agreed. "We will follow the Word of the One. How long do you think we have until we–?"

Sarah cut him off. "We'll have to strike hard."

Abraham nodded, took a deep, shaky breath. "Soon, then."

Sarah sneered. "Yes, it will have to be soon."

Outside their chamber, in the darkness of the hall, Aliqui listened, catching bits and pieces of their conversation, beginning to understand.

* * *

Standing in the Valley grass, Tyger looked at the folded Wing with some disbelief. It was so delicate looking, but she had to go out. She had to feel the Wind, and the Rescue Squad had taken all the Windboards. With a sigh, she checked to make sure that the crystal El Rod was hanging from her belt. Finding it secure, Tyger hefted the glider across her back, sliding her arms through the carrying straps. Carefully, she began to climb the Valley wall.

If Kestrel had been there, riding the air up, Tyger would have beaten her to the ledge by a heartbeat. Tyger unfolded and fit the glider together, just like Kestrel had shown her, and soon the twenty-foot Wing, the color of flame striped with black, with wide emerald eyes at the sail tips, was ready to fly.

"All right, Daggerwing." She slid into the front harness. "Let's see what you can do." A strong current of air dove down over the Wing and rider, and Tyger ran towards the edge, pushed out, then pulled back on the crossbar, and flew.

The leader of the Windriders, who was born of the Wind, rode as if she had always had wings. She soared through the Valley, dipping near the falls, gliding over the hole into Skynest, and then rising up at the Valley's end and turning with the breeze. She was one with her Wing and knew every movement it made and every message it sent her.

But the Valley was not what she desired. Not what she needed. So Tyger caught the currents and rose out into the Wind.

There had never before been a time when Tyger had cried at the beauty she saw around her, but now she did. Out of the green, Old World Valley she rose, feeling once more in touch with her soul. She was a child of the Wind. Her short hair blew back from her shoulders, and she shook her head and let it dance, laughing out loud because it felt so good.

She dipped the Wing low, and then lower, until the gold-white sand was close enough to touch. It rolled in soft waves, glistening with shining mica. There was a cactus close by. Its purple flowers had deep red centers. Tyger swooped over them, catching the rich, sweet fragrance. Everything was so different here. Felt so right.

Tyger's blood pounded, sang in her veins as her senses opened like the cactus flowers below her, like exotic children that could be found nowhere but in the Wind. She pulled up and felt the Wind's force, the sheer, clean power that was both her birthright and kindred. She caught a twisting current of the air and found herself flying with her back to the ground, her eyes on the glorious sky, the limitless expanse of bronze streaked with silver that had shades of every color imaginable hiding everywhere.

Tyger turned Daggerwing to the right and rode a fast current upward. She had thought that riding a Windboard was the closest she could get to the Wind itself, but this Wing, these wings made of shining cloth and transparent crystal, were so close to the natural ability to fly that Tyger thought that birds had not died with the Old World – they had simply been replaced with Butterflies and Wings.

The Wind was silent. But Tyger wanted sound, so she caught a swift current through the dancing air, closed her eyes and let her body take her where it would. She was Windborn and needed the Wind to live. Too many years in the domes had taught her that, and too many days underground and in green, lush grass had much the same effect – though the environment was certainly different. Her thoughts had become dulled and she'd felt the tension within her rising.

The Wind and her blood bore her steadily east though she was not aware of the direction. When she opened her eyes again, she understood why the Wind had brought her here. The Stone Forest lay before her with its groves of Great Stones that surrounded the site where her village had once stood. Where she had been a child. Where the Windriders had come, and where Sarya was buried. But Tyger did not go on to her empty village site or Sarya's grave. She stopped at the outskirts of the Forest, for she had all that she wanted right here.

She landed Daggerwing in the sand and stepped up to the nearest Great Stone. She placed her hands and her cheek against the blue, Wind-smoothed surfaced and whispered, "Great Stone, you who were once a tree, you who have seen the End and lived to give me this warmth, we are both children of the Wind. We are kin."

Tyger's words became part of the song, for the Wind was full now, passing through each great monument, playing each one like a marvelous instrument. The song was deep, mighty and gentle and Tyger felt as though it was welcoming her home. Finally home.

She moved then, and as the Wind sang through the stones, she wove a dance both beautiful and deadly, just like the brilliant but venomous Tiger flower that was her namesake. She leapt in a dance of battle, moving with the Wind on her side against a world of obstacles.

She drew her El Rod. One moment she was spinning with each kick, snapping with life at each feigned blow and then the crystal sprang to life and there was a beam of fire in her hand. A part of her, it grew brighter as she leapt with sharp slices and cuts, moving the blade as its element commanded. She twirled the blade, and it became white as the sand – a blade made from the element Air, quick and all-encompassing.

Next the El Rod turned blue, like her E.C. had once been. Now it was the power of Water, and Tyger's steps reflected the element. They moved forward and struck forward, for water never went backwards, only onward, over obstacles, over enemies. Finally, the blade shone green and

Tyger wielded Earth power. Her movements were low to the ground as if she were part of the earth itself. She felt as if the Earth below her were praising her in her display.

Though Tyger was deeply focused on the dance, she was aware that she was being observed. Ardyn, watching from a hollow near the top of the high blue Stone that Tyger had lain against and whispered to, praised Tyger's dance in silent respect. Her deep brown eyes watched the dance and saw the warrior who could never be only a woman and loved her still. Loved her like soulkindred, loved her because they were so very different, but still so much alike.

Ardyn watched Tyger's shortened mane swirl, watched her muscles move across strong shoulders, bare back and arms. The dark breasts, nipples small in the blowing Wind. The tight stomach, wide hips and powerful legs that delivered kick after kick with the balanced control of an artist. But Ardyn found her thoughts wandering and knew that she could watch no more. She had come here with an unnamed longing. Now that feeling had a name. And so she leapt down from her perch on the Great Stone and landed softly in the sand beside the dancing warrior.

Tyger's El Rod dropped to the ground as Ardyn came into her arms. Their lips met. To Tyger Ardyn felt like fire racing along her skin everywhere their bodies touched. Memories tugged at Tyger once more, building like swirling flames but when Ardyn's tongue touched her own, the flames became desire and nothing more.

They climbed to the top of the blue Great Stone and lay down together upon the soft blanket stretched there. The blanket had been a gift from Iahala, given to Ardyn at dawn that morning as Ardyn had prepared for her hike. The blanket was woven with colors and symbols. It told the story of their lives. Their legend.

Ardyn reached for Tyger and touched her face and Tyger bent and kissed her. Her hands went to Ardyn's tee-shirt and Tyger brought it over Ardyn's head. Tyger bent over her again, her hair falling about her shoulders as her lips met soft, warm, chestnut skin and her tongue traced Ardyn's collar bone and the nape of her neck.

Ardyn's breath came quickly, her voice shaking as she tried to say Tyger's name. She finally gave up and laced her hands in Tyger's hair, held Tyger's head against her breast as Tyger's tongue gently encircled her nipple.

Tyger unbuttoned and pushed away the woman's jeans, taking Ardyn's hips in her hands for a moment, feeling her tremble beneath her. Tyger brought her mouth back to Ardyn's, her eyes closed and her head filled with fire that was taking no form but need. Ardyn's hands went to Tyger's breeches but Tyger pressed her tongue between Ardyn's lips and a groan rose up in Ardyn's throat. Her hands fell to Tyger's back, pressing all of Tyger down upon her.

Their hair fell together and Tyger's mind flashed with a fragment of memory that she couldn't completely catch. Her claws sank into the blanket, touching the stone beneath. She closed her eyes, made herself calm. She kissed Ardyn's cheeks and her neck, nuzzling against her ear and listening to her breathing – uneven gasps that mixed with her own slow, deep breaths. Tyger took the small softness of Ardyn's ear between her teeth and nibbled gently like a small animal, or rather like a large but careful one, her hair falling over Ardyn's smile.

"Tyger," Ardyn's voice was soft with desire. "I won't break."

Tyger opened her eyes. She liked the strength in Ardyn's gaze, the breathless wanting, and again her mind's flames danced higher, her body tensing, burning where their skin met. As she lifted her hand from the blanket to touch Ardyn tentatively, Tyger's eyes never strayed from the other woman's face. Ardyn shivered. Tyger kissed her, then drew back to gaze again into Ardyn's eyes. Slowly Tyger drew her hand down Ardyn's shoulder and over her breast, found the nipple taut and continued downward. Over her stomach, fingertips tracing the curve of her hip and then lingering against the tender skin on the inside of Ardyn's thigh, leaving trails of fire on already hot skin.

Closing her eyes, Tyger willed her claws to completely retract, willed them to allow her to do this. To touch this beautiful woman.

"I want you," Ardyn whispered. Tyger opened her eyes. She slid one arm behind Ardyn's head, drew Ardyn against her. Ardyn reached back, took the hand that was resting on her shoulder, held it as tightly as she could. Tyger's claws disappeared.

"Ardyn," Tyger said just because she wanted to hear her name, and then her fingertips, soft fingertips, were in small, soft curls and Ardyn trembled in Tyger's arms and did not stop. Their eyes locked. Deep brown with deepest green, and there was nothing in either gaze that said beast or warrior. Only woman.

Tyger moved her hand, pressing just enough to make Ardyn's breath catch in her throat. Tyger saw something in Ardyn's expression, sheer surprise, breathless delight, and asked tenderly, "First time?"

Ardyn nodded, for there was nothing else to do. She had lain with Sarya, touched her, but the lovemaking had not been mutual. Because Sarya had never touched Tyger, she was unused to such sharing and so Ardyn had given. What she had received in return was not physical, but something deeper, something far more that had touched her soul, that would stay in her heart forever. It was there now. Very much alive.

But when she answered Tyger's question, all of her was focused solely on Tyger's body, the fire just beneath Tyger's hand, and her words were truth. "I'm glad it's with you."

Tyger kissed her again and this time when her tongue pressed between Ardyn's lips, her buried fingers moved as well, sliding down to become encased in warm wetness. In their kiss, Ardyn cried out, and Tyger drew away just enough for Ardyn to call her name when, gently, inside her, Tyger began to move.

Ardyn's eyes closed, and her lips parted in soundless discovery. All she knew was the tender rhythm of Tyger's hand, Tyger's warm breath against her ear. Then suddenly she knew something more. Tyger was whispering. Whispering slowly, as slowly as her caress, in time with their ragged breathing, what she was doing. Tyger murmured that it was her fingers inside Ardyn, her mouth that kissed Ardyn here and here, her tongue that.... And Ardyn was thankful for that solid anchor to reality, because the feelings were so strong, physically stronger than anything she'd ever felt before and she needed to know she was with Tyger. Strong Tyger who was always gentle in matters of love.

Then Tyger began to ask soft questions. Barely whispers. Could Ardyn feel this? Could Ardyn hold Tyger's fingers tighter? And the answer to both was barely a nod. Ardyn moaned as Tyger touched deep within her, sending a chorus of pleasure through Ardyn's body. And she did hold Tyger's fingers tighter. The fingers of both hands, those within her body and those without. The last question was softer still and Tyger's voice was silken and selfless in its desire to please. "Will you tell me what you want, Ardyn?"

Ardyn opened her eyes. There was warmth in Tyger's gaze that was utterly new. Tyger's face was calm, and there was a light sheen of sweat on her dark skin. Tyger moved again within her. Ardyn's eyes half closed; she made a small sound in the back of her throat. Tyger touched her lips to Ardyn's, very softly and when she drew away Ardyn whispered, "Deeper."

Tyger pressed slowly, carefully. Ardyn's hips rose to meet Tyger's hand. The Wind blew over both of them. Ardyn's eyes fluttered closed, then suddenly opened wide as Tyger created a new sensation that was like rippling fire. With the soft tip of her thumb, Tyger pressed down gently against the taut bud of nerves even as her hand continued to move within. Ardyn's breath came faster, matching Tyger's, and then suddenly she cried out as the Wind's song crested and soared and crested again through out her body.

Ardyn lay very still in Tyger arms. Lulled by the rhythm of the moment, Ardyn's eyes closed. Tyger thought the woman might sleep, but after a while, when Tyger shifted, Ardyn's deep brown eyes opened and fixed Tyger with a penetrating gaze.

But Tyger's thoughts had moved suddenly far from that place and deep into the past. She couldn't see how visible the longing was on her own face. But Ardyn could.

"I want you." This time when the words were uttered against the silken skin of Tyger's ear, they meant something different. Ardyn's voice was edged was a different kind of desire, a deep tone that brought Tyger's half-closed eyes open, revealing completely the flames of her need.

Tyger opened her mouth to refuse, to tell Ardyn that she didn't know what it was she longed for. That it was buried too deeply. But Ardyn's mouth covered hers; her tongue stroked Tyger's own. She pushed Tyger onto her back. Ardyn looked into Tyger's eyes and saw the unnamed desire. Then she kissed Tyger's eyes closed.

"Just let it happen," Ardyn whispered. "Just let me bring you there."

Dancing across her mind's eye Tyger watched images, memories that matched the fire of Ardyn's touch on her skin. She saw the lumi-lights of the Industrial District – purple and blue – casting shadows and colors into the night; the Currents blowing hard. She felt herself riding a Windboard – the old kind – before Ravyn's modifications. She remembered a battle, bright and sharp, her first battle against the Wheels. She saw people celebrating, the first Windriders, and Tyger was flooded with the feeling of being alien, unwanted....

Ardyn slid along Tyger's body, touching her with her mouth as she lowered herself between Tyger's thighs. She unbuckled Tyger's belt, slid her breeches off, slipped everything away until the Windborn lay bare and alive. Ardyn gazed at Tyger for a long moment, drinking in Tyger's exotic beauty with her gaze. The striped thick hair, the rich, dark skin, the incredible strength so like the Wind.

Tyger could feel Ardyn's hands on her thighs, even as memories continued to wash over her. She saw her old quarters at the Windrider's homebase, saw herself undressing, heard a voice so smooth and warm it could have been a caress. The flames of desire that had all but consumed her wove past and present together, making them one. In Tyger's mind, the flames became a woman. In her memory, Tyger turned to look at her. But she couldn't. She felt a wave of shame and thought suddenly that she was undeserving of these pleasures. But before she could move away from either her memories or Ardyn's touch on her skin, Tyger felt Ardyn's soft hair brush over her thighs and then Ardyn found Tyger with her mouth.

The flames took Tyger, consumed her, and at first she did not know who she cried out to, who she desired and dreamed of each time Ardyn touched her. And then, all at once, she knew. Tyger knew her name, her scent, her voice, and why Tyger had been able to risk everyone but her. And as this knowledge washed over her, she buried her hands in Ardyn's hair, feeling each sweet stroke, each deep caress.

Ardyn pressed deeper, drank rich wine. Tyger's legs shook and Ardyn touched them with soft hands, marveling at the changing tastes and textures of the woman beneath her. Tyger's hands covered Ardyn's. Then Tyger fell suddenly to shudders, her body uncoiling brilliantly. Tyger cried out a name. But it wasn't Ardyn's.

Ardyn moved slowly, repositioning her body against Tyger's. She held the Windborn until the shudders subsided and Tyger's eyes opened slowly. Ardyn smiled, stroking Tyger's short mane. She had wanted Tyger today and no one else, but she had come here with her own heart-secrets as well.

* * *

They were eight in number. One for each of the four directions and the four elements. A perfect balance. Iahala, Aliqui, Mouse, Mlinz, Tylon, Fox, Tamarin and the flock of baby Butterflies. The Windriders wore new cloths, Sky clothes, soft and patterned with swirling colors. They stood in a circle, among the standing stones of Skynest, gathered together to call a spirit. The babies flitted about their shoulders and hair.

"Let us cast the Circle," Iahala said.

Aliqui began. She walked to the center of the circle, raising her arms above her head and turning her eyes skyward. "Great Powers, hear us. Sun, Moon, Time and Earth. Four forces grant us strength. Earth, Water, Air and Fire. We come together in your name." She melded back into the circle.

Mouse took her place at center. He faced the east first and turned toward each separate direction as he spoke the name of each. "Mighty East, place of birth; Mighty South, place of strength; Mighty West, place of endings; Mighty North, place of protection, be here with us and stand as guardians for our task. We come together in your name." Mouse stepped back, becoming part of the circle again.

Mlinz came forward. It was his first time in a magical Circle. Precious time stolen away from his parents. Mlinz believed that the One had made all the great powers and so he did not hesitate to play his part. He went to the east first, raising his hands together, palms facing out. He traced the symbol of magic, the pentagram, in the air and sang his words. "I bring Light and Song to the East, to cleanse our Circle." Mlinz turned clockwise toward the South and continued in this manner until he had completed his rotation.

Tylon went next. Beginning in the east, he used a slim burning candle to light four larger ones set in nooks in the standing stones, each one marking one of the four directions. As he lit the first candle he said, "I bring Light and Fire to the East, to illuminate our Circle." He moved to the next, until he faced north and all the red and white candles blazed.

Tamarin went after him, a waving censer of incense in his hand. It smelled like New World and Old World flowers and herbs. Tamarin moved to the east, his waist-length hair, braided into a soft rope and tied with a ribbon of swirling colors, swinging gently behind him. "I bring Light and Air to the East to give breath to our Circle." Like the others, he greeted each direction, bringing breath into the ritual.

Fox followed him. She looked beautiful in a long skirt and full blouse made from brightly colored Sky cloth. She carried a wooden bowl of dark loam. "I bring Light and Earth to the East to give strength to our Circle." She placed a bit of soil at the base of each burning candle and moved on.

The Butterflies were next. One by one they dipped into the bowl of water Iahala held and, beginning in the east, fluttered their wings and sprinkled the water all the way round the circle. When they were finished, the entire company chanted together, "I bring Light and Water to give blood to our Circle."

The Butterflies settled back into hair and onto shoulders. Iahala put the bowl aside and drew a sword from the sheath at her belt. The silver-colored blade was very sharp and the weapon itself was perhaps three feet long. It had a black leather grip, gold-colored hilt and pommel. It was truly a beautiful thing and the power it emitted when drawn seemed bright enough to see by.

Carrying it with the point down, almost touching the stone floor, Iahala went to the east and began to trace the border of a circle from candle to candle. The border she drew was shimmering gold and completely visible. "I bring Light and Power to our Circle and give it life."

Then together they said, "Blessed be our Circle of Light. It is born. So mote it be."

Their hands joined and their eyes closed, they reached out to the spirit who had called the Wisewoman. They needed to make things right with it. Needed to find this lost spirit. Perhaps then the Great Butterflies would become calm. Perhaps then some mysteries would be answered.

They had called for so long without response that Iahala wondered if they should stop. Some part of her mind knew she would soon need to send Mlinz and Aliqui to see if Sarah and Abraham had left the Core. But just as she was about to break the trance-summoning, a gust of wind rose in Skynest and the Gold One landed alone at the heart of their Circle.

Iahala had suspected this. "Gold One," she asked as the others stared. "You have taken in the spirit that sang to me?"

The Gold One looked at Iahala. Its blue eyes were no longer as large as they had been and were growing lighter about the edges. Its face was more oval than round; its body no longer as straight and simple as a butterfly's. Its middle pair of legs were completely gone.

"Yes." It spoke in a voice both feminine and powerful.

A shocked silence followed. Everyone waited for Iahala to speak. Finally she asked, "Which one of you shall take control of the body?"

The Gold One smiled. Its slim black mouth was softening. "Share."

Iahala took a deep breath. To share, to compromise. It had never been done before. There was no way to know what the end result would be. Iahala knew there was nothing they could do but wait and see. What part would this creature play in the legend? "For whom do you sing, Gold One?"

But the Gold One did not answer with words. Instead, it rose up and out of Skynest.

Iahala was prepared for this. Without wasting a moment, she motioned to Mouse. The circle was broken as Mouse, Aliqui, Tamarin and Tylon ran toward Mouse's Wing. They carried the glider into the circle of stones, the Gold One's magical wind still strong in the room. Mouse kicked his legs into the back harness. The three lifted the small glider and the boy, tossing them both up into the air. The Wing, named Blue, caught the currents of Skynest, drawing him up into the Valley, and soon Mouse was soaring after the Great Butterfly.

Iahala watched him go. Before the day was over at least this mystery would be solved.

* * *

"I'm so glad I'm a woman." Tyger smiled as she lay against a rise at the top of the Great Stone, one knee raised and an arm draped across it. She closed her eyes and tilted her head back, letting the sun warm her naked body.

"I don't know how I ever thought you were something else." Ardyn said, kissing her lightly. Tyger opened her eyes as the other woman sank down next to her. Ardyn had donned her pants and tee-shirt, leaving her sneakers and jacket in the pile of Tyger's clothes.

Tyger smiled, snapping her teeth, then showing her claws. "Yeah, how could you have thought that? Me a beast? I only threw my partner around and swung an E.C. with a vengeance."

Ardyn looked away. Tyger, knowing she'd said something wrong, tried to make light of it. She drew a hand along Ardyn's tee-shirt. "Cold?"

Ardyn looked back at Tyger. Those bad times seemed like ancient memories, memories of a different Tyger. "No. I'm just not used to running around naked, like someone else I know."

They looked at each in silence for a moment. Then Tyger reached out and touched Ardyn's cheek. She knew why Ardyn had looked away. She said softly, "You know, I couldn't help it. I tried, but there was something about the dome. It twisted the Wind, made me... wild."

Ardyn nodded. She took Tyger's hand. When Sarya had died, she'd linked their hands together, knowing perhaps that with that gesture, she linked their lives as well. "I know. I don't blame you, now that I understand. But the memories can be difficult. The way you treated Sarya sometimes...."

Tyger lowered her eyes. The Wind rushed past them, carrying songs upon songs. The two were silent as they listened to the sound of freedom.

"You came here today for Sarya?" Tyger asked, motioning further east, to where Sarya was buried.

Ardyn nodded again. "I planned it that way. I didn't really realize how far it was. I left about dawn, but climbing a few hundred feet tires you out. By the time I got here I thought I'd lie down in the sun for a while. I went in the Stone to take a look around and the next thing I knew this beautiful warrior was dancing for me."

Ardyn smiled but it didn't last very long. Her face became serious and she looked east. "I did plan to go see her. I miss her, Tyger. I-I miss her so much. I know she was your partner. I tell myself that every day. But I know I'll never love anyone like I loved her. Like I do."

Tyger was silent for a moment. Then, "Today," she asked, "why me?"

"Because I wanted you. Because I wanted to see the woman in you and forget the beast."

Ardyn looked gently at Tyger, studying her face before continuing. "First love stays with you. I only have my memories of Sarya and they aren't many. I can never have a life with her. But you, you can go to the woman you love." Ardyn shook her head in some surprise. "And you must have loved her for so long. Since before Sarya even came into your life. Why isn't she with you now, Tyger?"

Tyger only blinked in surprise.

"Tyger." Ardyn touched her hand. "I know about Terri. Even if you hadn't called her name..." Ardyn trailed off. "I knew before now."

Tyger's face grew hot. "Great Wind." Her voice was a cross between embarrassment and apology.

"I don't mind, Tyger. If anything, I understand."

Tyger bowed her head to Ardyn's shoulder. For a moment, it seemed as though she was crying, but her shoulders shook with laughter, not tears. "Behold the mighty warrior! Unbeaten by her foes, an honored leader and conqueror who is bested by visions of a lover she hasn't had in years!"

"'Bested?'" Ardyn nudged Tyger's face up. "I'll be insulted if that's what you call today."

Tyger stopped laughing and asked, "What has today to do with

Terri?"

"It made you realize what you wanted, Tyger. Who. You're welcome, of course. I was very glad to oblige."

They laughed together. After a bit they leaned back against the Stone and Ardyn drew nearer Tyger, playing with a lock of her hair. "Will you tell me your story?"

Tyger looked down at Ardyn. Of all the pain she had in the world, of all the guilt, she felt as if the last bit was the secret that would be revealed in the telling of this tale. Spider may have forgiven her for what she'd done to the P3M. Iahala had showed her a kindness she had never imagined. But this was the last shame. Afterward, there would be only a warrior woman who had nothing to blame herself for. For a moment she weighed the consequences of telling this tale. Then, coming to a decision, she began to speak. "Do you remember the night you brought Sarya to the Windriders?"

"Yes. It was the night you claimed her. I've tried to forget."

Tyger looked into Ardyn's eyes. "Do you remember the night before that one?" When Ardyn shook her head, Tyger reminded her. "We were alone. You and I. Up on the roof. We had fought, which we never did then, and I had become so angry my claws emerged. I could have killed you. But when you saw them, you didn't even flinch, you kept right on screaming at me about whatever it was.

"It had been a long time since someone had stood up to me." Tyger smiled, remembering. "No one since... since Terri had dared such a thing.

"The Currents were wild that night, more so than usual, it seemed. We began laughing because we were so tense, and it was all so stupid. The lumi-light from the street fell across your face. It made you look so strong – the way it highlighted your eyes. I reached over–"

"–and you kissed me," Ardyn whispered the rest of the sentence. "Yes, I remember now."

Tyger nodded. "I kissed you because you were bold enough to stand against me. Terri was like that. She could stand up to me and everyone else, but she also loved me. She didn't just want me because I was different and wild. She loved me. And I loved her. Which was why I sent her away. To protect her. I wouldn't take her into the Wind to be enslaved. I wouldn't permit myself to see her for months at a time because I thought somehow I would ruin her.

"But until today, I never knew that the reason I wouldn't risk her was because I loved her too much. That the reason I kissed you that night was because you reminded me of her... and I missed her so terribly I couldn't even admit it."

"And I pushed you away, didn't I?" Ardyn asked. "You were my friend and my leader, but you were so... different. When you kissed me... I remember pushing you back so hard I almost fell, even though you barely moved. I guess Sarya was right, I was prejudiced."

Tyger pretended not the hear her last words. "When you pushed me away... you hurt me. So I wanted to hurt you back. I saw that you wanted Sarya, loved her, even when you first walked in with her. And I knew you couldn't stop me from taking her."

Ardyn was stunned, shocked. "You-you didn't love her?"

"No, not at first. But I grew to love her. If I hadn't, I would have let her go after the novelty had worn off. But how could someone not love Sarya? Our butterfly."

Ardyn's face became soft. "I hope she got her wish."

Tyger nodded. "Of all of us, she deserved to have it granted."

"It hasn't been very long since we buried her near the Heart. But it seems I've been without her forever. And you, you haven't seen Terri, haven't been with her for...." Ardyn's words faded.

Tyger looked down at the blue stone. It had been a very long time. Too long. She motioned around them. The sun was low in the sky and the air was full of the Wind's song. "The Wind blows away the pain, but sometimes it blows away memories as well. Once," she said, touching Ardyn's face with one soft hand, "we hated each other."

"I... I don't think you and I are meant to be these extremes, Tyger. Enemies. Lovers. We have to find a middle ground. We have to," Ardyn joked, her smile growing as Tyger gathered her into her arms. Ardyn melted into Tyger's embrace, remembering symphonies of passion, concertos of emotion. "Because I can't live through another day like today."

Their shared laughter became part of the song.

They were entwined together, almost asleep, when the Gold One found them, circling high above. Mouse appeared in the sky soon after and the Gold One's eyes gazed evenly at Mouse. Mouse looked down at the two and then back at the Gold One. Finally, not knowing what else to do, Mouse turned his Wing, Blue, and headed for home. Still no wiser to the mystery of the Gold One's song.

* * *

Back in Skynest, Iahala was alone. She moved through a routine check of each of the small nests, ensuring that each had enough soft bedding. As her fingers poked gently into the separate nests, something unusual happened. A voice sounded in her head.

"Iahala Snoqualmie, an urgent message awaits you. Please come to retrieve your urgent message."

Iahala's hand went to the IkioiHashi disc. "Thank you. I will come at once."

Iahala rushed from Skynest and out into the stone halls of Sky. She knew what this message must be and she knew it was not good news. She turned down corridor after corridor, moving forever closer to the Core.

Even though Sarah and Abraham had told Tyger that Iahala never came to the Core, Tyger had suspected they lied. It was as though Tyger could almost picture Iahala there, almost see her as she was now, stepping through what had been solid rock a moment before, stepping into the crystal colors, into the heart of Sky.

* * *

Night fell and class began.

"It's best to learn the El Rod at night. Night is a time of magic." Aliqui stood, her weight evenly balanced. The moon was directly above the Valley, spilling down like liquid silver over those gathered there. To understand the four elements was to understand power. And if they were to face the Patriarchy, they had to know all about power.

Ardyn shifted, casting a glance in Tyger's direction. It had become clear to Aliqui that Tyger had already mastered the techniques of the El Rod. So Tyger sat nearby in the grass, her brother Mouse at her side.

Tylon stood beside Ardyn. Tamarin and Fox were there as well. They turned their attention to Aliqui as she began to speak. "There are five stages in Phoenix: Warrior, Earth, Water, Air and Fire. Warrior stage is when you learn the art of fighting, the ability to connect with your inner Wild. The desire to protect. The second through fifth stages – Earth through Fire – are about mastering the four kinds of fighting: earth, water, air and fire. In Earth, fighting is about low, solid moves. Water concentrates on forward motion moves; air, on turns and leaps; and finally fire on using high movements and sharp slashes. Fire is also about bringing all the elemental aspects into one single focus."

Aliqui looked at the moonlit Windriders. They were antsy and shifting their weight from one foot to the other. They had learned to fight on the streets. Their idea of Warrior was very different from her own. Because of this she would teach them as she had her hotheaded Falcon – as few words as possible. They knew their Wild. They lived their Wild. She just had to show them how to control it.

"Let's begin with some sparring? Who'd like to–" she hadn't even finished her question before Ardyn stepped forward. Aliqui took a deep breath. "Remember," Aliqui said as much to Ardyn as to all of them. "Earth and Water are allied, as are Air and Fire. If someone strikes in Earth, parry with Air. If someone strikes in Fire, parry with Water."

Ardyn nodded and shifted again, lowering her body into a position that showed how many battles she had fought.

Aliqui realized this was going to be very, very interesting. They struck together. Tyger had always taught her warriors to strike first because giving your enemy a chance to take the upper hand could mean your death. Only Mouse and Tyger could see the actual beams, but Aliqui had showed them how to anticipate a blow from the power in the air and your opponent's movements.

Ardyn's red sword met Aliqui's blue beam and sparks flew that they all could see. The Windriders cheered.

Aliqui dropped away, spun to the side, and clipped Ardyn's wrist with her El Rod blazing Earth power. Ardyn would have a bruise, nothing more, but it was a strike nonetheless and Ardyn set her jaw. Ardyn struck high then dove low, feigning a blow at Aliqui's legs and sliding inside her guard, miming a clean slice at her stomach. "The teacher is dead!" Ardyn teased, dancing away from Aliqui's Fire move.

Aliqui followed after her, aware of the truth of her words. She cut across Ardyn's body, keeping her at a distance and then thrust at Ardyn's center. Ardyn doubled over, as if she were embracing the beam with her torso and legs, and managed to keep a pocket of air between her body and Aliqui's beam tip. Ardyn slipped to the right and danced behind Aliqui, striking her from behind. "Dead again," Ardyn laughed.

Aliqui opened her mouth to remind everyone that striking from behind was dishonorable, but stopped when she realized what Ardyn was doing. Aliqui spun, knowing she would never get the full respect of the Windriders until she learned how to street fight.

They circled again. This time, Aliqui attacked first. She slipped to the side as Ardyn brought her El Rod up to block Aliqui's stroke, but Aliqui did not strike with her El Rod. Instead, her foot lashed out at the last moment, forcing Ardyn to drop and roll to avoid being hit.

Ardyn snapped up from the ground and charged, her El Rod swinging in Water. Aliqui struck in Fire and cut through the attack. Ardyn kicked out, her foot crunching into Aliqui's ribs. Aliqui tumbled into a back somersault and brought her El Rod up just in time to block Ardyn's slice.

"We may just make a warrior out of you yet, Aliqui," Ardyn grinned.

"And I just might be able to teach you all about the power of the elements." Aliqui leapt up and their El Rods locked again.

"Don't hold your breath!" Ardyn answered.

Out of the corner of her eye, Aliqui saw Tylon rise suddenly. He dropped his El Rod into the grass as though it burned him and ran full tilt toward the hole of Skynest. She didn't have time to consider what this meant, however, as Ardyn was bearing down on her again.

* * *

Iahala sat in the darkness, listening to the voice of the Valley. She was trying to put her thoughts in order, trying to fit the information she had received at the Core into the tapestry of life all around her. Across from her, Mlinz sat with his parents who were reading their Book by moonlight. She wondered how dangerous Sarah and Abraham really were. Wondered if Sky could do without Tyger. She thought about what the Gold One had showed Mouse. Wondered if the Butterfly sang for both women or just one of them, and what any of these answers might mean.

She opened the small pouch in her lap. She touched the handful of crushed crystals there. If the Gold One sang for Tyger or Ardyn, why had the Butterflies sung in the Hidden Garden? Why had they destroyed the crystals?

Her thoughts were interrupted by Tylon's arrival. He sank breathless to the ground beside her. Leaning close, he whispered in hushed and hurried tones, "Wise One! I know now. I understand my vision. I need your help."

Nothing could surprise Iahala today; she simply nodded.

Tylon pulled at the cloth of his new tunic. "I need something heavier than this. Something stiffer. Like the leather jacket that Ardyn wears, or Tyger's breeches. But it would work like this...." His voice trailed off. Iahala watched him working out the puzzle, waited for him to enlighten her.

His hand touched the pouch of crystal powder. He looked into her face, his own awash with sudden insight. "Crushed crystals are still crystals. The powder could be affixed to cloth in patterns, self-containing patterns. It could be any shape as long as it had closed lines. Those shapes, those areas of cloth lined with, surrounded by crystal, could be filled with power. No armor would be stronger!" He looked at Iahala as if he expected her to understand. She gazed at him tenderly, but she could not quite grasp his meaning. Yet.

"Those areas of cloth, the spaces between the crystal borders, could be charged with the power of the elements." Tyger had shared with Tylon her adventures in the Core and so he had to know the truth. "But it can only work if the elements can really be conquered, if they really are magic." He stopped there and just looked at her.

Iahala understood. She had expected this question to come soon, but from whom she hadn't known. "Before the End, Tylon, there was an art called Microcrys. This art, this practice, made it possible to capture the power of the elements, including their essence and properties, and encase them in crystal. The dispute over who had created it – the scientists in their laboratories or those who practiced the art as magic – raged for many years." Iahala paused for a moment. Then she said, "Microcrys breakthroughs were made in many fields. The act of combining allied elements, or opposing elements, was truly groundbreaking. We found that everything could be traced back to one of the four powers. Every living or nonliving thing contained the pulses of either Earth, Water, Air or Fire.

"The results of this were stunning. Children were born to parents who could never have had children before, like same gender couples. Diseases were destroyed that had been thought incurable. All by combining the raw power of the elements. But the one thing we couldn't do was clean up the world we had desecrated. Because the world was made up of all the elements, and the opposing force against the elements was... us.

"So in the end, not even Microcrys could save us. We had to die for the world to be reborn. The debate was never settled. Some said science, some said magic."

There was a brief silence. Then Tylon said, "I think the two are one."

Iahala just looked at him. "Maybe you will be the one to combine them."

Tylon stared at the pouch of crystal dust. She handed it to him and he continued his explanation. "The encompassing design on the prominent arm of the jacket would be charged with Fire for quickness," he said. "The defensive arm would be charged with Earth for firm blocking. The front of the jacket would be Air to aid breathing and the back with Water to aid flexibility. Those would be the magical parts." Tylon paused. "The other part, the technical part, came to me just as you were talking. The jacket would be armor as well as enhancement. Aliqui told us each element pulses with attributes that create its genetic make-up. The heredity variation between the powers. If something strikes an area charged with an element, it reacts. If the pulses are the same as its own, it absorbs them. If the pulses oppose, then it attacks the foreign strike and destroys it." He paused to see if she understood him. Iahala nodded and so he continued.

"For instance," he said, "the jacket fronts are charged with Air. If the wearer of the jacket were hit with something aligned with Fire – Air's ally – the Fire would be absorbed. If the wearer were struck with Earth or Water, then the Air power would battle against the strike. Neutralize it. Nothing could get through."

"But what about a blow that's over-powering? Like a Water strike more powerful than the Fire of the armor? Would it then simply strike the leather of the jacket?" Iahala asked.

Tylon nodded vigorously. "Yes. But it would have to be a very powerful blow. The jacket's power would grow as it absorbed allied energies. It could even be charged on a regular basis to keep or build its power level." His face flushed with the ideas surging through his mind. He looked at her excitedly. "It would have to be tested. It wouldn't make a person invincible, but still..." Tylon grinned at her and she was caught up in his enthusiasm. "If everything can be broken into one of the elements, then maybe the armor could even stand up to the Patriarchy's lasers, or even the Users' guns." His eyes grew distant for a moment and Iahala waited for him to speak again. "I'll call them Skins," he said. "The Patriarchy created a body suit of New World animal hide that they called a Skin, but it was something evil, something used for death. I'll take the power of the name away from them. My Skins will be something used to protect life. It will be like wearing the Wind, because the Wind holds all the elements."

"I'll help you," Iahala said. Her eyes moved from Tylon to the Windriders and finally to their leader. She and Tyger would talk tonight. It was time for the journey to begin.

* * *

Tamarin sang out as he lunged at Fox. "Take that, you beast! Wild thing from the Wind, feel my blade!"

She growled menacingly at him. It was such a startling display of power that Tamarin screamed and ran away. Fox laughed. "Hey, this opposing opposites stuff really works! He plays around. I threaten to eat him alive, he takes off. I like it!" She took off after Tamarin into the darkening Valley and Aliqui watched as Fox tackled him into the grass.

"You got through to them," Ardyn observed.

Aliqui and Ardyn sat on the grass together, catching their breath after their match. Aliqui looked over at Ardyn with a smile and noticed the heated look that passed between Ardyn and Tyger. Aliqui looked away. She did not want to see their passion. She was brought abruptly from her thoughts when Ardyn asked, "You're Falcon's partner, aren't you?"

Aliqui nodded. She had been that. And more. She had rescued Falcon, soothed her nightmares. Falcon, always quick to anger and discontent. Falcon, who dared everything for what she believed in. Falcon, whose made love like she fought – brilliantly and utterly absorbed. Aliqui had been so much to her – tried so hard – and yet... Falcon still chose to leave. Chose to explore the tunnel where evil lived.

Ardyn said gently, "I understand your pain. I lost my love to the Wind."

Aliqui looked at her in confusion. It was no secret where – and with whom – Ardyn had been all day. Aliqui could not help the glance she gave Tyger.

Sensing Aliqui's unspoken question, Ardyn said, "Tyger and I are companions. She is part of me, but Sarya... Sarya is my heart. You know," Ardyn said, tipping her head back to look at the constellations, "we first discovered the Valley by noticing that the constellation called the Great Tears was gone from the sky. Tyger told us a legend about how–"

"–when the Tears fell, water would return to the world," Aliqui finished. "I know that tale. Falcon told it to me when I brought her into the

Valley that first day and she saw the River Sky. The stars are still there. Iahala says that the Valley makes clouds that hides them. Falcon always believed it was magic."

"You must love her very much," Ardyn said, purposefully not using the past tense.

Aliqui was quiet for a long moment. "Yes," she admitted finally. "Yes. I do."

"You're lucky, Aliqui. Falcon was with you for a long time. Even though I loved Sarya, she was partnered with Tyger. My leader. There was nothing I could do. She loved me, too. I think. But not like she loved Tyger. Tyger was her soul. But I... I was special to her."

"The way you speak, I would guess you were more than that," Aliqui said.

Ardyn didn't answer her directly. "No matter where life brings me, no matter where my heart leads, I'll always remember Sarya. Her laughter and tenderness. Her golden curls. Her ocean-blue eyes."

Aliqui didn't respond. As she listened to Ardyn's description, something tugged at her from the edge of her consciousness. She found herself thinking of another beauty with ocean-blue eyes.

And into that stillness, Sarah called in a sing-song voice, "Sleep well, everyone!"

No one answered her.

Sitting next to Tyger, Mouse's body became suddenly alert, shaking with tension. His face wrought with frustration and love, Mouse looked toward Mlinz as the young man walked with his parents towards the door into Sky. Tyger touched her brother's shoulder, her brow creased with concern. "Sarah's watching him, Mouse," she said softly. "He can't come to you now."

Mouse stared into the darkness as if willing the situation to be different. But then he sighed and nodded.

Ardyn rose from where she'd been sitting and joined the siblings. She looked at Mouse, seeing the pain on his face. "What scares you the most about Mlinz being with his parents?"

For a long moment, Mouse did not respond. When he began to speak, he stared at the door into Sky, as if willing Mlinz to reappear. His voice seemed weighted with understanding he did not necessarily want to have. "They called him Isaac when he was born. It's a name from their Book. In the Book, Sarah and Abraham were the names of Isaac's parents as well.

"The story of Isaac... " he faltered. Tyger and Ardyn waited for him to continue, letting their silence hold and encourage him. "In the story, the One calls to Abraham and tells him to... to sacrifice his son. To take him up top a mountain and... kill him.

"Abraham loves his son. But he loves the One more. In the end, the One spared Isaac. In that story, the One was merely testing Abraham's faith. Just before Abraham would have killed his son, the One stays his hand and gives him a beast to kill instead." Mouse's voice fell into the darkness that surrounded them. When he spoke again, his voice was dark as midnight. "I'm afraid that Sarah will tell Abraham that the One wants him to kill Mlinz. Here, with Mlinz, Abraham does not hear the One's voice – only Sarah hears it. Or at least she claims to. And Abraham, because he believes her and believes in the One, he would take Mlinz to an altar to sacrifice him. But just before he'd do it, Sarah would stop him. Sarah would say that it had only been a test. And as the beast, Sarah would give *me* to Abraham."

Mouse stared at them, his eyes wide in the starlight darkness. "And I would die for him. I would die for Mlinz because I love him that much. I would let them kill me so that he would live."

There was a tense pause. Tyger struggled visibly with her rage, but Mouse didn't seem to notice. His attention was fixed again on the door while Ardyn's gaze was fixed on Tyger. Mouse changed the subject completely. "They didn't just get sad, you know. It didn't just suddenly come to them that so many had died right in front of their eyes. It was like they were fine one day and crazy the next. Headaches and this spinning in their heads. They just went crazy." He shook his head as though he didn't understand.

"Who went mad, Mouse?" Ardyn asked.

"The children," he said slowly. "The children from the Village of Wind."

Ardyn looked at Tyger. She remembered what Tyger had told her about the west tunnel leading to the Patriarchy. About how the Users were Humans addicted to the Drug – Humans who seemed to be allied somehow with Sarah and Abraham. About how the Drug threw the body off-balance, shattered the mind and the emotions of the users – fragmented them into behavioral extremes. And, eventually, drove them mad. She shuddered. "We won't let anything happen to you, Mouse." Ardyn's eyes willed Tyger to be calm. Had Sarah and Abraham poisoned the Windborn children? Ardyn added, "Or Mlinz. We won't let them hurt you."

He looked up at her, eyes gleaming with tears and Ardyn couldn't tell if he believed her.

* * *

"You know something more," Tyger said, her voice tight. "Tell me." In the darkness, Tyger lowered herself to the grass beside Iahala, her every muscle ready to spring, her emotions, her rage at Sarah and Abraham barely held in check. She had felt Iahala gaze from across the Valley, had known secrets awaited her.

Iahala looked at Tyger. Tylon was back with the others, perhaps discussing his plan. They were alone. Iahala took the talking stick into her hands. "It's time to face the Wind. Humans have been running from it for too long. We must change or die, Tyger. Otherwise, we will never be part of the New World.

"I have known for a long time that every breed must have a voice if we are to co-exist, but that one of your kind must lead us. The Wind rules the New World and only the Windborn can truly know the Wind. We Pagans, here in Sky, have great respect for the Windborn. Those who don't can rot underground for as long as they wish.

"The Wind is in your blood, Tyger, and it is as strong and powerful as you are. It allows no lies and no evil. It will be – and has been – the rebirth of the world. The true Genesis."

Iahala paused, knowing that there would have to be a battle – and a terrible one – before the prophecy was fulfilled. She took a deep breath, knowing that these next words would set everything into motion, everything that would follow from now until the end of time. "I received a message today. A message of great sadness. We are destroying ourselves once again. But this time, if something isn't done to stop it, we will all perish – everyone of us. Across the world, governments are falling, nations are crumbling and people are dying. These countries of domes are not being overthrown – their leaders are going insane.

"As you know, domes are made of two skins with a layer of Cells between them; the Cells are living creatures, encased. Enslaved. They know but one thing and that is madness. Forever, they consume each other, eating then splitting and eating again. Their life creates power – chaotic energy. That power ebbs out into the domes, a little more each day.

"The Cells are dangerous. Through my work in the Core, talking to other Humans who exist in other Sky bases, I have discovered that we are once again on the brink of disaster. This world fell once before because we would not join together. This time I had hoped it would be different. But months ago, before I was sure exactly what was happening, I tried to talk to Sarah and Abraham about the problem. They refused to believe me, refused to help me organize and send out warnings to the domes. 'Let the Clones die,' they said. 'They are little more than animals anyway. Let the Cells poison them all.'

"Tyger," Iahala reached for her hand. "The domes were never meant to exist in the Wind, to stand against the Wind or to stand for so long. Some of them are collapsing, drowning Clones and Originals in Cells that consume them. But other domes, perhaps even more horribly, are slowly leaking their poisonous madness into the cities, dragging everyone into chaos and death. Sarah and Abraham believe we should allow this madness to run its course, to let the Clones die and then take over the empty domes.

"But I know – as you know – the Originals, and the Clones, deserve to know that the Cells destroy them."

Iahala's eyes burned with purpose. "The Users make their Drug from Cells. They tap it from the domes and dilute it with water from the River Sky. That is how ignorant we Humans can be. That some of us are injecting the very Cells that are killing us all over the world. The cities are falling, Tyger, and the Cells are sweeping into the Earth, into the land of Sky, and killing Humans as well. None of us is safe. We must leave the domes, and Sky, and find a way to live in the Wind."

Iahala was silent, her eyes on the ground, then she looked up and met Tyger's blazing eyes. "My message today confirmed a formula. A way to devise when a dome would fall by the way it affects the environment." The Wisewoman's face was covered in compassion and commitment. "The domes on this continent are beginning to fail. Nothing can stop it. New Seattle does not have much time left. A few weeks, maybe only days. When the catastrophe happens, it will happen quickly. One moment the Clones and Originals may experience physical discomfort – pains, aches. Then there will be disturbances outside the dome in the form of great storms as the Wind battles the poisons in the air. The Cells will either saturate the city with poison or eat through the dome and consume everything... everyone.

"They must be warned. If the leader of the Patriarchy will not listen, he must be overthrown. In other countries, many dome leaders have not heeded our warnings. They do not want to believe that their precious domes can kill. But the truth is that we may fear the Wind, but we should fear the Cells more. At least in the Wind, we may have a chance... with your help, the way you can read the Wind... I hope we have a chance."

When she was finished, Iahala set the talking stick down. She gazed up into Tyger's face and saw there the determination she had hoped to see. Tyger stood. "I have been waiting for six years to hear this," Tyger said. She turned her head as if listening for something in the Wind. As if knowing already exactly what she must do and how. "It's time." Tyger took a deep breath. "It's time for the Patriarch to fall."

* * *

# Part Seven

Terri sat awake in her room as night fell over the city of New Seattle. Another of her Spiders – twenty-two in all now – had complained to her of a horrible headache and she wondered if the Patriarchy had put something strange in the food.

There was a knock on the door. Terri debated not answering. She needed more time to think. Falcon's face was still swimming before her every time she closed her eyes. But ignoring the Spiders was not a luxury she had. "Come in."

Joanna opened the door, Ravyn and Byn behind her. "Ready to talk?" Joanna asked.

Terri just motioned them inside.

When the three settled themselves on pelts spread across the floor, Joanna spoke first. "Falcon's lying, Terri. They all are. They don't make sense. To have traveled so far with no weapons, no packs and no scars? They claimed they searched the Patriarchy compound as if were a playground, and then, just when you think the Patriarch would be wild trying to find the prowlers – they had to have set off alarms – instead of being angry, the Patriarchy's dumping food, new clothes and everything under the sun into the bins!"

"Not everything. There were no weapons, no ammunition," Terri pointed out.

Joanna fell silent.

"Joanna," Terri began slowly. "I trust your counsel, but I also know how much you hated Tyger. Her rule, her power. How can I listen–"

"I did *not* hate her! Terri, damnit, you know that! I loved Ravyn. I hated what Tyger was doing. Having Ravyn make death-weapons, then taking her from me! Don't discredit all I'm telling you just because it's easier than listening to the truth! There is something wrong, about those three – especially Falcon!" Joanna's dark face had grown dark scarlet with anger and urgency. She kept her voice a deep hiss that would not be heard outside the room.

Ravyn took her partner's hand and Joanna clasped it, looking away. Terri could tell how hard this was for them. How hard it was for Joanna to say she didn't trust people who had just arrived. But she could also see that something instinctual in Joanna was telling her that something wasn't right.

Ravyn spoke into the silence. "Terri, you must admit it's strange. They arrive by some secret means into New Seattle, but six years after the fact. Six years after Falcon claims she *saw* Tyger be taken. Why didn't she just follow the Hovercraft then? If she'd been close enough to see the pendant fall, why didn't she try to help? Why didn't she try to stop Tyger from selling herself to the Steel?"

"Falcon didn't even mention that," Byn added urgently. "It's like it doesn't matter that Tyger sacrificed herself for the Village... just because the Patriarch lied and attacked them anyway... Tyger tried!"

Terri looked at Byn. The girl appeared as torn about what to make of this as Terri was. "She looks a lot like Tyger, doesn't she, Byn?"

"She doesn't look anything like her!" Byn protested hotly. "They're like hot and cold – opposites. I don't even think they're sisters. I don't even believe Falcon's Windborn."

There was a short tense silence. Then Byn added, "But if I'm wrong, I've turned away Tyger's last kin. To know that I didn't help the last Windborn find Tyger... that would be worse than anything."

"No, Byn," Joanna said gently. "Worse would be telling a killer where Tyger was. Just look at Falcon. Her eyes, her body are filled with secrets and anger. And what could we tell her? That Tyger went to her Village and from there we don't know? Let Falcon figure it out on her own. I say we're traitors if we so much as open our mouths."

"Then close yours and let me talk with your leader." Falcon stood in the doorway. The lumi-light gave her an aura the color of an Original's night. Falcon smiled. "Terri, leader of the Spiders, may we speak?"

The four Spiders had jumped, startled, by Falcon's sudden presence. Terri saw a flush of anger race across Joanna's face and then recede. Clearly Falcon had only heard Joanna's last words and she must suspect they were trying to keep something from her.

Terri leaned back against the wall, closing her eyes for a moment. Joanna, Ravyn and Byn were watching her and she knew it. What harm could it do to tell Falcon what little they knew? What wrong, indeed, if she truly was Tyger's sister?

If Falcon could get into the city, she could get out. Terri swore to herself that if Falcon left, she'd be with her. She'd make Falcon take her to Tyger.

"We will speak," Terri said steadily, convincing herself that telling Falcon Tyger went to their Village couldn't possibly do any harm. Terri had no way of knowing that on the Heart Stone at the Village of Wind, beside the story of the Windriders and their leader, was a etched picture of the Valley that Tyger and Ardyn had seen in a dream. The Valley they had quested for, found, and inhabited at this moment. If Terri spoke, Falcon would be able to find Tyger and then she would kill her.

Joanna and the others stood to leave. When Joanna turned and faced Falcon, Falcon was smiling at her. It was clear from Falcon's expression that the Windborn didn't care what Joanna thought of her. She was beyond worrying about what weak Originals might do. They posed no threat to her.

"Your acceptance of difference astonishes me," Falcon murmured as the three walked by.

"Tyger is different and we love her," Byn replied with a child's conviction. "But you're not just different. You're evil." Byn closed the door behind as the three she left Terri's quarters, shutting out Falcon's burning glare without flinching.

"They don't trust you, Falcon from the Village of Wind."

Falcon turned to the Spider leader. For a moment her eyes flashed dangerously. Terri saw her rage and for a split-second, she feared Falcon might grab and shake her until Terri told her what she wanted to know. But then the fire in Falcon's eyes diminished and she reigned in her anger.

"And what of you, Terri?" Falcon asked, careful not to smile unpleasantly. "Do you trust me?"

Terri was surprised for a moment by Falcon's height and strength, but that thought was followed a moment later by the memory of Tyger and she was no longer awed. How many paled in comparison to the flamed-haired warrior? In Terri's eyes, all did. "Sit down, Falcon. I don't trust you, but I'd like to."

If Falcon was surprised by that statement, she didn't show it. She sat in silence, taking a place near Terri, staring into Terri's light green eyes. "I do wish you would. We have shared a common loss. I loved her as deeply as you did. When she left, I felt the pain that you feel now." She reached out with her good hand and touched Terri's cheek. Her hand was very cold and not altogether gentle. "Heartache always has the same face."

And then Falcon made her second mistake, and this one Terri did not forgive. The Windborn leaned forward and kissed her. Terri had never been the kind of woman prone to slapping someone who had stepped out of line. She was a fighter by instinct and by trade. Before she'd even thought about the ramifications of her actions, her rock-hard fist connected with Falcon's face. She was on her feet a moment later, her other hand tangled in Falcon's collar, hauling the startled Windborn half-way up off the floor. Her fury had not only made her bold, it had also made her incredibly strong and she shook Falcon as hard as she could.

"I didn't just love her then, Falcon! I love her now! Forever! My heart belongs to her, whether she is dead or alive, whether she walks the Wind or has become it. How dare you come here and tell me you feel my pain! No one feels as I do! And if you did, you would never have touched me as you have!"

Falcon shrieked wildly, her own rage exploding inside her. Someone was pounding at the door, but Falcon had locked it behind her and so the two were trapped inside. Alone.

Falcon threw Terri from her as if she were a speck of dirt. Terri flew toward the concrete wall. Her head hit with a heavy thud. But before she could fall to the floor, Falcon was there, pulling Terri up by her neck, the tips of her claws sinking into Terri's soft flesh. Terri felt the blood trickling down and knew how very easily it could become a river.

Terri's vision clouded. She thought she might pass out. But then Falcon released her. Terri's vision cleared and her eyes widened in sudden horror. Falcon held a black weapon that looked like a laser, but was slicker and newer, pointed at Terri's head, and Terri knew it would not just stun. It would kill. Falcon's next words struck Terri like the coldest ice and became fear freezing the blood in her veins.

Blood fell from Falcon's split lip as she spoke. "Stupid, Original bitch! I'm surprised my sister would choose you. I thought she'd have better taste. I thought she'd preferred women with some power. But I suppose she'd become as soft as her surroundings." Falcon leaned closer and her solid-colored eyes seemed to fill Terri's entire field of vision. "I'll give you four days, Terri, leader of the Spiders. One for each finger on my hand. No more. If you do not tell me by then where my sister has gone, I will let my soldiers use their own means of interrogation, on all your young women. And I think they'll begin with little Byn, because she loved Tyger and knows I'm evil."

Falcon smiled. "You'd be surprised how much pent-up aggression these soldiers have. The Silver Steel only lets them give Seed twice a month and they do that alone." Falcon *tisked*, then cocked her head. "Or perhaps I should handle the interrogation. Just you and I. Alone. How long do you think it would take me to break you?" Falcon moved the gun a fraction of an inch and fired. The bullet sped past Terri's face and blew a fist-sized hole in the concrete wall. The Currents burst into the room in a rush of air.

Falcon's smile became colder, but her voice was like molten steel. "Please, Terri, don't make me do it." She turned suddenly on her heel, reholstering her gun behind her back, under her vest. Terri didn't move or breathe. Falcon reached the door but did not turn around. She spoke to the stone. "Four more days, Terri. I'll be waiting."

Falcon flung the door open, coming face to face with all of the assembled Spiders. Falcon ignored them, her eyes searching for her companions, Duke and Liege. When her eyes found theirs, she grinned. She held up her hands as if to placate the restless crowd. "Don't worry, everyone," Falcon called out. "Your leader is a strong, wise woman. We agreed that she does not trust me, but now, at least, we have come to an understanding."

Falcon reached down and cupped Byn's face in one hand. Still smiling, she looked back at Terri. "A very strong, wise woman." Falcon let go of the child, leaving red impressions where her fingers had pressed Byn's face. Cutting her way through the crowd, she motioned for Duke and Liege to follow her. The Spiders crowded around Terri's door, leaving the newcomers to their far corner.

Joanna pushed her way to the front, dragging Ravyn and Byn behind her, and closing the four into Terri's chamber. She rushed across the floor to Terri, taking in the blood on her neck and shoulders. She took the rag Ravyn handed her and began to dab gently at the wounds. "I'll kill her," she growled.

Terri caught her hand. "Joanna, listen to me. I need you all to be warriors now. Spider warriors. Go slowly, one at a time. Don't let them see you leave. Don't let them know we're taking action. Go to the Rollers. Go to Speed and the Prowlers and the Climbers. Go to the independents who have no gangs.

"Ravyn, find the Wheels. Find Panther." Terri's eyes were as cold as the air that rushed in through the hole in the wall. "Tell everyone it's time to join together. The Patriarchy has come to the Industrial District, and now they have to pay."

* * *

Part Eight

They sat in the dark, not bothering to build up the fire too much. It wouldn't help. They would still be cold. And no one wanted to see by the light of the dancing flames what they had become. With no food and little to drink, there wasn't much they could do now but wait for death. It left them with chills, fire or no.

There were four of them. P3M. Originals changed by the Wind. The steel dome skeleton they had been issued to build was long completed, but there had been no food deliveries for two weeks. At night, when the survey cameras blinked off, they would go out into the Wind and collect what foods they could. But they never went far – where would they go? – fearing still the wrath of the Silver Steel.

Lark began to sing softly as he often had while they worked. The others closed their eyes and listened. Tonight's song brought visions of warmth and peace, but they didn't even dream of salvation anymore. Once they had shared visions of rescue. Of an angel with gentle eyes and curls tossed in the Wind. But even the vision was gone now. It was almost time to die, and all four of them knew it.

Petre was the first to walk between the steel beams and into the flickering firelight. His eyes were tender, hazel in color, and his hair was golden with bronze-touched curls. When they first saw him, standing so peacefully, he was dressed in white, color-swirled breeches, a jacket to guard against the cold and a matching headband. The cloth shimmered in the Wind.

"My name is Petre of the Windriders," he said. His voice was loving, angelic. It brought tears to their eyes. "Tyger has sent me to save you."

Out of the shadows, the others in the Rescue Squad stepped forward, hands extended, full of food and drink. The four stood shakily, crowding around Petre, touching his jacket, his hair, his face, taking what was offered with expressions of shock and awe and gratitude.

The Rescue Squad had been doing this for some time now, moving from dome site to dome site, relieving the desperate thirst and near starvation of the P3M imprisoned there. They always used the same approach: Petre would go in first and then the others would join him. When they had gone to the first site, the P3M had run to Petre as if he were an expected visitor, a man of myth and vision. The P3M told them that they had seen Petre in their dreams. That the Wind told them he was coming. The Rescue Squad tried not to show their surprise as all of the P3M shared that they had seen the same vision. Seen Petre and heard the voice of the Wind.

At this site, it was Lark who shared the tale with the Windriders. He said, "He would come to us from the skies. His eyes were kind, and his hair was gold and bronze like the sands and the heavens. He wore the colors of the cactus flowers and the Wind blew all about him. And the voice of the Wind spoke to us. It said, 'Go with him. He will lead you to freedom.'"

And just as Petre's arrival seemed the fulfillment of some magical promise to the slaves, it was also the beginning of Petre's destiny. When he had come to the first site, seen the emaciated faces of those waiting for him there, he remembered with sudden clarity his own dream. The faces before him were as familiar as those of his friends and he knew, with a certainty he could not explain, that this was what he had been born to do. But despite the adoration of the P3M, he refused to accept their insistence that he was something more than what he had always believed himself to be – a good man and a better Windrider. He had something to give them because he knew the evil that had enslaved them. There was as much gentleness in his heart as there was cruelty in Christopher Jarth's.

And it was this quality that Tryl the cowgirl was teasing him about before he fell.

"Hey, Petre, the storm's getting worse! You better come fly close to me where you'll be safe. You don't want to get your curls messed up!"

Petre laughed. All the Windboards were being used as well as the Wings, almost all of them carrying two passengers. Tryl and Petre were the only ones without another passenger. Petre slid his Windboard through the currents toward Tryl, coming to rest just under her left sail tip.

"We knew this was going to happen," he called over the gusts of wild Wind. "We should have tried to wait it out!" Although it was near dawn, it was very dark, and the storm had been growing worse as they drew closer to New Seattle. Tonight seemed as though the Wind was spinning in circles, creating funnel clouds of frightening proportions that sprouted suddenly and veered toward and away from them unpredictably. Both their Wings and their boards were battered and tossed by these currents and the blackness of the night was a wild animal trying to claw its prey from a corner. They ignored the headaches that tormented them. They had no idea that the Cells of New Seattle were leaking into the Wind... that the Wind was battling the poison... reacting to it, changing it, being changed.

Tryl shook her head. "We have to get to the last site! You said it yourself. They've been days without anything."

Petre nodded, squinting into the Wind. He couldn't see anything but the storm. "I know. I felt guilty about taking shelter while they waited for us – while they're not even sure if someone's really coming."

"We won't do anyone much good if we all get blown away."

Petre looked at her. "I know," he answered, but she didn't hear him.

Kestrel flew to join them, one of the P3M strapped to her Wing with her. "Wolf's Wing has a rip in the sail. It's bobbing dangerously. And Jaguar – you remember, the one who's so ill?"

Petre nodded.

"He's getting worse. I think we should land and decide what to do."

"All right," Petre agreed. He looked for a spot to set the company down. Just then, the storm intensified below them, hiding the ground, swallowing it. Never had there been a storm like this over these lands. It felt as if the elements were all going mad at once. "Let's wait this gust out," he called, and had a fleeting thought of how proud Tyger would be of his leadership skills. How proud Tylon would be.

He moved away from Tryl so he could be ready to dive when the gust passed. But it never did. Instead, the Wind grew wilder, and howled around their Wings, tossed their Windboards, threatening to consume them all. And in that moment, Petre saw something in the blackness. He saw the face of the Wind.

"Petre?!" Petre heard Tryl call to him but suddenly he could not see her. He could not find any of his companions. He hovered, or was held, at the center of a funnel of Wind and before his eyes, colors spun and danced in the darkness, images or visions swam within the column of Wind and he heard a voice. A voice that spoke to the center of who he was. The Wind spoke to him.

"Why do you need me?" Petre's voice shook uncontrollably as his head was filled with not words, but intentions, feelings and memories and flashes of the future. And he realized that the Wind was a living thing. He realized that science and magic were one and the same. He realized that he was the first Clone to change with the Wind and he realized that he was the last ingredient to the rebirth of the world.

Petre stood up as straight as he could on his Windboard. His fear was suddenly gone. Tears flooded his eyes and he opened his arms to the Wind. "Take me then," he said. "Take me."

The funnel of Wind spun open, and a geyser of sand shot up into the air, spraying the Flyers. Directly over the geyser, Petre's Windboard was slammed with its tremendous force and Petre was hurled into the air.

Seeing him thrown, Tryl screamed and dove toward him, ignoring her own peril. The geyser's sand, falling toward the earth again, covered her sails, bearing her down with its deadly weight. Kestrel dove past Tryl, but even she was unable to shake the sand's weight, as if it were the hand of fate itself. Everyone was screaming Petre's name, plunging after him, seeking the place where he disappeared in the swirling tornado of sand and Wind.

Then a flash of light split the air, separating the group into two halves. Later, everyone swore it was the most amazing light show any of them had ever seen – like the simultaneous blooming of all the flowers of the

Great Cactus – a long distance below them. It was beautiful and terrible at the same time. And when it was over, Petre was truly gone. The Wind had called.

The storm abated almost at once and they landed in a place that Tryl and Jyln remembered – the place where the Patriarch's Retrieval Squad had fallen. Like great dead beasts, the ruined Hovercraft offered the shelter they needed as the storm continued to rage. The sixteen P3M crawled into the empty shells of the Hovercraft, but the Windriders and Kestrel would not.

Tryl pounded her fists against the steel sides of one craft, as the Wind howled around them, blowing sand and nearly blinding them. "Damnit! We have to go look!" she argued. "He was right beside me! He has to be around here somewhere."

Spider grabbed hold of Tryl's shirt before she could strike out alone, trying to shake some sense into her. "Do you know how fast we were traveling up there? Great Wind, woman, get a grip on yourself! Even if we did find him, he'd be dead from the fall. There's nothing we can do except get inside the craft and save our own lives!"

Tryl pushed Spider away and tore off into the darkness. Jyln ran after her.

"She's crazy," Spider muttered.

Wolf and Kestrel stared after them. They were all crying and the sand struck their wet eyes and burned.

Wolf asked, "Have you ever seen a storm like this, Kestrel?"

Kestrel came closer to them and shook her head. "I can't believe I'm seeing one now. I don't know what it means. Was that light lightning? That's an Old World phenomenon."

They looked at each other. Death was an Old World phenomenon as well.

A short distance away, Tryl sank to her knees in the whirling sand and her tears spilled over the snapped pieces of the fallen Windboard. "No!" she shouted, her fist raised in angry protest.

Jyln sank down beside her partner and took Tryl into her arms, ignoring the other's shaking and cursing and flailing about. "Did you see the way they looked at him?" Tryl continued. "He was someone special. Someone rare. Never before has a Clone changed in the Wind. Never before has a soldier grown to be so kind. Tyger knew he was different from the beginning. They were friends even though they were supposed to be enemies. He was meant for something great, Jyln. Damnit, I should have–"

Jyln's eyes were very gentle when she spoke. "He was needed somewhere else," she said simply, feeling some certainty.

Together they made their way back to the others, Tryl lost in her own thoughts, turning Jyln's words over and over in her mind. *Needed somewhere else.* Jyln's words sounded so right. Because they were.

* * *

Part Nine

Tyger looked around the chamber that Iahala had given the Windriders. It had been home for a while, but now they had to leave. Tyger turned to the six who stood with her: Mouse, Ardyn, Tylon, Tamarin, Fox and Iahala.

"Revenge is on everyone's mind. I read in your eyes as I know it in my own. We have varied histories, but shared pain. I have waited for a very long time to stand before you and say these words." Tyger's voice filled the room. "Since the first time Jarth laid his hands on me and told me I was his. Since the first time I had to watch a friend die because I thought I was saving my Village. It's been a long six years, almost seven. I have faced so much. We all have. But now the day I have long awaited has come. It is time for the Patriarchy to fall."

The Windriders moved closer to Tyger, eager to pledge themselves to her cause. In this moment, all that they wanted was to lay the Patriarchy's shattered remains at the feet of the Tiger, the warrior who may have once worked for the Silver Steel but had never given them her heart.

"I know how it must be done," she said. "Doors have been opened. Secrets shared. Even if they were not meant to be. I have seen the Core of Sky and have returned... with these." She handed them several cloth sheets, the Core's print-outs. Aliqui had helped Tyger make hard copies of many of the maps, graphs and floor plans she had found. "These are pictures of the Patriarchy compound – which I know better than I would like – but which none of you have seen. There's also a map of the Patriarchy's prison and a mechanical breakdown of a soldier's laser gun – that one's especially for you, Tylon. These maps will aid us, but they will not win us this war." Tyger paused. The silence seemed to command attention and the gathered six turned their eyes away from the drawings and found the burning fire in Tyger's eyes.

"Only blood will win this fight," she said. "War is what the Old World did. It is a horrible act and has always been so. They tried to hide it by calling it different names, but the death was the same.

"Christopher Jarth must leave the dome of New Seattle. Everyone must leave. If Jarth won't give the order to evacuate, I'll kill him. Iahala has discovered that the domes – the Cells inside the domes – cause a terrible madness. All over the world people are dying. Clones and Originals alike must brave the Wind, take shelter in the Great Stones, or in the Valley, until we discover a way for them to live in the Wind. Iahala and her people have started to send out warnings to all the domes through their computers. Hopefully leaders will listen.

"But you all know as well as I that Jarth will never give up his rule, nor leave his kingdom. His soldiers will stand with him until they all lie dead with him, and so we will have to kill, and be killed, to win this cause.

We must put our lives in jeopardy in order to save the Clones and the Originals who want to leave the dome. They might well have turned to the Wind long ago had it not been for Jarth's lies which filled them with such great fear. We don't even really know what happens to Clones in the Wind. They haven't been exposed in over two hundred years. As for the Originals, we know that some of them can change in Phase Three; maybe with the help of water from the River Sky, they'll have even more of a chance. And if we can fell Jarth, we can open all the Patriarchy's domes, not just New Seattle. Everyone will be freed.

"We will take the first step towards a new way of living," Tyger said proudly. "Clone, Original, Human and Windborn, together. If we are victorious, we will build a new world."

Tyger looked at Iahala. "Iahala will speak with Aliqui tonight. Together, they will contact the Pagan warriors throughout the land of Sky who will join us in our cause. When we reach New Seattle, I hope that all the Originals will join us as well. It won't be easy. But it must happen. It will happen. And when the Rescue Squad and all the P3M return, there will be a message for them which reveals our whereabouts and our mission. A message asking them to come to us."

"Can't we wait for them?" Tamarin asked.

Tyger shook her head. "We need to go quickly, before the dome deteriorates. Iahala has made many calculations, but they are not exact. We may have weeks or days, I don't know. All I am sure of is that we can't wait any longer. There are too many lives at stake. The time to act is now."

Tyger's eyes seemed far away for a moment. She saw Terri in her mind's eye and her heart ached in her chest.

"I can have the Skins done by tonight," Tylon said. "Iahala has been helping me." He motioned to the pile of leather clothing that Iahala had brought from Sky's supply rooms. He was almost finished bordering the edges with crushed crystal, affixing the powder with the thin natural adhesive that Iahala had brought him. Already the Wisewoman had begun conjuring the elements, bespelling the clothes. Soon they would all have magical armor to face the Patriarchy.

"How do we get to New Seattle? How do we get in?" Ardyn asked.

Tyger looked at her. "We use the Underground."

The six looked at Tyger in complete surprise. Even Iahala had not heard this part of the plan. Tyger held up the last of the print-outs from the Core. "Sky's caverns cross the entire Earth. Made before the End, many of the tunnels travel under cities and pass beneath domes, but these corridors never reached New Seattle. Just before the End, when the governments were depositing their Answerers into Sky, these officials would travel here, to what was Snoqualmie Falls, and enter through a similar doorway to what exists now. Not connecting the Sky base to the city was an extra precaution to ensure that no one would be able to harm their precious Answerers. It also made it nearly impossible for Answerers to escape from Sky should they wish to.

"Even though Sky does not reach New Seattle, the city itself has hundreds of interlacing pathways running beneath it. During the Old World, it was called Underground Seattle. It's an older city that the newer city was built upon after a great fire destroyed the first one. Today, the domed city of New Seattle lies on top of Underground Seattle."

Tyger paused. It was obvious to everyone that the flame now burning in her eyes was one of hope. "The Core also told me that at some point in their exploration of the Underground's tunnels, the Patriarchy must have discovered a kind of gelatin-water which pooled in a passageway leading east – toward Sky. The gel could be mixed with New World food stuffs and chemicals, thinned to make drinks. So they dug. After a while they found crystals that they could use in the laser cores. So they dug farther and deeper until, eventually, their tunnel from the Underground connected with Sky. So, thanks to the Patriarchy's curiosity, there's a path for us to take. A path that will give us access to the inside of the dome without setting off radiation sensors that opening the dome wall would.

"The Sky tunnel that the Patriarchy connected to runs roughly west from the Genesis chamber. Its the tunnel believed to house a beast, and evil. And it does. That tunnel is the lair of the Patriarchy."

Iahala was staring at Tyger in amazement and the others were stirring with excitement. Tyger continued, "Sarah and Abraham told me that Falcon had been killed by soldiers. But as I thought about that, I began to put two things together. I remembered that Falcon's vest had been found in the west tunnel in shreds in a pool of blood. That pool of blood suddenly became the blood of a soldier, not my sister. The torn cloth – colored black and silver – became part of a soldier's uniform... shredded by Falcon's claws. I know now that I might not have to avenge her death after all. Falcon might still be alive."

Mouse gasped, his face suddenly radiant with hope.

"She's alive?" Aliqui was suddenly in the doorway. She was panting hard, her face creased with pain. He voice shook but her eyes searched Tyger's face, demanding the truth.

Tyger took a step toward her, nodded. "I can't be sure until I see the cloth in the tunnel, but there is a chance."

"Sweet powers," Aliqui murmured and her strength failed her. She stumbled into the room. Her vest was stained dark red as she held her hand, bleeding, against her chest. Iahala cried out, taking Aliqui into her arms. Fox was beside them in an instant, carrying a medical pack. She could already tell that bones were broken by the pain on Aliqui's face. Aliqui tried to push her away, tried to stand again, but Tamarin came forward and held her in place as Fox deftly began to tend to the wound.

"What happened?" Mouse demanded, sudden terror in his eyes. "Something's happened to Mlinz." It wasn't a question. He knew.

Aliqui grit her teeth. "Sarah and Abraham have taken him into Skynest. They managed to override the codes and get access to the room. When I tried to follow, the door came down... my hand was caught."

She looked from Mouse to Tyger. "I couldn't get in. I tried everything I could think of, but I couldn't get access. They've done something at the Core, locked out everyone from Skynest. Abraham... carried a knife. They're going to kill their son." Mouse choked back a sob.

Tyger felt something shift within her. She had planned to go to Skynest for a blessing but instead Skynest would be the place where the first blood was spilled.

"He is not their son," Tyger reminded them all as a growl rose in her throat. "And not even their One will be able to protect them if they harm him."

"Ardyn, Tylon." She motioned to them and they left together. She did not try to stop Mouse from following them.

"Go with them," Aliqui told Iahala and the Wisewoman did.

Together the five bore down on Skynest, with no plan except to stop the execution of the boy his parents called Isaac.

* * *

Standing in the Pagan space called Skynest, Sarah Terahson lifted her head and called out a series of numbers amid a jumble of what sounded like gibberish sounds to anyone except the Core. The computer processed the sequence, a sequence Sarah had named The Purification, and slowly Skynest began caving in piece by piece. First the sliding door, next the standing stones and soon the walls, then the floor. The green crystal lines that controlled the stones' stability shattered as they deactivated. The stone all around her seemed to be crying, crackling with sounds and shifting without support.

The Users were not going to return with more of the Drug. Sarah and Abraham's time had run out. If they waited any longer to act, they would surely go mad. For now they were in complete control of their senses. They had already commanded the One believers throughout the land of Sky to rise up. Now they must make the Great Sacrifice, ending their Earthly time with the cave-in. A cave-in that would also destroy Skynest, this powerful symbol of Pagan magic. When it was all completed, Sarah was convinced they would be remembered as saints.

Yes, Sarah thought, *it is time to leave*. Despite their prayers, this world had fought them relentlessly with its twisted ways and twisted people who refused to embrace the One. They would leave it all behind. Surely the One would forgive their suicides? After all, they were offering up their only son!

Sarah crooned, "We will go, leaving this place where people see power and truth in everything but the One! We will escape from these foul practices of magic and mysteries. The Book does not speak of this world. It does not apply to this Hell – so we will go!"

Abraham looked at his wife as the standing stones of Skynest began to tumbled down and they moved away from them, against the shaking walls. "I would only wish that our children..." he began, oblivious to the boy bound and gagged before him.

Sarah's glare silenced him. "We leave. You and I. The sacrifice of boy and the destruction of this Pagan place will wash us clean of any sin. The One is the Only and the Way."

"Yes," Abraham breathed, trance-like. He lifted Mlinz onto one of the fallen stones. Sarah came to stand beside him. They looked down at their Isaac, but it was Mlinz who looked back at them, his brown eyes wide with terror.

Mlinz looked into the faces of his parents – once familiar and beloved, now twisted and unrecognizable from the debilitating withdrawal from the Drug. Their eyes were red and glassy, sunken in their tense and twitching faces. He had tried to reason with them, tried to escape, but they had bound him easily, their strength unnatural even for two adults, and gagged his mouth against screaming. But still he thrashed, throwing his body from side to side in an effort to roll off the stone that had become a sacrificial altar.

"The first Isaac did not struggle," Abraham intoned. "He trusted his father to know what was best." Abraham's brown eyes were pained but unwavering.

Sarah said, "The One says this must be the Way and we must follow His command. Abraham, it is time."

Abraham nodded. For a moment it seemed that he would not complete the ritual, that like the first Abraham, he would hear the voice of the One calling to him to stay his hand. But this time, it seemed, no power would save the boy. Abraham raised the long knife above his son. His hands shook, but it was impossible to tell whether they shook from withdrawal or from the passion of his conviction.

Tyger rounded the final corner and came face to face with a dead end – the closed door into Skynest. In that same moment, she saw the Gold One. And although her mind registered the increased differences in the

Butterfly's body, she did not have time now to wonder at the cause. Iahala had once said that the Butterflies had their own ways of getting into closed places. Tyger hoped it was true. It was.

The Gold One moved to the Skynest door and gripped the massive stone wheels with two of its legs. Tyger lent her strong shoulders and back to the task as well. Together they pulled at the huge door, no longer supported by gears and wires, and a moment later the great stone rolled away.

The Gold One burst into the room, flying directly to the bound boy and covering his body with its own. Tyger pounced from the doorway, colliding with Abraham with enough force to send them both sprawling. Abraham's head struck the stone floor with a resounding *crack*. Tyger leapt away, but Abraham lay without moving. The knife, thrown from his hand, clattered to the stones.

"Great Powers, it cannot be!" Iahala cried as she and the others ran into the still shaking ruins of Skynest.

Sarah laughed. She still stood before the altar where her son and the Gold One lay. "We knew the demon would stay as long as your power lived! We had to destroy this place, your power, and so we did!"

Tylon steadied Iahala, one hand on her elbow. The Wisewoman was shaking like the walls around her, but not with fear. Her fury rose like a storm and swept through the room. "You have not!" she cried. "You want to destroy my power? Then you must tear *me* apart! My power lies within!"

Sarah retrieved the sacrificial knife from the floor. She advanced on Mlinz, snarling, "Wait your turn, old woman! The One shall have you all before the day is done!"

At Sarah's cry, Tyger bolted over a fallen stone, slamming into Sarah just as Ardyn crashed into her from the opposite side. Sarah was knocked aside, but the knife, still clutched in her fist, impaled Tyger's shoulder, buried to the hilt, the bloodied blade protruding behind her. Tyger roared and her claws shot out.

Grabbing Sarah by the hair, Tyger held her easily, her tender neck exposed. "You killed the Windborn children," she roared. "You infected them with the Drug and sent them into the west tunnel to be killed by soldiers. Your hatred and prejudice delivered them to madness. Where I come from, *we do not harm our children!"*

Sarah met Tyger's eyes with a blank calmness. Tyger saw no recognition there of her crimes, only judgment of those different from herself. When Sarah began to laugh, Tyger saw that her tongue was peppered with holes from her Drug use. "Falcon died in the same way, beast! I was there when she and the Drug first became acquainted." Her laughter rose hysterically, matching the rise of Tyger's rage. "Great One," Sarah cried. "Forgive her! She knows not what she does!"

Tyger bared her fangs; her claws gleamed. "That's where you're wrong. I know exactly what I'm doing!" Tyger's claws flashed, slitting Sarah's throat as if it were rice paper. Blood spurted and sprayed like a fountain. Tyger let the lifeless body fall from her hands.

The walls were quaking dangerously now. Skynest would not stand much longer. The Gold One took flight, its task complete. Ardyn and Mouse ran toward the blood-stained alter where Mlinz still struggled.

"Forgive me, son." Abraham's voice, weak and fading, floated across the stone floor.

Mouse ripped the gag from Mlinz's mouth as Ardyn worked to free him. Chunks of stone fell from high up the walls and crashed to the floor. Mlinz, free of his bonds, turned a cold eye on Abraham. "You are not my father."

With that, the room was filled with the shrieking wail of the entire structure losing its integrity. The floor heaved as if pushed up by the hounds of Hell, hungry for prey. Tyger and her allies were thrown off-balance and slid toward the ruined door, separated from the bloodied would-be altar and the followers of the One. The chasm spread and deepened, the floor buckled again, this time downward toward the spreading maw. Tyger and the others clung to the fragmented and broken stones, and as if by some magic, their anchors remained rooted in place even as Sarah's body slid across the floor as if drawn downward by an invisible thread, and Abraham, though he scrabbled for purchase in the rubble, could not close his fingers around anything. Then they were both were swallowed by that huge mouth of stone, and they fell headlong into their Hell.

* * *

Tamarin, Fox and Aliqui found them all just outside the ruins of Skynest, clustered together in the hallway, the dust still settling from the destruction.

Tyger made no sound as Fox pulled the knife from her body.

Iahala was the first to speak, "What do we do now, Tyger?"

Tyger looked at Iahala. The Wisewoman was on her knees, her back toward what once was Skynest. Tyger could tell that Skynest's fall was taking a heavy toll on the woman's heart.

Aliqui sank down beside her grandmother, covering Iahala's folded hands with her good one.

Tyger spoke carefully. "You two know the evils of the domes. I'm counting on you to gain allies among the Pagan people of Sky. Share what you know. Convince them to aid to our cause or, at least, to come up out of Sky because the Cells are leaking into the ground as well. Tell them to gather in the Valley and inside the Great Stones where they'll be safe. Ask them to join us in our battle against the Silver Steel."

Iahala took a deep breath. "I will do as you ask, Tyger. But I ask something in return."

Tyger waited for her to continue.

Iahala reached out for Tamarin and Fox. They came and sat beside her. "When Skynest fell, the young Butterflies lost their home. I assume that now they are scattered in the Valley. I will take them with me as I travel through Sky. They will bring the people hope. But I would like to take these two as well." Iahala looked at the two P3M. "The Butterflies mean much to the Pagans of Sky and you have found a bond with them as well, as they have with you. I want all of Sky to see that not only Humans are accepted by the Butterflies. The Butterflies see beyond the boundaries of race."

It was clear from Fox's and Tamarin's faces that they wanted to go with Iahala and so Tyger nodded. "All right. The four of you will go," she said, including Aliqui in her count. "And we'll meet up with you as planned, one week from now."

"Only three will go," Aliqui said.

Tyger looked at her in surprise.

"I want to go with you, Tyger," Aliqui continued.

"Because of Falcon," Tyger said, almost to herself. "This will bring you to the truth about her sooner – if she lives, if not, what state she is in."

Aliqui just looked at her. "Falcon was always wild, Tyger. She was always quick to temper. Her emotions ran in extremes. She wanted revenge. I know she would have killed any soldiers she came upon. But she wanted more. She wanted Jarth. She wanted to know the truth. Why he took you, where you were." Aliqui stared into the darkness of the corridor, perhaps imagining Falcon. "But if she has found Jarth, what would he tell her? And infected by the Drug, what would she believe? Who is she now? Does she even remember me...."

Tyger felt a sudden chill. She knew Falcon had been deeply scarred by the slaughter at the Village. There was a terrible rage within her sister. Rage and great power. There was no telling what she would do when she faced the Patriarch and heard a story sure to be full of lies. Tyger knew the Patriarch's lies first hand. How convincing they were. And how deadly.

Tyger nodded once, understanding Aliqui's importance in this quest. "You're the only one who may be able to reach her," she said.

Aliqui nodded. "Yes."

"All right then." Tyger stood. "The Riddler gave us a second chance. Let's not misuse it. Unity will be born. Even if we all must die for it."

They all took hands, their bodies becoming what Skynest had once been, a circle of strength and magic.

Iahala's voice rose in blessing. "We come together through the strength of the Powers and of the True One. We are the warriors and the heralds of the New World, the Unity. We willingly give our bodies to the cause that will bring us all together, despite what divides us.

"In the past, the conqueror has always rewritten the conquered's history. Let us be the first to tell the truth. Let us write a world of equality. A world of freedom. We will be the first, but we will not be the last."

Then they all said together, "Great Powers grant us this. Blessed be, so mote it be. Amen."

Iahala turned to Tyger. "I do not want to bring you fear, Tyger. There is one last thing you should know, and even I do not completely understand it. Prophesy says: *The birth and death of the Tiger will come on the wings of the Butterfly.* Do not forget these words, Tyger. Promise me this."

Recovered from the rubble of Skynest, Iahala pressed the sheathed sword that she'd used in her Circle into Tyger's hands. The sword was covered with symbols and runes and Tyger could feel the weapon's power pulsing in her hands.

"I won't forget," Tyger said.

* * *

They entered the west tunnel, the tunnel called Dark, and shone their lights into the shadows. Tyger went first. Ardyn and Aliqui followed close behind her. They were cautious, but moved quickly. They had three days, maybe four, to get to New Seattle. Any longer would be tempting fate.

Their lights flashed on the crushed-crystal lines of their leather jackets and breeches. Tyger could see and feel the magic that swirled over each surface. She knew Tylon's creation would save lives. Her light found something on the tunnel floor and the six came to a stop.

They had come far into the tunnel, past Iahala's now defunct magical wall, to the Patriarchy's steel barricade. At its base, where once there had been a pool of blood, there were only remnants of clothing. Tyger knelt. Everyone watched as she fingered the cloth. After a moment, she stood and said, "My sister has killed a soldier. She did not die here."

Had danger not lurked close by, Aliqui might have cried out in joy, but instead, she nodded silently and kept her own counsel. But the question that haunted everyone was: if Falcon lived, what was the Drug doing to her?

It did not take long to dismantle the wall that the soldiers had built. Mouse and Mlinz scaled steel and pried the clasps at the top away from the stone ceiling. Then Tyger, Ardyn, Tylon and Aliqui threw their weight against the silver metal and it fell away from them with a crash.

Beyond the wall there was darkness. After a moment's introspection, they crossed the boundary, boots echoing dully on the remnant of the steel wall, and they were swallowed up in a darkness that even their crystal lights could not fully dissipate.

"Our goal is of the Light," Tyger said in encouragement. "And that makes us warriors of the Light." The others, buoyed by the sound of her voice, felt hopeful. She was leader of the Unity and would be the death of the Patriarchy. Tyger would drink the silver wine.

They traveled on, moving beside the slow ebb of the weak stream from the River Sky and past the crystals set in the walls that the black and silver soldiers dug out to charge for their laser guns. The stone was rough and smooth in turns, peppered with holes from the soldiers' mining.

As Tyger walked, she asked herself what she fought for. For the first time her answer was not her people or even the P3M. For the first time she fought for herself. She would face Jarth for herself because she believed she deserved to have him fall at her feet.

After almost twenty-four hours of travel they settled to rest in a curve of the corridor, huddling closely together for warmth. Mouse and Mlinz lay asleep in each other's arms. Aliqui was sitting, her back to the stone wall, and it was clear from her expression that her thoughts were of Falcon.

When she saw Tyger watching her, Aliqui said, "I was just thinking of the last time I saw her." Tyger was silent so Aliqui continued. "She was getting ready to go flying. That wasn't unusual, she needed to be by herself often enough. But that day felt different. She seemed preoccupied, closed off.

"I went to her and kissed her. I said, 'I love you.' And she said she loved me too. A feeling crept over me then. It was as if I knew she wasn't coming back. I said, 'I hope you find what you're looking for.'

"She just looked at me." Aliqui's eyes glistened with tears in the shadows of the tunnel. "Then she kissed me again and was gone. For the longest time, I thought that she'd only found death. But now that I know she's alive I wonder what it was she did find."

Tyger didn't answer her. There was no answer to make. After a time, Aliqui drifted to sleep.

Nearby, Tylon tossed and moaned softly in the throes of a dream. In the dream, the young man saw Ravyn. She smiled at him and said, "I love you, Tylon." He shook his head.

"No," he answered. "I know that's not true."

And then the dream changed. Another voice said, "I love you." It was Petre. Tylon could feel Petre's presence just behind him. Tylon turned, knowing finally what he wanted to say to the other man. But Petre was not there. Instead, the figure before him was a man who closely resembled Petre with the same soft curls and rainbow-colored clothes, but his gentle, innocent eyes were different – they reflected a knowledge that was ancient and an acceptance of that knowledge that was new. "I am with you always," said the figure that was-and-was-not Petre. "For as long as the Wind blows."

Tylon was looking down toward the ground as if from a great height. Below him, Petre was falling toward the earth. There was no one to catch him and the ground rose swiftly closer. Then suddenly, beautifully, horribly, Petre's body burst into a million colors, colors that splattered across Tylon like an exploding rainbow. The colors spread everywhere, in the sky, over the earth, into the ground. What had been Petre – what was now a brilliant flash of rainbow light – was seeping into everything, slipping over dormant places of the World, and then, finally, touching a sleeper, an ancient presence more powerful than any other. A sleeping power that waited for the right combination of movements, molecules and magics to be awoken. And when this proper fusion had circled the Earth, seeping into everything, the colors that had been Petre woke the Wind.

Tylon shuddered awake for one sleepy moment. Tyger looked over at him, her gaze asking if he was all right. The young man only nodded and fell back into sleep. When he woke the next day, the dream would still be with him, in all its vivid brilliance, and Tylon would remember Petre's words and the promise he had made.

Keeping first watch, Tyger unsheathed Iahala's sword and held the weapon across her lap. She traced each symbol with her hand and realized that she knew some of them.

The sign for Wind was here, as was the symbol for sky. There was an etching of a tiger's face, another of a tiger's claws and one of the flower she'd been named for. There was a Butterfly as well, and Tyger wondered if it was the one that would bring her birth or death. She leaned back against the cold wall and let her mind wander. Her thoughts came to rest eventually on Terri, leader of the Spiders and one time Windrider. The only Windrider Tyger had never risked to the Wind. The only woman to ever have taken Tyger's heart in her hands when she had cupped Tyger's face. Terri had believed Tyger could never harm someone she loved.

But Tyger knew that wasn't true. For many years, employed by the Patriarchy, it had been her job to hurt those she loved. And even when she had turned away from the Silver Steel, she'd still hurt the one she loved most in the world when she'd sent the letter to Terri. The letter which said nothing of Tyger's true feelings. A letter she had not even delivered herself.

Tyger wondered how they would find the life of the Originals when they reached New Seattle. If Jarth was ignoring the dome sites, surely he was ignoring the Industrial District as well. What would kill them first? Cell madness or starvation? Tyger stiffened at the thought. If they were not successful, so many would die.

"Tyger." Ardyn's voice drew Tyger out of her thoughts. She looked at Ardyn as the other woman sank down beside her. "We're on the way to bring down the Patriarchy and instead of looking like the proud warrior you are, you look like you're going to be sick."

Tyger smiled despite her dark thoughts.

"I am a proud warrior," she answered softly, not wanting to disturb the sleepers. "But one with concerns."

"We may have to call you the Worry Warrior of the West Walkway."

Tyger grunted. It was as close to a laugh as she would get this night.

After a moment, Ardyn said more seriously, "What is it that concerns you?"

"So much rests on my shoulders, Ardyn. So many lives. I can't expect the others to carry this war for me. This war is my destiny. It is what I must do. What my bloodline, my birth, demands that I do. Mouse is barely a man. And Falcon... I know not what she has become or if she can be healed. We are the only Windborn left that I know of. If I am to fall in the battle ahead, there must be one of my bloodline to finish what I've begun. To fight for the Unity." Tyger fell silent for a moment. "We've been through a lot together, Ardyn. I know how strong you are. I know you would finish this, if I could not." She paused and looked directly into Ardyn's eyes. "I want you to be my sister."

Ardyn was stunned for only a moment, then, "I'd be honored," she said.

So in the darkness of the Underground they used the sharp edge of the Circle sword. They cut their palms, pressed their hands together to mix their blood and pledged a bond of kinship.

When the time for rest was finished, Tyger, who was not tired and had never woken the others for their shifts, woke everyone gently. They moved on without delay, their minds bent toward the future task of nothing less than the rebirth of the world.

* * *

Part Ten

Eight days had passed since the Rescue Squad had ventured from Sky when they returned to the Valley triumphant. All of the P3M had been found and freed.

And only one had been lost.

Kestrel led the mixed flock of Windboards and Wings down into the Valley of Sky. She landed Swallowtail and stepped away from her Wing as the others landed: twenty-four in all.

As everyone assembled for their entrance into Sky, Kestrel realized how much she had missed this place, despite her new-found love for the world of the Wind. Kestrel turned toward the falls, drawn by the excited exclamations of the newcomers. Wolf fell into step beside her and she smiled at him. Her eyes were as solid now as any Windborn's. They were as rich and brilliant a brown as his own. The change had occurred sometime after the storm and the fact that she could survive in the Wind showed in those eyes. Somehow the storm and the Sky water in her blood had made the transformation possible. "Think of what this means, Wolf," she said. "Humans can change. I'm not sure how, but they can."

Wolf smiled wordlessly at her as they were joined by Tryl, Jyln and Spider.

"I thought we'd never get back," Jyln said. Her appearance was changed as well. Her hair was now two-toned and her eyes were Windborn solid. Even her senses were heightened. "And yet, despite everything, here we are." She clasped Tryl's and Spider's hands in her own.

"The storm that took Petre... that was the worst," Wolf observed. "I didn't think any of us would survive."

"But every storm we saw, every one was worse than anything I've ever seen," Kestrel admitted. "Something is changing. I can feel it."

For a moment, each of the five seemed engrossed in their private thoughts. Then Spider broke the silence by announcing, "I feel like we can do anything now."

Kestrel smiled and took her crystal pendant from a pouch at her waist to open the door into Sky.

"It'll be good to see Tyger again," Tryl added. The cowgirl's newly solid eyes took in the now-familiar landscape. She was the first to see the Great Butterfly's approach.

She came from within the curtain of the falls. Her wings were gold with blue marks like eyes on the tips and they glistened as if bordered with crystal. She landed before them and said in a voice that was both strong and feminine, "Tyger of the Village of Wind has gone. She left a message for you within, but I will give it to you now."

"Great Wind," Tryl gasped. Silence followed. They all stared at the Butterfly who had transformed. No longer a Butterfly, this creature was two races – Butterfly and Windborn.

She had cream-colored skin, that bore just the faintest sun blush. Solid blue eyes deeper than any Old World ocean. Golden blonde curls cascaded down her winged back, wings that framed a body lithe and strong. She had diamond-shaped eyes, delicately pointed ears, a slender nose and a taut, pale-lipped mouth. From her temples rose velvety black antennae, quivering in the breeze.

And more than anything, her eyes arrested them for they seemed to hold the wisdom of two lives bound together – two sets of memories and experiences bound now into one incarnation.

She was clad in black leather breeches bordered with crystal powder, and upon her head she wore a thin stone crown that gleamed with crushed gems.

Tryl took a step towards her, and Butterfly-woman reached out to touch Tryl's face with a long, six-fingered hand. Her solid ocean eyes sparkled in recognition. "I know you. You are Tryl of the Windriders. The cowgirl. You are my friend."

Tryl gently clasped the hand that touched her. "Yes," she said. "I am." Tryl's voice was almost a whisper in comparison. "And you are Sarya."

"Yes, I am Sarya, the Gold One." There was a moment of stunned silence. Could it be true? Their beloved Sarya come back to them again? Jyln was the first to break the spell. Moving forward deliberately, she reached for Sarya's hands. Searching Sarya's eyes, she looked for the woman she had known and found her. But something else as well – something stronger, more confident, more complex than that singular creature Sarya had been. "So many friends to see again," Sarya said. "And many new ones to find."

Sarya touched each of those gathered with her eyes. She raised her voice to be heard by all. "Tyger, the one marked by my Power, has gone ahead to prepare the way. She has taken those called Mlinz, Mouse, Aliqui, Tylon and Ardyn with her. They will join with the Originals and be called First Force. The Pagans, Second Force, called Magic, followed shortly after them."

Sarya motioned with her arms and suddenly they were surrounded by the swarm of adult Butterflies each carrying garments of black leather with colored patterns, bordered with crushed crystal, enough for everyone.

"The man Tylon created these and left them for you. He did not have time to complete them all, so what he had not finished, we did. Once you have donned your armor, we will depart for New Seattle. We will travel overland. Each of you will be borne by one of the flock so that we may reach New Seattle as quickly as possible."

"Wait," Tryl asked. "Tyger has gone? Why New Seattle?"

"War, Tryl. War has come to the Patriarchy." Sarya looked to the sky above them as if she could see the currents of the Wind that would carry them. "I will lead us there. Astride the Butterflies you will truly be Windriders. We are the Third Force of Four. History will remember us as the Force called Butterfly."

* * *

Part Eleven

Jarth dreamed of doom. In his dream, he faced four warriors. One was called Tiger; the second, Magic; the third Butterfly and the fourth – the most frightening of the four – destroyed him with claws of fire and eyes of flame before he was allowed to know its name, or even understand its awesome power. When he awoke and felt his sweat-drenched skin, he thought for a moment he lay mired in his own blood and screamed himself hoarse before he realized he was finally awake.

Shaking in terror, he called for the lights which had gone off automatically when he'd ceased to move, about an hour before, when he'd fallen to sleep at his desk. But even their brightness could not dispel the encroaching feeling of dread that he had not been able to shake for days.

The P3M were gone. Inexplicably. Disappeared without a trace. He could not understand where he had gone wrong. They should have been dead, or at least living out the last moments of their pitiful lives in terror, but something – someone – had found them and convinced them their fear of him was undeserved. Someone had led them, as the Tiger had lead those others, to escape to the Wind.

Jarth wiped the sweat from his face and neck and pivoted his chair to gaze though the glass wall. Something was brewing in the darkness of the Industrial District. Something that he could not control. Somehow, he knew, a piece of that same power that had freed his slaves would seep in through the dome walls and incite his Originals... then his Clones as well. Little did he know that he had less than four days until it would do just that. Four, one for each of the warriors of doom.

He groaned as the sharp pain of his familiar headache began again behind his eyes. This day had simply been another in what was beginning to seem an endless pattern of nightmarish moments all linked together – almost as horrible as his terrifying dream.

Today, the continuing nightmare had begun with Wenright's report that Petre Tarrl's bio-stat chip had ceased transmission. Tarrl was dead and so was Jarth's link to the world outside the dome. He hoped that Falcon – whom he had code named Butterfly – would bring him the information he craved about the renegade Tyger. But was it a foolish hope? At another time, Falcon's employ would have comforted him, but the dream was still fresh in his mind and he could not shake the image of the third warrior. The Butterfly. He hoped his two soldiers were self-possessed enough to aim their lasers well once he'd obtained the information he needed. But a seed of doubt bloomed inside him. It would be too fitting to have this botched as well. Too much in keeping with the continuing string of annoying little problems which, put together, were quickly becoming overwhelming. And frightening. And so he fretted. Fretted and dared for doom to come.

* * *

She had given Terri four days and that was more than enough. Falcon could not afford to be lenient. Once, lifetimes ago it seemed, she had been a child running in the Wind with her sister, etching Tyger's face in the Heart Stone so she would always remember Tyger was the person she loved the most.

Once, lying in the arms of a Human woman she had given her heart to, Falcon had told her of Tyger, of how brave she was as a child, and of how brave Falcon believed she still must be.

Falcon did not believe in magic and she did not believe in the One because neither had come to the aid of her dying people. There was only herself. Once, there had been more. Back in Sky, but now, she was alone. Sky seemed like a distant dream. A memory that belonged to someone else. Through the whirling in her skull, she couldn't remember that once she'd been respected, that once she'd been loved.

But those times were very far from now. Past and present were separated in her mind by a strange and churning wall. Now Falcon knew the only bravery was within herself, and Tyger, her sister, had been the greatest coward of them all. Tyger had saved herself from death by selling the lives of others. She was filth to be wasted.

Earlier that day, Falcon had marched into Terri's room, grinning in pleasure as the other woman tried to hide her shudder. When Falcon reminded Terri of their "agreement," recalling in vivid detail all she would do if the forth-coming information were not what she required, the so-called leader had started to cry.

Falcon waited for Terri to compose herself, a sly smile playing about her lips. Finally, Terri had named the meeting place – the intersection of Jefferson and Terry where the roads crossed under the permanent shadow of the Ramp.

Falcon had seen the fear in Terri's eyes and believed she had won. Even now Falcon was writing her own history in her head. But unfortunately for Falcon, she was unaware of another history – the history of that particular intersection. The blood that had once been spilled there and the honor that had been won. Jefferson and Terry were legendary for what had happened there. The great Battle of Fire. Every gang knew the story. Every Original had, at one time or another, come to gaze upon the scorched street and blackened buildings with a certain amount of awe. Jefferson and Terry. The last battleground of Tyger and her Windriders. This was the place where the Wheels had fallen from glory after reigning on the streets for many years. Falcon did not know this, nor did her two soldier companions. But they had their own histories – their own futures – to contend with, futures that centered around their orders to kill.

But what Falcon could not know and did not see was that Terri was relying on precisely the information that Falcon lacked to lead Terri to victory. If there was anything Terri had learned in the world of the Originals, it was how to survive. Even if survival meant shaking in the eyes of a beast and crying heavy tears – tears meant for the woman she was ultimately protecting, but misinterpreted as a sign of weakness. Terri would do whatever it took to survive and do it so well that not even Falcon, who could pick the truth from lies like one picks dead flowers from a flowering bush, could see through the masquerade.

"You should have demanded she tell you everything right there!" Falcon's musings were interrupted by the Duke's irritating voice. Falcon, Duke and Liege stood now beneath the Ramp, where Jefferson Street crossed Terry. Falcon turned slowly toward him as he continued, "Letting her make us trek all the way out here and stand in the night for her to–"

Falcon didn't feel like letting him finish. She hit the man in the face and he toppled to the ground. Blood streamed from his broken nose.

"Shut up," she said. Wisely, he didn't reply.

Falcon stared down Terry Street toward the Spider homebase. Soon she would see a single figure walking to them. Soon, or she would follow through with her threat.

Outside the dome a storm raged. It had raged there for many days and Falcon could feel it. The churning pain in her head increased and subsided, as if the storm were in her blood and she was fighting it off. The pain was irritating, like a burr beneath her skin. Her normally short temper was nonexistent as she simply moved from silence to rage. She had no idea that behind her, Duke was taking aim at her head.

"The Original must be humiliated that she caved in," Liege said into the tense quiet, pushing Duke's laser away, shaking his head adamantly at the other soldier behind Falcon's back. No matter how arrogant Falcon was, killing her too soon would not put them in Jarth's good graces. "She probably couldn't bear to talk to us at her base, hm? All her followers would think she was a coward. I'd think–"

Falcon held up one hand as a warning to Liege. She turned only her head toward him. Her solid-colored eyes bore into his and she felt him shrink from her. "I will do the thinking here. Understand?" Her claws glistened in the faint lumi-light.

Liege just set his jaw and nodded.

As Falcon turned back toward the street, she saw them. For a moment, Falcon squinted down the Street in disbelief. Beside her Liege tightened took out his own laser and Duke scrambled to his feet, ignoring his pain.

The road was full of warriors. Terri lead them – six gangs plus her own, and all the Originals not members of a gang as well. They came on, a solid wall of seemingly unstoppable fighters, united for a common cause for the first time. The Climbers with their grappling hooks and sharp throwing discs; the Prowlers, haunting in blue face paint wielding metal staffs; the gang called Speed, who, although they had just fought the Spiders, had called a sudden truce. Even their leader, her knee bandaged from the recent scuffle, marched proudly toward Falcon, shoulders squared and head held high. The Rollers with their crossbows also walked among the force, and in numbers rivaling even the Spiders came the Wheels.

Clad in black leather, astride their motorcycles painted in flames, the Wheels were ready for this fight. Leading them was a man who no one had seen for many days. A man who rode now without his helmet, his dark eyes burning. He had no hair anywhere on his head or face, and his skin was slicker than it should be, as if he had once been melting.

Panther was indeed a fearsome sight. Once he'd promised Tyger no more bloodshed on the streets but this was different. He'd only promised her he wouldn't shed Original blood. Clones were a different story. And fighting for their lives against the Patriarchy was more important than anything.

The warriors walked together in a terrible silence, shoulder to shoulder and armed to fight legions. Amid them a banner had been hoisted high over their heads, a banner that filled Falcon's blood with cold fear and hot fury. A banner with a golden orange background and stripes of black that read in fiery letters, *Tyger*.

Duke was the first one to panic. "This is Sergeant Maurer!" he spat into his implanted communicator. "We have a full scale revolt on our hands. Request immediate reinforcements. Corner of Jefferson and Terry!"

The two soldiers leveled their lasers. Each weapon had a full six shots, six bullets filled with death. Falcon's laser had only five, but she made no attempt to ready her weapon. Instead, she watched the approaching onslaught with eyes blacker than night and her body as still as stone.

"In the name of the Patriarch, woman," Duke screamed, "take out your weapon! We're going to be slaughtered here!"

Falcon ignored him. Terri stopped the gathered warriors directly across the street from Falcon and the two soldiers. Terri held an E.C. in one hand and a Thread was mounted on her other wrist. Her green eyes blazed and Falcon was reminded again of Tyger. Always Tyger.

"These streets are ours," Terri called out, her voice unwavering and strong. "We will not tolerate the Silver Steel in our world. You have four seconds to turn and leave."

"Fools! If we go, more will come!" Duke and Liege said in unison, drawing the masks that had covered the identical Clone features away from their faces. They spoke over each other, their voices the same, as if only one man spoke. "Don't you know what you've done here? The Patriarchy will squash you now. You have pushed Jarth too far. He'll destroy you all and begin again!"

"We'll be waiting," Terri growled. Her words were nearly drowned out by a roar of approval from the gathered warriors.

Falcon looked at Terri with a level gaze. Terri did not flinch away from her this time, and Falcon knew that she had greatly underestimated this warrior. "You loved her that much?" Falcon asked, her voice filled sarcasm and hate.

Terri raised her head defiantly, but before she could speak Joanna answered, "We all do."

Falcon looked at Joanna, finding it strange that Joanna, who obviously had such anger toward Tyger, would be the one to defend her. But then Falcon understood. Tyger had been the only one to stand up to the Patriarchy and win. The only one to taste the silver wine.

Falcon was smiling. Already the hum of the Hovercraft bringing reinforcements filled the air. This battle at least would be fairly matched. She looked at Terri again. "If you loved her that much, then you will die for her." She reached for her laser and shot at Terri in one fluid motion, but Curn dove in front of his leader and took the bullet that killed him.

Duke and Liege fired, and twelve more Originals dropped to the ground. Blood flowed over the street. Death had come to New Seattle. The gathered warriors rushed forward as the Hovercraft landed and soldiers spilled out on to the streets of Jefferson and Terry. Spilled out like silver wine.

* * *

Part Twelve

In the darkness of the tunnel, Tyger and her companions fell silent. The stone walls shook above them, vibrating with the familiar sound of Hovercraft speeding overhead. When the sound had died away, they all turned to Tyger, whose face was hard in the crystals' light.

"We'll follow the craft," she said. "And see where they go."

They followed her into another narrow pathway. The ancient buildings of the Old World blurred by them as they ran to catch up with the speeding crafts.

"Could just be ration patrol," Tylon said.

Tyger shook her head. "Too fast. Too many."

"The Patriarchy soldiers are armed with stun-guns, yes?" Aliqui asked.

"But don't underestimate them." Ardyn held up a hand still disfigured from their torture, the wrist still wrapped. "They know about close fighting and have no qualms about striking after you're down."

The sound of the Hovercraft stopped just ahead. They ran a bit further through the debris. Dirt and rocks, dislodged by the sudden tumult above, fell from the ceiling. Mouse and Mlinz took out their El Rods and the others did the same.

Tyger held up her light and searched the ceiling, her emerald eyes darting. Then, she led them a bit further away from where the Steel had set down and handed her light crystal to Ardyn. "The silver wine has been poured. It either ends here or it begins. May the Powers be with us."

Tyger gestured and Ardyn shone the light onto a set of metal rungs set into the stone wall. The ladder rose through a narrow stone tube, all the way to the ceiling. Tyger looked up for a moment, then took a deep breath. She stripped off her jacket – it would restrict her ability to climb – and handed it to Ardyn. Tylon started to protest, but a glance from Ardyn silenced him. Now was not the time to question their leader. Tyger would face the Silver Steel in her own way.

She moved away from them, a shadow moving out of shadow, muscles moving beneath her dark skin. The delicate mark of the Butterfly between her breasts glinted briefly in the feeble light as Tyger grabbed the first rung, some eight feet up and hung there by one hand. She touched Iahala's sword which hung at her belt, then curled her fingers into her palm, touching the new scar, the mark of her blood bond with Ardyn. She looked down at Ardyn. Ardyn nodded at her, the hint of a smile playing about her lips, her eyes dark and courageous. Ardyn was ready. They were all ready. That was all Tyger needed.

"May the Wind be with us all," she said and climbed all the way to the top.

* * *

Soldiers spilled around Falcon like water around a stone. She was no longer smiling. The street was a chaotic mass of screaming, fighting bodies. Blood pooled on the concrete. The soldiers, equipped only with weapons that could stun, used every fighting technique they knew to take as many Originals as they could out of the battle. And the Originals, for their part, were fighting to kill.

Ravyn and Joanna fought back to back, parrying the blows of two soldiers' stun rods. Ravyn swung her staff with deadly precision while Joanna kept her opponent at bay with bolts of Thread. Suddenly, Speed's leader, the girl Ravyn had struck not many nights before, rushed forward and pushed the two women down. The two death bullets, both from Falcon's gun, missed them by inches.

Panther did not flinch as a laser beam cut by his face, leaving a trail of blood. It was not a direct hit so it only burned, and Panther had stopped feeling fire after his entire body had been an inferno. He shot two soldiers with his crossbow as he tore around the battlefield on his black bike. He downed another soldier and swerved wildly to avoid a laser shot.

When he brought his gaze back to the battle field he saw Falcon rip out the throat of one of his Wheelers. Panther opened his mouth to bellow the beast's name but changed his mind when he saw her target – Byn – and screamed the child's name instead. Alerted by Panther's warning, Byn hit the ground. She heard the bullet pass above her, sizzling in the air. Crossbow bolts whizzed overhead and suddenly Panther was beside her, scooping her up, banner and all. They rode together, the banner bearing Tyger's name streaming above them.

Terri, her E.C. blazing, rushed towards Falcon. Her auburn hair fanned about her face like flames. Her green eyes flashed dangerously, and there was blood on her coveralls.

Falcon heard her coming and turned calmly to face her. Falcon had one shot left and she smiled as she aimed.

The ancient sewer cover was made of solid cast iron and weighed two hundred-fifty pounds. Bracing her feet in the metal rungs and her back against stone, Tyger lifted the cover from below, throwing it aside. It clanged onto the street above her head, spewing up loose chunks of concrete where it landed.

Like something out of ancient legend, Tyger rose out of the Underground into the battle. Everywhere, eyes turned toward her, but she saw only one thing – Falcon, her death weapon raised and Terri in her sights.

Tyger was like a stone dropped into still water. From her, a wave of power rippled through the crowd as every fighter felt her presence. Both

Original and Clone alike knew she had arrived, that Tyger of the Windriders, of the Village of Wind, had returned to New Seattle. And with that, everything changed.

Falcon turned directly to her sister. Black ice met emerald fire. "How convenient, sister," she spat the word like a curse. "You came to me."

Tyger looked at Falcon dressed in black and silver, with a pendant Tyger had once worn hanging from her neck. "Falcon," she said, taking a step toward her kin.

Falcon raised her laser. Tyger was unprotected. No one stood close enough to save her. Falcon's voice was even colder than her eyes. "The Patriarch gave me a special gift, and I saved one shot for you."

The Butterfly smiled at the Tiger and pulled the trigger.

* * *

About the Author
(Photo by Carol DiMarco.)

Born in Seattle, Washington, in 1973, Jennifer Anna DiMarco has been writing and publishing since before she could legally drive a car. She is the author of over a dozen novels, stage and screen plays, in addition to several children's books and board games. She insists this is proof that having lesbian parents has many advantages.

Though she has been employed as a martial arts instructor, a construction worker and a chase-driver, Jennifer is currently the driving force behind Pride Publications where she intends to stay.

To contact Jennifer, or any other Pride author, write to Pride Publications, Post Office Box 148, Radnor, Ohio 43066-0148, or email PridePblsh@aol.com.

Pride Publications
bringing light to the shadows
voice to the silence

Pride Publications
Post Office Box 148
Radnor, Ohio 43066-0148

Our History
Pride Publications was founded in 1989 by a circle of authors and artists. A publishing house dedicated to shedding light on misconceptions, challenging stereotypes and speaking for those not spoken for. A press created for the authors, artists and readers, not for profit. With several imprints and divisions, Pride publishes books in all genres by all kinds of authors, regardless of gender, orientation, race or age. We are always looking for new projects that others might consider "too wild, too risky, too truthful." At Pride we believe that risk and diversity are part of life. We believe in opening eyes.

Our Facts
Pride Publications works with artists, authors looking for publishers, authors self-publishing who want help, and authors in need of agents. Authors published with Pride receive 10-15% of gross monies received and retain the rights to their book. Authors will also have say in all edits, artwork and promo done for their book.

Authors co-publishing with Pride's help pay only half of the paper costs. Pride pays for all other costs and offers all standard services including accounting, advertising, storage, tour planning, representation and international distribution. Authors receive 50% of all gross monies received.

Authors working with Pride literary agents will receive complete industry representation for 12% of gross royalties received.

Artists working with Pride novels receive advance payment for their art in addition to royalties on all two dozen products that will feature their art. Artists working with Pride children's books receive royalties equal to the author's.

Author submissions: Send complete manuscript, typed, single-sided, double-spaced on white paper. Resume and bio. Summary of entire manuscript. SASE for return of manuscript.

Artist submissions: Send five to ten color and black-and-white samples of artwork. Resume and bio. Cover letter discussing what types of projects you are interested in working on. SASE for response.

If you enjoyed
Fall Through the Sky...

Ask your local bookstore to order
Escape to the Wind
the first book in the *Wind Trilogy*
ISBN 0-9628621-5-0.

Or send check or money order to
Pride Publications for $11.95
plus $1.50 for shipping.

Show Your Pride!

Pride Publications offers many products featuring our full-color book covers including tee-shirts ($15.00), mugs ($15.00), canvas tote bags ($18.00), baseball caps ($18.00), 20 by 30 inch posters ($15.00) and 2 1/2 by 3 inch cloth patches ($12.00).

Send check or money order to Pride Publications. Please specify size (if necessary) and design desired. Thank you!

Matters of Pride

Pride books are available to bookstores through distributors
as well as direct for 50% off retail, payment due in 60 days, free shipping.
** designates forth-coming titles.

Books and Plays

The Redemption of Corporal Nolan Giles. Historical Fiction. Jeane
Heimberger Candido. A rich, haunting tale set during the Civil War by a
talented writer and Civil War enthusiast. The Civil War has never come alive
as it does on these pages. Perpare yourself for the truth.

ISBN 1-886383-14-6 $11.95

Annabel and I. Romantic Fantasy. Chris Anne Wolfe. Set on Chautauqua
Lake, the tale of a love that transcends all time and all categories. Jenny-wren
is from the 1980s but Annabel is from the 1890s. Features thirteen interior
artplates by Chris Storm.

ISBN 1-886383-17-0 $10.95

Bitter Thorns. Adult Fairytale. Chris Anne Wolfe. Magical, sensual retelling
of Beauty and the Beast with two heroines. *From the Muse Fairytale Series*,
#1. Features eight interior artplates by Lupa.

ISBN 1-886383-12-X $10.95

talking drums. Prose Poetry. Jan Bevilacqua. Lush prose-poetry plus. Love,
life, sex and empowerment. Exploring gender and butch/femme in our society
today. Features fourteen artplates by Kateren Lopez.

ISBN 1-886383-13-8 $9.95

The White Bones of Truth. Science Fiction. Cris Newport. In a future where
film stars are owned by the Studio and independence is illegal, revolution
brews. A novel of rock 'n' roll, redemption and virtual reality. Features five
interior artplates by Pride Publications.

ISBN 1-886383-15-4 $10.95

**Queen's Champion.* Adult Fairytale. Cris Newport. A classic and enticing
retelling of Lancelot and Guinevere's love affair and the legend of Lancelot.
From the Muse Fairytale Series, #2.

ISBN 1-886383-20-0 $11.95

1000 Reasons You Might Think She Is My Lover. Erotica. Angela Costa.
Romantic, rowdy, tasty and titillating. A red-hot, pocket-sized collection that
will make you laugh, blush... and look for a lover.

ISBN 1-886383-21-9 $9.95

Fall Through the Sky. Science Fiction. Jennifer DiMarco. In this stand-alone sequel to the future-fiction adventure *Escape to the Wind*, Tyger and her gang the Windriders discover incredible secrets and prepare to face the Patriarchy.

ISBN 1-886383-16-2 $12.95

At the Edge. Play. Jennifer DiMarco. You'll laugh out loud. You'll shout hallelujah. Terease Weaver is a poet giving new meaning to the word "melodrama," and Daniel O'Donald is an HIV+ construction worker and activist. When these two women meet tectonic plates shift.

ISBN 1-886383-11-1 $9.95

Games
These role-playing games are brought to you by RAMPANT Gaming,
Pride's gaming division. Portfolio bound.

Arena Warriors. Battle adventure where you command a fighting team through the challenges of the Great Arena. Play with friends, alone or through a national club!

ISBN 1-886383-04-9 $9.00

Jewel Fighters. Build your fortress, create your fighting force. A game of strategy and skill. Infiltrate your opponent's kingdom and steal his or her Jewel while protecting your own!

ISBN 1-886383-03-0 $9.00

Kingdoms. For everyone who loves or hates chess. Play on a regular chess board, but each piece has new names, powers and abilities. An age-old tradition made new!

ISBN 1-886383-01-4 $9.00

Children's Books
This book is brought to you by Piccolo Pride, Pride's children's division.
Full-color interiors and exteriors.

The Magical Child. Carol DiMarco and Connie Wurm. In the days of castles and kings, dragons and things, there lived a little girl named Angela Marie who was magic but didn't know it... yet!

ISBN 1-886383-19-7 $10.95

Send check or money order to:
Pride Publications
Post Office Box 148
Radnor, Ohio 43066-0148

Readers, remember!

To honor Gay and Lesbian literary excellence, vote in
the 1997 Lambda Literary Awards!
(Before February 1998)

Categories are: fiction, poetry, mystery, biography,
anthology, humor, sci-fi/fantasy, stageplay/drama,
children's, non-fiction studies, and small press book.

Lambda Literary Awards
1625 Connecticut Avenue Northwest
Washington, D.C. 20009-1013
Fax: 202-462-7257

Vote for *Fall Through the Sky*
in the sci-fi/fantasy and the small press categories.

Your writers thank you!